Texas Twilight

Other Books by Caroline Fyffe

McCutcheon Family Series

Montana Dawn
Texas Twilight
Mail-Order Brides of the West: Evie
Mail-Order Brides of the West: Heather
Moon Over Montana
Mail-Order Brides of the West: Kathryn
Montana Snowfall
Texas Lonesome

~~~*~~~

Prairie Hearts Series

Where the Wind Blows
Before the Larkspur Blooms
West Winds of Wyoming
Under a Falling Star

~~~*~~~

Stand Alone Western Historical

Sourdough Creek

Texas Twilight

A McCutcheon Family Novel

Book Two

Caroline Fyffe

Cover design by Kelli Ann Morgan
Interior book design by Bob Houston eBook Formatting

Proudly Published in the United States of America

ISBN # 978-1-4664235-9-6

This book is dedicated to the incredibly brave men (one of whom is my son, Adam) and women of the 373D MI Battalion of the United States Army now serving in Iraq—the last Military Intelligence Battalion to serve there. It is your dedication, determination, and honor that make this country great! Thank you for your service.

Chapter One

Texas Badlands, 1886

The stagecoach lurched. John Jake McCutcheon opened his eyes and saw the young woman next to him grasp the leather loop that hung from the coach's ceiling to keep from being tossed around. She tipped precariously to the right, then left, bumping forcefully into his shoulder. With an apologetic glance she moved away, then dabbed at her brow with a folded handkerchief. She looked at her elderly aunt.

"*Tante* Harriett? Are you all right?" she asked in a soft German accent. She opened the fan she held and swished it back and forth in front of the tiny woman. "Your face is extremely red."

"Of course, Lily," Harriett Schmidt said in a raspy voice laced with exhaustion. The old woman's hair was swept up atop her head and fastened in a bun, but after the miles and miles traveled on the dusty, sun-baked road, it looked more like a weather-blown tumbleweed after a storm. She patted her niece on the knee. "Thank heavens we're almost there. Just one more day and we'll be out of this oven."

John glanced away, not wanting to seem impolite. He'd met both Harriett Schmidt and her niece, Lily Anthony, when they'd boarded the stage together in Concepción. He'd seen them on the train from Boston, too, but they'd kept to themselves, never speaking with anyone else.

John gazed out the window, thinking. He was finally finished with his medical training and heading to West Texas. Anticipation coursed through him.

Rio Wells was a long way from his family ranch in Montana, but he'd get used to it. His plan to return to Y Knot after graduation hadn't panned out. His hometown already supported two full-time physicians. If he really wanted to make a difference in people's lives as a doctor and surgeon, he had to strike out in a place where the townsfolk were in need. At least he wouldn't be a complete stranger in Rio Wells. Uncle Winston and his family were there. And his fiancée, Emmeline Jordan, would be joining him this fall.

John closed his eyes, recalling Emmeline's elegant profile and dark, alluring eyes. In his mind's eye, her mouth drew down into a seductive little pout, a manipulation he knew all too well, but one that fueled his blood all the same. She was like a beautiful, exotic bird, needing care and affection.

"Oh, just to take this corset off," Harriett said to no one in particular, then chortled softly at her niece's shocked expression at her bluntness. "It pinches horribly. I think I'll throw it away for good." She paused, thinking. "No..." Her eyes twinkled mischievously. "Actually, I'll burn it."

Cyrus and Jeremiah Post and Abigail Smith, the other passengers cramped uncomfortably on the opposite seat, just smiled, now used to the old woman's antics. Miss Smith, a teacher, had been hired by the same town council that had hired John, and he felt a small kinship with her.

"You know, Dr. McCutcheon," Harriett Schmidt went on, trying to catch his eye, "my Lily doesn't need a corset. Her waist is eighteen inches without one."

"Tante Harriett. *Please.*"

John chuckled and shrugged his shoulders. He'd tried not to notice something like that, but it had been difficult, if not impossible. The girl had practically been snuggled to his side for several days.

Without warning, the driver called out sharply to the horses and the coach picked up speed. The two guards riding on top of the stage scuffled around and one shouted something unintelligible. John glanced out the window.

A shot rang out. A second later, one of the guards fell from the top of the stage, past the window, landing with a thunk as the stage rolled on. Lily gasped and threw her arms protectively around her aunt. Abigail screamed and then fainted, flopping over onto Cyrus's shoulder.

The driver bellowed to the horses again and the stagecoach heaved forward as the six-horse team was propelled instantly into an all-out gallop. Three more shots were fired, and the sound of horses' hooves thundered from behind.

John looked back through the dust to see a number of riders racing toward the stagecoach, eating up the distance between the two. What the hell was he supposed to do now? He was a doctor. He'd taken the Hippocratic Oath to heal not three weeks before. His job was taking bullets out, not putting them in. But then, he'd also been raised on a rugged Montana ranch, where the unwavering reality was hard. Sometimes staying alive meant killing someone else. Besides, everyone's lives were on the line, not just his. It would be especially bad for the women aboard. These hills were a common hiding place for Comancheros. They used women in the worst ways and then sold them into prostitution in Mexico. As pretty as she was, Lily Anthony would fetch top price. Hell, they'd sell the skinny teacher and the old woman, too.

Smoke and dust filled the coach.

Pop. Pop. Pop.

Lily covered her ears. Her elderly aunt coughed as she struggled to hang on. Abigail, now fully awake again, filled the small space with one shrill scream after the other, never even pausing to take a breath. John reached for his satchel under the seat, withdrew a Colt 45, and strapped on his holster. Carrying his guns was a habit he hadn't been able to break even after his years at school. With hands nimble from experience, he loaded and fired several shots out the window. Two riders fell.

"You have another gun?"

John was surprised to see old Harriett Schmidt eyeing him expectantly. One hand was outstretched while the other grasped the windowsill as the coach careened down the road, jerking violently this way and that. "I'm not letting those filthy dogs take my Lily!"

"Can you shoot?"

"I wouldn't ask if I couldn't. My derringer's not worth diddly."

John squeezed off three more shots, then pulled another gun from his bag, handing it to Harriett. He pushed the bag toward Lily. "Bullets."

Cyrus Post fired out the other side of the coach just as a bullet hit Cyrus's brother in the chest, slamming Jeremiah violently against the back of the seat. Jeremiah gasped several times as he tried to hold back a rush of crimson that spurted through his splayed fingers, soaking his clothes. With just a glance, John could see he wasn't long for this world. Abigail's eyes grew round as she took in the blood. With a gasp, she fainted again, blessedly putting an end to her screams.

"Hell and damnation!" Cyrus cried out. "There's too many. Prepare to meet your maker."

"Hush your mouth, you old coot," Harriett shouted as she hefted the heavy gun and shot out the window. "I have more faith in God than that."

The coach rounded a corner dangerously fast and then slowed a bit as it began an uphill climb. One side of the road dropped off, falling some forty feet to a bed of jagged rocks.

Seizing the moment, John holstered his gun and opened the narrow door. He climbed the side of the rocking coach using the window as a step and, grasping the luggage rack, pulled himself up. He flopped onto his stomach, facing the oncoming killers and picked up the fallen guard's Winchester. He took aim.

He was able to cock the rifle, shoot, and pick off three Comancheros. One thing about a McCutcheon was that their father took great pride in teaching them all how to shoot well. Even his sister Charity was a sharpshooter.

Two bullets whizzed by John's head so close he felt a trail of heat. He hunkered lower behind the cargo and steeled his nerves. A third shot took the life of the driver, forcing the remaining guard to jump into the driver's box and grab for the multiple reins before they were lost completely. The man scooped them up and slapped the leather across the backs of the charging horses, demanding more speed.

John paused to reload. He wasn't ready to die! He'd worked his tail off to get into Harvard and get his medical degree. And now this? Angry at the turn of events, he unloaded his chambers, bringing down two more outlaws.

"Help me up," a female voice shouted over the ruckus.

Lily Anthony dangled from the side of the stage, her white knuckles grasping the iron rod of the luggage rack to keep from falling under the steel-rimmed wheels. Her dress swished around her legs as she struggled to secure footing. John reached down, took a firm hold under her arms, and pulled her up next to him. "What the hell are you doing?" he yelled over the sound of gun-shots and galloping horses.

"Helping you," she shouted back as she scanned the area. She picked up the abandoned Winchester, reloaded it from a bag of ammunition, and handed it over to John. He grunted his understanding, took aim, and fired three times, sending more outlaws into the dirt.

As the coach slowed, the seven remaining desperados prepared to come aboard. John grabbed for his Colt and brought down the two closest. Taking aim on a third, he squeezed the trigger, only to have the chamber click empty. The rest of the ammunition was inside with Harriett. At this range the Winchester was nearly useless.

He swung to his left as a man leapt from his mount and began climbing up. With his empty gun, John bashed him in the face, knocking him off. Lily hefted the Winchester to her shoulder and fired, taking down a rider who was bringing up the rear.

Lily screamed and again grasped the luggage bar. One of the Comancheros had her by the ankle, pulling her toward the side of the rocking coach. John fought to keep his balance as he swung around. Grabbing the Winchester, he struck the outlaw's face several times, but the man was mad with evil intent, and hung on relentlessly.

The coach lurched as the hind right wheel spun off the road. John scrambled to keep from being pitched off the top. The outlaw faltered. Quickly dropping the rifle, he grasped Lily's upper body and heaved. She bucked and kicked, finding the outlaw with her boot, the kick glancing off his temple, but still he clung fast. Again, the careening coach swayed violently, almost toppling all three.

A volley of shots sounded from within the coach and from the corner of his eye he saw one of the remaining two mounted riders fall. The final rider fired once, then pulled up and stopped, abandoning his companion who still rode the stage.

John yanked Lily behind him as the Comanchero stood and pulled out a knife. With the agility of a cat, the man slashed out and John dodged to the side. Emboldened, the outlaw sprung forward, catching John around the middle. The two fell to the roof, wrestling for the weapon. John reached for his empty Colt and brought it down on the man's head, but not before a searing heat flashed down his face from temple to earlobe. Hefting the unconscious man up, John threw him off the cliff side of the rollicking coach then slumped down, pressing his palm to his face.

Chapter Two

The driver let the horses run on for a good quarter mile. Then he hauled back on the reins, bringing the lathered animals down to a trot, then a walk, and finally to a halt.

Everything was quiet. The hot sun beat down and the landscape wavered before John's eyes. Lily's stricken expression gave him pause. Had she taken a bullet he hadn't seen? "Lily, are you all right?" he asked, struggling to get the words past the confusion in his brain. "Are you hurt somewhere?"

"No. I am okay," she answered, climbing to her knees.

The driver came back and took John by the arm. "Come on, McCutcheon, let me help you down."

John shook him off. "I can manage. Check on the passengers below." It was then he realized his hand was pressed to his face and blood dripped onto his shirt. Instantly the side of his head began to sting with excruciating pain.

"What the...?" He pulled his hand away to see it covered with blood.

"Dr. McCutcheon," Lily said as she stood carefully and took his arm. "You have been cut badly. Let us help you down before you fall." She looked to the driver who again took John's other side, and this time John let them help him to the ground.

When Lily turned to leave, John caught her wrist. He held tight as she strained to get free. "How bad is it?"

"Looks like everyone's dead," the driver answered.

Lily let out a cry. She twisted and turned in John's grasp. "Let me go!" With force, she jerked her arm free then ran to the other side of the coach where she pushed past the driver and climbed in to find the limp and pale body of her elderly aunt. "No," she wept. "You cannot be dead! Wake up. Please, wake up."

John followed with his handkerchief pressed to his face. He reached in and hefted Lily out of the coach and held her, feeling the wetness of her tears. Her hands curled around the fabric of his shirt as sobs racked her body.

John swung her into his arms. "Shhh, now, Miss Anthony," he crooned gently. "It's a pity, I know. I'm sorry this had to happen. Don't cry so." Her hair, free from its bonds, was a mass of blond locks cascading down her back. Improper or not, he stroked it, marveling at its softness. He rocked for a few moments until she quieted. Through the open doorway, he could see that a bullet had penetrated the stage and Miss Abigail Smith had taken it in the side. The teacher's eyes were open wide in surprise, and her mouth formed a little O. The stain on her blue calico dress gradually grew larger.

He set Lily on the ground. "I need to check them," he said. "You wait here." The fatal wounds of the two brothers left no doubt as to their condition. Feeling for Abigail's pulse confirmed her demise. Harriett Schmidt was slumped in the corner, no apparent wounds visible. He pressed his index finger to the artery in her neck. Several moments ticked by. "Actually, she's alive."

Lily's eyes widened in hope.

Without hesitating, John cleared away guns, hats and other personal belongings and carefully laid Lily's aunt out on the bench and undid several buttons at the neckline of her blouse. He inspected her head, looking for any sign that she'd been hit by something. Without anything left to do for her but wait for her to wake up, he climbed out of the coach.

"What's wrong with her?"

"I can't find any wounds and she doesn't appear to have hit her head." He looked into Lily's face. "You understand?" It took a moment before she nodded and wiped her tears with the sleeve of her dress. She looked too young and small to be out here in the badlands of Texas. "Why don't you sit over there in the shade of that rock for a moment while Hank and I take care of them." He motioned to the stage with the tilt of his head.

"No. I want to stay with her. In case she wakes up."

John looked at her for a long moment. He climbed back into the coach and gathered up her aunt, then carried the tiny woman over to the shade and laid her down. With his knife he sliced a section of cloth from her skirt and soaked it in water from his canteen, placing it on Harriett's forehead. He looked at Lily, who'd followed behind. "There. Now, you sit." He gave her a little nudge. "Go on."

Dazed, Lily sat on a large slab of granite next to the body of her aunt. Beyond, where the sun beat down on the rocky surface, speckles of black and white sparkled brilliantly and heat waves rose to the sky. An enormous red ant crawled across Lily's hand, but she just watched it with swollen eyes. Somewhere a locust buzzed.

Why had her *Tante* insisted on leaving Boston in the first place? Returning from a mysterious meeting, she'd insisted they leave that very night. When asked, she'd said she needed a drier climate for her health, but she had never mentioned that before. When pressed further, Harriett, totally out of character, snapped at her telling her not to question her so much. If only they had not come west...

Lily glanced back at the coach and her heart did a somersault. All those people were *dead*. She and Miss Abigail had been discussing sarsaparillas and how they wanted one as soon as they reached Rio Wells. The thought of the teacher with the blood spot on the side of her dress made Lily's throat threaten to close and her eyes felt as if hot coals were wedged behind them.

The coach rocked slightly. She didn't want to think about what they were doing in there. She tried to look away, over the desolate, dry lands, but couldn't tear her gaze away. She watched Dr. McCutcheon as he approached, then set her cloth satchel at her feet.

"Miss Anthony." He looked uncomfortable. "I'd like to make it to the safety of the swing station before nightfall. I think it best if you ride up top with us."

"What about my *Tante?*"

"She'll need to ride inside."

"But what if she wakes up? She will be frightened if she cannot find me." But I do not want to look at those dead bodies another time, she thought, suppressing a shudder.

"She's still unconscious." His expression was soft but his tone said his decision was made. "Do you have a bonnet, or parasol, to keep off the sun?"

Her emotions were all jumbled up inside and she struggled to understand. At her silence, he squatted down and opened her bag, rummaging through it.

"Here." He placed the bonnet on her head and tied the sashes. The ugly gash of his wound stood out on his tanned cheek, and the purple stain of iodine confirmed he had done some doctoring to himself. Finished, he sat back and studied her face.

"I killed a man," Lily said under her breath. "I shot him dead. Maybe even more than one man. I am not sure."

Dr. McCutcheon nodded thoughtfully. "That you did." He reached out and straightened her bonnet as if he were searching for the right words. "And, if you must know, I'm glad you did. Those men were killers. As bad as that might sound to you, it's just the way it is out here. You have to be tough to survive."

He stood. "It's best not to think about it too much. Now, up you go." He took her hand and pulled her to her feet, then gathered her aunt into his arms.

At the coach, Lily stopped him with a touch to his hand before he could open the stage door. "Please bring her up on top with us, Dr. McCutcheon. I'll make a spot for her between the luggage. Watch over her. The fresh air will do her good and…"

His jaw clenched and released. "Hank," he called, and the man ran over and helped Lily to the top of the coach where just a few minutes before they'd been fighting off the Comancheros. Dr. McCutcheon climbed up with her aunt in his arms. After laying her down, he took his spot as lookout.

Chapter Three

By the time they reached the swing station the moon was overhead and the sky filled with stars. Not much more than a rundown shack, the stage stop had several corrals holding a dozen or so horses. It was the property of Wells Fargo, run by an employee who met and fed passengers along the routes. Smoke wafted from the chimney, attesting to the fact that there was indeed an able-bodied occupant within.

In the soft moonlight, John watched a stout little man hurry out, followed by a shaggy black dog. The man took hold of the horses as the driver set the brake.

"Hank, I was getting worried. Did you have trouble? Where's Sam and Dalton?"

"They're dead, Chester."

John climbed down and reached up for Lily. Taking her hand, he guided her down, then made sure she was steady on her feet before releasing it. "We were attacked. They killed three of the passengers, too."

"Those Comancheros are getting as bold as brass around here. I fear for my safety near every day and night. Just a couple of nights ago I saw two up on the hill, watching. I'll miss those boys..." His voice broke and he shook his head.

"You have some supper ready for this miss?" John asked. "She's had a rough go of it."

"That I do. Stew and cornbread. Come inside." The man walked ahead and opened the creaking door.

Lily waited for him as he climbed back to the top for Harriett. It was strange the woman was still unconscious. Inside, he laid her on a small cot on the far wall.

"Go ahead and dish up Miss Anthony's dinner," John said. "Hank and I have business to take care of outside."

"Understood. There's a small graveyard out back. If you use the lanterns on the porch you won't have a problem finding it. You can bury them there."

John motioned to the cot. "Come and get me if she wakes up."

It took the better part of two hours before John and Hank had the bodies of Abigail Smith and Cyrus and Jeremiah Post buried in the sandy loam and covered with rocks. John had gathered the few personal belongings off the men's bodies and stuck them into their luggage, along with some blood-soaked sheets of a letter. They'd been loose in Jeremiah's breast pocket, and John had folded them and stuck them back into an envelope addressed to the sheriff of Rio Wells.

He and Hank washed up and hurried inside, hunger gnawing their bellies. Lily had changed and now sat by her aunt's cot, holding the older woman's hand.

Chester dished the men's food and watched as the two wolfed it down, refilling their bowls to the brim for a second go-round. "That's a nasty cut. Are you going to do something with it?"

John swallowed. "Just as soon as I eat I'm going to stitch it up."

"How you gonna do that?" Chester asked, skeptical.

"He's a doctor," Hank responded, over a mouthful of potato and meat.

"It'll hurt like hell," Chester said as he came close to get a better look. "I suggest you take some whisky first." The dog followed his master over. He whined once, then made a small circle and lay down by John's chair.

"Don't I already know that, but I have to be steady." Finished, John went to his black leather bag and pulled out the things he needed, along with a pie-sized mirror. "Bring me all the light you have in this place, if you don't mind."

He was surprised when he found Lily standing next to him with a lantern. "I can do it, Dr. McCutcheon," she said, her eyes assessing his wound. "I am a seamstress. I have a year and a half of experience working for my *Tante*, as well, before coming to America." She put the lantern on the table and picked up the needle in a steady hand, the one that had been shaking not all that long ago. "You can trust me."

John looked down at her slim fingers holding the needle. They were lean and long and a bit roughened at their tips.

"Okay. Let me get prepared."

He washed up, then slicked his hair away from his face. Taking a tub of clean water and soap, he tackled the painful job of cleansing the wound thoroughly, having to stop several times to slowly breathe in and out through his nose. He then irrigated it over and over with handfuls of water. Afterwards he swabbed it generously a second time with iodine, bracing against the pain. He took the needle and held it in the flame of a lamp for several seconds. Looking into the mirror, he pointed out to Lily where he'd like her to make the stitches. When he was finished, he took the bottle of whisky Chester held out to him and took a long drink.

"Take another one, son," Chester said. "Can't hurt nothin'."

He did, ignoring the burn as it slid down his throat. He looked at Lily. "Ready?"

When she nodded, he settled in a chair. She sat opposite and pulled in close between his legs, studying his face.

Just yesterday he'd been thinking how pretty her wheat-colored hair looked sparkling in the sunshine and how her blue eyes reminded him of hyacinth in spring. Now, with her up close and personal, he noticed a light sprinkling of freckles over the bridge of her nose and a minute beauty mark at the outside corner of her left eye. He was surprised he'd never seen it before.

She softly cleared her throat. "I think you should close your eyes." Her warm breath, laced with coffee and sugar, tickled his senses. "Dr. McCutcheon?"

Although reluctant to lose sight of her pretty face, he complied, willing himself to relax. When the sharp prick sent fire into his temple he sucked in a great draught of air, stilling her hand.

"Go on," he said through gritted teeth. "Don't mind me. I'm toug..."

Pain ripped through the hours-old wound. He clenched his jaws tighter, breathing through his nose. Lily pulled the thread through, making sure it was snug, then tied the knot and snipped it, again making him grimace. With a clean cloth, she applied a little pressure as he'd told her to do, to keep the bleeding down and allow her to see the wound easily.

"There. The first one is done."

Lily held up the mirror. A perfect little knot, done exactly as he had instructed. It was tied off at the top of the slash in his skin, still oozing a little. "Very nice work," he said. She blushed and he couldn't stop his mouth from curling up into a smile. "That wasn't so bad." He looked over at Chester. "But—I think I'll have another drink now."

"Thought as much," Chester said knowingly, handing him the bottle.

Time crawled, marked by the ticking of the clock. The sound kept Lily's thoughts straight, as if it were directing her hand. After each stitch was finished, Chester would hand Dr. McCutcheon the bottle of whisky. After the fourth round, her patient didn't even flinch when she poked the needle into his cheek, and she knew he was feeling no pain. Chester picked up the bottle, intent on giving the doctor with the charming smile another swig, but she motioned for him to put it away. He was going to be in enough discomfort in the morning without a pounding headache and rolling stomach to contend with.

"I'll say it again, Lily. You have a fine, steady hand. Are you sure you've never been to medical school?" John asked in a teasing tone.

Hank and Chester chuckled.

"No, Dr. McCutcheon, just many hours stitching dresses, but I respect doctors very much. It is the noblest profession. At least, that is what I believe." Her comment drew another chuckle from the men.

Lily tried to concentrate, to keep her mind on what she was doing, but it was proving extremely difficult. Dr. McCutcheon was the most handsome man she had ever seen, let alone been this close to. He was the epitome of everything western, with his long legs and muscular body. Why, he didn't look like a doctor at all. His fine, straight nose complemented the hard angle of his jaw. And his hair, oh—it was so silky and smooth; it practically begged to be touched. When she felt her face warm she hardened her resolve not to be distracted, but his intriguing scent—of outdoor freshness mixed with something else she couldn't put her finger on—circled around her. Without even taking her gaze from what she was doing she could feel that he'd opened his eyes and was looking at her.

"Ouch!"

She pulled back, embarrassed. "I am sorry. I—"

John chuckled. "I'll let it pass—but, just this once." He scrunched his face, as if working to relieve the pain. "You're a regular little Florence Nightingale, aren't you?" He winked at his spectators, drawing more laughter from them. "I'll be your pin cushion anytime."

She smiled. He'd loosened up considerably since drinking all the whisky. His face was flushed, his eyes a bit glassy. With relief, she tied off the last knot.

"All finished." She handed him the mirror.

He inspected her handiwork closely as she dabbed it again with iodine. "We need to cover it," she said, more to herself than to the three other people watching with interest.

"I'll be right back." Lily went behind the screen and lifted her bag onto the log-cabin-patterned quilt of her cot. She hurried, digging around inside until she came to the small squares of fabrics she had brought along. They were wrapped in brown paper and tied with a yard's worth of twine.

She went back to the table and untied the bow, sorting through the contents until she found the gauze. She handed it to John, along with a small roll of gummed paper for hemming.

"Sure you don't mind?" he said, his eyebrows lifting in surprise. "I'll be sure to replace it when we get to town."

"No need. You saved our lives today, Dr. McCutcheon. I am happy I can repay you at least by helping."

"Lily? Where are you, girl?"

Lily hurried to her aunt's side. "You're awake," she said, holding back her emotions. "I was afraid—" She stopped and exhaled. "How do you feel?"

John gathered his stethoscope from his things and followed, his legs a bit wobbly, and hunkered down beside the old woman. He felt her forehead, then took her pulse. Putting the ends of his stethoscope into his ears, he leaned close to her chest, listening to her heart. "She's getting stronger. I'm still concerned, though, that she was out for so long." He lifted each eyelid and looked into her pupils. "Does anything hurt?"

"I've a terrible headache, young man."

"Have you a history of passing out for long periods of time?"

"No, I don't."

Alarmed, Lily spoke up. "But, what about the times..."

"Hush, Lily. I'd had too many sips of champagne. I've explained that to you several times. My Lily," she laughed softly, as she regarded her niece. "Always so worried about her feeble old auntie."

Lily bit the inside of her cheek. She'd found her aunt passed out more times than she'd like to remember. Lily had been petrified each time it happened, but she usually came around pleasantly rested and calm. Her doctor seemed unconcerned, telling Lily not to worry so much. "Just old age," he'd say before leaving. She wasn't so sure.

John's head throbbed painfully. The sun was already hot for the first day of May; it blasted the stage and its inhabitants like a furnace.

"Whoa," Hank shouted to the horses as they pulled in next to Rio Wells' stage office midway down Main Street. Several people milled about on the boardwalk waiting for the stage to arrive.

When John climbed down and stood in their company, opening the coach's door for Lily and Harriett, they gaped at the sight of his face and some turned and backed away. In the heat of the day the bandage had curled and fallen off, leaving the raw flesh exposed. The puffy skin, pulled together with sixteen stitches, was enough to make the strongest stomach lurch.

A heavy man in a dapper hat stepped forward expectantly and peered inside the coach. "Miss Abigail Smith?"

"Miss Smith is dead," John said, as gently as he could under the circumstances. Several bystanders gasped in horror. "She's buried out at the swing station along with Cyrus and Jeremiah Post." He helped Lily to the ground, and then reached for her aunt.

"John McCutcheon. Is that you?" a deep voice called out.

John turned to find three men striding up the boardwalk. They were tall and rugged and the oldest bore a strong resemblance to his father. "Yes. You must be Uncle Winston."

The man gripped him in a strong embrace, then set him away to get a look at his nephew. "You've been hurt. By the bullet holes in the stage, I can guess what happened."

"Three passengers and two employees have been killed."

"Comancheros?"

"A whole band of them."

Uncle Winston shook his head angrily. "They get more brazen every day. Thank God you made it here in one piece. Here, meet your cousins. This is Dustin." John gripped the hand of his older cousin who was his brother Luke's age, the two standing eye to eye. Then Chaim, who was John's age, also twenty-five. While they talked, John was conscious of Lily scurrying around, gathering their things while holding onto her worn out and disheveled aunt.

He motioned with his head to the women. "Give me a few minutes, please." He turned to Lily, who was holding her aunt's elbow while staring at her trunk with a perplexed look. Her cloth satchel, and that of her aunt's, sat close by.

"What are your plans?"

Startled, she looked up. "Oh. Dr. McCutcheon. Are you still here?" She smiled, but he could see something different in her eyes, as if somehow he'd ruffled her feathers. How, he couldn't imagine.

"Our plans? Well, for tonight we will secure a room at the hotel. Then tomorrow we will settle into the shop we have leased at 33 Spring Street. It has living space upstairs."

"Let me help you take your things to the hotel."

"We can manage."

They bent at the same time, both taking hold of the two smaller bags. Her eyes challenged his as the satchels were pulled back and forth between them.

"Stop being so stubborn, Florence," he said, chuckling. Her annoyed expression said she didn't appreciate the name. "What's gotten into you?"

"I am not being *stubborn*."

"*You are.*"

"Children. Children. Is this really necessary?" Harriett said, placing the back of her hand on her forehead. "This heat is stifling."

"The hotel is just across the street," Lily said, her chin raising a notch. "We can manage. But, thank you all the same."

Ignoring her remark, John lifted his hand and called to a Wells Fargo employee standing nearby. "Can I trouble you to take this trunk over to the hotel for the ladies?" Then, one by one, John pried Lily's fingers from her hold on the bags, then took Harriett's other elbow.

In the hotel, John tapped the bell several times until a man hurried out of a door.

"These ladies need a room for the night."

"Certainly," he replied, eyeing the side of John's face. He produced a large ledger and held out a feather pen to John, who handed it over to Lily.

"And once they're settled I'd appreciate it if you would have the restaurant send them up a hot meal. Charge it to me."

"Doctor," Lily sputtered at the exact same time Harriett said, "Thank you kindly." Startled, the women looked at each other for a moment.

"Stop being so prickly, Lily," Harriett admonished. "If he wants to send us dinner, let the man."

Finished with signing in, Lily put down the pen and opened her mouth to object further, but John silenced her with a smile and a finger pressed to her lips. "Ah-ah-ah, your aunt was my first patient. It's just a small gesture of thanks."

"But, we should be paying you..."

"Your name?" the little man asked him. "For the food bill."

"John McCutcheon. I'm the new doctor in town."

The hotel clerk scribbled a little note and held it up for John to sign. Finished, John leaned close to Lily and whispered, "Will you two be okay?"

She nodded, then after two heartbeats her lips curved up into the soft smile that he'd come to know so well in such a short time. Aunt Harriett reached out and laid her hand on his forearm. "We'll be just fine, Dr. McCutcheon. Thanks to you."

"Anyone would do the same," John replied.

"Perhaps," Harriett said, letting her hand fall away when a baldheaded man picked up their bags and headed for the stairs. "But, it wasn't anyone, was it, Dr. McCutcheon? Will we see you again?" she asked over her shoulder as she and Lily turned to go.

John took another fleeting glance at Lily. "Without a doubt."

Chapter Four

Uncle Winston and his two cousins helped John find overnight storage for his two boxes of medical equipment, books and small safe that they had unloaded from the stage while he was getting the women settled. As soon as that was accomplished Uncle Winston presented John with a horse, chosen from their best stock, and gave it to him as a gift. When John tried to refuse, Uncle Winston's face fell so far John reversed direction immediately and thanked him kindly.

"He's beautiful, Uncle Winston. What's he called?" John asked as they rode down the trail. He liked his glossy chestnut color and fine conformation. A white blaze ran down evenly between the gelding's eyes.

"Hobo, but I call him Bo," Uncle Winston said. "He's a four-year-old and is as intelligent as all get-out. Was keeping him for myself until I got your last letter. We're all excited to have family moving to Rio Wells. Aren't we, boys?"

"Yep," Dustin replied after several beats.

"Sure," Chaim added.

Was it his imagination or was there a lack of sincerity in their tone? Who knew, maybe he'd feel the same if one of them was moving into Y Knot. John shrugged it off. His uncle was glad to see him and that was a fact he couldn't deny.

"I like him, Uncle Winston. But like I said before, it wasn't necessary."

"Of course it was necessary. It's twenty-nine years since we had a Montana McCutcheon come to visit. Last one was my little brother Flood. He brought your two older brothers with him when they were just wee lads…" His uncle's voice trailed off and it was a moment or two before he continued in a sober tone. "Your pa wanted them here while he was off searching for your mother after she'd been abducted." He shook his head. "That was a few years before you were born. Regardless of the reason, we enjoyed having them. And now, it's been much too long in-between. We're glad you made the decision to take the job in our town and make Rio Wells your home. I couldn't be prouder if you were my own son."

Embarrassed, John looked off the side of the road at the dry lands so different from what he was used to. Prickly pears, as well as bluebonnets, were everywhere. Plus an overabundance of rocks. "How are things at Rim Rock?"

"We've been better. But, we can't complain. Texas has always had its problems—be it water, weather, drought or some kind of pestilence. There's always something to kick the snot out of us. But we're tough and it'll take more than any of those things to beat us. Isn't that right, boys?" The last question, thrown over his shoulder to Dustin and Chaim, went unanswered.

"That's the same with us. The Heart of the Mountain always has something that needs fixing or doing or driving. I miss it, though, and that's a fact." John thought he heard a soft snort when he said the fanciful name his mother had given their ranch all those years ago, but he couldn't be sure. "It takes a lot of sweat to keep things moving forward."

The sun was low in the west and the thought of laying his head on a clean pillowcase was inviting. He reminded himself he still had a passel of introductions to go through and a welcoming party, he was sure. If these McCutcheons were anything like his family, it'd be hours before he could retire.

"The ranch is just over that hill. Go on boys and give the women a heads-up. We'll be right behind you."

Dustin galloped up the hill, with Chaim directly behind.

Uncle Winston gave John a look. "No one in this family has ever been to the university before. They don't know what to say. Give 'em time to get to know you."

John looked up, surprised. He hadn't thought of that. Never even considered it. Except for him, no one on his side had been to university either. It did make him somewhat of an anomaly. "I don't know what to say."

"Nothing to say. Just wanted to make you aware of the situation. They're usually welcoming."

Chaim, the younger, and of his own age, might be a bit shy, John thought. He seemed a nice enough fellow with his sandy blond hair and easy smile. But he'd hold out judgment on Dustin for the time being. His older cousin made him uneasy for some reason, and John didn't know why that should be.

John could now make out the ranch house in the distance. It was large with white adobe walls and big glass windows. Several earthen pots filled with flowering bougainvillea plants and a few cacti sat in front. "Uncle, she's beautiful. That must be Aunt Winnie waiting out front."

"It is. And here come Becky and Madeline," Winston went on, raising his arm and waving. Dustin and Chaim were nowhere to be seen.

The three women rushed over as the men dismounted. They crowded in, and for a moment John felt a flash of homesickness for his family in Montana.

His aunt went to embrace him, but pulled back quickly. "You've had an accident, John." She placed her cool palm on his forehead, making him smile. "You're warm, too."

She took his arm and pulled him toward the house. "And you're tired. You'll take your supper in bed after you have a bath and a shave, where you can relax. You've had a long, exhausting trip."

That was music to John's ears and he wasn't going to argue.

"But, but...Mother?" the younger girl spoke up, a note of disappointment in her voice. "What about the dinner we've been planning?"

"It'll wait until he's feeling up to it, Becky. Another time."

"Don't we even get to meet him?" The two girls were following closely behind. Uncle Winston brought up the rear, carrying John's saddlebag.

"Just briefly," Aunt Winnie replied. She stopped and turned to the girls. "John, this is Madeline and Becky. Girls, this is your cousin, John."

With his free hand, John tipped his hat. "It's nice to finally meet my Texas relations."

Their faces turned pink. Madeline was the eldest, with an oval face and big brown eyes. Her hair was dark like his and she was slender and very pretty. Becky, the younger of the two, looked a lot like Charity. She had the same strawberry-blond hair and was the same age as his little sister. Pretty, as well.

Becky giggled and Madeline's blush deepened. He shuddered to think how they would fare even a day at the ranch amidst his brother's teasing, if a little statement like that embarrassed them. They nodded in return as his aunt took his arm, and led him away.

Chapter Five

After washing up, Lily went to the window in her bare feet. The rosy, golden sunrise waxed poetically over the mountaintops and spread throughout the town, but today the beauty of it brought little delight.

Why on earth Texas? The question was still there. With each passing day, as they got farther and farther away from Boston, the only home she'd known since coming to America a year and a half ago, her anxiety grew.

She glanced over to the bed. Always generous, her mother's older sister had sent for her in Germany. The ocean crossing had taken two months. Since her arrival, Lily had made many friends. Learning to be a seamstress had been her dream. But the puzzling truth was, throughout the time spent with her aunt she'd never once mentioned anything about leaving.

It wasn't until the night they'd left that she had shown Lily the agreement between her and a Mr. Bartlett here in Rio Wells for the lease of his shop on Spring Street.

She sighed. It was a mystery. For now she'd let it be.

And now there was John. And her attraction to him. She needed to remind herself often that he was engaged. Her conscience prickled for the childish way she'd treated him when they'd arrived. Especially after all he'd done for them. But, she'd not been able to help herself. She'd grown used to sitting at his side, as distracting as it was, and she would miss him horribly now that the trip was over.

Somewhere a door slammed, making Lily jump. People passed down the hallway and were gone. Tante Harriett stirred under the quilt, then reached for her spectacles on the bedside dresser. She put them on and blinked.

"Why, Lily, you're up."

Lily came close. "Yes, a new bed in a new town. You know."

"Yes, indeed I do," Harriett said, scooting up. She positioned her pillow behind her back and leaned against the shiny brass headboard. "That's exactly what you said your first day here in America. I'm sorry, dear. I can say it had little effect on my sleep, though." She reached out and stroked Lily's hair. "Tell me what's troubling you."

Lily didn't have the heart to voice her concerns. She knew her aunt would never hurt her intentionally or break the law in any way. She was just going to have to be patient, until she could figure this out on her own. She wouldn't burden her aunt's already weighted shoulders.

"I just feel bad Abigail is dead. She was such a wonderful person." She felt her eyes well up but blinked back the tears. "Now she's gone. And the two men. How can people be so cruel?"

"That's a question I don't have an answer for. It's strange, isn't it? How humans can protect their own with such fierceness and loyalty, yet not blink an eye when it comes to destroying someone else. I wish I knew, Lily. I really do."

Harriett flipped the cover back and swung her spindly legs over the bed. Her pink flannel nightgown swirled around her feet as she went behind the dressing screen and used the chamber pot. A moment later sounds of water pouring and splashing, then quiet. "Let's go get a nice cup of hot coffee downstairs and then go and see what kinds of things our new home has to offer," she called past the blue and white gingham fabric stretched taut on the wooden frame. "How does that sound?"

"Fine."

Harriett peeked around the screen. "Just fine? Would you rather have a hot cocoa and strudel?"

Lily smiled at her aunt's efforts to cheer her up. She went to her trunk and debated on which dress to put on. "I doubt they have strudel here," she responded as she took off her nightshirt and donned her undergarments. Gathering yards of blue material, she pulled her dress over her head and took a moment of shifting this way and that to get it straight.

"Perhaps John McCutcheon, with his flashing green eyes, will be at the restaurant this morning. I think that would cheer you up."

Lily was fixing her hair but stopped to gape at the screen in the reflection of the mirror. "What are you saying? You heard him speak of Miss Emmeline Jordan. He's engaged to be married."

"I'm saying I'm getting hungrier by the second. If I don't have my coffee soon, and maybe some toast, I'm going to evaporate into thin air and float away." Lily heard a bang and a swish and then a scooting sound. "There. I'm ready."

Tante Harriett came around the screen dressed for the day. She picked up her parasol and her small clutch, then stuffed a white cotton kerchief up the sleeve of her dress. She went to the door and waited patiently.

It was amazing how fast her elderly aunt could get ready. Lily pushed away a wispy golden strand that danced before her eyes and hurried to the door.

She took Lily's hands into her own. "I don't want you worrying about a thing, child. I can see it in your pretty blue eyes that you're pining away about something, and that only sets off my anxiety and makes me dizzy. You don't want to do that, do you?"

Of course Lily didn't want to distress her. Fine, then. Until something horrible happened, she'd put her suspicions aside and consider this a new chapter in her life. She'd read novels about the wild American West when she was a little girl. She'd dreamt about the handsome cowboys and the ruthless outlaws. Today she'd concentrate on all the new things in her life.

John was finishing his breakfast of sliced beef, potatoes and gravy, and a cup of strong coffee when Dustin came through the front door. He hung his Stetson on a peg and pulled up a chair opposite John, next to his sister Becky.

Dustin nodded and picked up the china cup that Maria, their maid, had just filled. He took a sip then replaced it with a loud clatter, causing Becky to flinch.

"You're a moose," she said, giving Dustin a look of chastisement. "When are you going to learn some manners? You were saying, John?" She dabbed her mouth with her napkin. "Still single, Charity likes to ride and tend to cattle?"

John pushed away a small niggle of irritation, realizing Becky was just curious about her cousin. "She's had a longtime beau that's just waiting for the right moment to ask for her hand." He sliced a portion of beef and forked it into his mouth. He chewed and swallowed. "You see, we all know they'll end up together—well, all of us except for Charity. She's as hard-skinned as an armadillo." He laughed to himself, knowing how Charity would react to that description.

"Who's the beau?" Dustin asked.

"Brandon Crawford. Sheriff of Y Knot."

"A sheriff?"

John glanced up from his plate, wondering at his question.

"Hardly a match for a McCutcheon, do you think?"

John glared. He was about to tell his condescending cousin to go to hell when Becky beat him to it.

"Mind your manners," Becky gasped, looking to see how he'd taken the offhand comment. "That's a rude thing to say."

John stood when Aunt Winnie came into the room, then helped her with her chair. "That's nice of you, dear," she said, getting comfortable. "But unnecessary. I want you to feel like family. Which, of course, you are." She leaned in close and looked at the slash on his face and all the stitches holding it closed. "How's it feel this morning?"

John had stared at his wound long and hard in the mirror. Surely Emmeline wouldn't care about something superficial, would she? He'd cleaned it again and put on the disinfectant. That was all he could do. The rest was up to fate.

"Aches some. But nothing I can't handle."

"It's a nasty one, all right." Dustin was leaning back, staring at him. His mouth was a hard, straight line.

Winston and Chaim came through the door together. They hung their hats and hurried to the table, scraping their chairs across the cool tile floor.

"Are you heading out this morning?" Uncle Winston asked.

"Yes. I hope you don't mind. I'd like to head into town straight away, retrieve my things and start setting up." He also wanted to check on Lily and Harriett. He'd hated going off without getting them properly settled.

"I thought as much," Winston replied, digging into the breakfast Maria set in front of him. "Just stay right at the two forks and that will dump you at the end of Dry Street, next to the school. Dr. Bixby's office—er, I mean *your* office—is just down the street. It's not hard to find. Didn't you say something in your last post about a young woman?"

John glanced at Dustin. "I did. We've been keeping company and she is planning to follow sometime in the next few months."

"You're engaged?" Aunt Winnie exclaimed, looking between John and the rest of the family at the table. "This is exciting news. Congratulations!" She shook her finger at her husband. "You never tell me anything, you bad man. We're going to have a wedding to plan. How wonderful!"

Chapter Six

Lily's feet stopped when she saw Dr. McCutcheon riding down the middle of the street, toward her and her aunt. It was still early in the morning and there were only a few people on the boardwalk. They had taken breakfast in a little restaurant called the Apple Dumpling, across the street from where they'd stayed.

"Look who it is," her aunt whispered into her ear.

"I see," Lily answered quickly, embarrassment warming her cheeks.

"Be sure to say hello to him when he rides by."

"He's almost a married man, Tante. Surely, you haven't forgotten so soon."

"Oh, pooh. I know your intentions are good, but things out here in the West are different. He's not married *yet*."

Dr. McCutcheon reined up in front of where they stood, tipping his hat. "Mornin', ladies."

"Good morning, Dr. McCutcheon," Harriett said. She walked to the edge of the boardwalk, closer to the street, bringing Lily along with her.

"So, how is little Florence this morning?" he said to Lily, his smile teasing. "Did you sleep well?"

"Very," she fibbed, hardly getting the word out. Sitting on his horse, he looked even more devastatingly handsome than she remembered. He had bathed, shaved and it looked as if his hair had been trimmed. His mischievous green eyes reminded her of the foamy sea, deep and all-knowing. Her gaze briefly touched the spot she had so recently, and somewhat intimately, tended for him and heat rushed to her face.

"And you, Harriett?" he said, looking to her aunt. "Do you feel rested?"

"Oh, much better, Dr. McCutcheon. I guess the sight of Abigail Smith getting killed right before my eyes was just too much for me. Today I'm fit as a fiddle, thank you kindly."

"That's good. Still, I'd like you to stop by my office later this week so we can make sure you're all right. Will you do that?"

"Where would that be, Doctor?"

John sat back in his saddle and looked up the road, which was gradually coming alive with people. A large wagon, pulled by four horses, plodded by slowly, and he had to wait until it passed so they'd be able to hear his answer. "I'm told it's just up this street a ways." He chuckled. "Actually, I'm not sure yet myself."

"Well, don't you worry, we'll find you. We're on the way now to our own new shop." She held up a large silver key. "Looks like we'll be neighbors."

"So it does." He smiled and tipped his hat again. "Good day."

John rode down the street, taking it all in. This was his new home. Rio Wells wasn't huge, but it was much larger than Y Knot. Just on Dry Street alone he'd seen a yellow school house, a livery, the Cheddar Box restaurant, an undertaker, the Station House Hotel, and he wasn't yet halfway down. The street was lined with gaslights, and there were lines running from pole to pole that he suspected would lead to a telegraph office.

John reined up in front of a building. "Jas Bixby, MD." He read the sign aloud. Gray paint curled off the bat-and-board siding like shavings piled on a woodcrafter's floor. The dingy front window was opened just an inch, from which a curtain fluttered pathetically, as if trying to draw attention. A random gust of wind sent the sign wagging back and forth and bringing the faint odor of rotten eggs.

Dismounting, he tied Bo at the hitching rail. On the porch, John reached up and pushed up on the sign, slipping the hooks from the eyes that fastened it to the underside of the overhang. The previous doctor had forgotten to take it with him when he left. He leaned it against the wall and proceeded inside a few steps, then stopped.

The waiting room was a cluttered mess. A bookshelf ran the length of one wall overflowing with books, as well as a variety of other things of every description. This was his new office? The town council had promised it would be ready, and the upstairs fit to live in. If the condition of this room meant anything, it would take days to get all this disorder thrown out to make room for his medical books and supplies. Removing his hat, he searched for a clean place where it wouldn't get covered in dust.

"Who're you?"

John swung around to find a man standing in the doorway to another room. He was old and had a piece of toast in one hand and a newspaper in the other. A worn cardigan sweater was haphazardly buttoned across his thickened belly, and his white hair stuck out from his head.

"John McCutcheon. Dr. McCutcheon," he corrected, his hat still hanging in his fingers.

The man's shoulders relaxed. "In that case, I've been expecting you. I'm Dr. Bixby." He shuffled toward John, switching the toast to the hand with the paper, and stuck out his right.

Bixby eyed the wound on John's face as they shook hands. His spectacles teetered on the end of his nose. "Come in and I'll get you a cup of coffee." He turned without waiting for an answer and went back into the room from which he'd come. John stood for a moment before following behind.

"Dr. Bixby," John said as he watched the man set an extra cup and saucer at the table and go back to the stove for the coffeepot. "I was under the impression the office was vacant."

"That doesn't surprise me. That town council is always getting ahead of itself." As he poured the coffee, his hand shook violently and John feared he'd spill it all over the yellow and green plaid cloth. Dr. Bixby set the pot on the table and pulled out a chair, gently nudging a little white kitten from the cushion. He motioned for John to take a seat.

Sitting, John tried again. "Dr. Bixby…"

The man pointed to the right side of John's face with his fork. "Knife wound?"

John nodded.

"Whoever sewed you up did a darn fine job."

He was at a loss. The council had said that Dr. Bixby was retiring after forty-five years as Rio Wells' doctor. They'd said he'd be gone and the office would be cleaned out and newly painted. As it was, the place was in a shambles. He clenched his jaw several times before answering. "What exactly are your plans for moving out?"

Chapter Seven

"Moving out?"

Bixby looked up at him as he soaked up egg yolk with his toast. "Never said anything about moving out. Just handing the reins over to someone with a few less miles under his saddle. But that's *only after* I make sure he's well prepared to take care of the people here."

John opened his mouth to speak but Bixby held up his hand, silencing him. "I understand you've completed your medical training. But that's a far cry from knowing what to do if Millie Banks delivers three weeks early, like she has with the last two. Or how to treat Frank if he gets the gout in his other leg, or, or...," he mumbled, scratching his forehead. "Or, Cradle Hupton crushes his hand for the umpteenth time in his blacksmith's forge. You get my drift?"

The kitten mewed then hopped up onto John's lap. It looked around, then stretched its neck curiously, trying to see over the rim of the table. Jumping up, it went straight for Dr. Bixby's plate.

"You little scamp." Bixby scooped up the kitten and went to the back door and put it out. He pulled the door tightly closed and returned to the table. John stood and met the doctor eye to eye.

"I was told that this place would be vacant." He brought his arm up and covered his nose. "What's that smell?"

"Mineral spring. It's a block down Spring Street. Gets a bit pungent when there's no breeze to clear it out. You'll get used to it soon enough."

Jas Bixby sat back down and took up where he'd left off cleaning his plate. Seemed as if he hadn't heard what John had just said. Or maybe he did and didn't care. Possibly, he was just ignoring him completely. John strode to the door. "I'll be back."

"What do you mean there isn't anything you can do?" John leaned palms down on the mayor's desk, the shiny mahogany wood reflecting his frustrated face. "This whole situation is asinine, and if I had any good humor at all this morning, it's now gone." After leaving the doctor's office, he'd gone over to the mayor's office where Mayor Fred Billingsworth was sipping his coffee and reading the morning paper.

"I sympathize with you, Dr. McCutcheon. As soon as Jas gets his thinking on straight, he'll remember that it's this week that he's supposed to be moved out."

"Has anyone talked this over with him?" John asked firmly. "Was it his decision to retire?"

"Of course. It's been discussed for almost three years now."

"Does he have a place to go?"

"I don't know, Doctor. I suppose he does."

"*What?* He's been the town's doctor for all these years and you don't even know what he's planning on doing when he quits his practice, or if he even has someplace to move to?"

What a hypocrite. He wanted the old man out, too. He swiped a hand over his face in irritation. Going into practice with another doctor, especially one as old as sin, was not the set-up he'd been dreaming of.

"How come no one has kept on top of this? I was told the building would be ready."

The door opened and Lily Anthony came in, closing the door behind her. The mayor looked up from his desk, peering around John's body, to see who had entered. He looked much more interested in Lily than he had been in him.

"May I help you, young lady?"

She came forward and stood a few feet from where John was. He noticed a slight brightening of her expression as she glanced in his direction. "Dr. McCutcheon."

"Miss Anthony," he said, taking his hat off. "We meet again."

She handed the mayor a piece of paper she was holding. He opened it and scanned the page. "Yes, I hope you can. My name is Lily Anthony and I am looking for Mr. Bartlett," she announced before he had finished reading. "In his last post to us he said to inquire about him here."

"Mr. Bartlett? He no longer lives in Rio Wells."

Lily's sharp intake of breath echoed in the quiet room. "There must be some mistake. We have entered into a business agreement with Mr. Bartlett. And traveled all the way from Boston."

"Who is we, Miss Anthony?"

"My *Tante*, Harriett Schmidt, and me."

John moved a step closer to Lily, giving her moral support.

"If he is no longer living here, may I ask where I can find him? Where he has moved? We have already paid to him a year's lease of dollars and in return he sent us the key." She held the key up for the mayor to see.

It seemed the stressful situation was causing her to struggle with her normally good English. Her accent thickened considerably and her words jumbled.

The mayor sat back in his chair as if thinking hard. "Miss Anthony, Mr. Bartlett left town and didn't tell anyone where he was going. For all we know he up and got himself killed."

"Who took ownership of the building when Mr. Bartlett moved?" John asked. Lily looked up at him quickly, appreciation written in her eyes.

"Norman Shellston, the banker." He folded the paper in two and handed it back to Lily.

For a moment the name seemed to ring a bell to John, but the thought was pushed away by an inward groan. Most of the bankers his family knew were known to be overly concerned about themselves more so than the interest of their clients. Bloodthirsty, Flood used to call them. "Where's the bank?"

The mayor pushed his heavy body away from his desk and stood, possibly because he could see that the two newcomers were getting ready to leave. "A little way up the street on the corner of Church and Dry."

Lily and John turned to go. "Dr. McCutcheon," the mayor said. "Give Jas a few days to get used to you and used to the idea of retiring. He'll comply. Right now I'm trying to find someone to temporarily oversee the school until we can find a new teacher. It was truly a shame about Miss Smith." He shook his head. "Well, good day."

They stepped outside. "Let's go see the banker," John said as he escorted her up the plank walk.

"No, no. You have already been so generous with your time. I cannot ask this thing of you, Dr. McCutcheon. You have your own business to attend to without my problems adding to that worry." *You also have a fiancée and I enjoy your closeness much more than I should.*

"Nonsense. You're new and I'm new. The way I see it, we both need a friend about now." His arms swung loosely by his side and his crooked smile was endearing. Every now and then he'd nonchalantly grip a post as they passed, as if looking for something to do. "What happened this morning after I saw you? You were on your way to the shop."

"When we got there the key wouldn't open the door. It looked as if someone had recently changed the lock. We tried until my aunt was exhausted. She said she was tired and wanted to lie down. But I know she is also upset. And worried."

"She's back at the hotel?"

"Yes, Dr. McCutcheon. I walked her back and went straight to the mayor's office."

"Please, you *must* call me John. We've been through too much together to keep to such formalities. Don't you think?" He pointed playfully to his face and the many stitches she'd so carefully made.

Lily felt a thrill of happiness as she walked by his side. "Only if you stop calling me Florence." In her way of thinking, the name was a nickname—something you would call a special friend, and it just didn't feel right. "Please just call me Lily."

John looked at her skeptically, then chuckled. "Um, I'll try."

"I insist."

"Well, okay. If you put it like that. Did I ever tell you I thought you very brave to climb onto the top of the moving stage, between flying bullets and rampaging outlaws? Where did you learn to shoot like that?"

"From my brothers, Roland and Sigmund. They are great sportsmen."

His brows lifted in interest. "Well, it's a good thing they did. How old are they?"

"Roland is the oldest. He is twenty-seven, married and has three little children. Sigmund is twenty-five and still a bachelor. *Mütti* says he will never settle down and give her any grandbabies."

"So," John said, chuckling again. "You're a miniature Annie Oakley—as well as a Florence Nightingale." He quickly put up his hands defensively. "I'm not calling you that, mind you." He shrugged. "Just observing the truth. Do you have any more talents I should know about?"

"Why? So you can tease me?"

"Maybe."

When he gave her a playful wink Lily couldn't help remembering how he'd held her so gently in his arms. All her sisters would think him the handsomest man in the world.

And truth be known, she did too. Emma would love his hair and Giselle his strong, manly jaw. His sensitive green eyes would be what Gretchen would notice first. Ida and Louisa, being only twelve and eight, would just love the "whole idea" of him—the cowboy doctor.

"Not unless you count the ability of balancing a plate on my head while dancing the waltz."

He stopped and his eyes opened wide. "Seriously? That's something I'd like to see."

She laughed, continuing down the boardwalk. "Perhaps you shall." He had to hurry to catch up. "And, I also play the harpsichord." His expression was one of amazed amusement. She could not recall him ever looking so happy.

They were passing a leather tannery and a small speckled hen darted out the front door. It smacked wildly into John's leg then made a dive for Lily's hemline. She gasped, pitching towards John off balance.

John clasped her by the shoulders. "Easy. It's just Chicken Little."

Lily laughed again, enjoying this new, more easygoing Dr. McCutcheon very much. "You know that story, too? My mother used to tell us girls if the sky is not falling, things cannot be all that bad. Be peacekeepers. There are two sides to every story."

John laughed appreciatively, nodding his head. "Us girls?"

"Yes. I have so many sisters that most young men are too nervous to come to the Anthony home. Emma is twenty-three, and she, too, is married, to our landlord's son, Jürgen. They are expecting their first child this winter and are hoping for a Christmas baby. Then me. I am nineteen. Then comes Giselle, sixteen, Gretchen, fourteen, Ida, twelve and Louisa is the baby. She is only eight."

"Holy cow. That's some brood. And I thought I had troubles fighting for my very survival in my good-sized family."

"Fighting to stay alive?"

"That's just a figure of speech. Although my three older brothers and one younger sister were a force to be reckoned with sometimes. The thought of eight children is hard to comprehend. What does your father do for a living?"

John seemed keenly interested in her answers, and she felt satisfied to while away the whole morning just as they were doing now. "He is one of the best watchmakers in all of Germany. His shop is in the town square and we live a short distance out in the country. Our home is small, and we all had to share, but that is all we have ever known. It is quite beautiful. Picturesque, as you would say."

They walked along in a moment of silence. "That is why my *Tante* sent for me to come to America. By teaching me a trade that is one less mouth to feed and one less *Madchenkind* to worry over."

"*Madchenkind?*"

"Girl child." A warm flush moved through her again and she hoped he could not see the telltale signs on her face.

"Do you ever get homesick?"

Lily glanced away. That was something she struggled with often. "I do. But, I know I will eventually go home to my family."

They stopped in front of the bank and John opened the door. A young man rose from his desk and met them at the counter.

"May I help you?" His hair was slicked back from his forehead and he was nicely dressed. His skin glistened from the uncomfortable warmth of the room.

"We'd like to see Norman Shellston, please," John said.

"Is there something I can help you with? Mr. Shellston is busy at the moment."

"No. We need to speak with him."

"One moment." He hurried off and came back a moment later. "He's busy and won't see anyone until afternoon. Would you like to make an appointment?"

Chapter Eight

John looked at the clock on the wall and counted slowly to three. They'd have to come back for a ten-minute conversation? Darn, if this wasn't turning into the most aggravating town. But, he had to keep his head about him since he was a doctor now and needed to stay in a good standing in his new community. "Seems we have no other choice."

"Will two o'clock work for you?" the teller asked.

John glanced at Lily. "Yes, that will be fine."

Back outside, the town was alive with the mid-morning business. Three wagons passed in the street, followed by a man with a big stick driving two cantankerous cows. What to do now? They had a few hours before they needed to be back. "Come on, Lily, I'll walk you to the hotel," John said. "How did you like living in Boston?"

She nodded and they started up the boardwalk. "The whole way here we talked about me. I want to know about you. Did you get your things settled in your office?"

John stifled an inner groan. "Not exactly. The prior doctor hasn't left the premises yet even though I was told he'd be retired and gone. That's what the mayor and I were discussing. I want to be able to get my things in but the place is in bad shape and needs a lot of work. And now I find out the doc wants to stay around to make sure I know what I'm doing. Actually, I'm at a loss. I can't just kick him out, but I can't get on with my life with him there. I don't know." He stopped and removed his hat, running his hand through his hair and down the tense muscles in his neck. "I know what my mother would say, though." He settled his hat back on his head and leaned against a post.

"What would she say?"

"She'd say be patient. And respectful." He shrugged. "And kind."

"Your mother sounds a lot like mine."

Lily was not only beautiful and brave, but had a good sensible head on her shoulders. She was smaller than Emmeline and her nose had a dainty little slope. He glanced away. Why the heck did he keep comparing the two? Lily was his friend. And thank God he had her. He'd thought the process of moving to Rio Wells was going to be easy. But, so far, it had been the exact opposite.

"Does she?" He hitched his head and they continued on. "I've come to learn the hard way that she's right almost one hundred percent of the time. Okay, so the ol' doc stays awhile, what could it hurt? But, will he let me clean up the place and get it into shape? I don't think I could stand it for long the condition it's in now. It needs paint and a whole hell..." John stopped and pointed across the street. "There's the place now."

Lily shaded her eyes with her bag to get a better look. "Oh." Her face took on a pained expression. "I see what you mean."

"Go ahead. Say it. The place needs more than paint and a cleaning. It needs three sticks of dynamite and a match."

John was surprised when Lily started to laugh—because he hadn't said it to be funny. Soon she was laughing so hard others were looking their way. She waved her hand in front of her face, trying to get control, but high-pitched squeaks kept escaping.

"Oh, I am sorry," she finally said between gasps. "It is just..." She pointed. "It is as horrible as you said. You were not exaggerating in the least. I can see it blasting into the sky, boards raining down this way and that, finally ending in a big messy pile."

"Well, laugh all you want, but I don't think it's all that humorous," he replied, trying not to smile. The only other girl he'd ever seen laugh so hard was his sister Charity, and only after a good tickle. But Lily's laughter was contagious, and before long he was laughing so hard tears ran down his face.

"Well, I guess there's no help for it now," John said, wiping his eyes with the back of his hand. "All in due time." He took Lily's elbow and continued on until they were in front of the post office directly across from the Union Hotel.

"Mind if I check the mail before we cross?"

Lily drew away. "I am certainly capable of crossing a street on my own, John. I am not a baby or a weakling."

"I know. I know. But as soon as I see if I have anything, I'm crossing too. I need to get a room for a few nights until I can figure out what I'm doing. Where I'll be living."

A distant gun blast sounded and Lily flinched.

He raised a brow. "I'll only be a moment."

"In that case." She smiled and nodded and John went into the post office while Lily waited on the walk.

The tiny building looked deserted. John swiped his hat from his head and went up to the counter. He tapped the bell several times. "Anyone here?"

A scuffling came from the back room and a young woman hurried out. She was of medium height and weight with dark braids twisted up like cinnamon rolls on either side of her head. Her attention was focused on a mound of papers in her hands.

"I'm sorry, I didn't hear you come in." She stopped for an instant, then proceeded forward. She quickly stuffed what she'd been carrying under the counter, then reached up to pat one side of her hair. "May I help you?"

"Can you see if you have any posts for Dr. John McCutcheon, please?"

"You're the new doctor?"

"Yes. Arrived yesterday."

"Let me check." She rushed away but was soon back. "This is for you. It arrived two days ago." She held tightly to the post when he tried to take it from her fingers. "My name is Louise Brown," she said, smiling into his face. "I'm pleased to make your acquaintance."

"The pleasure is mine, Mrs. Brown." She finally let go and he slipped the letter into his front pocket.

"*Miss* Brown," she corrected, dipping her head shyly.

John replaced his hat, giving it a polite tip. "Good day, Miss Brown." As he stepped away, she cleared her throat. Against his better judgment, John glanced back to find her gazing up at him through a barrage of fluttering eyelashes. He hastened out the door.

John settled into his hotel room after retrieving his medical supplies and books from the stage office. He unpacked just the bare necessities, believing he wouldn't be staying long. He hoped that within a couple days he'd have the mix-up with Bixby resolved and have things back on track.

With his letter in hand, he flopped down on the goose feather mattress and got comfortable, plumping the pillow before doubling it over and sticking it behind his head. For a brief moment, he closed his eyes.

As was usual, the face of Bob Mackey, the man he'd killed when he was nine years old, popped into his thoughts. Although the number of times the vision awakened him in a cold sweat had lessened over the years, they still occurred occasionally. Like an old, unwelcome friend showing up at odd times, not quite ready to give up the relationship.

It had been a stormy August night and John was home alone having missed the social and barn dance because of a stomachache. At the sound of the door opening—and then an eerie silence, John grabbed his gun and snuck down the big staircase in the darkness. A tall figure loomed in front of him, seemingly larger than any bear he'd hunted with his father. His trigger finger trembled. A moment later, an earsplitting crash made him flinch. When shards of glass sprayed his skin, his gun discharged accidentally. In the close proximity, the blast was deafening. It wasn't until the smoke cleared and John was able to light a lantern that he saw who it was. He'd tried to stop the flow of blood, but the effort was futile and soon the man was dead.

Bob Mackey was a merchant from town and a friend to all. He'd been delivering a new pane of glass and it had slipped and broken. Flood had told Mackey to drop it off anytime, and since no one appeared to be home it was speculated that he was putting it inside the front door.

His parents had paid restitution to Bob's brother and business partner, and after time, he'd forgiven John, but the shooting weighed heavily on his little boy's heart, regardless of his mother's assurance that it had been an accident. And, truth be told, it was still as heavy a burden today as it had been sixteen years prior. His mother looked for ways to help him through his pain, to heal, but there hadn't been a magical fix. As he grew older, his ache turned to anger, and he began letting his temper get the best of him. Longtime friends whispered behind their hands. He started getting into fights. The betrayal of his friends hurt. It was only after he'd decided to become a doctor that the horror of it lessened. He'd pay his debt by saving a life, then another, and another, and another...until his debt was gone. His moving away from Y Knot had been a relief of sorts, finally free from the stigma he still felt, even if most people had forgotten.

John held up the letter to divert his thoughts. It was from Charity. She'd written to him unfailingly while he was at Harvard, keeping him updated with all that was happening at home.

The most recent news was a new baby girl, born to his brother, Luke, and his wife, Faith. The first two grandbabies for his parents had been boys. Billy and Adam were older now and were becoming a real help on the ranch. Then there was Colton, Faith's feisty eleven-year-old stepson. John stifled a chuckle thinking how the boy had knocked Luke out with a frying pan the night he'd found Faith.

John glanced at the letter again, looking for the little one's name. Holly Lace McCutcheon. Pretty. But before Holly there was Rachel and Matt's little Faith, named after Luke's wife, and Mark and Amy's Cinder. He was having a hard time keeping all the names straight. And who could forget baby Dawn, the little filly Luke had actually delivered? His nephews were seriously outnumbered, although Amy and Rachel were expecting again and perhaps they'd give the boy's team one up. There was a lot going on at the ranch these days.

Skimming the pages, Charity reminded him that she was ready for a visit. Now that he was out of school, she wanted to come and stay for a few months. He knew she was going to be upset seeing his face. Knowing her as he did, he knew she'd take it hard.

No. He wasn't quite ready to have Charity see it. He'd write and postpone, at least for a few months. By then, it was conceivable the bright crimson two-inch line would fade a little and be easier for her to take.

He read further. She thought Brandon was going to propose to her soon. She wasn't sure what she'd say. John looked up at the ceiling, perplexed. Why couldn't she see how much he loved her? More importantly, why couldn't she feel it? They were a perfect match. Brandon was totally devoted to her. And Charity, even if she didn't recognize it, set the sun by him.

The last paragraph was a complaint about how their ma and pa still wanted to send her to a finishing school for three months in Denver. She couldn't fathom why their parents kept saying that in this day and age a woman needed to know more than shooting and riding. Someday Charity might be put in a position of power and would need some "social skills." She didn't want anything to do with it. A vague comment about running away finished the letter. John knew his dramatic little sis would never go as far as that, but it was her way of getting attention. They'd work it out, and hopefully while they did it would take the pressure off him for a while.

He laid the letter on the quilt and slung his arm over his eyes. He needed to send a telegram to Emmeline and tell her he'd arrived safely. Regret pinched his insides as he thought of the others who'd been killed. He'd meant to send a message first thing yesterday when they arrived into Rio Wells and had forgotten in the aftermath of the attack.

Emmeline had been persistent about announcing their plans to marry. He would have preferred to keep their plans to themselves for a while longer, at least until he was settled and had some money coming in. Unfortunately, Emmeline wouldn't listen to reason. His lips turned up remembering the night she'd practically begged him to let her tell her parents. He'd felt uneasy since they'd not been courting for long.

Rolling over, he reached for his book on the bedside table and withdrew the picture he'd put there for safekeeping. He held it above his head, just looking. She was beautiful, without a doubt. He did worry a little about her age. Eighteen was usually a perfect age to marry, but she was immature. He'd noticed right away, but he'd been charmed. When the day came for her to join him in Rio Wells, how would she handle leaving her family? Her friends? Her social life? How would a rough cattle town like Rio Wells compare to Boston? A sharp rapping on his door made him jump.

Chapter Nine

"Dr. McCutcheon," a voice called, "you there?"

John rolled from the bed and hurried to the door. Opening it, he found a sandy-haired boy, perhaps fifteen or sixteen years old.

"Doc Bixby sent me to find you. He wants you to come over to the office right quick. He told me to tell you it's urgent."

"Absolutely, just let me pull on my boots." That done, he followed the boy down the stairs and out the front door of the Union Hotel. They turned left into an alley, between the hotel and the saloon, where piano music pounded.

"It's a short cut," the lad called over his shoulder. It was only then that John noticed that the cuff of the boy's left shirtsleeve hung empty, dangling loosely where his hand should have been.

After emerging from between the two buildings, they turned right and hurried past the back of the sheriff's office where two horses hitched to a post dozed in the warm sun. John took the steps into the back door of Dr. Bixby's two at a time.

"Doc, we're here," the boy called loudly.

John followed through the messy kitchen where he'd been earlier this morning. Turning into a door he hadn't seen before, he stopped short at the bright and clean examination room. The countertops were neat and tidy, and it looked completely organized. A frightened young girl was lying on the examination table, and her teary-eyed mother held her hand with a tight grip.

"Ohoo," the girl cried between loud gasps of breath. Her blue calico dress hung over each side of the examination table and her worn brown boots protruded from beneath her hem, each toe pointing to an opposite wall. Her other hand was pressed on the lower right side of her abdomen.

Dr. Bixby looked up. "Glad you found him, boy."

John came forward and put his hand on the girl's forehead. She was hot. He cautiously palpated her torso not wanting to cause more discomfort. Every time he came even remotely close to her midsection, she'd scream out in pain and double forward. It looked like a classic case of appendicitis. He'd done the surgery in Boston, but always assisted by his teacher. "Appendix?"

"That's my guess."

Does Bixby want me to assist—or to do the actual surgery? John couldn't tell by the look in the old-timer's eyes.

The boy hustled into the room carrying a deep basin of water clutched with his one hand and pressed to his body. Bixby took a smaller bowl and scooped some of the steaming water out and started scrubbing his hands. "Get her undressed, Martha, but leave her in her petticoat."

The girl was now crying uncontrollably.

"It's gonna be okay, honey," Dr. Bixby said as he prepared the operation room. "Tucker'll put you to sleep and you won't feel a thing."

The patient began begging her mother to take her home, saying it didn't hurt anymore at all. The poor woman's face was white as a sheet. "Go on, do as I said, Martha." Bixby set out a canister of ether and a scalpel onto a clean piece of white cotton.

John took a newly laundered apron and looped it over his head. He rolled up the white sleeves of his shirt, then went to the water, and with a bar of lye soap, scrubbed his arms and hands vigorously.

The boy picked up the canister and shook a little of its contents onto a cotton handkerchief and waited for a signal from Dr. Bixby.

Lily tapped on John's door for the third time and pressed her ear against the varnished wood to see if she could hear him moving around inside. Still nothing. Only the piano music from the saloon next door. She'd tried ten minutes before with the same results and knew she couldn't wait any longer. When they'd returned from the bank this morning, and after he'd gotten a room, John insisted on going back to the bank with her at two o'clock. At one thirty, Lily had freshened up, put the lease agreement into her satchel, then snuck out without waking her aunt. She'd found his room as empty then as it was now.

She'd have to handle this matter on her own. Setting her resolve, she hurried downstairs and stepped out into the harsh afternoon sun, looking down the two blocks to the bank. She needed to hurry. It was almost two o'clock and she didn't want to start off on the wrong foot by being tardy. She picked up the hem of her dress and crossed the dusty street.

She arrived with four minutes to spare. When she approached the counter, the same teller who'd been there before met her with a smile now that John was nowhere to be seen.

"You're back."

"For my two o'clock appointment with Mr. Shellston."

His forehead crinkled. "That's right. Actually, he's not back from lunch yet. Do you want to check back in, say, half hour?"

Lily felt her face heat. In Germany, people were respectful of appointment times. "He is expecting me?" she asked, trying to keep her annoyance from showing. She wasn't going to leave and come back. She needed to get this resolved. "I'll wait, thank you."

"Suit yourself." The teller went back to his desk.

Lily seated herself and tried to be patient. Twenty minutes passed without Mr. Shellston or anyone else coming in. She withdrew her handkerchief from her bag and pressed it to her damp brow, reminding herself that they needed Mr. Shellston's cooperation. He held ownership of the property they'd leased. She must remain level-headed. Looking down, she noticed a centipede moving quickly across the dusty wooden planks in her direction. Its legs moved like a wave as the creepy insect sped directly toward her.

She stood and went to the door and looked out. *Where is he?*

On the opposite side of the street two men stood in front of the Land Office, talking. Soon they parted ways and a tall, thin man started for the bank. He walked through the common area without looking her way and continued down the hall to his office. The teller got up and followed him. When he came back, he motioned Lily forward. "Mr. Shellston will see you now. Follow me."

All her indignant feelings evaporated and Lily was instantly filled with resolve. What if he wouldn't hold to the bargain Mr. Bartlett had made with her aunt? What would they do to support themselves? All they knew was sewing. They needed this shop.

The teller closed the door behind him, leaving Lily conspicuously standing. Mr. Shellston was seated behind his desk, shuffling through some papers. He'd put on a pair of spectacles and it seemed he'd forgotten already that he had a visitor.

Lily cleared her throat.

"Oh, please, take a seat." He put away the papers and looked up. "Miss…"

"Anthony," she said, settling herself in one of the two chairs in front of his desk.

"Now, Miss Anthony, what can I do for you today?"

Now that she had his full attention, her heart thumped against her chest and her mouth felt as if it was full of sand. She pulled the paper from her bag and handed it over the large desk to his waiting hand. "This," she was able to get past her thickened tongue, "is an agreement, a lease, Mr. Bartlett made with my aunt. We've traveled far—from Boston—to find that he no longer owns the building in question. You do."

Mr. Shellston opened the rumpled paper and pushed his spectacles up closer to his eyes. Lily assumed he was reading it because he held it before his face while making little sounds. She was conscious of the ticking of his clock.

Mr. Shellston folded it and handed the lease back to her without a comment. She didn't know what to make of it.

"What do you want of me?" he finally said.

His face was expressionless and warning bells went off in Lily's mind. "We want you to honor it. Let us in so we can set up our shop."

"That's impossible, Miss Anthony."

Lily wasn't sure she'd heard him correctly. He'd taken his spectacles off and was now squeezing the bridge of his nose as if he was dealing with an impetuous child.

"Why? You own the building. You can do with it as you please. Can't you?"

He sat back and stared at her, making her feel uncomfortable. "In a sense, yes. And no."

"What do you mean?"

"It is mine to do as I please, you're correct when you say that. But I've already leased it to someone else. He's to move in next week."

Lily sat forward so fast she nearly fell out of her chair. Embarrassed, she righted herself but not before seeing his lips curl in amusement. Was he playing with her? Bringing her along like a trout after a fly? Most assuredly he was. And enjoying it immensely as he wielded the power over her head like a blade ready to fall.

"Mr. Shellston," she said in a clear, confident tone. "You could honor it if you were so inclined."

"And your point is, Miss Anthony? I'm a businessman. I didn't get to be president of The First National Bank of Texas by sitting on my hands. I've worked hard every day to make the right decisions. And the right decision now is to lease 33 Spring Street to Arlin Ames because he's paying me twice what Mr. Bartlett leased it for to you."

Lily stood. She knew his decision was made and she'd not change it. "Very well. I expect to be refunded all the money my aunt sent to Mr. Bartlett. Every last dime."

"You make the mistake of thinking Mr. Bartlett gave that money to me. He did not. I'm certainly not going to give you money I never received. Now, I'm a busy man, Miss Anthony. If that is all." He stood, signaling for her to leave.

"That is not all. I will take this up with the mayor. I am sure he will not side with you treating the citizens of Rio Wells this way."

"Oh, you mean my brother-in-law, Fred Billingsworth?"

He was so smug standing there. His pinched face and wide set eyes reminded her of the dreadful bug in the lobby. Turning, she flounced out of his office and then out of the bank. She stopped when the door closed behind her. She breathed deeply, trying to calm down. Now what? She couldn't tell her aunt what had transpired. It would not only break her heart but might even make her sick, or worse. She needed to get Mr. Heartless Banker to change his mind. Or else, find another building and come up with the money to rent it. Both ideas, she knew, were about as farfetched as a trip to the moon.

Chapter Ten

Y Knot, Montana

Charity McCutcheon bounded down the massive staircase of the ranch house when she heard the door downstairs open and close. Her waist-length hair flowed around her arms and shoulders freely as she'd been brushing it out after a washing. Dressed in a serge blouse, tucked neatly into her riding pants, she looked much younger than her eighteen years. She'd been waiting impatiently for her brothers to return from Y Knot all morning and was anxiously anticipating a letter from John. It had been a long time since his last post and she was more than worried, a sentiment no one else in the family seemed to share with her.

She hurried over to her brother Luke. "Anything for me from the post office?"

Luke placed his hat on a peg and shrugged out of his jacket. Even in spring the elevation of the ranch made the Montana air quite chilly this time of the day. "Hold on, Charity. I haven't even looked through it yet. Can't a man get a cup of coffee first?" She ignored his knowing smile. He softened his tone. "I'm sure there's something for you today."

She reached for the saddlebag he held in his hands but he hoisted it over his head out of her reach. "Ah-ah-ah," he said, with a no-you-don't tone in his voice. "Where's Faith? I thought she was here with you today."

Charity fought to be patient, crossing her arms over her chest and tapping her toe. The virtue was something she was supposed to be working on. "She was until Rachel and Amy decided to make cookies. They're over at Amy's with all the little ones."

Esperanza, the cook and housekeeper, came into the room carrying a tray filled with cups. There was also a dark brown confection and a stack of folded napkins. The heavy front door opened again and Mark, Matt and Roady entered the room.

"Hey, Char, how're you?"

"Fine, Roady," she answered. Roady was more than a hired hand. He'd been with the McCutcheon ranch for years and was Luke's best friend. He smiled at Esperanza and tipped his hat, making her smooth, dark complexion take on a rosy hue. The newcomers discarded their outer coats and hats and took a seat by the fire.

Luke settled into the sofa and slurped his coffee with gusto. "Nice and hot. Thank you, Esperanza. Charity, how was Holly today?"

"Crying all morning. Faith has to carry her all the time. The second she sets her down, Holly starts in. God forbid I ever have a colicky baby. I don't know how she does it."

"Holly?" Matt asked.

"No, Faith," Charity corrected. She settled next to Luke with a wistful glance at the tan leather saddlebag at his feet. Absentmindedly, she gathered her hair and pulled the mass of locks over one shoulder.

Luke reached for the saddlebag. He unbuckled the clasp and withdrew a handful of letters and papers and started shuffling through them. He handed the first post to Mark, who reached for it with the hand that wasn't stuffing a big chunk of chocolate cake into his mouth.

The posts to his ma and pa he set on the table and several he slipped into his shirt pocket. Charity felt her heart dropping as he came to the last white envelope. He looked up at her, his forehead crinkled and brows arched over his dark eyes as he handed the last one to Matt.

She struggled, trying not to let her disappointment show too much. "I'm really worried about John. He used to write so often. It's been months since his last post and I'm afraid he might be in some sort of trouble."

Roady sat forward. "Probably just forgot, Charity. With graduation, and moving to Rio Wells and all. He's trying to set up a practice, too. That must take some doing."

Charity shrugged. "What if he's hurt or something? We wouldn't even know it. I just have this feeling inside that he needs me."

Matt took a refill when Esperanza came back with the coffee pot then turned his attention to his little sister. "You need to face the fact that he's not returning home to Y Knot. He's a grown man. And he's chosen something other than ranching. No crime in that." He took a sip and set the cup back on the table. "I know Ma and Pa were relieved that he got the position in Rio Wells close to Uncle Winston and the family. Aren't you going for a visit soon?"

Charity glanced away, hurt. That's what the plan had been, but he'd not gotten back to her with the dates. It just wasn't like him to do that to her. Something inside told her that he needed her, but her other brothers would never understand that. "Yes. We just haven't firmed up the dates yet."

"Well, stop. Your letter will come any day now when he finds a free moment to write," Matt responded. "By the way, we saw Brandon today. He asked when you're planning to come to town."

She stood. Everyone had been throwing her and Brandon together for years, ever since she was a girl and they realized she was sweet on him. To be truthful, she *was* partial to Brandon and every single thing about him, but sometimes she worried it was her brothers and the whole idea of being part of the family and ranch that attracted him to her. Marrying up would be an easy way to be part of the McCutcheon clan.

How could she know if he really loved *her*? Being an orphan without much knowledge of his past must make a man yearn for roots. It was understandable. Ever since he'd ridden into Y Knot and taken up residence, he'd been all but adopted by all of them it seemed, and she was glad for it. She hated to think it, but maybe he just wanted to make sure his spot was permanent. "How is he?" she asked.

"Fine. Been working hard. Just hired two new deputies," Mark added.

"Two? Why?"

Luke reached over and sliced himself a piece of cake. "That's what I wondered. But, he says the place is growing and he needs 'em."

Charity stood, just looking at the men. She couldn't calm the feeling growing inside her chest. John was in some sort of trouble. She needed to find out what it was. "Oh, by the way, I've finally decided to go to the finishing school in Denver Ma and Pa have been after me to attend. Lacey's School of Proper Lady's Etiquette. You remember?"

They all looked up at her in surprise. "What?"

"Are you serious? I was led to believe you'd die a despicable death before going there," Luke said, seemingly over the initial shock of her statement and wiping the crumbs from his hands onto the napkin. "I can't believe it."

"Well, it's true. Mother and I talked it over and she left the final decision up to me."

Luke glanced around at Matt and Mark. Both men shrugged their shoulders. Luke continued, "Aren't you too old?"

"That's exactly why I've decided to go. Mother has had her heart set on it forever and since this is my last chance, I wanted to do it for her, to make her happy. The three months will fly by. Right? Just so you know, I'm leaving day after tomorrow."

Luke stared at her for a few long moments. "You're sure Ma knows about this?"

"That's what I just said, isn't it?"

"I think you should wait until they get back from their trip to Cheyenne," Matt suggested.

"Can't." Charity started up the stairs. "The semester starts in a week. If I leave day after tomorrow, I'll have a few days to get there and a couple more to get settled in. The next time you see me, gentlemen, I'll be a changed woman."

Dr. Bixby picked up the scalpel and studied the little girl's exposed abdomen where he'd scissored her undershirt down the middle and laid it open. As a result of the ether, she was in a deep sleep and her mother paced in the other room, her footsteps making the old floorboards creak softly.

"Guess we're ready," Bixby said, looking up at John.

Disappointment gripped him. Of course Dr. Bixby would do the surgery. He was still the doctor here. Had been for many years. But the tremor John had seen earlier in the old doctor's hands had him more than worried. Before he could voice his concern, Dr. Bixby held the tool out to him. Surprised and humbled to his core, John held the old man's gaze for a moment before Bixby nodded his approval.

The sharp metal instrument felt good in his hand as he took a moment to gauge its weight. He'd done this exact operation thrice before. He shouldn't be nervous. However, the other patients had all been adult males, and glancing now at Candy's peaceful face and miniature-sized abdomen made John's stomach tighten up. There was no going back.

Placing the tip of the scalpel on her soft skin directly above her appendix, he made a straight incision with little effort. Dr. Bixby reached forward with a wad of cotton and dabbed away the blood that sprang instantly to the surface. Several kerosene lamps hug from the ceiling, giving John plenty of light, but after ten minutes their warmth made perspiration break out on his forehead.

"Good," Bixby said quietly, their heads almost touching as they leaned forward over the incision. "Go slowly, boy. You don't want to puncture the infected organ."

When John cut through the muscle and then the sac-like covering of the abdominal cavity, the purplish-black appendix, no bigger than his little finger, popped up like a little marching soldier, making it easy for him to remove. He made the cut and removed it with tweezers, placing it in the pan Dr. Bixby held out to him. Carefully probing the area, John looked for signs of infection. The boy reached up and wiped a drop of sweat that was getting ready to fall.

"Almost done." John laid the scalpel and tweezers down and picked up a pre-threaded needle. Slowly he closed the clean incision, taking time with each little knot. Finally finished, he straightened and stretched, relieving the muscles in his back.

"You did fine," Bixby said as he went about cleaning up the blood. "You have a good, steady hand..."

"Your hands were steady, too," John replied in contemplation. "At breakfast I noticed they were quite the opposite. No offense intended," he added quickly.

"None taken."

Bixby finished cleaning up and covered the child with a white cotton sheet from the closet. He tucked it lightly under the child's chin and brushed back her hair from her forehead, never taking his eyes from her face. Turning, he came out of his thoughts to address what John had said.

"I don't know why that is. About my hands, I mean. I've been shaking for about ten years now, but never when I'm in surgery. Just something the good Lord understands."

"Then why did you decide to retire if you're as steady as you've ever been when it counts? A lot of doctors practice till their dying day."

Dr. Bixby removed his apron and threw it in a pile of bloody rags on the floor that would be sent out to the laundry.

"Makes some people nervous. I guess I understand that. I'm getting up there in age. Can't deny it."

John shrugged.

"My Maker could call me home any day or night. Before I go, I wanted to test out the man that replaces me. Make sure he's up to the job. This here ain't an easy place, boy. People have to scratch out a living from the dirt and rocks. They have to live past the outlaws and desperados. Rio Wells is hell on earth. You may as well know it from the get-go."

There was a tapping on the door. "Doctor Bixby. Can I come in now? Tucker said you were all through."

He went over and opened it, motioning for Candy's mother to enter. "Of course, Martha." He pulled up a chair so she could sit by her daughter's side. "It went well. There were no complications."

The woman visibly relaxed, releasing a long, wobbling sigh. "Will she be out for long?" The words were unstable as Martha picked up Candy's hand and held it between her own.

"That's hard to tell, exactly. Maybe an hour or two."

Martha stood back up and hugged the old doctor. "Thank you for saving her life. I was so frightened. Now that Daniel is gone…"

"Shh. It wasn't me that saved her. It was Rio Wells' new doctor. Here, meet Dr. McCutcheon."

It was as if the young widow was now just seeing John for the first time. She came over to where he was leaning against the counter, still wearing his bloody apron. "Dr. McCutcheon? Are you relations to the Rim Rock McCutcheons?"

"Yes, ma'am, I am. Winston and Winnie are my uncle and aunt."

"Well." She looked pleased. "That's wonderful news." Her face brightened, making her look years younger. She was trim and pretty and her head about reached the bottom of his chin. "Thank you, Dr. McCutcheon. My daughter means the world to me."

"That's okay, Martha, that's what us doctors do," Bixby said, ushering her back to her chair and sitting her down. "I'm sure Dr. McCutcheon was happy to oblige."

At that moment, the clock on the wall chimed and John glanced up, remembering Lily's appointment at the bank. He was an hour and a half late. He'd forgotten all about it, not that he'd have been able to go even if he had remembered. He hoped she'd rescheduled when she couldn't find his whereabouts.

"Come on, Dr. McCutcheon," Bixby said, opening the door again and going into the kitchen where the boy was straightening up. With a clatter, the lad dumped the morning dishes into a pan of soapy water. "We'll be right out here, Martha. Just give a call if you need anything."

"Have you two met?" Jas asked, gesturing to the boy. "Formally, that is?"

John went over and stuck out his hand to the youth that had been so helpful during the operation. "No. But I'd like to. He really knows his way around with medical things and what to do. John McCutcheon."

The boy smiled and grasped John's hand with a firm grip. "I'm Tucker Noble. And I appreciate your kind words. I've been working for Doc for a while now."

"Glad to make your acquaintance, Tucker. I really valued your thinking ahead in there."

"No problem. It's what *I* do."

Bixby cleared his throat. "He's the best assistant I've ever had. If you tell him what to expect he don't mind bending his back none. He earns five dollars a month." He paused and looked away before saying, "Now, if *you're* smart, you'll keep him on when it's my time to go."

John looked at Bixby suspiciously. "Where're you going? I was under the distinct impression you were sticking around for a while."

"Thought you wanted this place to yourself?"

Tucker watched the exchange with interest.

Feeling sheepish over his actions this morning, John shrugged. "I guess I did come off that way. But, after today, I see there's merit in the idea of you staying around for a while, just while I get settled. Show me the ropes. Is there enough room upstairs for me?"

Bixby's eyes narrowed a bit behind his spectacles. "Well, Tucker lives up there, too. But there's a free bedroom. We might be able to fit you in."

"What about my medical things and books?"

"Push mine aside, make room."

John groaned inwardly as he tried not to look around and draw attention to the mess. But he knew this was how it should be played out. Besides, maybe he and Tucker could get this place straightened up a bit more. It wouldn't be half as bad. He nodded. "I'll bring my things over later this afternoon."

After her confrontation with the banker, Lily took her time going back to the hotel room, not knowing what she was going to tell her aunt.

She crossed over Main Street and crossed again at Dry. Where the streets intersected, a black iron bench was placed surrounded by two olive trees and a tall saguaro cactus that stood a couple of feet above Lily's head. It also had a beautiful six-foot-tall clock making it one of the prettiest spots she'd seen in town. And, with its pinch of much needed shade, it gave pedestrians a spot to get out of the heat on the sun-drenched street. Coincidentally, it was also one building over from the doctor's office that John had pointed out to her this morning. Was John over there now? She stopped for a moment, looking.

Shouts drew her attention down to the swinging doors of the Black Silk Garter Saloon where a man staggered out and stumbled back and forth. Luckily, he hooked a post with his elbow, swinging around a couple of times before sitting down hard on the edge of a watering trough, spooking several of the horses tied there. A voice shouted from within that he wasn't to come back until he'd sobered up.

Darn. She'd crossed Main Street too early. She should have remained on the bank's side of the street and crossed in front of the hotel. Now, if she wanted to go back to her room, she'd need to pass by the saloon, and the drunken cowboy on the way. She glanced south at the two wagons coming her way, and north at the three mounted riders. Pondering her situation, she didn't hear the footsteps approaching.

"Looks dangerous to me."

Chapter Eleven

Turning, Lily found a tall cowboy standing a few feet away on the boardwalk. He was nicely dressed, and clean. His eyebrows arched over his eyes, amused, as he gestured to the man swaying on the trough, loudly giving the horses a dressing down.

"I wouldn't want to walk past him alone, either. Never underestimate a man in his cups." There was a tinge of humor in his voice and Lily couldn't help but smile at her own actions, clearly evident to others. "You're staying at the Union Hotel?" he asked.

"I am."

The cowboy stepped closer when she answered and she noted his crisply ironed red shirt and expensive-looking boots. He tipped his hat. "I'm Dustin McCutcheon. Didn't I see you arrive on yesterday's stage?"

She was so surprised at his name she had a hard time finding her voice. "Why, yes. My aunt and I traveled from Boston. My name is Lily Anthony."

"I heard what happened on the way here—with the Comancheros. I'm sorry. It must have been frightening for you."

Dustin McCutcheon looked much too young to be John's uncle, so Lily deduced that they must be cousins. He was taller by an inch or two, a handsome man in his own right, though not nearly as handsome, charming, or wonderful as John. His hair was dark and wavy, and there was a lot of it if she judged by what she could see around his collar. His smile was attractive, to say the least.

"It was. Miss Smith and I had become friends during our travels. The others, too. I was very sorry when they were killed."

He held out his arm. "May I escort you past the drunkard?"

She nodded as she glanced one more time at John's office, then placed her hand in the warm crook of his elbow.

"You must be Dr. McCutcheon's relation," Lily said as they walked along.

"John's my cousin. Although, this is the first time we've ever met. Actually, I'm older than John by a few years. Luke, his older brother, is my age."

"Luke? John hasn't said anything about Luke. He just mentioned he had four siblings."

"I suppose he wouldn't, being that his brother is..." He stopped and looked down into her face, then smiled innocently. "I guess it's not for me to say."

As they approached, the disheveled man stopped scolding the horses and looked their way. He stood and watched them draw near. His eyes narrowed into slits.

"Francine," he said, then hiccupped. "I told you to stay at *home*, woman. What're you trying to pull, sashaying all over town?" He took a step in Lily's direction, but stopped abruptly when he glanced up into Dustin's face, self-doubt getting the better of him.

He was a big man, tall and husky. His fists looked like frying pans and his arms bulged in their sleeves. His ruddy complexion darkened as his face twisted into a sneer. "*McCutcheon!*"

The man grabbed for Lily, but Dustin swept her effortlessly into his arms. There was just enough time for Dustin to place her behind before he had to duck the punch aimed at his head. Missing his mark, the drunk lost his balance and crashed into the side of the building, sliding down the wall.

Dustin turned to her and smiled. "You okay?"

Before she could get the words out of her mouth, the drunk was back, and charged. "Watch out!"

Dustin stepped aside with the grace of a dancer. The giant ended up in the water trough head first. His feet kicked back and forth as he struggled to get out.

Taking Lily's arm as if nothing of consequence had happened, Dustin escorted her down the boardwalk to the hotel.

"Here you go." He opened the door and stepped back, letting her pass. "It was a pleasure meeting you, Miss Anthony. May I call you Lily?"

She nodded. "Of course, Mr. McCutcheon."

"Dustin," he corrected, then smiled mischievously.

"Dustin," she repeated, then felt her cheeks heat under his close scrutiny. "Thank you for the escort."

He tipped his hat. "My pleasure."

Lily hurried toward the sweeping stairs at the back of the lobby. She was just about to go up to her room when she heard her aunt's voice calling out to her.

"Yoo-hoo, Lily dear, over here."

Lily looked over to the parlor area of the restaurant where there were a few tables set up for teatime. Her aunt sat at a small table next to the window. She looked rested and happy and was dressed to the hilt. Her gray hair was swept up beautifully and her face had a nice amber glow. She and Dustin had walked right past that exact window. She motioned for her to come over.

"There you are," Harriett said, setting her cup down and offering Lily her cheek for a kiss. "Who was that nice young man?"

Lily placed a light peck on her cheek and sat down opposite, then nodded when a waitress looked her way, holding up a tea-cup.

What was she supposed to say about the lease and the money? Her aunt was nearly eighty-six. The last thing Lily wanted to do was upset her.

"So do tell," Harriett asked with interest. "Who was the handsome stranger? Where did you two meet?"

"Dustin McCutcheon. We met outside a few minutes ago. And thank heavens we did. He all but saved me from a man who thought I was his wife. He was drunk, you see."

"McCutcheon?" Harriett's eyes opened wide. "Another McCutcheon? Maybe I should send for Giselle, too. So many single—"she said, looking at the waitress as the young woman set another cup and saucer in front of Lily and then a pot of hot tea, "—men in Rio Wells. He is single?"

"Tante Harriett," Lily said in a scolding tone. "I do not know. I assume he is. He acted like he was, but then one can never be sure. I certainly did not ask."

Harriett lifted her teacup to her lips and took a tiny sip. She looked at Lily across the rim of her cup. "I think coming to Rio Wells was the best idea I've ever had. I can definitely see you as a doctor's wife."

Right then John came hurrying through the heavy glass door and went directly to the staircase. He took the stairs two at a time. Halfway to the second story balcony he glanced over his shoulder and his gaze met Lily's. Lily quickly looked down, but it was too late. She was sure he'd seen her watching him. She didn't have the nerve to look and see if he was on his way over. It was less than a second that she had to wait to find out.

"Lily. I'm sorry I missed the appointment. There was an emergency and it couldn't be helped. "

Lily glanced up from her teacup where she was pretending to be interested in a tiny sliver of tealeaf floating at the bottom. His clothes were rumpled and when he removed his hat his hair was damp around his ears.

"Would you care to join us," Harriett asked.

"No, thank you. I only have a moment. What happened with the appointment, Lily? I hope you rescheduled so I can accompany you."

Lily patted her napkin to her lips. "Actually, Mr. Shellston and I did talk. He's leased the Spring Street building out to someone else." Her aunt's sharp intake of breath was like a knife in Lily's heart. Harriett's teacup rattled so violently John reached out and helped her set it back in its saucer.

"Lily, dear, you didn't tell me that. You mean 33 Spring Street is not going to be our shop? Our home? But we've prepaid Mr. Bartlett for the full year's lease." Her aunt sat forward and grasped the white marble tabletop, her cup of tea forgotten.

The look on John's face spoke volumes. He realized his mistake as her aunt's distress grew.

"Everything is going to be fine, Tante. Mr. Shellston said he had another building that he is going to get ready for us. It will only take a few days. That is all. He will apply our lease money to it."

Tante Harriett's hand fluttered to her chest as a sigh whistled through her lips. "Well, thank goodness for that. Without a way to support ourselves, what would become of us?"

John's expression was hard to read. "I have to get back to the patient," he said, glancing at the clock in the lobby. "But first I'd like to know if you two would have dinner with me tonight. And of course, it's my treat."

Lily was about to decline when her *Tante* nodded. "We'd love to join you, Dr. McCutcheon."

"Six thirty?

Tante Harriett nodded again.

"Done. I'll meet you in the lobby."

John sliced into the mouth-watering filet as it sizzled and popped, releasing the rich mesquite flavor. He pushed a large hunk through his mashed potatoes, then placed it in his mouth. He chewed, swallowed and wiped his mouth with his napkin. "How are your dinners?"

"Delicious," Lily said. "I did not expect such fine cuisine here. One can survive on tea and crumpets for only so long."

"I'm glad. I hope you're not offended by the artwork?" He chuckled as he looked around the walls of the Lillian Russell Room at the twenty or more paintings of nudes. All the subjects were ivory-skinned beauties, partially draped in velvets, silks or some other finery.

"Oh, I think they're beautiful. Every single one," Harriett said. She took a small sip from her wine goblet and looked about. "Now, in Europe, we lean more toward impressionism, mind you. But, we have our risqué painters, too. The prototypes for these artists here, I'm sure."

John smiled, enjoying the conversation. In Boston, Emmeline hadn't been too enthusiastic over the arts. She would rather spend her time shopping at Faneuil Hall, looking for the latest bauble or a new pair of finely made shoes. "Do you like them, Lily?"

"I do. They're all so different and yet, a woman is a woman, yes?" she said without the least hint of coyness. "I especially like that one."

She pointed to a medium-sized painting hanging above the door to the hotel lobby. A scantily clothed young woman lay on her back in the tall grass, with her horse grazing nearby.

Just then, the door swung open and Dustin came through. He looked around the dining room and, with the few diners on this Thursday evening, spotted them easily. He nodded to John. Hanging his hat on the rack, he sauntered to their table.

Chapter Twelve

"This must be your aunt?" Dustin said as he approached, looking between Harriett and Lily. "The one who traveled with you from Boston."

"And you must be the young man who so graciously saved my Lily from the drunken sot." Harriett's eyes gleamed in the lamplight. Her face, an interesting maze of wrinkles, powder and happiness, was alight with pleasure. "Lily told me what happened. It sounded like something straight out of a novel."

So. Dustin and Lily had met. John motioned to the empty spot at the table, opposite Lily. "Care to join us?"

"Thank you, but I've already eaten supper." That said, he continued to stand there, as if waiting for another invitation.

"We're finishing up, ourselves," John stated. "Have coffee and dessert. We've hardly had a chance to get to know each other since my arrival."

"As long as the ladies don't mind."

"Of course not." Excitement sparkled from Harriett's eyes, making her look years younger. "We would love to have your company."

"And," Lily added, "I have hardly had the chance to thank you properly for what you did for me. I am very grateful."

Dustin pulled out the empty chair and seated himself. "It was nothing. You weigh next to nothing at all. And, if I'm going to be absolutely truthful, I enjoyed the moment more than I can say."

Lily's face flamed scarlet. She glanced at John and he shrugged. "What happened?" he found himself asking against his will.

"Well," Dustin began. "I found Lily on the boardwalk contemplating how to get past the saloon. Billy Burger was sitting out front, drunker than a skunk, giving the horses a tongue-lashing. All I did was escort her by without incident."

Lily started to laugh. "Without incident to me. But not to, ah, Billy Burger. I could not believe he went head first into that water." Her eyes scrunched at the corners as she tried to hold in her laughter.

Dustin was watching her with interest. "It was nothing, cousin."

It didn't sound like nothing to John, but he'd not question further.

The waitress was back with a tray and picked up the used dishes. "Did you save room for dessert?"

"What do you have?" John asked, a bit defensively.

"Bread pudding, berry pie, peach cobbler and two slices of granny apple."

"Lily?" John looked at Lily, seated to his left.

"Oh, I couldn't possibly. You've been much too generous already, John. You can't keep treating us to dinner like this."

"I insist. Don't go looking to Harriett for help, either. I won't take no for an answer."

"In that case, I would like a slice of berry pie, please."

"The same for me," Harriett said.

"Apple," Dustin added.

John leaned back in his chair. "I'll take a large piece of the cobbler."

"John had to perform an operation today," Lily said after the waitress left.

Dustin's eyes narrowed almost imperceptibly. "Today? On your first day in town?" He stared openly at John. "You sure the poor victim really needed it?"

"Victim?"

Dustin laughed. "I'm just kiddin', John. It just seems strange. You know—your very first day and all. Who was the patient?"

"Candy Brown."

"I know Martha, Candy's mother," Dustin replied.

The waitress was back and served the desserts.

"*That* would go without saying." John cut his cobbler with the side of his fork and raised a brow at his cousin.

Dustin's fork stopped halfway to his mouth. "What's *that* supposed to mean?" He completed his action and chewed vigorously.

John shrugged. "Just that Rio Wells is a small town. I'd think you'd know just about everyone. It was her *appendix*."

Dustin was swallowing and the strange word made him cough. "Append...what?"

"Appendix. It's a little organ on the right lower half of your abdomen. If it gets infected and isn't removed, it ruptures inside, spewing infection everywhere—then kills you."

Harriett gasped.

"That sounds difficult, John," Lily added. "And dangerous. As I said before, being a doctor and saving people's lives is a noble profession."

She was listening with rapt attention and John felt a little surge of victory. "She's as good as new."

"Thank goodness," Lily breathed. "What a blessing you got to town when you did. I hate to think of that happening to anyone."

"Dr. Bixby could have done the same if I hadn't been here."

A moment passed. Dustin grunted, then pointed to John's stitches. "Still hurt? Looks like you put something on it."

John figured Dustin must have seen Lily arrive on the stage yesterday and took a shine to her. Well, Dustin needn't worry about *him*. He and Lily were just friends. He wished Dustin would back off.

"Actually, *Dustin*, I did. Dr. Bixby suggested a salve he makes from cactus juice. It heals a wound quickly. And it also soothes." John scraped his empty plate with the bottom of his fork, getting every last crumb.

"My treat," Dustin said as the waitress approached with the bill.

"Oh, no. That's not necessary."

"I can't let you pay for your own dinner your first night in town, cousin. Texas McCutcheons may be a little rough around the edges, but we do have *some* manners." He took the paper from the waitress' hand, glancing at the total. Withdrawing a twenty-dollar bill from his pocket he handed it to her. "Keep the rest."

"Dustin," Harriett gushed, "that is so kind of you. Thank you very much."

"Yes, thank you *again*," Lily added.

Knowing there was nothing he could do or say to change Dustin's mind, John thanked him, too. "That's thoughtful of you, cousin." As the word "thoughtful" passed his lips, he realized he *still* hadn't yet telegrammed Emmeline. What in the devil was wrong with him? At this hour, the telegraph office was closed.

John helped Lily with her chair as Dustin did the same for Harriett. After thanking Dustin again, the three went up the stairs and then, at their room, Lily produced the key from her bag and put it into the lock.

"May I talk to you for a moment?" John waited until Harriett went inside after kissing him on the cheek.

"Of course." She followed him back a few steps to the balcony railing that overlooked the lobby.

"What happened at the bank today? I know you didn't tell the whole story this afternoon."

"Mr. Shellston is…an arrogant, cold-hearted man. He has let the building out to someone else because he can get more money for it."

"But, you said he's finding you another shop?"

"I am ashamed to admit that I lied to keep Tante Harriett from worrying. He is *not* finding another building for us and he is *not* refunding the year's rent that my aunt sent to Mr. Bartlett. He said he had never received any funds and he would not return money out of his own pocket."

"So. What now?"

She shrugged. "I am not sure. I do not know exactly how much money my aunt has, except that it is not much. She keeps it from me so I will not worry. But, I *am* worried. Somehow I need to find a new building and discover a treasure chest full of money at the end of a rainbow. Nothing impossible, mind you." Her hands were placed on her hips and her expression resolute.

John racked his brain for a solution. "I wish I knew more people around here. There has to be somewhere you can use at least until I get that banker to return your money."

"I do not wish to keep involving you with my problems. You have done so much already. And for hearing me out tonight. A problem shared is half the problem solved."

"Come on," he said, turning and going over to her door. "Get some rest tonight and tomorrow things will look brighter. And I'll also see what can be done with this matter."

"Be sure to look after yourself." She gestured to his wound. "I think you are busy doing for others. Do not forget to do for yourself."

He waited till she closed the door, then descended the stairs and went out into the dark street.

Chapter Thirteen

A candle flickered on the nightstand as Lily went directly to the screen in the corner of the room and slipped behind it. Her emotions were too close to the surface to let her aunt, who was already in bed with the covers pulled up to her chin, notice her distress.

Reaching behind her back, she unclasped the row of hooks and eyes holding the green muslin fabric of her best dress together, and let it fall away, feeling the cool air glide across her warm skin. She lifted the garment, which she'd made herself, over her head and hung it on a peg on the wall next to Harriett's gown. Taking the wide-mouthed pitcher from the wooden shelf, she poured water into her basin.

Gooseflesh raised up on Lily as she stood, barefoot in her pantaloons and chemise, and washed her face and neck with a clean cotton rag dipped in the cool water. After rinsing the cloth, she went about washing her arms. Stripping off her underclothes, she finished up the rest before donning a long sleeping gown. Lastly, she brushed her teeth and quickly braided her hair, not caring if she missed a strand or two.

She peeked around the screen. She didn't want to talk tonight. She didn't have any answers for the questions her aunt might ask. Thankfully, she had rolled to her side and seemed to be sleeping soundly.

Lily went to the open window and sat in the chair, thinking. Dinner tonight had been special. She had enjoyed John's company very much. And, if she were honest, Dustin's too. Would Emmeline really come from Boston to a town like Rio Wells? John believed she would. Feeling a bit melancholy, she sighed. A breeze wafted down off the mountains that rimmed Rio Wells from the north, cooling her skin and making the lanterns that stretched across the street sway gently.

A shot rang out. The piano music stopped abruptly and the double doors of the saloon swung open and smacked against the walls with a bang. Two men ran out, darted into the alley between the buildings and disappeared into the night.

Harriett sat up in bed. "What was that?" she asked, frightened. "Lily? Lily, dear, are you there?"

Lily ran to the bed and sat down. "I'm here. I'm here. Don't be scared."

Harriett reached for her spectacles on the bedside table and put them on with trembling hands. She then took Lily's hands into her own. "Did you hear something, Lily?"

"Yes. Something happened next door in the saloon."

"Was it a gunshot?"

"That's what it sounded like. But, maybe the cowboys are just having some fun." *I will never get used to America. Dime novel stories are a far cry from the grisly reality of dead bodies riding in a stagecoach.*

"Oh." Harriett blinked several times and looked around the darkened room. She lay back onto her pillow and smiled up at Lily. "I'll be so happy to move out of here, Lily. Think about it. Our own home again. It will be good to get settled and set up the shop. Don't you agree?"

Lily, still holding onto the older woman's hand, patted it softly. "Of course. It will be just as we planned. Soon all the ladies of Rio Wells will be coming to us for their clothing needs."

"I haven't seen too many ladies, Lily." Anxiety was back in her tone.

"No worries tonight. They are just hiding away, out of the hot Texas sun. Once we set up shop, they will flock to see our newest creations."

Harriett nodded. Her eyes shone with tenderness before slowly drifting closed. "You're such an angel, dear. I don't know what I would do without your pretty smile," she mumbled.

After a moment, Lily removed her aunt's spectacles and set them back on the tabletop. Tomorrow she would find a building come heck or high water. She *had* to. They needed a safe place where gunshots and piano music didn't disturb. Rio Wells was wilder than anything she'd ever read about, and she'd only been here for one day. She circled the big bed and climbed in on the other side. Looking across the room to the open window, she knew it would be hours before sleep would come.

Finished checking on Candy and her mother, John was just about to climb the stairs when a gunshot shattered the stillness. He crossed the room in three strides and opened the door, stepping cautiously out onto the front boardwalk. He couldn't tell from which direction the sound had come, but he looked up and down the street for anything suspicious. Dry Street was quiet, except for a black cat that jumped from a barrel to the shed roof of the mercantile next door. Antsy from his first night in town, he decided to take a short walk down to the livery and check on his horse. The breeze blew in from the north, bringing with it a feeling of rebirth.

When he arrived in the livery, the animals were dozing with their heads hanging over the stall doors. Several chickens nesting in the hay clucked nervously as he approached, pulling their heads from under their wings and blinking their sleepy eyes in his direction.

"You're out late tonight, John." Cradle, the owner of the livery, came in through the back doors of the barn, pulling his suspenders up over each shoulder.

He seemed like a genuine sort with the way he handled John's horse with gentleness and affection. He must have noticed him walking past and into the front doors of the livery from his residence on the second floor.

"Heard a gunshot earlier and thought to take a look around," John said. "This town always this noisy?"

Cradle lowered his hefty body onto a sawhorse and stuck a clean piece of straw between his teeth. The moon's light shining through the loft opening gave John ample luminosity to see him.

"You know, I just have a feeling. A niggle deep down in my gut," the smithy said. "Seems like I've seen a few strange faces these past two days. More than I should."

"What do you mean?"

"Not the usual newcomers arriving on the stage like you and Miss Anthony. I'm talking about the kind of man you don't want to run into in an alley at night." Cradle got up and went over to the hay he kept in the corner, giving each expectant horse a handful. He stopped at the last stall and ran his hand down the animal's neck.

"You've met Lily Anthony and her aunt, then?"

"No. No, I haven't. But news travels fast when a young, single woman comes to town. Especially one as pretty as she's reported to be."

John pushed away from the wall and went and looked out at the corrals where a few horses dozed. He turned back. "How'd you come by the name Cradle anyway? Don't think I've ever heard it before."

Even in the moonlight, John could see Cradle's face take on a wistful expression. "I guess my pa had a sense of humor. I was a big baby when I was born. Gave my ma a horrible time, almost killed her. Right from the get-go I was bigger than the cradle my pa had built. He started calling me that over the protests of my ma and it just stuck. Real name is Herman."

"Cradle," a man said, walking into the barn.

"Sheriff."

John swung around to see a tall man walking his way. So this was the sheriff, Dexter Dane. John had stopped at the sheriff's office today as it was right across the alley from his back door. He'd met the deputy, Pete Miller, but the sheriff had been out. John stepped forward. "I'm Dr. John McCutcheon, Sheriff. " He put out his hand.

Sheriff Dane took it into his own. "I heard of your arrival but haven't had a chance to drop in. I went out to the Wells Fargo swing station today to get a statement from Chester about the three passengers and two employees who were killed. I'll want to get your statement too, in the next day or two."

The sheriff was an older man, probably his father's age. He was tall and thin with a pitted face. He must have been in a fight sometime in the past because several of his front teeth were missing.

"Well," John said. "I need to get back to my patient. You know where to find me."

Chapter Fourteen

The smell of coffee drew John out of his sleep. He stretched, relieving all the tensions that had been building in his body for the past week, then laid back, staring at the ceiling of his new, tiny room. After a moment, he found a match and lit the lantern by his bed. Checking his pocket watch, he found it was almost five o'clock.

He pulled on his pants and a shirt and descended the stairs to find Tucker in the kitchen, reading the paper with a hot cup of coffee on the table in front of him.

"Morning." John ran his fingers through his hair as he looked around the quiet kitchen. "You're an early riser."

"Reckon so."

John motioned to the examination room with a nod and asked, "They awake yet?"

"Haven't heard a peep."

John glanced around the kitchen.

"Bottom shelf of the cupboard."

John went to the back of the kitchen and retrieved a cup. He filled it with dark, fragrant liquid. The first sip burned all the way down, just the way he liked it. At the table, he pushed some of the clutter to the side and sat down. "You like doctoring?"

Tucker looked up. He nodded and reached for his cup. "Yup. I do."

The row of books in the other room caught John's eye. "Read any of Bixby's medical books?"

The boy straightened, as if surprised John was interested in him. "As a matter of fact, I have."

John sipped his coffee then asked, "Really. Which ones?"

"Robley Dunglison's Practice of Medicine."

"Mmm, that one is good."

"Elements of Surgery, by Robert Liston and Samuel Gross. Really liked that. It has a lot of good illustrations."

John was impressed. Those two books were hard reading and took attention and determination to get through. Only someone who really loved the subject would be able to complete them. "Any others?"

Tucker's cheeks deepened in color. Then, as if he'd decided to trust John, added, "Midwifery Book, by Thomas Ewell."

"I'm *very* impressed, Tucker. Good for you." Should he encourage the boy toward medical school or would that road only lead to frustration? He didn't know. His handicap was somewhat limiting, but sometimes a determined spirit could find ways of getting around almost anything. "I have some others I brought with me. Remind me later to show them to you."

The morning flew by as the two doctors and Tucker prepared the patient to go home. A buckboard for transport was rented and Martha was all smiles with the quick recovery her daughter was making. Dr. Bixby insisted on going and taking Tucker along with him, to help get the child settled in.

The moment the buckboard rolled out of sight, John headed to the telegraph office. It took twenty frustrating minutes to learn that the lines had been down for a few days and the only way to communicate was with a letter.

John realized in his present frame of mind he should probably eat before he went looking for the banker. It might improve his mood. Although he doubted it. The bank was just across the street and he'd like to resolve Lily and Harriett's problem as soon as possible.

The teller that he'd talked to yesterday stepped out on the boardwalk and lit a cigarette, taking a long draw. Their eyes met over the smoke as he exhaled. *So much for having breakfast first.*

Stepping off the wooden planks, John made his way across the dusty street. The temperature was rising and a trickle of sweat slipped down the side of his face. The teller must have known by the look on John's face that his break was over because he dabbed the top of the cigarette on the post, and put the rest into his shirt pocket.

"Is Mr. Shellston in? I'd like a word with him."

"Yes he is. Let me go check if he will see you."

Who in the hell did this banker think he was? Grover Cleveland? No one should take themselves so seriously.

In a moment the teller was back. "I'm sorry. He's quite busy. Would you like to make an appointment?"

Though John was the youngest male McCutcheon, he was known by all in Y Knot as the one with the hottest temper. Growing up, he'd gotten into trouble more times than he'd like to remember because of it, and he'd been marched out to the woodshed by his father, each and every time.

"Absolutely," he said in a pleasant tone. "I'd like to make an appointment for…" He flipped open his pocket watch to see the time was now eleven twenty-five. "Eleven twenty-six."

The teller backed off a step, peering at John to see if he was joking. "But…that's in one minute?"

"Exactly."

Chapter Fifteen

After the big night they'd had, it was no wonder Harriett slept soundly past seven o'clock without any signs of waking. Lily snuck from the nice warm covers and peeked out into the hallway until one of the chambermaids came by. She requested some hot water and a tub sent up. In no rush to go out, Lily enjoyed bathing and washing her hair. The hotel even availed her at no extra charge a tiny bit of rose water for rinsing.

Today she needed to "make opportunities" happen. That's what her mother always said. People who sat around waiting for good fortune to find them never achieved anything of value. Something of worth was never gotten easily. If you depend on yourself, then you only have yourself to blame. She could go on and on remembering all the sayings. Her mother and father had been extremely hard workers, never wasting a moment of time or energy. She would be like that. She would make her opportunities happen.

When Lily came around the screen fully dressed, she was shocked. She went to the side of the bed and gazed at Harriett. Stirrings of fear began in her mind. She bent close to her aunt's face, checking to see if she was still breathing.

"Tante," she whispered, lowering herself to one knee so she could get closer. "Are you awake?" She rubbed her aunt's shoulder, then gave it a soft shake. "Tante Harriett?"

This had happened three other times since Lily had come to live with her aunt in Boston. Fear gripped her as she shook the small frame of her aunt with more force but no result.

Falling to her knees, she reached for her aunt's satchel under the bed. She rummaged around, looking for the cylinder of smelling salts that her aunt usually had nearby for emergencies. Not finding it, she rifled deeper into the clutter, carefully setting aside the tiny derringer her aunt always carried, and the knitting needles that she had yet to use since departing Boston. As Lily was about to close the bag up, something new caught her eye. It was a little black lacquered box etched with flowers and a tiny pink butterfly. Lily opened it carefully, finding several packs of paper containing a small amount of white powder. Confused, she slowly closed the lid and put it back where she'd found it next to a pair of black knitted stockings. As she pushed them to the side, she noticed that something appeared to be stuffed inside one.

Lily sat back on her heels for a moment, thinking furiously. Slowly, she took the sock and reached inside. Her fingers closed around a wad of soft fabric. Instantly her heart quailed in trepidation. When she withdrew her hand and unwrapped the mysterious lavender cloth, a glimmering blue stone lay in her palm. It was the size of a buffalo nickel and had a little gold loop so it could be put on a chain. It looked incredibly expensive.

Quickly, she rewrapped it and stuck it back in the sock, then replaced it in her aunt's bag. She backed away from the bed, still staring at her aunt. She'd heard hushed stories about opium and laudanum before, but no one in her family's history had ever suffered from any kind of dependence. Was the white powder medicinal? And where had the gem come from? Was it stolen? Was that the reason for their hasty departure?

"I don't take kindly to anyone barging into my office, Dr. McCutcheon, no matter who they think they are." The shocked look on Mr. Shellston's face was worth the regret John would feel later over his temper-fueled actions. "I'm a busy man and can't abide being sidetracked every other minute of the day."

"What I have to say will only take a minute. I'm sure we can come to an understanding. Rio Wells isn't so big that you don't have a moment for me. Or Miss Anthony, for that matter."

Mr. Shellston's eyes narrowed. "Oh, you've come about her. There isn't anything more I have to say on the subject. If her aunt was careless enough not to check references before wiring such a large amount of money across the country, then she deserves what she gets."

"She's an eighty-five-year-old woman, for God's sake. Have some compassion. This bank can easily make their bad situation better if you choose to."

Both men stood glaring at each other with the massive desk between them. The tick of the lobby clock and their breathing was all that was heard in the small office.

Mr. Shellston's features softened. "If I had received those funds from Mr. Bartlett, then of course, I'd be apt to rethink my decision. But, am I just supposed to give them use of a building for a whole year for free?"

"With the many places I see vacant that they could use, and I know must be owned by this bank, yes. Your bank could easily afford it."

"Even if I saw fit to agree, the board of trustees would never concur. Besides, as a result every person would come in here looking for charity. This bank does not give away free handouts. My answer remains as it did yesterday, Dr. McCutcheon."

John left the bank as frustrated as when he had entered. He strode down the walk on his way back to his office, his mind racing over every possibility he could think of. He could lease a building for them himself, and he would if it came down to it, although he knew Lily and her aunt wouldn't like feeling beholden to him.

He could ask his uncle to talk to the mayor and city council. Surely Uncle Winston had some pull in this town. His ranch was the largest spread around these parts and was one of the major reasons this town was prospering. If either of those ideas didn't pan out, he might be able to help Lily find a job. That would be a shame, though, given her skills as a seamstress. John lightly fingered the stitches on his face. They pulled when he drew his mouth up into a fake smile to feel the tautness of his wound. The tiny, well-placed knots were a testament to her fine needlework. He wasn't going to just roll over and give up.

He rounded the corner and stopped, facing the doctor's office. As he waited for a wagon to pass he stared at the dilapidated place, then his gaze moved across the small alley on the left side of the building to the structure next door. Was it a storeroom? Striding behind the wagon, he hurried the rest of the way and tried the doorknob, finding it locked.

Bixby and Tucker were back from taking Martha and Candy Brown home, and startled when he let the door slam behind him.

"They get settled okay?" John asked abruptly.

The old doctor eyed him for a long minute. "They did. I'm happy, too, with that little gal's progress."

John only grunted. He hitched his head to the side. "What's the building next door?"

"Storage room. Can't even get into it any more. Has thirty five years of *stuff* packed inside." He chuckled and shook his head. "Some of it payment for services, some just things I couldn't live without. Now it's a millstone around my neck."

"It's part of the doctor's office building, then? What if I wanted to use it for something?"

"I reckon you could. But, like I said, it's near on full."

"What kind of stuff? You want any of it?"

"You name it. Glassware, cloth, gadgets and gizmos. Horseshoes, saddles, tools, furniture, whatnots." He laughed. "See what you have to look forward to? Guess I don't want any of it since I've not even gone in there for years. And I don't need it for anything. You really want to clean it out?"

"Depends. Does the bank hold any title?"

Bixby whistled and shook his head. "I'm not indebted to that snake. I like that man about as much as a cat likes to swim. Since he's come to town a handful of years ago, more people than not have up and lost their properties. Don't trust him a bit."

"Well, we agree on something, then. What about living quarters? Any upstairs?"

"Of sorts. But very small."

"I have friends in need of a place to start a business in. Problem is, they don't have much money now. In return for them cleaning up the place and fixing it up a bit, maybe you'd offer to let them sell the contents—since you say you have no need of them—and split the profit with you. What do you think?"

Bixby stared at him for a long moment. "I'd be relieved. And grateful."

The building might just be a solution for Lily and Harriett's problem. He could feel his anger abating, at which point he noticed the gnawing hunger in his stomach. He needed food before he did another thing.

"I'm starved and don't have the volition or the time to fix anything myself. Where can you direct me to get a good, fast noontime plentiful plate of food?"

"The saloon does a first-rate steak or stew. Or the Cheddar Box down the street across from the livery usually has some palatable specials. There's also the Union Hotel, but I'm not taking responsibility if you go there. It's on the road out to the McCutcheon ranch. You most likely passed it on your way to town."

"You're a wealth of knowledge, Bixby, thanks. Anyone interested in joining me?"

"Martha fixed us breakfast this morning," Bixby said. Tucker just shook his head.

"Okay then, I'm off to the Cheddar Box, just in case anyone's asking."

On the way, John ducked into the mercantile to introduce himself to the Gradys. Nel and Betty were friendly enough and had a nice selection of goods. John was impressed. As he gazed at the knickknacks behind the cash register, a porcelain figurine caught his eye. No mistaking the German dress and kerchief. The petite maid was holding a milk bucket and there was a small periwinkle flower at her feet. It was the exact color of Lily's eyes. A slow smile formed. Did he dare? Why on earth would he buy her a gift?

"May I see that?" He pointed to the figurine and Mrs. Grady quickly brought it to him.

"This is a beautiful piece we just got in last month. It's imported from Germany and is hand painted." She carefully put it into John's hands.

Instantly he knew, for whatever reason, he had to buy it. Perhaps her birthday was coming up? Or, maybe a gift when she and her aunt had gotten their shop up and running. They were friends. Had been through so much together already. It didn't mean anything more than that.

Holding her skirt off the ground, Lily ran toward John's office. She opened the door and hurried inside. "John," she called while trying to catch her breath. "John, are you here?"

An old man met her in the waiting room. "Is Dr. McCutcheon here?"

"You just missed him." Lily could see his mind twirling like a windmill. One of his bushy gray brows lifted when he said, "You can find him at the Cheddar Box having his midday meal." He pointed past her and out the window. "Across from the livery."

When she finally reached the restaurant, she rushed inside. She spotted John and one other table of customers. John hadn't seen her enter. A waitress had just set a plate filled with food before him and he was cutting into it with relish. His eyes were on his plate as he lifted a forkful of meat to his mouth.

He looked up, surprised. "Lily. Hello." He set down his fork and knife. His smile faded as she struggled to catch her breath. "Would you care to join—"

"It's Tante. I can't wake her up."

He stood abruptly, his napkin falling from his lap to the wooden floor. "She's at the hotel?" Lily nodded. He took two coins from his pocket and placed them on the tablecloth, then rushed out the door.

Chapter Sixteen

John set Harriett's black box into his doctor's bag. "My guess is morphine, a powerful pain reliever. Maybe she had some sort of accident when she was young and is still addicted to what she was given for the pain. Many of the soldiers after the war have become dependent."

Lily only nodded.

"Do you have any idea where she's getting it?"

"No." Her voice was low, like a child's, and her teeth chewed on her lower lip.

"No, I guess you wouldn't." John folded his stethoscope and put it away. "Does she ever complain of having pain?"

"Yes, sometimes she complains about her back. I just thought she meant pain in general. Maybe she fell off a horse or something?"

Lily's brows were drawn down in a worried line over her eyes. She glanced at her aunt's travel bag. "What am I supposed to tell her when she wakes up and sees her box is missing?"

"The truth. That I have whatever this is locked up in my office for safekeeping. Then send for me. You don't have to deal with this alone."

Lily turned and walked to the window. He followed but stopped short, giving her the space she seemed to need.

"Have I upset you?"

She shook her head, making the mass of golden hair ripple and reminding him of aspen leaves in the fall. "No, you've done nothing wrong. I am just worried about my *Tante*. She is old. I think she might die."

John took her shoulders and gently turned her toward him. "At her age, you know that that is always a possibility. Right?"

"Of course." She regarded him intently. "I just wish I had known about the drugs before. Maybe there was something I could have done to help her."

John tugged her into his arms and held her close. Her body was compliant, and she didn't pull away. On the contrary, her hands came up and circled his neck.

"Or perhaps I could have worked harder to talk her out of this idea of coming to Texas," she murmured close to his neck, as if it were the most natural thing on earth for them to be embracing. "It seemed so farfetched at the time and even more so now."

When he felt her fingers playing with the back of his hair, John bent his head and found Lily's forehead, kissing it softly. "Why did she arrange the trip in the first place?"

"She said she needed a drier climate for her health. However, she has never been sickly in that way. She has never had a cough or suffered from the influenza. If I may be so bold to say, I think that she was making that up."

John knew it must be terribly hard for Lily to imply that her aunt had lied. He wished there was something he could do to make her feel better. He'd help in any way he could, especially be a supportive shoulder for her to lean on. "I may have solved one of your problems."

She lifted her head to gaze into his eyes. "What do you mean? Did you change the banker's mind?"

She slid from his embrace and instantly his arms felt empty. "Uh, not quite. I did talk to him, but we didn't quite see eye to eye."

She nodded, knowing what he was implying.

"But I have found a building for you and your aunt to set up in. You can use it free of charge." When her face clouded over he added quickly, "That is, until you're on your feet financially, so to speak, and then you can start paying rent."

A spark came back into her eyes as she searched his face. "Where?"

"Let me just say first that it's small and needs considerable work. But there's a living space upstairs, too."

Lily clapped her hands once and went up on her toes in excitement. "Where is it?"

"Remember my office? The run-down, ramshackle of a place? Well, it's right next door. Actually, it's part of the medical buildings. Dr. Bixby is using it as a storage room."

Lily glanced across the room at her aunt. "So you are the landlord, then?"

"I will be when Dr. Bixby retires. But for now, it's his. He said he hasn't even been in the building for five years, though, so don't worry about putting him out. I think he was even anxious to get the responsibility of it off his mind."

She smiled, and held his gaze for several long moments. "It sounds like an answer to my prayers. If it is available, I will work hard to clean it up."

"Well, don't make any decisions now. Wait until you come over and go through it. It might be more work than it's worth." He went over and picked up his black bag and moved toward the door. "I'll be back in a little while. Just keep your eye on her." She nodded as he let himself out and closed the door.

Charity climbed into the stage in Y Knot and straightened her plain brown skirt around her legs. She smiled at the woman she was seated next to, and the young son sitting on her lap. Luke reached in and handed Charity her small satchel, which she took and placed beneath her seat. Mark waited on the boardwalk, having already given her a brotherly hug.

Luke winked as he patted her knee. "Ma's going to be real happy to know you've finally decided to go. Like you said, three months will fly by. Besides, you may even enjoy yourself." He smiled as if trying to convince himself of his own words. "Consider it an adventure."

"Ten minutes," the stage line employee shouted from the office doorway. His worn-out Levi's were stuffed into tall black army boots and a green vest hugged his body. He snapped his pocket watch closed and disappeared into the dark interior. The driver moved around, getting comfortable. Luke backed away for a moment to let another passenger into the coach. The young man sat opposite Charity and the other woman and child. Luke gave him a no-tomfoolery look. "You behave yourself, Theodore Browning. Understand?" He was a couple of years older than Charity and the son of the only attorney in Y Knot, the man who did the legal work for the ranch.

"Yes, sir," he answered, clearly intimidated by Luke's hard look.

"Out of the way, McCutcheon," a voice said from the boardwalk.

"Brandon," Charity said in surprise. She tamped down her pleasure at seeing him as she took in the sight of his strong, handsome face and earnest eyes.

"Thought you'd get away without saying goodbye?" He leaned into the door. "Why didn't you tell me you were going? I had to hear it from your brother this morning. I can't believe you're doing this. You always said you'd never even consider going to that silly school. I'm confounded. You already know all the manners you'll ever need."

"That's a lot to say in one breath, Sheriff," she teased with forced humor. "I guess I changed my mind." Brandon looked so serious she had to glance away. It was impossible to hide anything from him. He seemed to know everything she was thinking, what was in her heart, and all her dreams. It had been like that since she was just a girl. She'd miss him for sure, more than she'd let herself admit.

"Five minutes!"

People were milling around and Charity felt the coach move an inch or so as the horses danced in anticipation. Lacey's School for Proper Ladies was located in the northern regions of Denver. The road there was safe and well-traveled, but tiresome and boring. She'd covered the same route with her family many times in years past. Why then did this feel so permanent? She hadn't thought at the time she was dreaming up her idea that leaving would be so hard.

Brandon looked over his shoulder briefly, then back at Charity. "Since you're set on going, I'll wish you Godspeed. Take care of…" He stopped as the station man came up to close the door. Brandon stepped back and joined Luke and Mark on the boardwalk. His expression was bleak, and…she wasn't sure…maybe a little angry? She hated to leave under these circumstances.

Charity leaned out the window and waved a gloved hand. "Goodbye," she called, flashing the brightest smile she could muster. The other passengers leaned out their windows, too. Luke and Mark both smiled and waved, oblivious to her true intentions. But Brandon just stared. She'd bet he knew something was up, he just didn't know what it was. The coach lurched once when the driver called out to the four-horse team, then rolled away.

Chapter Seventeen

A week had come and gone since the decision to make the dilapidated storage room into a real shop. Lily carried a brass spittoon through the main room, out the door and onto the boardwalk. Looking around carefully to avoid tripping, she searched until she found a spot between several other items and carefully set it down.

Tucker came through the door behind her with two axes and dropped them next to a bucket. "Whew, can you believe all this stuff?"

Lily stretched her back muscles and wiped her arm across her moist brow. "No. I can't. I've never seen such a mismatch of things in one place in all my life. It's amazing. But, I can see just how cute this building is going to be once it's cleared, cleaned and painted. With the big window, and all the ideas John is suggesting, I think it will be *charmant*."

Tucker gave Lily a funny look and she laughed. "Charming."

Just then John exited the doctor's office next door with his arms full to overflowing. He headed for a wagon sitting directly in front in the street and dumped the papers in the bed. Taking a handkerchief from his pocket, he swabbed his face, being careful of his stitches.

"Never said this was going to be easy," he called to Lily and Tucker. Tucker was doing Dr. Bixby's share of the work and John was helping Lily with her share. The idea was to get both parcels of real estate fixed up at the same time. It was a lot of work.

Cradle Hupton stepped out of Grady's Mercantile, letting the door slam behind him, and headed toward John. The livery owner smiled at Lily and waved her over.

He hitched his head, gesturing to the building he'd just left. "You know you got the Gradys bent clean out of joint, don't you, with this sale you're having tomorrow? They are about fit to be tied with the good deals you're offering." He shook his head as he looked at all their stuff and then back at Lily. "I don't know if that's the way to make friends or enemies."

"I was afraid of that," John replied. "But there was no better way of disposing of all this stuff quickly. Besides, the extra money will be put to good use. It's only for one day."

"I never thought of that," Lily said. "Do you think they are really upset?"

Cradle smiled. "Yes. But then Nora Grady is always upset with someone. Today and tomorrow it's you and John, then Monday, it'll be someone else. She'll get over it. She always does."

Mrs. Grady came out of the mercantile and threw a bucket of water into the street. Turning back, she eyed the sale items as if she were taking stock, and then slowly made her way back into the store.

Cradle pulled the Saturday edition of the *Rio Wells Republic* from his back pocket. He unrolled the brown paper and scanned the page. "I like your advertisement. I think you'll have a good turnout tomorrow since most people are in town for church." He looked around. "Where's your aunt, Lily?"

"John gave her strict orders to stay at the hotel," Lily answered, trying to sound nonchalant. "Whenever the temperature soars, she fairly withers." Besides, Tante was weak and emotional. Lily would never forget her expression when her aunt had learned she had been discovered. But, Tante had agreed to go along with John's suggestions for weaning herself from the morphine. She said she'd wanted to rid herself of the desire for it for years, but was always too ashamed to ask anyone for help. Her doctor in Boston had given it to her whenever she asked.

Thinking about her aunt brought to Lily's mind the blue gem she'd found hidden away in her aunt's sock, and her suspicions resurfaced. She knew she needed to confront her, but Lily wasn't sure she was quite ready to hear the answers. Besides she seemed so fragile. She'd give her more time to get past the worst, then insist she tell her everything.

John waved her inside. "Show me what big items you want out next, Lily. With Cradle here, they'll be easy. May as well put him to work, too."

"This extra dresser can go."

"Fine." John bent down and took a firm hold. "You just find the spot where you'd like us to put it. Ready, Cradle? On three."

With Cradle helping John and Tucker with the heavy lifting, the storage space was cleared in no time. Dr. Bixby walked around with Lily and helped suggest asking prices for each thing. The main purpose, along with raising money, was to make sure the things were gone by the end of Sunday evening, or soon after. Many prices were way below the objects' worth.

Bystanders watched with curiosity. Some were even poking around the hodgepodge mess of eclectic goodies. Tucker planned to sleep outside, to make sure nothing walked away on its own. By the time nine o'clock chimed on the town clock, Lily could hardly keep her eyes open.

"Come on, I'll walk you to the hotel," John said. "This has been a long day."

"You are right about that. I'm tired." Plus, she needed to get to the hotel and get a bath tonight while there was still someone in the hotel to warm some water. She was filthy and couldn't go anywhere in this condition.

"I'm so excited," Lily said as they walked along. "I think the building will be perfect. It is small, but cute." It was a short walk from John's office to the hotel and they were almost there. She stopped. "There is something I want to tell you."

He'd stopped also and looked at her questioningly. "Yes?"

"Remember the day I found my *Tante's* drugs, the day she passed out?"

"Of course."

"Well, there was something else I found too, but I've been hesitant to say anything about it. I was hoping my aunt would share with me what it might be. But she has not and I am getting more worried by the day."

The temperatures had cooled considerably and the cold desert air put a chill on the skin. Most people had gone home but there were still a few out on the street. John removed his light jacket and placed it on Lily's shoulders. "Go on, Lily. You can tell me anything."

"Thank you." She ran her hand over the fabric, thinking. "I think it is a sapphire or some other expensive gem. I found it hidden in her travel satchel stuck inside one of her socks."

John eyes opened wide. "Could it be rightfully hers?"

"Maybe. That is why I did not want to say anything. I do not want to think she has done anything wrong, if she has not. Maybe she bought it with her life savings. Or perhaps it was a gift from someone—a rich someone she has never mentioned to me—it is possible, I guess. But I thought it strange when we left Boston in the darkness of night without telling a soul. Plus, she has made it clear that the money she sent Mr. Bartlett was, more or less, all she had in the world. I am just really confused. I think she may be in some kind of trouble."

She could tell he was considering her words carefully. "I didn't know you two fled Boston. You've never said anything like that before."

"I know. I have not wanted to think the worst, but now…"

"We'll ask your aunt about the stone you found. Maybe it's fake."

"No. I don't want to make her any more upset than she already is. She seems fragile to me."

"Well, I don't like to think of the both of you living in the same room with a priceless jewel, especially in this unruly town. Perhaps someone is out there looking for it. Let me lock it up in my safe."

Just the words she was hoping to hear. She smiled. "I am sure she will not notice if I sneak it out to you tomorrow."

"Fine, then. The sooner you can bring it over, the better I'll feel. And, no worries. We'll get to the bottom of it." He laughed, a low rumble from deep in his chest, making Lily's smile grow. "Life can be surprising sometimes, that's for sure."

It felt wonderful to finally tell John about the gem. She trusted him with her life. She reminded herself again that he was engaged to be married. He was just a friend. But, he was the best kind of friend. One with whom she could share her fears and joys. One who wanted to help her and protect her. John McCutcheon was a remarkable man, and Emmeline was a lucky woman. Lily hoped the young woman knew just how lucky she was.

Settling Lily at the hotel, John headed back to the office. As he approached, he saw Tucker wrapped in a blanket and lounging on a cot. John wasn't sure if this was the wisest thing to do, but the boy wanted to make sure no one made off with their items. There had been no talking him out of it.

"You set for the night, Tuck? Need anything?"

"Nope. I'm fine right here."

John nodded and made his way inside the cleaned-out building. With much of the excess accumulation removed, the rooms appeared bigger.

"Lily home safely?" Bixby asked from his seat at the kitchen table.

"Yeah." John went over to the sink and leaned forward, peering into the plate-sized mirror hanging on the wall. He tested his sutures gently. "These are ready; I'm going to take them out."

"I was thinking the same thing today. Would you like me to do it?"

That thought hadn't even crossed John's mind. He could see the old man in the reflection, looking at him in eagerness. "Sure."

Bixby's chair scraped back nosily, causing the kitten to race out of the room. Bixby laughed. "Come on into the examination room where there's more light."

The senior doctor pulled out a stool for John, who sat down submissively. Bixby moved around the office with ease, gathering cotton, antiseptic and tweezers. Pawing through a drawer, he extracted a tiny pair of scissors. He washed his hands, pulled a stool up close to John, then picked up a magnifying glass. Leaning in close, he examined the wound.

"I'm still impressed," Bixby said softly. "Who done the stitching?"

John couldn't suppress a smile. "It was Lily. I don't know if I could've done better myself."

Bixby set the heavy glass magnifier down and picked up the scissors, pushing his spectacles up the bridge of his nose. "I have to agree with you on that. You using the salve I gave you?"

"Every day. As a matter of fact, I'm almost out."

"I'll mix up some more tomorrow."

There was a little stinging when Bixby pulled the first suture, but John ignored it with effort. "What happened to Tucker's hand?" he asked through clenched teeth.

"Comancheros cut it off. For fun. His parents and some other folks were traveling somewhere, to California I think, from what I could get out of the boy. They were attacked and robbed. Everyone was tortured and killed. They left the boy for dead, but a miner stumbled upon the grisly site and brought him here to Rio Wells. He was just a little pup, about five years old. Cute as a bug's ear." Bixby pulled out the last stitch and leaned back. "He's been with me ever since."

John thought about the energetic youth so eager to help and a thought crossed his mind. Perhaps some of the savages who mutilated Tucker were the same ones who attacked his coach. The ones he'd killed. He hoped so.

Opening up a drawer, the older doctor handed John a small hand mirror. "What do you think?"

The wound had closed up and the tissue wasn't quite as bright red as it'd been for the last few days. For as bad as the slash had been, he was pleased with the healing progress, though there clearly was going to be a noticeable scar. "Looks good. Without the stitches it feels better, too."

Chapter Eighteen

Now that the stage was in the homestretch and the driver said they'd reach Rio Wells in the next hour, Charity's stomach felt queasy and her mouth was dry as straw. Her idea had sounded so clever when she'd decided to surprise John, just show up on his doorstep, but now that she was almost there, she wasn't so sure. The trip had been a long and body-jarring experience. She'd much prefer to travel the distance on a horse. Oh, how her back and neck ached. Plus, she was worn out and grimy.

Sadly, the mother with the cute little boy who'd boarded with her in Y Knot had stayed behind in Denver, leaving her trapped with Theodore Browning smiling at her in his every waking moment. If she'd known Theodore was going to follow her all the way to Rio Wells, she would've told him to not bother. She didn't need a chaperone, and while she didn't think her brothers had put him up to it, she wasn't sure. But she was sure of one thing. She had tired of making conversation with him days ago. Thank goodness he was nice and had an engaging way about him. And with his thick black hair and handsome face, wasn't hard to look at either.

"Excited?" Theodore asked. "We're almost there."

Charity nodded. "Extremely. It's been almost three years since I've seen John." She twisted the hankie in her hands until it was as narrow as a ribbon. Would John be furious at her arrival? The last thing she wanted to do was get into a fight.

"He knows you're headed his way then? This isn't a surprise?"

Astonished, Charity gaped at Theodore. "Actually, it is a surprise. How did you know?"

He looked down at the white-knuckled grip she had on the piece of cloth she held. "Don't be nervous. I'm sure he'll be awfully happy to see you."

Charity smiled in an attempt to convince herself. "Yes, he will. We're very close. I can't remember a time he's ever been upset with me." Well, except the instance she'd opened a matchbox filled with grasshoppers in his bedroom, or when she'd told Mary Lou he wanted to marry her, or spilled the beans to Pa that he'd gone fishing when he was supposed to be minding the herd. A half dozen other times paraded through her mind but she pushed them aside.

"Well, all brothers and sisters have a tussle of some sort or another, don't they?" Afterwards, she and John always made up and were conspirators all the same.

"Of course."

She glanced out the window in an attempt to clear her mind of worry. Then there was the family back in Montana. Had anyone discovered yet that she wasn't in Denver, as she'd told them she'd be? Had Brandon?

"I think I'll drop in on him as soon as we get into town," Theodore said, straightening his sleep-rumpled clothes.

"Why? For your sleeping sickness?"

He let out a chortle. "You're funny, Charity."

"I'm sorry. That wasn't very nice of me." She gave him a teasing smile.

He chuckled on for a few more seconds. "I never got a chance to really know you very well in Y Knot. You always had all your big brothers hanging around. Heck, I don't think we've ever even spoken to each other, have we? I mean, besides this trip?" He gave her a puppy dog look of love.

Oh, brother. "Don't think so. Why do you need to see John? Don't you feel well?"

"I'm fine. Well, maybe he can do something about this bunion I have growing on my foot, but I was thinking about a job. Maybe he needs an assistant. Since I know you, maybe he'll give me a try."

She shrugged.

Theodore's brows crumpled in disappointment.

"You're probably right," she corrected quickly. "Do you have any experience working with the sick or injured?" She hadn't meant to dash his hopes.

He shook his head. "Not really. But I've helped my father for years in his office. I file and take notes. I also have a good head for doing sums. And I'm a fast learner."

"In that case, he might well need you. I don't know. I think he's all alone in his practice. And he's just gotten to town so maybe he hasn't hired anyone yet. But, understand, I'm just guessing at all this. We'll just have to wait to see what the future brings."

Lily and Harriett hastened over to the sale area, where a crowd of people were eagerly waiting. John was there, with Tucker and the old doctor. Dr. Bixby lifted up the long rope that circled the items and men and women rushed in. Lily hurried to John's side.

"Good morning. I saw you at church but didn't get a chance afterwards to say hello. How are you?" he asked when he saw her.

"Excited."

"You should be. Look at this turnout." He gestured to the many people milling through the sale items. "All your hard work is going to pay off."

"*Your* hard work," she corrected, and then laughed when he gave her a stern look. "All right, *our* hard work. This really is beyond my wildest expectations." She sucked in a deep breath as her eyes wandered over his face. "Your stitches. You took them out." She couldn't stop a murmur of approval that slipped from her throat, but suppressed her impulse to reach up and caress the punished spot. "It looks *so* much better."

"Last night. I'm happy with the way it's healing up. Not even a hint of infection."

Harriett, who stood patiently by Lily's side, sighed wearily.

"Come inside, Harriett. You can relax in the waiting area while we work the sale." John took her by the arm.

"Thank you."

Lily noticed the edginess of her aunt's voice. She had snapped at Lily this morning, but then apologized profusely afterwards, all but heartbroken. When Lily suggested that she might be more comfortable staying home today, Harriett was adamant that she was ready to venture out. Now Lily wasn't so sure. Her aunt's wrinkled hands shook as she clutched her handbag to her chest and clung to John's arm.

"I'll be right back," John said over his shoulder. "Tuck and Bixby are over there taking the money, in case you're looking for them."

Quickly Lily reached into her handbag and surreptitiously handed the carefully wrapped stone to John. He nodded his understanding, folding his hand securely around it, and then proceeded to take Harriett into the office.

Lily turned a half circle, trying to take it all in. She'd worn her best blue dress today with her matching suede shoes. This was the first time she would meet most of the towns people and she wanted to make a good impression. In church, there had been more women than she had been expecting from her experiences here the last week. Dustin was seated a few pews in front of her, with four others to his left before John had joined them. It was impossible not to notice the quality of the dresses of the three women she assumed were John's aunt and female cousins. Surely they had traveled to a city to purchase such well-made fashions.

"Lily," a male voice called out. She turned to find Dustin and the others coming her way. "I'd like you to meet my family. My mother and father. My brother, Chaim. My sisters, Becky and Madeline."

"I am pleased to meet you," she replied. Their keen interest made her feel special.

"I've told them all about you and your aunt and the shop you're starting in Rio Wells. This is the building, then?" His eyes glanced over the tiny structure, then landed on the doctor's office.

"It is. After everything out here is sold I'll clean it and paint it."

Winston took a small step forward. "That's a fair amount of work, young lady. How 'bout I give my boys the day off tomorrow to come and help?"

Lily's mouth opened to object but he'd rendered her speechless.

"We want to help, too," Madeline said. "With all of us working it'll be easy."

"That's a wonderful idea," his mother added. "And I'll stay home and help Maria with a big dinner. You'll be hungry when you're all done. We never did have the welcome party for John. We'll incorporate the two." She clapped her hands together in excitement. "I can hardly wait."

"What's all this I hear?" John was back with a wide grin on his face. "Lily, I see you've met my extended family. What are all you cooking up without me?"

Madeline batted her long dark lashes. "We're all coming to town tomorrow for a work party. We're going to help Lily get her shop in tiptop shape."

"And then we're having the welcome party we never got to have the night you arrived in town," Becky added.

Lily was moved by all the attention and the fact that near strangers were willing to spend a long, hot day helping her. Her cheeks heated up so much she was tempted to reach into her satchel and find her fan. When she glanced up, she found both John and Dustin watching her.

"I don't know what to say. It is such a generous offer."

"Mother, look," Becky said, coming forward. She shyly touched the cuff at the end of Lily's sleeve. "Did you notice the lace work? Lily, I hope you don't mind me pointing this out. We were looking for rose point lace the last time we were in Abilene. Did you do this work yourself?"

"Go on, Lily," both John and Dustin said at the same time. They looked at each other for a fleeting second and then looked away.

An awkward moment of silence descended.

"Yes, I did. My sisters and I all learned to make lace from an early age in Germany. By hand with only a needle. My mother is incredibly talented. She handed her love of it down to us."

"It's beautiful," Winnie said, taking a closer look. "The finest I've ever seen. I'm sure we'll be some of your first customers when you open."

John's smile sent tingles down to her toes. "It was Lily who sewed up my wound," he said, pointing to the red line, which was still tender-looking, on his face. "She did a fine job, too."

Uncle Winston jumped in. "Tools and such, do you have any? Paint brushes, scrapers, hammers and saws. Nails and screwdrivers. If not, the boys can bring 'em out."

She looked at John for the answer.

"Yeah, that would be helpful. I don't know yet what Bixby has around here in the way of carpentry things," he said, then laughed at the absurdity of the statement as he waved his arm wide. "Except all this."

Everyone laughed.

John looked over to where Tucker and Bixby were taking in money quickly, then glanced back at Lily, his eyebrows arched in question.

"I guess we better get to work," Lily said. "While there's still something to do. It was a pleasure to meet all of you."

The group moved away. "See you tomorrow," Becky said, as she waved.

Chapter Nineteen

"**W**hoa," the stage driver shouted out, pulling back on the reins. The tired horses came to an abrupt stop in front of the same Wells Fargo stage office where John and Lily's coach had halted eleven days prior. The stage jerked a couple times, settling in, and Charity heard the driver press the foot brake down with crushing force. "Rio Wells," he called out sharply.

An employee came out and opened the door for Charity and Theodore. "Have any problems between Draper Bottom and here?"

"Trouble?" Theodore asked. He'd been the first one out and reached up to assist Charity.

"No," she said, waving Theodore's hand away and climbing out easily on her own. "Why do you ask?"

"Three people were killed not too long ago coming in from the East."

Charity looked around, taking in the dirty-looking street and the hotel across it. Well, that was certainly reason enough to ask. She was glad she hadn't known that news before, during the hours of solitude out in the badlands. Then when his words registered, she gasped. "From the East?"

He nodded. "Two men and a woman. She was to be the new teacher here in Rio Wells. Come all the way out from New York only to be murdered the day before reaching town."

Charity grasped the man by the arm as he turned to go back into the stage office, stopping him in his tracks. His surprised face gaped at her.

"Do you know the men's names? The ones that were killed?"

"No miss, I don't." He pulled free and walked quickly away.

In a panic, Charity glanced around the town but didn't see anyone else to question. She ran into the stage office as she heard her trunk hit the dirt behind her, tossed down by the guard. She was disappointed to find that the man she'd already questioned was the only one there.

"Is there anyone else here who might know the names of the men who were killed?"

"No, miss, it's Sunday. I'm the only one here."

Theodore came up to her side. "Charity, what's wrong? Why are you so upset?"

"Because I've had this bad feeling for a while that something awful has happened to my brother and now this man tells me that three of the passengers last week were killed. What if one was John?"

"Where is everyone today, anyway? The town seems deserted," Theodore asked, without answering Charity's question.

The clerk reached under the counter and brought out a two-sheet newspaper and opened to the centerfold. He turned it upside-down so the newcomers could read it. "Big sale today down on Dry Street. That's just around the corner. Lots of things being sold off at a fraction of the cost. Everyone's over there."

Charity ran out without saying another word. "Come on, Theodore," she called, picking up her trunk with strong arms, intending to take it with her.

The driver stopped her before Theodore could. "Give me that before you hurt yourself, miss." He grasped it and had to tug several times before she finally let go. "I'll take this to the hotel across the street and they'll hold it for you until you decide what you're going to do." His eyes were still round that she'd handled the heavy box so easily.

"Thank you," she called as she took off at a run. Theodore was following behind. Within moments, she was close to the corner and she could hear laughter and talking. Rounding the street, she stopped dead in her tracks. Why, it must be the whole town of Rio Wells and then some. If she had to guess there must be nearly three hundred people looking at a street full of junk. She plunged into the throng of townsfolk, looking back and forth.

She stopped in front of a man who was examining an extraordinarily large bottle of molasses. "Excuse me, sir. Do you know a man named John McCutcheon?"

He paused to look at her. "John McCutcheon? No. I know Winston and his sons, though."

"Do you see them here anywhere?"

He straightened and looked around for a few minutes. "Sorry, no. But that don't mean they aren't here. I can't see everyone, you know."

"Yes, I know," she answered as she moved on. Her heart was getting heavier by the second.

"Charity, wait up," Theodore called as she pushed her way through the crowd.

"Why, Bixby, you ol' goat. This man wants to give you two dollars for that old clock. I think you're getting a heck of a deal."

Charity stopped at the sound of familiar laughter. She turned in the direction and scanned the people. Gasping, she all but ran and vaulted into John's arms, almost knocking him over.

He had to set her away to see who it was. *"Charity!"*

"I was so sure you were dead," she said, barely getting the words past her strangled throat. She squeezed tightly, making sure he wasn't a figment of her imagination and would be gone when she opened her eyes. "You're alive. You're really here." She stepped back and opened one eye slowly, fearfully. "Aren't you?"

Just then Theodore burst through the crowd and ran into Charity's back knocking her back into John's arms.

"What the heck is going on here?" the old man next to John asked loudly. "Who is this young woman?"

John set Charity away again but by the stricken look on her face he knew that she'd noticed the ugly red line running from his hairline to the center of his ear. "*This* is my baby sister," he said proudly. "Charity, meet Dr. Bixby, the man I'll be replacing someday." He winked at the old man. "We don't know when that day is just yet, but that's all right."

"It's a pleasure to meet you." She reached up as if she were going to touch John's face, but didn't. Her expression was soft, sad. "What happened?"

"Our stage was attacked. I made it, but three others didn't."

Lily was watching from a few feet away. He waved her over.

"This is Emmeline, then?" Lily asked, coming to stand by his side.

John let out a bark of a laugh that grabbed everyone's attention. Heads turned in their direction. He shook his head. "No. This is my *sister*, Charity McCutcheon. She surprised me. She made the trip all the way from Montana by herself." He looked at her and then glanced around at the people. "You did come alone, didn't you? I haven't seen Luke or Matt or anyone."

"No," a voice called out. "I came with her, John. Do you remember me?"

A tall young man stepped forward, a worried expression marring his face. The face was familiar to John but he couldn't quite place from where. "Uhhh..."

"It's Theodore Browning," Charity piped up. "You know Leonard Browning from Y Knot. He's the attorney for the ranch."

"I'll be, Theodore. You've grown two feet since I saw you last. I have to admit I would not have placed you on my own. How old are you now?"

"Twenty."

"Well, welcome to Rio Wells. You too, Charity. Gosh, I'm happy to see you." He gestured toward Lily. "This is Lily Anthony from Boston. Dr. Bixby." He pointed past Bixby. "That's Tucker Noble. All the townspeople that have come out to support our sale." John caught sight of Mr. Shellston watching them from the other side of the street with interest. When the man noticed John looking his way, the banker walked off.

"Where're your things?" he asked.

"I left them at the hotel."

"Good. I think that's the best place for you now unless you want to be crowded in with us at the office." He shook his head. "Don't think you'd like that. Depending on how long you stay, we'll work out other arrangements." He laughed, still delighted at seeing his baby sister. "For now, we have to get back to work."

"Dr. McCutcheon," a female voice called, as a slender young woman made her way through the people.

"Hello, Louise," he replied. "Louise is the postmistress and works across the street from the hotel," he said to Charity. "What can I do for you?"

"I'm looking for some new dishes, at a good price, of course." Her brows rose in hopeful interest.

John pointed. "Right over in the corner. I think there are several sets."

A smile blossomed on Charity's lips. She gestured at Theodore. "We can help, too. With more of us working, these things will be gone all the faster."

Chapter Twenty

A handful of shoppers mulled around, the majority of Dr. Bixby's collection of eclectic stuff, gone. "Okay," John said as he motioned the workers to gather around. "Let's finish up and get the remainder of the items off the street before night falls. We don't want to be accused of creating an eyesore. There's not much. We can put it 'round back, in the alley for now."

"I've been thinking about that," Bixby said. "Why don't we give the remaining things to the Gradys to sell in the mercantile? To make amends. Maybe we'll get back into their good graces. They've been fine neighbors all these years and I hate to see our friendship deteriorate over this."

John nodded. "Good idea, Bixby."

"I haven't seen 'em leave yet," the old doctor replied. "I'll go ask. If they agree, we can take it over now and be done with it. "He handed John the cash he'd been collecting and headed down the boardwalk toward the mercantile. Tucker also gave the cash he had to John, who combined it with the money in his pockets. The wad was so large he had to use two hands. "I'll take this inside. Come on, let's go in."

Harriett greeted them at the door looking rested and happy. "How did the big sale go?" she asked the young women as they entered.

"Good, Tante. It was a success."

The group crowded into the waiting room and filtered into the kitchen, where a tea kettle was just starting to let off some steam. Whistling pierced the air. "I'm having tea. Would anyone else like some?"

John opened the cupboard drawer and stuffed the cash inside. "I think Doc Bixby should have the honors of counting the take when he gets back. Without all his stuff, this wouldn't have been possible."

John pulled out a chair for Lily and she sat at the table with the two boys. "So, Theodore," he said, "what brings you to Rio Wells?"

Theodore's face reddened a bit then he spoke up. "I wanted to try something new."

John looked over his shoulder at Charity to see if she had anything to add. She'd traveled in the stage with him for the past week. She shrugged.

"I'd like to find employment," the young man added. "You wouldn't need any help in the doctor's office, would you? Help of any kind? I'm good with numbers and office-type work. I've had experience at my pa's place." The young man's gaze moved slowly over to where Charity was standing and all of a sudden John thought he might know the reason for Theodore's journey.

"Hmm. We have Tucker here, already. That's something I'd have to give some thought to, being I'm so new. I'll let you know."

Just then Bixby came in the back door. "Boys, girls, the Gradys will be happy to take the rest of the stuff off our hands. Let's get it moved to their back door. They'll take it inside."

Everyone stood up to go, including Lily.

"Wait, Lily, I want to talk with you," John said. He signaled for the others to go ahead.

"You should take your aunt back to the hotel," John suggested. "It's been a long day and she looks tired."

"But I'd rather help with the cleanup."

"I appreciate that, but now with Charity and Theodore we have plenty of able bodies to help. And, besides, what else do

I have to do today? I don't see a drove of patients breaking down my door for services." He laughed. "Just get Harriett back and get her something to eat. Soon your dream of having your own shop will be realized. And, tomorrow is going to be a long and busy day. You should rest up, too."

"All right. But only because of my aunt. It does not feel right to have all of you doing all the work."

"I understand."

"Good. I am not one of those little figurines of a milking maid I have seen in china shop windows. You know the ones, with a little kerchief on her head and a milk bucket in her hand? I am not made of porcelain. I will not break."

John couldn't stop the grin that was wobbling his mouth.

"What?"

"Nothing." She was eyeing him suspiciously. "Oh, just in case you'd ever need it, the combination to my safe is ten, ten, thirteen"

"Why?"

"Just to be cautious. One never knows when trouble might strike. It's the numerical equivalent to JJM—John Jake McCutcheon—in case you forget. If anything were to happen to me, I want you to be able to get to the jewel. Who knows, it could actually belong to your aunt." He placed his hand on the small of Lily's back and encouraged her toward the door. "Now, go on."

The sun dipped behind the distant peaks as John sat relaxing on the porch of his office, enjoying the peacefulness of the now quiet street. It felt good to rest and just do nothing. Gave him a moment of solitude to examine his feelings about his life and living it in this new town, among other things. In about an hour, after Charity had time to clean up, he'd head over to the hotel and pick her up and they would go to dinner and catch up on things at the ranch. He was glad she'd taken the matter into her own hands and come for a visit, even if she had almost surprised the life out of him. Still, he couldn't get over his parents letting her come all this way on her own—well, with the company of Theodore Browning, he corrected himself.

"You're quiet tonight," Bixby said, striking a match and lighting the lantern hanging next to his shingle. John had yet to hang his.

John scoffed good-naturedly. "You don't know me well enough yet to recognize if I'm being quiet or not."

"I do, indeed," he replied matter-of-factly. "What's on your mind?" Bixby took his time pulling another chair closer to where John lounged, and sat down.

A few moments passed before John said, "A lot of things." He crossed his legs out in front of him and laced his fingers behind his head. The street was near vacant being it was Sunday and most people would be sitting down soon to supper. The pungent air, thick from the mineral spring, coiled around him. It was a far cry from the crisp mountain freshness he'd grown up with, filled with scents of pine and wild grass, but he was resigned to embrace his new life with an open mind.

"Lily Anthony being one of them?"

John looked over at the old man and slowly shook his head, amazed at the old man's astuteness. "Could be."

"She's a pretty one, McCutcheon. Nice, too. You could do a lot worse."

Was he that transparent that everyone could see what he was thinking? And feeling? He'd made no overt advances toward the young woman or spent that much time with her since reaching Rio Wells—well, maybe he'd spent a lot of time with her, but her aunt *was* his patient. What was he supposed to do? "I suppose you're right."

"So. What's stopping you?"

"You're one irritating old man, Bixby. Anyone ever tell you that before?" The white kitten jumped from the roof of the telegraph office across the street, landed on some crates stacked three high, and then made for her master. "I'm just sitting here minding my own *personal* business and you come out and give me the third degree."

Bixby picked the kitten up when she reached his feet and stroked her back. She started to purr. "Well?"

"There's someone else."

He stopped stroking and looked over at him. "Who?"

"My intended in Boston."

Bixby gave a low whistle and resumed the affection he was giving to the kitten. "Well, that changes things, don't it?"

"Yes."

"Do you want it to change things?"

John looked at the man. "What do you mean? Change things so I can proceed with Lily or change with Lily and proceed with Emmeline?"

"You tell me. In my way of thinkin', a man is free until he's married."

"Even if there's an understanding? An engagement?"

Bixby removed his glasses and swiped his hand across his face. He resettled his spectacles on his nose. "That's right. Engagement is a time of discernment. It'd be dishonest to marry someone if a person has fallen in love with another. Now, running around and looking for it is something different entirely, of course. I'm not talking about that—sometimes things just happen. But, breaking a promise is a lot kinder than a life of misery, regrets. Just my opinion." The kitten squirmed and jumped from the old man's embrace, hiding beneath the boardwalk when a dog trotted by. "But once those vows have been said, that's another story entirely."

John grunted, thinking about what Bixby had just said. What were his feelings for the two women? Both were beautiful and strong in their own right. Falling in love with Emmeline had been easy, and fun. But life wasn't all lollipops and roses and was never meant to be. Protectiveness for Lily surfaced and he had to tamp it down, reminding himself that most likely it was the highly-charged Comanchero attack that made him feel so.

"You ever been married?" he asked, looking at the old man.

"Nope."

"Why not? I'm sure there were plenty of women around Rio Wells that would've loved to have hitched up with you."

"Just never meant to be. Time marched on and then I found myself ready to retire. Be careful, boy. Days are long, but years are short."

"I can't believe that." It was a moment until Bixby returned his look. Even in the fading light, his haunted expression couldn't be masked and John wished he hadn't started this line of conversation.

"Actually, I was in love once," Bixby finally admitted. "But that was many, many years ago. She was a married woman."

John wanted to ask if she still lived in this dustbowl of a place. If he ever ran into her from time to time. He wanted to, but wouldn't. His ma was big on not prying into other people's business. You might learn something you didn't need—or want—to know. The proverbial Pandora's box, so to speak.

Tucker opened the door and stuck his head out. "I'm going down to the livery to see Theodore, see if he needs anything."

"I'm sure Cradle has him all set up. Sure glad he had that inexpensive room for that young man to rent. I like him, he's nice," Bixby said. "But, go. Have some fun. Just be sure the two of you stay out of trouble." The door slammed and Tucker disappeared back inside, apparently intending to use the quicker route to the livery out the back.

John hitched his head. "He's a good boy, too. It's a shame about his hand."

"It is indeed."

The atmosphere had turned a little depressing, so John decided to ask the question he'd been curious about for several hours. "So, did you count the money?"

Bixby straightened. "Sure did. I can't believe how much hard-earned cash those townsfolk were willing to throw my way to haul that junk away." He laughed. "Never thought anything good would come from my collection. One hundred dollars and seventy-three cents." He shook his head in disbelief. "I have you to thank. I'd never have gotten that place cleaned out on my own and it would've fallen to you or someone else after I'd died to—"

"Now, wait just a minute," John said, cutting him off. "Who said anything about you dying? I'm just glad we had such a great turnout."

"Tomorrow I'll give Lily and Harriett their half. It'll be a good start for them."

"That's generous of you, Bixby, and I for one, appreciate it."

Three men walked up the boardwalk in their direction from Main Street. When they were closer, John recognized Sheriff Dane and the deputy, Pete Miller. The third man was unfamiliar. John and Bixby stood.

Chapter Twenty-One

"**H**ow're you, Sheriff?" John asked, shaking the sheriff's hand while taking in the hard expression of the third man. He wondered who he was. Uncertainty swept through John's mind as he looked at him.

"Good." He nodded a greeting to Bixby.

"Just making the rounds?" the old doctor asked.

"No, actually. Wanted to introduce you all. This is Lector Boone. Seems he's investigating a robbery that he's followed all the way to Rio Wells. I'll let him fill you in."

Boone was dressed in all black, which in a way matched his demeanor. Hard lines accentuated his face and his build was tall and strong. Twin Colt 45s were holstered on his thighs and tied in place with leather strings. The man slowly stepped forward with the confident swagger of a gunfighter who relied on the persuasion and power of the weapons strapped to his legs.

"I'm here to retrieve a jewel that was stolen from my client in Boston," he said, barely above a whisper. "It's taken some doing, but I'm positive it was smuggled to Rio Wells on the last stage from Concepción."

John masked his surprise, though moisture instantly slicked his palms. It was just this morning after church that he'd locked the subject of the conversation into his safe, not ten feet from where they all stood now. *Is Harriett a jewel thief?* That was unthinkable. Granted the woman was addicted to drugs, which sometimes led people to do things they wouldn't normally do, but still. He didn't believe it. And it wasn't Lily. Even if she hadn't brought the gem to him, proving her innocence, he wouldn't have believed her capable of such a deed. Still, the women would be suspects to Boone. And he knew he'd be a prime suspect too, as he'd traveled said route that the precious stone had to reach town.

"Who's your client?" John asked to keep the conversation moving. "I didn't catch the name?"

"That's of no importance to you, Doctor," Boone replied. So, the sheriff had already told Boone who he was, had been discussing him, and possibly Dr. Bixby, too. This wasn't just a chance meeting.

"No?" Irritation bubbled inside. Bixby gave him a long look, so he changed tack. "Guess you're right. What can we do for you?"

"Just answer a few questions."

"I will if I can."

"Me too," Bixby added.

"Have you seen or heard anything unusual? Any new faces?"

John glanced at Bixby, who shook his head. "Can't say that I have."

"Me either," John said. "But I'm relatively new in town. Can't say I'd be able to distinguish between new or old. On the other hand, Cradle Hupton, the livery owner, told me he's been seeing a lot of new faces around Rio Wells lately. Some he wouldn't want to meet in a dark alley."

"We'll talk to him next," Sheriff Dane said to Boone.

"Is this robbery common knowledge? Was it in the papers?" John wanted to know if there would be other bounty hunters showing up in Rio Wells looking for clues, as he was sure that was what Boone was.

"A crime of this size is hard to cover up," he replied. "But to answer your question, yes."

The men looked around at each other, then the deputy spoke up. "I guess we can expect more visitors to Rio Wells then." His hat was tipped back and his eyes were clearly visible. "Maybe we should deputize more men."

"That's not necessary, deputy." Boone lifted his lips in a cold smile as he glanced around in the darkness beyond. "Shouldn't take me long to find the guilty party, if they're still here. I'm not about to muck up my perfect record now."

The town clock clanged seven times. "Gentlemen, I'm off," John stated. "I have a dinner date with my sister and I don't want to keep her waiting. If you have any more questions, Sheriff, you know where to find me."

John walked away. His mind whirled, trying to figure out just where the stolen stone had come from. Thank goodness Lily had done as he'd asked and brought it to him. At least it was locked safely away. He'd have to get to the bottom of this before the gunfighter did. If not, who knew what the outcome would be.

The workday on Monday went smoothly with everyone's help. Their new shop, the little storeroom, now christened Lily's Lace and More at Tante Harriett's insistence, had been gutted, washed inside and out, stripped of its old paint and paper, and then painted a cheery yellow on the outside, with a soft cream tone on the inside. All the door hinges were tightened and oiled, windows were washed, floors were mopped, the indoor water pump checked, re-worked and greased, and wall lamps hung.

Tucker had returned from Grady's Mercantile with two strong locks and keys, one for the front door and one for the alley door. Even with only one hand, he was able to remove the old locks and install the new. Being tall, Dustin did most of the outside painting, using a buckboard and ladder when he needed to reach the high spots. His sisters had a grand time laughing at his yellow-speckled face.

Mrs. McCutcheon donated a beautiful pair of pale emerald curtains made of velvet. Becky said her mother had stored them away after she'd redone her bedchamber at the ranch and wanted to give them to Lily. They fit the front window perfectly, and looked so beautiful Lily was barely able to hold back tears. She'd been overwhelmed several other times throughout the day too, as when she'd seen the two small beds for her and Tante in the two bedrooms upstairs. There was also a small table with a couple of chairs in the back of the McCutcheon's big buckboard.

Theodore, having an artful touch, was chosen to make two signs—a large one for the front of the building, and another smaller one to hang on the boardwalk.

John and Chaim, working well together, built a small dressing room in the main body of the shop, which was finished off with another matching curtain from the emerald set that garnished the front window. Once the two got to building, they were impossible to stop. Next, they constructed an elevated platform by the window, so Lily could adjust hemlines with ease. Then they made a cutting table and some shelves to show off her fabrics, and put up a handful of pegs on the opposite wall to display spools of different types of lace she'd made.

With the shop taken care of, they continued working and updating the tiny kitchen area in the rear of the first floor. They quickly built a wall that went halfway across the room, so the kitchen had a little privacy and a homey feel. Lily was amazed at their speed and skill. Then, just for fun, they fashioned together a large frame, the size of a window, on which Lily could stretch fabric. Later, when she had time, she would add handfuls of old buttons, sequins, glass beads and such that she and her aunt had collected over the years. It would be a piece of novel decorative art. It was a clever idea Charity had dreamed up and Lily looked forward to starting work on it.

Within the day, Lily's Lace and More was done and ready for customers. Lily and her aunt's belongings had been moved over from the hotel and put away upstairs. When she and Tante Harriett had gone to pay the bill, they found it had been taken care of and nobody would tell them who was responsible. The day had turned out better than any fairytale she'd ever been told.

Lily moved around the upstairs rooms getting ready for the big party out at the McCutcheon ranch. She'd been thinking about it all day, and now that it was almost time to go, she was filled with excitement. She had grown close with Charity today, and with Becky and Madeline, as well. The cousins were so much alike, yet different, too.

"Tante Harriett, would you like some warm water for a bath?" Lily asked, looking at the little clock on the bedside table. She dried behind her neck with a fluffy towel, another generous gift from John's aunt, then padded to her closet for her wrapper. "We will be leaving within the hour."

"Please forgive me if I don't go. The thought of snuggling into my bed holds much more appeal." She had already removed her heavy, purple dress and presented an adorable picture in her petticoat and stockings.

"Of course you are going," Lily insisted, donning her housecoat and all but running to her aunt's room. "I would not have a good time if I left you at home."

Harriett yawned as she patted Lily's arm several times. "Of course you will. I'm so pleased you now have three wonderful girlfriends."

Lily admitted to herself that staying home was probably better for her aunt. "Well, if you're certain. I will have Doctor Bixby check in on you later. He is staying home, as well."

"Fine, dear. But only if it will make you feel better. She bent over slowly and picked up the kitten. "See. I have all the company I need."

Chapter Twenty-Two

John pulled up in front of Rim Rock Ranch and set the brake with his foot. The buggy rocked forward and back several times as it settled to a halt in the gravelly dirt and the gangly old bay in the harness nickered to the animals in the corral. John had rented a two-seat buggy from Cradle so they could all ride together. Lily sat beside him, wearing a pretty pink dress with a shawl draped over her shoulders. Charity was wedged in back between Theodore and Tucker and had been conspicuously quiet ever since they'd left town. John looped the reins around the bar in front running the width of the carriage, then hopped out, extending his hand to Lily.

With his help she stepped to the ground and straightened her dress as the others descended. The house was ablaze with light from within and a ranch hand came out of the barn and took the horse and carriage away.

The ranch house door opened and Becky looked out. "They're here," she called out excitedly and ran to meet them. She hugged Charity and Lily, then went straight to Theodore's side. "How are you, Theo?" she asked in a shy voice. She laced her fingers together behind her back and looked up at the young man with worship shining in her eyes.

Theodore looked embarrassed. "It's only been a few hours since I've seen you, Becky. I was fine then and I'm still fine," he replied stiltedly, slipping in next to Charity as they all walked to the front door.

"Welcome, come in," Uncle Winston boomed in a voice that echoed through the room. John found it amazing how much of his own father he recognized in his uncle. Not just in his physical attributes, but in his actions and expression as well. "How was the drive out?" he asked, looking directly at John.

"Good. It's a nice, easy ride." John shook hands with the three men, ending with Dustin. They looked each other in the eye, not knowing what to say.

Aunt Winnie came dashing in from another room. "Where is she?" she asked in excitement. Spotting Charity, she pulled her into a hug. "I was so surprised when I heard you'd come to town on Sunday. I guess we just missed each other." She backed up to get a good look. "You're beautiful! I can't even begin to tell you how glad I am to have you and John here. It's just…" Her words trailed off as her eyes welled with tears.

"Just too much emotion," Winston said, laughing. "Calm down, woman. We have the whole night ahead of us and you're going to wear yourself out in the first five minutes. Charity is going to be staying on in Rio Wells for some time. I'm sure you'll have plenty chance to get acquainted."

Winnie dabbed at the corner of her eyes with the tip of the apron. "You're right. Tonight is not a time for tears, but one of joy. A celebration. To welcome John and Charity to Rio Wells and to congratulate Lily on her fine new shop."

Again Winnie marshaled her emotions. "I know Tucker here, welcome, young man. But who is this tall fellow?" she asked, looking at Theodore.

"A friend from Y Knot," John answered. "He made the trip south with Charity. Seems he'll need a job."

Everyone nodded and Theodore's face went scarlet.

Winnie smiled at Lily. "Where is Harriett? I hoped she would be joining us tonight. I haven't yet met her."

"I wanted her to come along, also, Mrs. McCutcheon," Lily said. "But all the activity the last two days has completely worn her out. She sends her regrets."

Winnie nodded. "That's totally understandable. Rio Wells *can* be exhausting. Now," she said, gesturing to everyone. "Come into the dining room. Maria and I have cooked up a feast you'll not soon forget."

The sight of the beautifully decorated table almost took Lily's breath away. It was opulently laden with china and sterling and eye-catching linen finished off with intricately stitched lace that Lily longed to inspect. Two candelabras held six candles each, giving the room an enchanting amber glow.

"It's stunning," Charity gasped. "You really shouldn't have gone to so much trouble, Aunt Winnie."

"Of course we should have," Madeline corrected her. "You're family." She proceeded to walk beside the long table, glancing at the place cards above each plate. "John, you're down here."

Lily glanced at the table, noticing the name cards for the first time. Dustin was on this end of the table, at the head. She was next to him, on the corner to his right, with Chaim on her other side. John proceeded to the opposite end of the table where Mr. McCutcheon was already standing at the other head spot. It felt like a mile away. John pulled out Madeline's chair for her and pushed it in as his cousin got settled. He looked up and his gaze met hers.

Tucker and Theodore sat opposite each other in the middle. Becky waited patiently, gazing at Theodore until he grasped her meaning and pulled out her chair, making Lily smile.

"Lily?" Dustin said, as he pulled out her chair for her. Chaim took hold of the back of her chair also. After she was seated, her chair fairly flew forward as both men pushed her in.

When Lily looked up, John was smiling at her. *Again.* The nod of his head was so imperceptible she had no doubt no one else noticed. Maria came in with a tray laden with slabs of meat still crackling and popping with a detectible, buttery scent.

"It's beef," Winston assured the guests. "Of the finest cut. Porterhouse for the men and filets for the ladies. There's plenty more in the kitchen, so don't be shy."

Dustin stood and went to the sideboard. Taking a decanter full of wine, he went around the table, filling everyone's glass. Tucker looked up in surprise. "Go slow, young man," Dustin said. "I don't want Bixby coming after me."

Mr. McCutcheon picked up his glass. "A toast. To family. And to friends. And to knowing what life is really all about."

Glasses were raised and the clinking began. Becky laughed and so did Charity. The two girls were so much alike it was remarkable. Madeline glanced at John longingly as he reached his own glass toward his sister for the toast.

Chapter Twenty-Three

"Lily?" Dustin said, gaining her attention. He touched her glass with his. "To good times ahead. Success for Lily's Lace and More. To long and lasting friendships."

Chaim reached over to find her glass, too. "To weddings and children." He winked at her, then broke into a grin.

This time when Lily peeked from the corner of her eye, John wasn't smiling. It was evident he had heard what his cousin had said and it was more interesting than the toasting on his end. She brought her glass to her lips and took a small sip.

"So," Mrs. McCutcheon said, looking at John and then Charity. "Is this like The Heart of the Mountains?"

Charity set her wine glass on the tablecloth as Maria continued to bring in bowls and platters. "Very much. It's amazing how at home I feel. The only real difference is that we have a passel of little ones, too. Someone is always crying, or needing changing or a nap or something," she said, laughing. "At the present, Matt and Rachel have three and one on the way, Mark and Amy have one and one on the way, and Luke and Faith have three. Mother had to hire more help for Esperanza this past fall. She just couldn't keep up."

"Flood and Claire must be so proud. We're waiting for the day one of this brood gives us a grandbaby," Winnie said.

"In all fairness, our oldest is Luke's age," Mr. McCutcheon added quickly. "Flood, even though he's younger, got an earlier start. We're not that far behind."

"And Luke came with two built-in, if I understand the explanation of the fiasco correctly."

Lily was surprised at Dustin's remark. It was clearly an insult.

"If any of us do as well as Luke, we'll be fortunate," John shot back, the timbre of his voice deeper than Lily had ever heard it. "He's a lucky man, in my opinion."

"Have you even met Faith?" Dustin asked offhandedly, scooping a large spoonful of mashed potatoes onto his plate and then holding the bowl out for Lily. "I was under the impression you haven't been home for years."

"Of course he hasn't, with his medical schooling and all," Charity spoke up. "But I kept him informed with letters and the others did, too. We all love Faith. There isn't a more giving person on the face of the earth," she said, "and beautiful as well."

"Then indeed, Luke is a lucky man. *Mother*," Dustin chuckled, "you look like you've bitten into a lemon. I didn't mean anything by my observation. John understood what I meant."

"Absolutely, Aunt Winnie," John added, dryly. "No offense taken."

The situation was so tense Lily could not bear to look up. Instead, she stabbed at the creamy sauce-drizzled asparagus that Chaim offered by her side.

"Boys," Winston said sternly. "This is a celebration. I'll have you remember that. Winnie has worked all day in preparation and I intend to enjoy it. Do I make myself clear?"

"Sorry," John said, ignoring Charity's disapproving look that said he hadn't defended Luke enough. He took a bite of sweet potatoes mixed with cranberries, chewed and swallowed.

"Tell us about what life in Germany is like, Lily," Dustin said.

She smiled. "I have a large family, with two brothers and five sisters. Times are difficult sometimes with so many mouths to feed, but my parents work hard to provide a good life for us. It is not like this," she said, and made a small sweeping gesture to take in all around them, "but, we are all happy and well."

"And is there school there like here in the States?" Becky asked.

"Of course. It is structured differently, but, nonetheless, a good system. My parents also require all of us to either learn an instrument or a trade. I learned to make lace."

John was captivated. But so were the rest of the male occupants at the table, it seemed. Lily looked like a princess. Her blond hair was swept up on her head, but some strands had worked free and floated around her face like a halo. When she spoke, it was unhurried. It seemed she'd relaxed as her eyes roamed from face to face, recalling her life back in her homeland. Her voice spread over John like an intoxicating balm. He longed to sweep her up and away, and not share her with anyone ever again.

"…is proficient on the organ and plays in church all the time."

John snapped out of his reverie, realizing he hadn't heard what she'd just said. He was engaged, he reminded himself with a shake of his thoughts. He had no right to fantasize about Lily at all. She was his friend and he'd better remember that. Emmeline was a good woman. She didn't deserve this.

"It sounds so beautiful, Lily," Charity said, awe written on her face. "I'd love to go there someday. Meet the rest of your family. I think that would be exciting."

Lily laughed. "I think my family would enjoy having visitors from the Wild West. But, be warned. There are many more people compared to here. Everything is much smaller. Our house would fit into your front room." She wiped her mouth with her napkin. "Let me correct myself. The houses and apartments are smaller, but our church is huge. St. John the Baptist is many stories tall, with a bell tower that is even taller." She laughed again, and everyone still stared, fascinated. "It overlooks the village square protectively like a lofty army soldier."

As Maria cleared the dinner dishes from the table, another young woman came into the dining room to help.

"How long have you been in the United States?" Aunt Winnie asked.

"I have been here a year and a half, all the while living in Boston while learning to become a seamstress."

"We're wearing Lily out with all these questions," John interrupted. He tasted the coffee Maria poured into his cup. "She needs a break. Dustin, what do you do with your days? Besides ranching, that is. Are there any issues in Rio Wells that have become contentious?"

"What answer do you want first, cousin?"

"Boys," Aunt Winnie said wearily. "Must you really? What is this between the two of you?"

"I think she's sitting at the end of the table," Madeline added sulkily, then patted the corner of her mouth with her napkin.

Maria's appearance broke up the uncomfortable hush. John's mouth watered as the maid served large slices of chocolate cake. Tucker, in an effort to help, reached out with his good hand, but upset the tray. He tried to rectify the situation, but his left arm made the circumstances worse. The cake fell onto the white tablecloth. It rolled onto the shocked boy's lap, then plopped to the floor. Gooey chocolate frosting was everywhere. His face clouded over and he bolted from the room.

Chapter Twenty-Four

"**T**ucker, come back! It's okay," John called sharply as he sprang to his feet and ran through the living room and out the open front door. Lily rushed to his side and the rest of the family followed close behind.

John hurried to the barn. "Tucker, come on, let's talk," he called. "No harm was done. We've all had accidents." Unlatching a gate, he ran into the trees behind the barn and paddocks, looking for prints. Finding nothing, he continued on. Almost ten minutes passed. Tucker was fast and smart. They wouldn't find him until he wanted to be found. When John turned to go back, he caught a glimpse of Lily's pink dress where she was searching in the trees. The last thing they needed was for her to go off into the wilderness and get lost. He headed in her direction.

She startled when he called out to her.

"John, I did not hear your approach. Have they found Tucker?"

"I haven't been back yet. But I'm thinking that we're not going to find him tonight. Humiliation is a potent emotion. Especially at his age. He's either hiding or on his way home."

Lily's eyes were dark with worry. "I feel so bad for him. He is such a good boy, kind and caring. I want to help him. There must be a way."

"Are you talking about finding him or something more?"

"Both. It is such a shame about his hand. There must be something that can be done. There must be some kind of operation."

John stepped closer, drawn by her concern. He took her chin in his fingers and tipped her face up, gazing into her eyes. A current of attraction passed between them. "Some things we just have to accept. Life is hard. Things happen."

That statement gave her pause. "Maybe he is watching us now, hoping we think enough of him that we will not give up so easily. Sometimes just knowing that a person cares is all that is needed to heal a broken heart. I am not giving up." She picked up the hem of her dress, meaning to run up the rise, when John pulled her back until her lips were a fraction away from his.

"I admire your desire to find him, Lily," he said, feeling his world somersault with her so close. Just the two of them, alone, in the trees. "To help him. To hurt for him. To love him." He moved closer knowing he was going to kiss her, wanting it more than the air he breathed. His senses thundered, making it hard to think of anything but her.

"John," she whispered, her mouth looking soft and ripe as a strawberry. Then her startled blue eyes went wide, and her gaze moved to his lips.

"John. There you are." Charity ran forward, then stopped.

He pulled back quickly. "Have you found him?"

Charity shook her head.

John wrapped his hand around Lily's, afraid she'd run off again in search of Tucker. "I promise you he's okay. He is. He's just embarrassed. Let it be for now. Okay? And if he's watching us, then he knows how much you care about him. That alone may be all he needs. Agreed? Lily?"

Several moments passed before she looked up into his face and nodded. "Agreed."

The ride back to Rio Wells took almost an hour with the slow pace in the dark. There was moon glow for guidance, but John still had to search the road carefully, not wanting to hit a rut and take the chance of breaking a wheel. There was one part of the road that had been washed out by heavy rains, which left two big boulders in the center and made the going difficult for the buggy. On horseback it would be easy, but tonight he had to navigate off the road carefully and go around the washout.

As they approached Rio Wells, the strains of piano music floated out to meet them. Laughter from the Black Silk Garter was clear all the way down Dry Street, where they were approaching the livery. They passed Cradle's place on the way to drop Charity off at the hotel, and the old bay slowed, thinking he was finished for the night. John had to slap the reins a few times to get him moving.

He pulled up at the hotel. "Mind if Theodore walks you up?"

Charity gave him a look. "That's fine."

The two climbed out of the buggy, leaving John alone with Lily. Her hair fairly sparkled in the moonlight, and the warm evening air wrapped around them like a soft, finely-knit blanket. "Did you have a nice time tonight?"

She looked at him with her soft blue eyes, and he felt her tumble even more deeply into his heart. "I did. Your family is so kind. Everything was perfect." She looked at her hands folded in her lap, troubled.

"I know. I'm worried about Tucker, too."

She looked surprised he'd been able to read her thoughts. He longed to put her thoughts to rest. "I'm sure this isn't the first time he's been embarrassed by something he's done. He'll get through it and be better for it, stronger. That's how it works." He reached across the small distance between them and touched the tip of her nose, making her smile. "Life is hard. There's no getting around it. All we can do is try to make each moment count."

"What about the je…"

Before she could finish her question, John put his finger on her lips. "Shhh. Mum's the word. I'll find out how it came to be in your aunt's luggage. But…remember—" She was nodding, wide-eyed. "—don't discuss it with anyone. Not even Harriett." He wouldn't worry her tonight about the bounty hunter that had shown up in town yesterday. She had enough to think about with her aunt's health and opening the new store, and now Tucker, too.

Theodore bounded out the hotel door, seemingly exuberant from his time with Charity, and hopped into the back seat. "She's back in her room safe and sound. Checked it all out myself." John turned the buggy around and started back toward the doctor's office. "She sure is offish, though. It's like I've done something wrong to offend her. Don't know what that could be."

John smiled to himself. Maybe Charity was finally facing up to the fact that she was in love with Brandon Crawford. Probably missed him all to heck and back but would die before admitting anything of the kind. This visit of hers was going to prove to be her downfall, John figured. She'd probably go running back into his arms.

Another week passed and all the while Harriett's health went up and down like the rollercoaster Lily had once seen in Boston. After moving into the rooms above the shop, she had taken to her bed and they had a hard time getting her to eat anything at all. It was as if she'd lost her will to live. Lily pleaded with her to eat and John gave her an elixir to fortify her blood, to keep her strong. Even with all the coaxing, nothing seemed to work.

Lily went about straightening the several fabrics that had arrived with the day's stage. There was indigo blue silk, heavy jade velvet, a taffeta of the most gorgeous color of lilac she had ever seen, chocolate brown corduroy for more serviceable, everyday clothing, and a thick cotton with a small floral pattern of greens and pinks any little girl would adore. She now had eight bolts in all, plus all the other necessities she needed to complete several gowns, purchased with the money Dr. Bixby had so generously paid her to get the place in shape. She understood that his action, spurred on by John, was more an act of charity than born of real need, but there was nothing she could do, with the impossible exception of leaving town, to change their minds. She had accepted, but had written down the amount in her book of accounts and planned to save a portion from each sale and pay the doctor back. She'd also pay rent, no matter what they argued.

She gazed around in satisfaction. Now all she needed was a customer. Tomorrow was the official grand opening, and Charity had insisted that she put a small advertisement in the *Rio Wells Republic*, even if it had cost her fifty cents. You have to spend money to make money, Charity had told her.

Excitement—and a little bit of fear—hummed through her veins. For the past year and a half, she and her aunt had been working side by side, measuring and stitching and doing alterations. Together they had created some of the most beautiful gowns circulating in Boston today. If Tante Harriett did not get stronger, and her mental state did not improve, Lily was going to be on her own. That was a frightening thought. She knew she could do it, but didn't want to have to. She and her aunt were a team.

The little bell that Tucker had fastened above her door tinkled as the door opened, and he came striding through the doorway. Since the night of the party, he had not said a word about his accident with the cake.

"I see everything is ready for the grand opening tomorrow. You excited?"

"Very much so." She held out her hand and they laughed as it quivered unsteadily.

"You'll do fine. John wants to know how your aunt is this morning. He and Doc Bixby are going to be going out in a while to Martha Brown's place to check on Candy. Said he'll check on your aunt as soon as he gets back."

Lily couldn't stop her smile and the pleasure she felt at Tucker's question. John checked in on her and her aunt so many times a day it was almost getting to be a joke. "Tell him she's about the same. That she took several big spoonfuls of soup this morning and is now taking a nap. She'll be just fine until he comes by this afternoon. Also, tell him we can string a wire from my apartment to the doctor's office with two cans on the ends, like we used to do back in Germany. Then we can just talk person to person."

"I know what you mean. I think I've worn the leather off the bottom of my shoes, but I'm not complaining. I like visiting."

"What is going on over there?" she asked, meaning the doctor's office. "Any patients?"

"No. And I can see John's getting restless. Charity came over early and is making them breakfast before they leave. Theo's already been in and out a couple of times for no reason at all except to look at Charity. I don't think he likes his new job at the livery."

"Is that what he said?"

"In not so many words, but yeah."

"Well, it was good of Cradle to hire him on, especially since he is giving him free room and board. He's lucky to find work so quickly."

Tucker laughed. "Maybe. But, I think his goal is to win Charity's heart. How can he do that smelling like horse manure?"

John and Charity stepped into the shop. The hat dangling in John's fingers gave Lily a nice view of his freshly shaven face and his hair, which was still damp around the edges. Lily's heart flipped over, as it did every time he was near, and she had to glance away before he saw the truth in her eyes. He came in further and looked around nodding, apparently pleased at how the shop had come together. "You all ready for tomorrow, Florence?"

Lily narrowed her eyes as Charity hugged her. He chuckled.

"What's this?" John looked at the length of fabric she'd cut yesterday and had left out on the cutting table.

"The fabric for the frame you built. You know, my button art piece. It is the last thing on my to-do list. I want to have it hung up by this evening. At least, that is my intention."

Charity came forward and ran her finger along the green velvet. "It's going to be so pretty, Lily. I can't wait to see how you finish it off."

John pointed upstairs. "Thought I'd drop in before heading out to the Browns' place."

Lily was thankful John had not told anyone about the morphine. Everyone just thought her downward turn was due to old age and deteriorating health. "She is asleep right now. I tried to get her to come down this morning, but she complained that she had not slept well." They exchanged a look.

"I think it's going to take a little more than your coaxing. I'll see what I can do after she wakes up."

The tiny bell sounded again, and the banker, Mr. Shellston, flanked by the mayor, Fred Billingsworth, came in. Another man unknown to Lily followed close behind. He was tall and foreboding, and dressed in all black. The shop seemed to shrink before her eyes as they looked around.

"I see your problem worked out just fine, Miss Anthony," the banker said confidently, looking the place over, a coveting gleam in his eyes. "And, with ease it seems. There was really no need for all your panic over my Spring Street building, now was there?"

"Things have a way of working out," she responded coldly. She noted the way John drew himself up and the tightening of the muscles in his jaw. The reddishness around his scar appeared to deepen a little as he looked the newcomers over.

"Maybe it seems that way to you, Shellston," John said, "that this place transformed itself overnight, but Miss Anthony has been working night and day to get it presentable. I'm positive you remember how it looked not that long ago." Charity seemed to pick up on her brother's mood and stepped closer to him. Her chin tipped up as she looked the men over.

The banker had the audacity to laugh at John's remark and pass it off as polite conversation. "Nothing of value ever comes easily, my father always told me. I live by that rule."

Lily was having none of it. "With the help of the good people of this town, all this work got done. It was because of them and none other."

Mr. Billingsworth spoke up saying, "It's because of those good people that we're here this morning. We still have the problem of the vacant teaching position, and the children are becoming a nuisance running over this town like a horde of locusts. We wanted to ask your sister, Dr. McCutcheon, if she'd take over the position just until our replacement gets here," he said, looking first at John and then over to Charity. "We'd hoped to have the problem solved by now, but teachers are scarce."

Chapter Twenty-Five

"**N**uisance? Problem? Horde of locusts?" Charity asked, taken aback.

Her toe started tapping and John almost chuckled, getting ready for the explosion he knew would soon follow.

"This is the mayor, Mr. Billingsworth," John said, introducing them and trying to defuse his sister. "The banker, Mr. Shellston, and Mr. Boone."

"Really, Mr. Billingsworth," Charity scolded. "I'm surprised at the way you feel about the children of the so-called 'good people' of this town. Aren't these the children of the same citizens who pay your salary? You should be ashamed of yourself. And, if they're as rambunctious as you say they are, I'm not sure I'd be capable of controlling them."

A few moments of uncomfortable silence filled the room as the mayor's face turned scarlet. "Uh, I'm sorry, I didn't mean…"

Charity glanced from one man to the other as her expression softened. There was something going on in that head of hers.

"Forgive me, Mayor. I *am* pleased to make your acquaintance," Charity replied, now going all ladylike. "I heard the news about Miss Smith. I'm sorry."

"Yes, it was a horrible tragedy for everyone concerned." The pudgy man wiped his forehead with a white handkerchief he'd pulled from his pocket, then dabbed at his upper lip. He seemed undecided if he should go forward with their offer.

Mr. Shellston gave him a look and he continued, "What do you think of our proposal?"

Charity smiled, turning on her charm full force as she gazed from one man to the other. John didn't like in the least how Lector Boone was looking back. "She's not interested," he interjected, feeling protective.

"I'm not so sure about that, John. I've yet to hear what the offer is. Just what would be required of me and how much does it pay?"

Taken aback, John started to object, but she stopped him with a tip of her head. "Let's hear what the mayor has to say, John. It might be a way for me to fill my time. You know how the days have been dragging on." Oh, geez, she was laying it on thick. He heard Tucker chuckle.

"It's a temporary position until the new teacher we hired from Abilene can pack her things and get here. I predict it shouldn't be more than three weeks to a month."

"The pay, Mayor?"

"Two dollars a week."

Charity tapped her finger on her chin, making them wait. "Hmm, the teacher in Y Knot is a friend of mine and she makes twice that much. I don't know…"

"It's only for half days," Mr. Shellston said. "Just keep them in for the morning, give them some homework and send them home. How hard can it be? Two dollars a week is more than generous."

"In that case, I decline."

The mayor gaped. "But, we need you. Won't you reconsider?"

"I would if I had the support of the town for the education of the children. I don't want to be just a babysitter. What good is that? And, if I'm teaching them something, then my time is worth more than pennies a day."

The two men looked at each other as Mr. Boone watched from the back.

"The town will pay you four dollars a week, Miss McCutcheon," Billingsworth said.

"Five. Temporary positions always pay more."

The bank owner frowned. "That's robbery."

"Pay the woman," Lector Boone said, stepping forward. "She's educated. And smart. Maybe the locusts will learn something."

Charity turned on him, eyes blazing.

He laughed, making her all the madder.

John reached out and put his hand on Charity's shoulder, calming her youthful anger, and disliking the whole situation intensely. What was Charity thinking, taking this job? She was here for a visit and that was all. He stared back at Boone until the man dropped his gaze.

Boone was silent for a moment, then asked, "Any information on the gem I asked you about Monday evening?"

Lily gave a small gasp and Boone immediately looked at her. A bird caught between two cats couldn't have appeared more uncomfortable. John groaned inwardly. "No, nothing."

"I need to check on my *Tante*," Lily said, going at once to the back of the store. Her slim figure disappeared around the partition and her steps were heard quickly ascending the stairs.

"I'll take the job, Mayor."

"At that pay, I should take the job," Shellston grumbled.

Mr. Billingsworth smiled and wiped his head again. "Good. Good. You can start tomorrow, if that's acceptable with you." He seemed oblivious of the interaction that had just occurred between Lily and the gunman. He held out his hand. "Here's the key to the supply cupboard in the school house."

Charity took it. "I presume there are books and slates?"

"To a degree."

"Chalk?"

"Yes."

"By the way, Mayor, what made you think of me? I mean, I haven't been in town but a few days and have met only a handful of people since coming to Rio Wells."

Mr. Billingsworth looked more relaxed now that the negotiations were concluded and Charity had agreed. "Because you're a McCutcheon and I learned through the grapevine that you're well versed and smart."

John wondered where that information had come from.

"What about my cousins, Madeline and Becky?"

He shrugged. "They seem more ladylike. I don't think they could handle the children. Any woman who can travel from Montana to West Texas on her own has to have some grit."

A blush crept up Charity's neck and onto her face and kept going until it reached her hairline. The comment was meant to be a backhanded compliment, John was sure, but it looked as though Charity didn't take it that way.

Mr. Shellston stepped to the door, opened it, and then stopped and turned back. "Tell Miss Anthony good luck tomorrow. The shop is now one of Rio Wells' finest." He went out, followed by Mr. Billingsworth and Mr. Boone.

John turned on Charity as soon as the door clicked closed. "What are you doing? You've never expressed interest in teaching."

She straightened defensively.

John pointed his finger in her face. "I never know what to expect with you."

Tucker made his way to the door, and slipped out. Now that John had Charity alone, he intended to get some answers. "I mean it, Charity. Since the day you arrived I've been a little on edge, feeling this mysterious energy from you. And now this? Are you planning on staying longer here than you let on? Has something happened between you and Brandon? Out with it. What's the big secret?"

"Why are you so upset? I have no ulterior motive, like you hint at, except to help the children of this town while I'm spending time with you. That's all. You can put your speculations to rest." She plunked her hands on her hips and glared back at him. "You're not the boss of me."

"You damn well better believe I am," he retorted. "At least while you're here in Rio Wells."

Lily's footsteps sounded overhead, then descended the stairs. John breathed deeply, then gave his little sister an all-knowing look of authority. Lily seemed to have recovered from her shock. He needed to talk to her, but not in front of Charity. No need to put his sister in jeopardy by knowing about the gem's whereabouts. The fewer who knew about it, the better. He was now having serious doubts about Boone's proclamation about working for the robbery victim in Boston. For all they knew, the man was out to steal it himself. Just because it was hidden in Harriett's things didn't mean the object wasn't with its rightful owner. There were more possibilities to this story the longer he thought about it.

"The men are gone?" Lily asked.

"Yes," Charity answered. Her face was still red with annoyance. "Mr. Shellston sent his good wishes for tomorrow."

"That man," Lily said with aggravation. "He has the nerve to come here and wish us luck." She picked up the green velvet and carefully laid it over the back of the wooden frame. "He is one person that sets my blood to boil."

"Here, let me help," John said, reaching forward to hold the edges as she stretched it taut across the frame. "Get the hammer, Charity. Please."

Still looking sullen, Charity picked up the hammer and tapped two small nails through the fabric and into the wood. She edged around his way as she worked, forcing him smack up next to Lily, and the sweet scent he'd become familiar with in the stagecoach. Lily's fingertips brushed his forearm accidentally in an effort to fit the velvet to the opposite side, and tingles of fire raced up his arm.

"There. There—hold that," Lily said close to his ear, then laughed nervously. Every fiber in his being surged in pleasure and he fought the impulse to take her into his arms. He knew, without a doubt, that she felt the electricity humming between them, too.

Charity yelped as the hammer glanced off a nail, clattering to the floor.

Lily went for the tool at the exact moment he did, and unexpectedly they were face to face. Their gazes locked, and held, as his hand enfolded hers on the hammer. They came up slowly with it between them.

A second passed. Charity cleared her throat.

In conspicuous silence, they finished up and John turned the now-covered frame over and held it up for inspection.

"It is beautiful," Lily gushed. "Even without anything else, I think the velvet picks up the light so nicely. Can you imagine how it will look with buttons and glass beads and other pretty things? Thank you so much." She pointed to a spot on the wall. "I think it will go right over there."

She looked questioningly to Charity. "What do you think?"

"Nice." Charity narrowed her eyes at John over Lily's unsuspecting head. "Really pretty."

The door banged open, barely giving the bell time to tinkle. "Remind me to find you a doorstop," John said, as Dustin stepped into the shop. "You need one before the wall gets worn out."

Dustin removed his hat and held it in his hands. "Mornin'," he said, looking around. "Just thought I'd drop in since I had some business at the bank." He gave a low, satisfied whistle. "The place looks great. Ready for business."

"It is due to your help, too."

John couldn't help but smile as the color of Dustin's face deepened. The silence in the room was palpable.

Finally, Dustin turned. "I guess I better get to my appointment." He hesitated, then put his hand into his pocket. "Here, Lily. This is for luck."

He placed a small item, sandwiched between two pieces of delicate paper, into Lily's open palm. "It's a four-leaf clover. It's been dried. A fresh one is nonexistent around these parts."

Lily's eyes opened wide and she looked at the gift for several long moments. "We used to hunt four-leaf clovers for hours. When I was a little girl," she said, turning it over and looking more closely. The tone in her voice spoke volumes. "It is an especially thoughtful gift. Thank you, Dustin."

She walked to the door and pulled up a chair. When she stepped up, both cousins hurried over to assist her, each steadying a side. Extracting a pin from her pocket, Lily carefully secured the clover in place a few inches above the front door.

Turning, she smiled. "There. We will see what the future brings."

Chapter Twenty-Six

Charity gripped the rope hanging from the bell tower and pulled it to her knees. The good-sized iron bell pealed out its announcement that class would resume this morning. A bit nervous, she ran her hands down the front of her dress and smoothed the apron she'd fastened around her waist. Her...a teacher? *Who would've thought?*

All the way down Dry Street was Lily's shop, open for business for the first time. She hoped Lily would have a customer today. Maybe even two. She liked Lily. There was something brewing between her and her brother. Dustin had set his sights on her, too.

The night she arrived in Rio Wells John had told her about his engagement to a young woman in Boston. It had been a surprise. And now this. Charity wished there was something she could do to help. But, with things of the heart, one had to travel the perplexing road alone.

Next to the school was an open lot where the children played at recess, and next to that was the Cheddar Box Restaurant. Hers was the last building on this side of Dry Street, with nothing but land as far as she could see until it ended at the base of the hills. The old Station House Hotel and the old stage stop were directly across, with Cradle's livery next door. At that moment, Cradle stepped out of his barn doors with pitchfork in hand and looked around. Catching sight of her on the school house porch, he smiled widely and waved.

The sight of him made Brandon Crawford pop into her thoughts and she wondered what he was doing right now. Was it quiet in Y Knot? Was he having a cup of that horrible coffee he boiled at the sheriff's office? Or was he hanging out at the ranch with her brothers?

She closed her eyes, bringing to memory his smile, and her heart fluttered. No one else had the power to do that to her, and she relished the sensation as she missed him all the more. Had he discovered she wasn't in Denver? Had the rest of the family?

She needed to let them know where she was. Of course Luke was going to be furious when he found out, as were Matt and Mark. She didn't even want to think about her mother and father, and what they might do. But, she reminded herself, she was an adult and free to go wherever she wanted. Still, saying and doing were two different things.

A wagon pulled up in front of the school. A man garbed in farm clothes tipped his hat to her and a boy about seven hopped out and helped his sister to the ground. The child ran up to the porch steps as the little girl tried to keep up.

"Good morning," Charity said, as he came close. "Welcome."

"Mornin'," he answered in a raspy little voice. He hurried into the schoolroom, apparently too shy to talk. His brown hair was slicked back and his face scrubbed clean. His dungarees had such a big roll at the cuff Charity was sure they were meant for someone much taller than his small frame.

The man watched until his children were inside. "Thank you. I'll be back later to pick them up," he called in a thick Texas accent. He slapped the long reins across the team's backs and the wagon rolled away toward the town center.

"Good morning," Charity said, going to the front of the room. "How are you this wonderful Thursday in May?" She had thought the girl younger, but now with a better look at the two, she realized they must be twins.

"My name is Miss McCutcheon and I'm going to be your teacher for a few weeks. Since I'm new in town, I'll need your help with names and such. Do you think you can do that?"

Both nodded.

"Good." She looked to the boy first because he seemed most outgoing.

"My name is Jedediah. And this here is Jane."

Charity relaxed and clasped her hands behind her back, getting used to her new position. "What's your last name?" She pointedly looked at Jane, trying to draw the little girl out. She wore a tattered blue-checkered dress that looked as if it had been fashioned out of an old tablecloth. Her hair was brushed and pulled into two pigtails, just above her ears, which were equally as scrubbed as her brother's. Her hair was so long that even in pigtails it fell down past her shoulders.

"It's Cole, ma'am." The child's face turned beet red and she giggled.

"Where do you live?"

Jedediah sat up straight. "'Bout a mile outa town toward the Rim Rock."

"In that case, I believe I passed your place the other evening. It was on the right-hand side with a big brown barn right off the road. Is that right?"

"Yes, ma'am."

"How many children usually come to class?"

Both shrugged in unison and Charity saw more of a resemblance between them.

"Five or more?"

"It depends," the boy said. "Sometimes it's just me and Jane, because my ma sets the sun by book learning. Sometimes there can be ten students, though, too."

Charity walked to the chalkboard and wrote her name in big letters. As she was writing the twins' names below hers she heard footsteps, then someone taking a seat. When she turned there was an older boy sitting in the last chair of the last row, closest to the door. It was as apparent as a colicky calf that he wasn't happy about being back in school.

"Good morning," she greeted. She waited a moment for a reply, and when there wasn't one she asked, "Your name, please."

"Harland Shellston."

"The banker's son?"

"Yeah," he shot back disrespectfully. "The famous First National Bank of Texas. You're pretty smart."

So, here was the problem Mr. Billingsworth had been talking about. Harland Shellston's very own son. His gaze challenged her even now. What would he be like once they were more familiar? Charity smiled, looking forward to the test. He had no way of knowing she had three nephews, all around his age. If Harland wanted to give it a go with her, she'd be happy to take him on.

Chapter Twenty-Seven

Lily stood safely away from the wood-burning stove as she stirred a pot of oatmeal. It was almost time to open and she wanted to make sure her aunt had something in her stomach before opening to the public for the very first time. Excitement rippled through her at all the possibilities that lay ahead. She dearly wanted her aunt to be a part of this day. Lily had high hopes that Tante would agree to be helped down the stairs and sit in the rocker by the front window. There was a beautiful spot of sunshine just waiting for her.

Lily scooped a ladleful of the creamy oats, already doctored with milk and sugar, into a bowl and placed it on a wooden tray. She added a napkin, spoon and cup of lukewarm tea and proceeded up the stairs, peeking into the bedroom. "Tante, are you awake?" She was lying on her side, and Lily couldn't see if she was still asleep.

"Yes, my dear." She reached for her spectacles and rolled over. Lily came in, set the tray carefully on the highboy, and assisted her as she sat up.

"Would you like to get up and sit in the chair for your breakfast?"

Lily noted the violent shaking of her aunt's hands as the old woman straightened the sheet on her lap and smoothed down the lace trim. She should be getting better every day and it looked to Lily as if she were getting worse. She was shrinking away right before her eyes.

"I think I'll take it here," she said, as she patted the sea-green eyelet comforter. "If that's okay." Her voice was soft, uncertain.

Sitting on the side of the bed, Lily took her hands into her own. "Yes, anywhere you would like." She paused, thinking. "You will be better soon, Tante. I'm sure of it."

Harriett's eyes, clouded with desperation, looked into her own. "A day never goes by without me thinking about...it." Her voice trailed off on the last word as if speaking about the drugs would make them materialize right before their eyes like a raging demon. "I'm so sorry you have to take care of me as if I were a baby. I—"

"Stop now," Lily said softly. She gave her aunt's hands a little shake. "You have nothing to be sorry for. You did not know that morphine was addictive when your doctor gave it to you. You trusted him. He is to blame. I love you."

Lily got up and placed the tray onto her aunt's lap. She unfolded the napkin, positioning it on her nightgown, over her chest. Resuming her seat, Lily stirred the cereal to make sure it was cool enough to be eaten, then handed the utensil over. "After you eat I want you to come down into the shop. Do you know what today is? It is our grand opening. And it is less than an hour before we open our doors for business for the first time."

Harriett's face darkened and the spoon slipped from her fingers, clattering onto the tray. "Oh, I'm sorry." Her voice was tiny, like a child's.

Lily straightened the things on her tray.

"I don't want to come down. Not yet." She looked away.

Lily was heartbroken at the sight of the once independent woman. She was so tiny and scared. "Do not think another moment about it, Tante. We will wait for the day that you are ready."

The older woman cautiously picked up the teacup and took a small sip, then replaced it in its saucer. "Lily..."

"Yes?"

"You do understand that I'm eighty-five years old, don't you? You realize what that means?"

Lily couldn't meet her gaze.

"Lily? You do, yes?"

"Yes, Tante."

"Good. I don't want you to be surprised if I fly away one day. I'm looking forward to it, so don't be sad when it happens. You'll do fine now, with all our new, caring friends around to look after you. And, you have John. He *loves* you. I couldn't be happier about the match if you were my own daughter."

Lily looked out the window, not seeing the bustle of the town at all, but rather the inner workings of her heart and where they longed to take her. She couldn't deny that what her aunt was saying was exactly how she was thinking about John, too. *I love him. With every fiber.* He was the man with whom she longed to share her every dream, plan for the future and build a family. Her face warmed just thinking about intimate moments and what they might be like. The thought of kissing him made her shiver, but, sadly, she pushed that image away. John would never be hers.

"Tante Harriett, you remember that John is engaged to another woman? She is coming to Rio Wells. To be married." She needed to make her understand the truth of the matter at hand and not keep indulging in her fantasy about the two of them.

Tante smiled and nodded. In her eyes was a great secret that Lily couldn't decipher. "Love can't be denied, Lily. It is inexhaustible and all-knowing. It is patient, too."

She hugged her aunt and then left the room. It was past ten o'clock and she heard voices outside on the boardwalk. Her biggest regret was that her *Tante* was not well enough to enjoy it, as well. To see the fruits of her years of toil.

John made his way from the post office and headed back toward his own place. He'd finally found the time to get a post off to Emmeline.

Turning, he saw Aunt Winnie's buggy tied in front of Lily's shop. She and his two cousins were there, apparently waiting for Lily to open. He was grateful they'd taken a liking to Lily—but then, that wasn't hard to do—and were going to help support her endeavors. Especially today, on her grand opening, he was happy she would have some business to celebrate.

Lector Boone approached. "McCutcheon." The toothpick clenched between his teeth dangled precariously when his lips twisted into a smile. "Your sister teaching school today?" he asked casually.

That put red before John's eyes. "What's it to you?"

"Just wondered." Taking the toothpick between his fingers, he rolled it a few times, then flicked it into the street. "She's about as feisty as they come. I enjoyed seeing her in action negotiating with the mayor. She's a smart one, all right."

"You'd do well to remember she's none of your business."

Across the street, Lily stepped out onto the walk and opened her front door, hooking it back with the fastener he'd installed himself. A broad smile wreathed her face when she saw Aunt Winnie, along with Becky and Madeline as they descended the buggy. They talked and hugged, then went inside. Now was not the time to take on the gunfighter, John reminded himself. Reining in his irritation, he crossed the street without another word.

Chapter Twenty-Eight

"**M**other, look at this one," Madeline said, running her fingers down the bolt of lilac taffeta, her expression pure delight. "I'd adore having my gown for the Cattlemen's Ball made from this." She leaned forward, putting the fabric close to her face. "What do you think?"

Mrs. McCutcheon came closer. "I think it suits you. It brings out the color of your eyes."

Lily couldn't believe her ears. A ball gown. For her first order. She clamped her hands tightly behind her back to keep them from shaking with excitement as the women made over her fabric.

"What do *you* think, Lily? Is this a good color for Madeline's darker complexion?"

Lily thoroughly agreed with the assessment. It would be stunning on her. She thought back to how Tante used to help assist women picking fabric and patterns that would best show off their beauty—and minimize their flaws. This color would bring out the young woman's earthy glow and add some sparkle. "I think it would be beautiful, and it is the one I would choose for her myself."

"That settles it. One gown for the Cattlemen's Ball, please. Do you have any patterns we may look at?"

"I do. Right over here." Lily went to the wall and pulled out a drawer that held eight different Butterick patterns. Only three were for fancy gowns; the others were of everyday clothes for men and women. Madeline and Winnie hurried over while Becky looked around the shop.

"Three only?"

It was Madeline and she was holding the patterns in her hands.

"Yes. But the options of the things I can do with them are almost limitless. I just use the pattern as a start." That brought a smile back to the girl's face. "I have a book of sketches of the gowns and dresses we made in Boston. All you have to do is look through them and tell me what you like."

Madeline's expression turned serious. "Can you have it finished in time for the ball? I know it's a lot of work for the few weeks remaining."

"What is the date? I've never heard it mentioned."

"That John," Winnie said with exasperation, and then laughed. "Just like a man not to say anything about the most important event of the year. It's on the Fourth of July. We all thought that's why you were hurrying to get your shop open. It'll be such a treat to have someone who's able to create beautiful clothing. We do have a tailor in Rio Wells, but he makes everyday clothing. The kind we can sew at home."

Lily did a mental counting. She could have it completed if it wasn't too complicated and she didn't run into any problems. "I can do it, depending on the kind of dress you want." She smiled, then added teasingly, "I will be sure to question John the next time I see him. Perhaps he has a reason why he's kept the celebration a secret."

John stepped through the open door without warning. "Did I just hear my name mentioned?" In the flutter of excited greetings, Lily could not help but think about her *Tante*'s proclamation about love just a few minutes before. She glanced up through her lashes to see him watching her as his youngest cousin wrapped him in her arms. His conspiratorial smile and wink made her face heat up unbearably. He was so handsome she feared she might swoon away right now on the floor. Her face must have given her feelings away, because he laughed in pleasure.

"You most certainly did, young man," Mrs. McCutcheon said, shaking her finger at him. "You're getting more and more like Dustin and Chaim every day. How come you didn't tell Lily about the Cattlemen's Ball on July 4th?"

He turned his gaze from hers and looked at his aunt. "Possibly because this is the first I've heard of it. I know, I know, that's impossible. But it's true. I've been busy working all this out," he said, sweeping his arm wide.

Adoration shone from Madeline's eyes. "Then you're forgiven. Look at the fabric we've chosen for my dress." She took him by the arm and dragged him over to the bolts of fabric. "The first gown Lily will make here in her new home."

Lily watched as John patiently took his time looking it over. "Very pretty, Madeline. I'm sure you'll be among the belles of the ball. Which fabric did you choose for Becky's dress?"

Lily had to stop the gasp she felt in her throat.

"I found a dress in Abilene on our last visit there, or I'd be commissioning one today also."

He looked over to Lily and shrugged, giving her an "I tried my best" look.

"I am actually a bit relieved to hear that, because without my aunt's help I do not believe I could finish two gowns in time. As it is, I'm going to have to get busy today. We'll take measurements, go through sketches and I'll need to get it pinned and ready to be cut out." She tried to hide her excitement about her first project but knew she was failing miserably.

"Then you best get going," John said, moving toward the door. "I won't hold up your progress any longer."

It was only a few steps from Lily's shop to his office, and soon John was in the cool, dimly lit kitchen, looking around for something to eat. This small-town doctoring wasn't much doctoring at all. Since the operation two weeks ago, he'd more or less been biding his time, waiting for something to happen. He found a loaf of bread in the sideboard and sliced off the end, spreading it with peach jam. He and Tucker were off somewhere now, doing something, and with a big mouthful John found himself drawn to the small safe he'd stuck in his corner of the office.

Twirling the dial, John set the numbers to the combination and listened, hearing it click open on the last spin. With a pull, he opened it.

Looking between the few drugs and possessions he had locked away, he spotted the fabric that held the mysterious stone. He unwrapped it and held it up. It wasn't costume, he was sure, and from the weight he figured must be worth a small fortune.

"You Doc McCutcheon?"

John spun, closing his hand around the jewel to find a boy about thirteen standing before him with a disgruntled expression on his face. "Who're you?" John asked, a bit defensively. He couldn't tell if the kid had seen what he'd been looking at.

"Harland Shellston. There's a rattlesnake trapped in the school outhouse. Miss McCutcheon wants you to come remove it. I told her I could kill it myself, but she said no."

"Go tell her I'll be right there."

The boy went out the door as if in no particular hurry. John rewrapped the stone and put it back into its hiding place. He retrieved his pistol from upstairs and started toward the school.

Charity was on the porch, watching his approach. As he got closer, he saw two children and Harland Shellston, sitting on a log a safe distance from the outhouse, probably forbidden to get up until the threat was taken care of.

She ran down the steps to his side. "I didn't have a gun or I would have handled it myself."

That sounded funny to John and he laughed, realizing how much he was enjoying having Charity's company again. He pulled her into his arms and gave her a hug. "Sorry about yesterday," he whispered into her ear.

"Me too."

A small quiver ran through her body and he looked at her questioningly. "It must be a big snake?"

"Huge. From the sound of its rattle I'll bet it's almost eight feet long." He saw her try to hide another shiver. "I can't imagine how it got in there with the door closed.

"Let's go have a look." Before he got within ten feet of the tiny structure, a buzzing sounded that was almost demonic. He'd never heard anything like it. He looked at her astonished expression and felt his mouth go dry. "A real doozy."

"So?" She glanced over her shoulder to check on the children. "What do you think?" She had to raise her voice to be heard.

"Well, I could just shoot through the wood and hope to hit it, but I'd have to fire several times and the whole town would come running." He removed his Stetson and swiped his arm across his wet brow, then settled it firmly back on his head. "I'd rather not do that."

"How about I get you a stool and you shoot through the moon." She looked doubtful. "Can snakes climb up wood?"

"I'd rather not find out." The rattling stopped as if the snake was preparing some sort of counterattack on them. "Any rope in the school house?"

She shook her head.

"Harland," John called. "Go over to the livery and get a length of rope from Cradle. If he's not there, just find something that'll work."

"Why can't you?"

"Because I asked *you* to do it."

Harland looked at John for a long moment, then got up.

"What's the rope for?" Charity asked.

"I'm going to tie it around the latch, back up a few feet and pull it open. I'll have a clear shot and be out of striking range."

She nodded. "He's being awful quiet in there."

"We haven't moved. He can feel our vibrations in the ground." John took a step and the hellish buzzing started up instantly.

Charity stepped away. "I'm really glad you're here. I don't ever remember a rattler sounding so deep before. Our Rocky Mountain rattlers get big, but I'm debating if I even want to see this one. It'll haunt my dreams for months."

"Yeah, and I remember how much you love snakes."

Charity nodded, her face a pasty white.

"Who found him?" John asked to change the subject.

"Poor little Jane. She came running back into class like the wind. I shudder to think if she'd opened the door."

Harland returned with a ten-foot rope and John wondered if he'd chosen the shortest one he could find. "Cradle there?"

"Nope." The boy ambled back over to where Jedediah and Jane watched.

John fastened it to the piece of wood that served as a door handle. Surprisingly, the snake remained quiet during the process. "Go on, Charity. Get back. I'd feel better if you go sit with the children."

"But…"

"Don't argue." She consented quickly and John backed up, feeling as if the ten-foot rope was really ten inches. He gave a pull.

Chapter Twenty-Nine

The outhouse door squeaked open. The sun was in the perfect position to shine directly inside, giving John full visibility of the structure's interior. His gun was cocked and ready as he peered intently.

A few heartbeats later he dropped the rope, stepped closer, then walked up closer still.

"Stay back," Charity cautioned.

"It's gone." Now confident the reptile was nowhere to be found, John took a hold of the doorframe and leaned inside, his Colt 45 grasped lightly in his hand in case he'd been wrong. "Nope. Not here anymore." He walked around the back, making a full circle.

Charity and Harland came forward, followed by Jedediah and Jane. "You sure?"

John smacked the side of the building with an open palm. "Yeah." He went inside and found a good-sized hole in the flooring. "There's where he got in and out. We'll board it up. He won't be able to get back in."

Charity's look was bleak. "But he's still around."

"I don't like that either. We'll all just have to be careful until, and if, he decides to show up somewhere else."

They were all still crammed into the outhouse, looking at the hole into which the snake had disappeared.

"John, is that you?" a voice called.

John peered through the door as the others piled out of the structure, giving him room to exit. He still held his gun, the hammer uncocked, and his hat was pushed back on his head for better snake hunting. He thought he was seeing things. "Emmeline?"

"Yes, it's me. Who else were you expecting?" She ran up the incline and flung herself into his arms, hugging him tightly.

She leaned back and gazed into his face, her expression falling dramatically. "Oh, my Lord, John. What happened to your face?" She pulled back farther to get a better look. "It's horrible."

"It's a long story," he said, taking a small step away. She looked as beautiful as he remembered and not at all worn from the long trip she must have endured. "I'm surprised to see you."

"Is that all you have to say?" Again she laughed as if she hadn't a care in the world. "*Hello, darling* would be so much nicer."

She did have a way about her, he realized, remembering all the reasons he'd fallen in love with her in the first place. She gazed at him through her long, dark lashes, smiling all the while. He chuckled, then gave her a kiss in front of everyone. "I'm just shocked to see you here without any warning."

"Didn't you receive my letter? I gave you the timeline and details when I should reach Rio Wells. Oh, my gosh, John. The country here is so different from Boston. Nothing could have prepared me for the move. Not even a letter from you—if you'd been so inclined to write."

"I did write. It, uh, went out yesterday."

"I see. Well, mail doesn't fly, you know." She laughed gaily. "I think I'll invest in carrier pigeons. The knights and princesses of England and Ireland had a much better system. I just love those stories."

He glanced at his sister who was watching with curiosity. "She's an avid reader, Charity."

"This is Charity? I've heard so much about you."

"All good, of course," Charity said, her startled expression looking past the petite brunette, up into her brother's face.

Emmeline laughed again. "Of course all good, silly. All John ever talks about is his family in Montana and how amazing you all are. And, of course, all his ranching stories."

"I do not," John replied with a chuckle.

"Are you settled in Rio Wells, too?"

"No," Charity replied. "I'm just visiting for a few weeks. It had been so long since John had been home I couldn't wait any longer to see him."

"I know what you mean." She reached over and touched his arm. "I've missed him too. You're a teacher?"

"Just filling in until the new teacher arrives. This is my first day, actually."

Emmeline clapped her hands together. "That's wonderful. I've always fancied myself a teacher."

"You have? I didn't know that," John said surprised. He pulled his hat lower to shield his eyes from the sun.

"Men," she said, giving Charity a wink. "They always think they know everything, don't they?" She waved her gloved hand in front of her face in an effort to cool herself. "It's quite hot." She turned back and placed her hand on John's arm. "Mama and Daddy send their love."

He smiled and nodded but his gaze drifted all the way down Dry Street. "That's nice," he replied, patting her hand. "Are your things at the hotel?"

"Yes."

"Let's get you out of this heat and let Charity get back to work." He'd noticed a fine sheen break out on Emmeline's forehead, and her cheeks had flushed a deeper shade of pink than he thought healthy.

"What were you all doing in there?" she asked, gesturing to the outhouse.

"A rattlesnake was trapped inside. I planned on shooting it, but it got away. Just stay aware—"

Emmeline's eyelashes fluttered several times and she wilted like a piece of day-old lettuce. John caught her just in time and swung her easily into his arms.

Lily was saying goodbye to Madeline when she noticed John coming down the street carrying a woman in his arms. Her head rested on his chest, and one arm hung down toward the ground, limp. The full blue skirt fluttered around John's legs each time he took a step and her little booted feet bobbed up and down. People gawked, trying to see who he carried.

"Look," Madeline said excitedly. "Someone's fainted. Let's go see who it is."

Lily held back. "You go."

Madeline grabbed her hand. "Come on. It will only take a second."

John reached the doctor's office and Madeline ran and opened the door for him. He went into the examination room and laid the dark-haired young woman on the recovery bed in the corner.

"Who is she?" Madeline asked. "I've never seen her before. Is she going to be all right?"

Lily watched as he straightened out her legs, making her comfortable. He loosened a few buttons at the neckline of her blouse. The young woman's skin was flawless. Her features looked as if they were made of porcelain. Her complexion, the most unusual shade of rose and sunset mixed, reminded Lily of the picture of the Madonna back home in St. John's. She was one of the most beautiful women Lily had ever seen.

"She's fainted is all," John finally said. Going over to the window, he opened it and then repeated the process with the one on the opposite side of the room.

"Do you know her?" Madeline stepped into the room a little farther, trying to get a better look.

John straightened and turned, looking straight at Lily. "This is Emmeline Jordan, my..." His sentence trailed off. "My friend from Boston."

Madeline gasped. "Your fiancée? Did you know she was on her way? You never said a thing."

"Not exactly. We had made some open-ended plans but that was all."

Madeline stepped closer, trying to get a better look at her. "What happened? Why'd she faint?"

"There was a rattlesnake in the outhouse at the school. I guess hearing about it was too much after her long trip."

Lily's mind reeled in shock as she took in the sight before her. She was here at last—and *so beautiful*. Despair, darker than she'd ever known before, swallowed her.

The door banged open and Dr. Bixby and Tucker came in behind Lily and Madeline, moving around the two women to see who was on the bed. The old doctor stopped at John's side. "She all right?" He reached down and felt the pulse in her neck.

John looked a little annoyed. "Yes. Just some talk of a rattlesnake."

Dr. Bixby nodded, then turned to the other women, ushering them out with open arms. "No woman I ever knew liked to wake up being gawked at by others of her own species. Now, out with you both."

"Of course, Doctor," Madeline said. Before leaving the room she added, "She's beautiful, John. Congratulations. Be sure to bring her out to the ranch for a visit real soon. Mother and the rest of the family will be anxious to meet her—and hear all about life in the big city. And about the wedding."

"Go on, now," Bixby said.

Blood pounded through Lily's head as she tried to get a hold of her emotions. In a fog, she said goodbye to Madeline and went back into her shop, this time closing the world out behind her door. Tangled thoughts jumbled in her head, and her heart felt as if it had been ripped from her chest and thrown into a bottomless pit. She'd never feel it again. She took several slow, calming breaths, then tried to put the whole situation from her mind, recreating the delicious feel of excitement and awe she'd had this morning, just before opening her doors for the first time and actually contracting a substantial commission.

Life was good, she reminded herself sternly.

She was no different now than she had been the day she and *Tante* Harriett climbed into the stage in Concepción. She'd known almost from the first moment she met John that he had a fiancée and that the woman would be joining him. *This* was no surprise.

Lily couldn't stop the burning or the tears that now flowed unchecked. *Oh, God, this hurts.* She brushed at her cheeks as a tiny sob escaped between her lips.

Getting a firm hold of her emotions, she reminded herself she'd prepared herself for today. Just because they'd survived the Comancheros together and he'd been helping her from the day they arrived, and that she felt a closeness and oneness with him that she had no way of describing...none of that meant anything at all.

And what about the kiss? Well, he hadn't actually kissed her...but he would have if Charity hadn't shown up. She closed her eyes remembering how his lips, hovering so close, had drawn her like a magnet. Looking into his eyes, so expectant and deep, caused her heart to flutter around her breast like a trapped bird.

She'd dared to think they might actually have a chance. Frustrated, she opened her eyes wondering if she'd imagined the whole thing. Emmeline's arrival wasn't a shock, she reminded herself. *It was not.*

Lily flopped the bolt of lilac taffeta over, wrapping it back into place and set it on the shelf. She picked up the collection of sketches that lay skitter-scatter on the small table and carefully placed them back into the leather-bound book. She was alive and happy. And so was her aunt. They were going to be secure in their new home with a business to support their every need. Maybe when she had paid back all the money to Dr. Bixby, and they were on their feet financially, she could send for Giselle or Gretchen and teach one or both of them to become dressmakers. Her world was *open* to any direction she wanted to take it.

Chapter Thirty

In her misery, Lily didn't hear the bell so when she turned it was a shock to see John standing there. A quick glance in the mirror confirmed that her eyes were red and puffy, her nose wet.

"Mind if I check on Harriett?" he asked stiffly. He looked directly at her. It seemed his gaze touched her very soul.

Warmth washed over her. She was swamped with conflicting feelings. She wished she could run to him and throw her arms around his neck and hold him close, tell him everything he meant to her and how much she loved him. But that was clearly impossible. Emmeline was now in Rio Wells and was a visible, living, breathing reason why she shouldn't, and would never be able to. She tried to smile but knew her expression fell short. His expression was unreadable.

"Of course. I was just doing that myself. I'm worried. She still refuses to come down."

"We don't want to rush her."

"No."

"Upstairs is the perfect place—she can feel close to you and yet she's out of the curiosity of others while she regains her strength and mental health."

Lily turned without answering and preceded John up the narrow staircase. "Can I make you a cup of tea?" she asked over her shoulder. "I'm already making one for myself and my *Tante.*" He always shared a cup with her on his mid-day visit. They used to joke that it was the only way they made it until supper without going nutty. The little white kitten—who had abandoned the doctor's office completely for Lily's shop— trotted up to her when she arrived in the upstairs parlor. Lily bent and picked her up.

"I better not. I have lots to do, but thank you."

The regret in his tone was impossible for him to mask, at least that was what Lily thought. If she couldn't be more to John than she already was, then she wanted to be a help to him. As he'd been for her. Not a stumbling block. Not someone to make him unhappy or feel uncomfortable around.

He turned and opened the bedroom door slowly, tapping on the doorjamb. "Harriett, you awake?"

Lily went in and said hello to her aunt, and then went back downstairs, leaving them alone. She checked the water in the teakettle, knowing full well it wasn't hot yet. Then, with her iron poker, she stirred the glowing embers in the stove, giving them some air.

By the time the kettle was whistling, John was just coming back down the stairs.

"She seems less shaky today and even a little stronger. I want you to keep giving her the molasses and iron elixir to build up her blood."

Lily reached for the teacups, needing to do something to keep from staring at him. "I will."

"Good." He seemed as if he was stalling, looking for something to say.

She glanced at him as she poured the heavy kettle, holding it with two hands and a potholder. "Is there anything else? "

"Guess not." He headed for the front door.

"She is beautiful. Emmeline, I mean."

He turned back, nodding. "Yes, she is."

What on earth had possessed her to say that? She shrugged, feeling like an uncertain child looking for reassurance from her mother. "Just wanted to tell you."

As if understanding her motives completely, he nodded.

His smile was as warm as his gaze and her glance strayed to his wound. "It is so much better this week. Pretty soon it will just be a little line."

"Not quite, but the wonder salve Doc Bixby makes is working better than anything I've ever seen. I think he should bottle it up and send it all over Texas. Heck, maybe even farther. I think he'd be a rich man if he did."

"Who'll be a rich man?" Emmeline said, stepping through the door and looking around. "You took so long, John, I wanted to come find you. This is your patient?"

Lily smiled the best she could.

"No," John replied. "She's upstairs. I've just finished up and was heading back over to the office. How do you feel? Are you still dizzy?"

"I'm fine, you silly worrywart. I'm sorry about fainting. Just the thought of a big snake makes my knees go weak." She directed her answer to Lily. "You know what I mean?"

Lily nodded.

"This is Lily Anthony," John said quickly. "And this is Emmeline Jordan."

"It is a pleasure to meet you," Lily said, taking the opportunity to look more closely at the beautiful fabric of Emmeline's skirt. It was expensive and finely made. A beautiful piece of clothing.

"The pleasure is all mine. Doctor Bixby mentioned that you and your aunt are new to town also. How do you like Rio Wells so far? I can say I've never been anywhere so hot and dusty before."

John stepped over to Emmeline, taking her by the elbow. "Let's get you over to the hotel and settled. I'm sure you're worn out by your long trip getting here. There'll be time later for talk."

"Actually, I'm famished. There was so little food at the stage stops I feel as if I've not eaten anything substantial for days. Do you think we could go and get a bite to eat first?"

"Absolutely. The hotel has a fine dining room." They stepped to the door and John tipped his hat. "Lily."

"Good day," she replied, knowing the hard part of meeting Emmeline was over, but also that the pain of watching the two of them together would never, ever be any easier.

Finished for the day, Charity walked down the street toward the hotel. Teaching was hard work, mentally and physically. As soon as she was back in her room, she was going to remove her boots and put her feet up. She'd never really stood in one place before for so many hours at one time.

The moment she'd said class was over, Harland Shellston had taken off without a by-your-leave or even a glance over his shoulder. The boy unsettled her. Usually there was a reason for such incivility. Perhaps she could win him over and be his friend. Surely, he wasn't all bad.

She glanced back as the Coles' buckboard left town with the children chattering away to their father. After class, she'd waited with Jedediah and Jane for him to pick them up. The snake was still fresh in her thoughts and she didn't want to trust that the children would keep a keen enough eye out for it.

As she drew near to the Cheddar Box Restaurant, Lector Boone stepped from the interior. He tipped his hat as she approached. "Miss McCutcheon. How was your first day of class?"

Something inside Charity told her to keep walking, to ignore him, but that would be out-and-out rude. Several people were inside the restaurant and she didn't want to seem impolite being the new teacher.

"Fine, Mr. Boone. Thank you."

That was until the snake decided to show up for class, she thought to herself, causing her lips to tip up in reflection.

Seemingly encouraged by her smile, he swung into stride next to her and took the books she was carrying from her hands.

"These look heavy," he drawled. He boldly reached over and swept a stray lock of her hair behind her ear.

"There's no need," she said, jerking back. She reached for her books but he held them from her reach. Out of the corner of her eye she saw Theodore, who was sweeping off the walk in front of the livery across the street, stop and stare.

"Have you seen the hot springs?" Lector asked, pointing down Spring Street to the rocky area a few hundred feet away. There was a bridge that spanned the swampy area of bubbling water and mist.

"No. And I'm not interested in seeing them with you." His forwardness had her blood boiling. "Now, if you'd hand my books back, I'd like to be on my way."

He let out a sharp laugh. "I guess that answers my next question."

Charity was still facing Main Street, where her brother's office and Lily's shop were now only a block away and plainly in view. A rider coming down the middle of the street snagged her attention and her heart did a somersault of excitement. There was no mistaking who it was as the rider made a straight line to her with the intent of an eagle after its kill. He was now within thirty feet, and the anger around his mouth and his dark shuttered eyes made her want to run for cover.

Chapter Thirty-One

Brandon Crawford reined up next to her and Lector Boone. "Charity." His tone was curt. "I'd like a word with you."

"The young lady is busy." Lector took a step toward the street and closer to Brandon on his horse.

Charity bristled at Brandon's tone but knew it was warranted. He had every right to be furious with her. It looked as if he'd been riding hard for days and his horse appeared spent. Several days' growth of beard covered his normally clean-shaven face and his clothes were dirty from living on the trail. His gaze raked Lector from head to toe. Knowing Brandon as she did, she realized if she didn't act swiftly, things could get dangerous. Reaching for her books, she took them from Lector and stepped back.

"Thank you for your assistance, Mr. Boone. I can manage the rest of the way on my own." She started to step into the street to cross, hoping to separate the two large men, but Lector took her arm, stopping her.

Brandon swung from his saddle and stepped forward. He pulled Lector's hand from her arm, causing Boone to throw a punch that Brandon dodged.

"Stop this instant," Charity shouted. She stepped between the men and pushed on Brandon's chest with both her hands, but he didn't budge. Boone's hot breath scorched the back of her neck and a mad bull, wanting to charge, came momentarily to mind, unbidden. "I said stop!"

"You know this man?" Lector said from behind her.

"You're damn right, she knows me," Brandon answered for her in a low, dangerous tone. His unreadable gaze left Boone only for a moment to singe her to her toes.

"The two of you stop this foolishness and calm down." Charity stomped her foot in an attempt to make her point.

When she felt Lector step back, she thought it safe to turn around and face him. "Again, Mr. Boone, I thank you for your help. Now, I'd appreciate it if you'd please leave. I never asked you to take my books in the first place. I'll thank you to leave me alone in the future."

She stepped into the street and marched toward the hotel, all the while praying the men would turn and go their separate ways. When she'd seen Brandon riding down the street, she thought her eyes were playing tricks on her. She'd wanted to run to him, the way she used to do when they were kids, and throw herself into his arms. He was her knight in shining armor, always showing up at the exact right moment. He'd lifted her spirits when she felt sad. Dried her tears if she cried. Just a glance from Brandon could cause her heart to float like a snowflake or melt with desire.

Then, when he'd taken the job as the sheriff of Y Knot four years ago, her adoring heart believed it was his way of staying close to her until she was old enough to marry. Well, she was eighteen now and it had been one misunderstanding after another, and all the while her doubt that he wanted to be part of the family—more than her husband—grew until it was all-enveloping. She'd seen the desire to belong lurking behind his eyes, more times than she'd like to remember. Everyone loved Matthew, Mark, Luke *and* John. Her parents, the ranch hands. Everyone. Brandon was the fifth brother and was loyal to the McCutcheons to a fault. Problem was, she wanted to be loved for who she was, not for the family she came from. Doubt was always in the back of her mind, gnawing away at her confidence.

She glanced over her shoulder. Boone was gone, thank goodness, and Brandon just stood there with his reins in his hand, watching her. She wished fervently she could talk to him now and tell him how sorry she was for not letting anyone know she'd left Denver and traveled on to Rio Wells. Her desire to live told her this was not the right time, however. She couldn't remember ever seeing him as furious as he looked at this moment.

John waited a moment before pounding on Charity's door again, for the third time. "Open the door, Charity! I'm not leaving until you do. I know you're in there."

The door flew open and Charity flung her arms wide. "Why not just go tell the whole town what's going on? My goodness, you're loud."

"Don't try to change the subject on me." He charged into her hotel room and slammed the door. "Sit," he said, pointing to the chair by the window. She did his bidding without question and waited for what she knew was next.

"I can't believe you took off without permission or even telling anyone that you were coming to Texas. My God, do you know what could have happened? I'll admit I was more than surprised when everyone allowed you to travel to Texas alone, but held my tongue. Now that I know you came without telling anyone, I'm furious. How disrespectful of you. How thoughtless. Frankly, Charity, I'm appalled."

She flinched at his words. Too bad if he hurt her feelings. What she'd just put the family through was reprehensible. She'd been getting her way since the day she was born. It was about time she grew up and realized that actions had consequences.

"Let me explain."

"I don't want to hear it. When I saw the condition Brandon was in I thought something horrible had happened back at the ranch. That someone was dead. Hell, I don't know what I thought, but it scared the hell out of me. Then he explained that he'd gone to Denver to check..." He stopped and shook his head. "No. You're going to have to hear it from him." He paced to the window and then back to where Charity sat. "I think you've really done it this time, Charity. I wouldn't blame him if he rode out of your life forever."

Charity stood, her face as white as a sheet, and hurried to his side. "Don't say that. It's not true. I needed to see you. Please listen to me. I kept telling everyone that there was something wrong, since I hadn't heard from you in so long, that I had to come and see. Mother and Father were away and I knew no one would agree to my going. So, I made the plan to go to Denver and then just keep going."

A tingle of guilt for not writing to her as he knew he should jabbed him hard in his conscience, telling him to ease up, that he was partly to blame. Still, what Brandon had just gone through was inexcusable.

"Where is Brandon? I want to talk to him, to explain."

"I don't know."

"Are you just saying that or don't you really know?"

"I really don't know. I've never seen him this upset. Seriously, he is livid."

She sank down on the side of the bed and stared at the wall. She looked wretched. If he'd done what he should have, she wouldn't have taken off. He reached up and ran his fingertips across the healing and still-tender tissue on his face. Moments turned into minutes. Finally, he stepped forward and sat down next to her, sensing her anxiety.

She glanced at him through tear-filled eyes.

"We all make mistakes, I guess," he mumbled.

With the back of her knuckle she wiped away a single tear from her cheek, then slowly shook her head. "No. I always seem to mess things up. Sometimes I don't know if I do that on purpose just because things start to go right."

He placed his arm around her shoulders and drew her close. She seemed so small and he was pulled back in time to when the two of them had had to fend off the three older siblings. They'd been a pretty good team back then.

"I have a confession," he said softly. "I knew I should send word to you, to write, but I guess I didn't want you to come out and see this." He pointed to his face. "Until it was healed a little more. I was being vain. I thought about it several times and kept putting it off. I could have written to you and eased your mind, but I didn't."

He waited a few minutes to let his words sink in. "I'm as much to blame for this mess as you."

"So, everyone at the ranch now knows?"

He nodded.

"Did Brandon go all the way—"

"That you're going to have to hear from him. But, if I were you, I'd give him some time to cool off. I'd wait until tomorrow, at least."

"I don't know if I can."

John had a bad feeling. He hadn't exaggerated when he told Charity he'd never seen his friend so angry. Over the years, Brandon and his sister had had their ups and downs, with plenty of antics and theatrics from Charity, to be sure. But Brandon was a man, and one that could just be at the end of his rope. "Well, I don't think you have a choice."

She nodded, then gave him a wobbly smile. "You're right. I don't have a choice. But, tomorrow I'll explain, make him see why I had to come. He'll understand. He'll forgive me. That's just his nature."

She leaned over and kissed John's good cheek, making his heart lurch. He hoped it was true. It would be a sad day indeed without Brandon around. The sheriff was already part of the McCutcheon clan, and it was too strange a thought to even think of anything different.

Charity went over to her pitcher and poured some water into the basin, splashing her face. "Tomorrow is a new day," she said.

He nodded sympathetically. That it was. A new day for him, too. For him and Emmeline.

Chapter Thirty-Two

Shots woke Lily in the middle of the night. Sitting up, she brushed the hair from her eyes with shaking hands. Blinking to adjust to the darkness, she looked across the hallway. It was difficult to see, but the tiny bit of moonlight coming in through her aunt's window showed that she still slept soundly.

Flipping her covers back, Lily rose and pulled on her heavy wrapper and hurried out of the bedroom. The white kitty, which had been sleeping beside her, hopped down and followed behind. In the upstairs sitting area she lit one candle and looked around to see that everything was as it should be.

Loud voices came from the alley, and a door banged. She hurried down the stairs, careful of the flame, and lit the lantern in the kitchen. First she tried the front door to make certain it was locked. Then at the back, when she pulled the curtain aside to peek out, she saw several men gathered around as two more carried a person toward John's office. Tucker was out there too, and when he saw her looking out, he hurried to her door.

"What happened?" she asked, letting him in and closing the door. "I heard gunshots."

"Don't know exactly yet, but someone at the hotel took a bullet."

Lily gasped. "It wasn't Charity, was it?"

"No."

"Or Emmeline?"

Again Tucker shook his head. "No. A man. They carried him into Doc's office."

"Is it bad? Do they have the gunman?"

Again Tucker shook his head, causing his tousled brown hair to fall into his eyes. Apparently quite comfortable with her now, he used his stump to brush it away.

"What?" she asked. "There is more you are not telling me." Her imagination took flight, cooking up all sorts of horrible things. "What is it?"

"Well, a woman seems to have been roughed up some, too. She's already at the doc's office. Looks like she'll die."

"Was she from the saloon?" Lily felt guilty for having voiced such an indelicate question, but saloon girls lived a dangerous life.

"No. She was a guest in the hotel. Someone broke in, then stabbed her when she woke up and screamed. That's when the other man came to help her and got shot. She was in the same room John used to have." He gave her a strange look and started for the door. "I better go now and see if they need my help. Keep your doors locked. Sheriff Dane and the deputy are out doing a search. You'll probably see 'em walking around, so don't be scared."

Lily stifled a shiver. The kitten wound around her legs until she picked her up. "Thank you for filling me in."

"John asked me to check on you, and also Charity and Emmeline at the hotel."

After letting him out and securing the lock, Lily made the rounds again, checking the windows even though she was confident they were bolted.

There were footsteps out front and then a knocking on the front door.

She hurried over and pushed the curtain aside just enough to see the sheriff. She unlatched the door and opened it a few inches.

"Sheriff?"

"Good evening, Miss Anthony," he said. "I'm sure you've heard the commotion going on the last few minutes. I was wondering if I could come in and have a quick look around."

There were several men waiting by their horses.

"Now, Sheriff?" Lily glanced over to a small clock on the fabric shelf and saw that it was fifteen minutes until three. "It's late and my aunt is sleeping."

"I understand, but we're conducting a search. I must insist."

Reluctantly, she opened the door and let him in. He walked around the shop, glancing in corners. He pulled back the drape to the dressing room and when he found it empty, let the curtain swing back into place. He nodded as if satisfied.

When he placed a foot on the first step leading to the bedrooms, Lily came forward. "Please, Sheriff. My aunt has not been well. If she wakes up and sees you, she will be frightened to death. I just came from up there and assure you there is not anyone there who should not be."

His shoulders relaxed and he took his hat off and ran his hand over his face, then exhaled. "Fine, then. I want you to let me know if you see anything suspicious."

John pulled the sheet up over the woman's face then stood, looking at her. When they'd brought her in, she'd been clinging to life by a thread, and a frail, worn one at that. He and Bixby had tried everything to stop the bleeding from the stab wound, but it was like trying to dam the Mississippi.

With nothing else to do for her, he went over to the examination table and looked at the chest wound of the other patient Bixby was preparing to work on.

Tucker was holding the ether cloth over the man's nose and mouth.

"Get me the tweezers," Dr. Bixby said. "Cotton and the bottle of alcohol."

John did as he asked, and the older doctor poured the clear liquid into the bleeding wound, then swabbed it with the cotton. He took the tweezers and forceps and explored around inside the man's chest until he stopped, then felt again.

Moving his hand slowly, he worked the instrument until he had the bullet and pulled it out. A fresh wave of blood bubbled up from the small hole. "Pour some more whisky in there. Then cover it with cotton and bandage it."

"Everyone okay over at the hotel?" John asked Tucker, as he did as Bixby had asked him to do.

"Scared but alive."

"And Lily?"

"She was awake and peeking out her window."

Just then Brandon came into the examination room, pulled a chair from under the desk, and turned it around. He straddled it, then watched John mop up the blood from the man's body. Bixby left the room.

"You look like hell," John said, meaning it. "You been drinking yourself to death?"

Brandon shook his head and motioned to the man on the table. "He going to make it?"

"Too soon to tell."

"Was he able to say anything before he went under?"

"Don't think so. But, then, I was working on the woman."

Brandon grunted. His bloodshot eyes looked tired and his face strained. John knew this man as well as he knew any of his brothers. He could see he was hurting.

"I spoke with Charity tonight." John tried to see where his comment might take him.

The nickel Brandon was twirling in his fingers stilled.

"She's extremely upset about the whole mess."

"That's a mite hard to believe. Charity always has things under control. Don't you know that by now, John Jake?"

John, finished with the patient, went to the basin and washed up. He let the comment go while he dried his hands and went to the door. "Come on. I'll put on a pot of coffee. I don't think we're going to be getting any sleep tonight. Got some things I want to talk to you about, anyway."

"If one of those things is Charity, don't waste your breath."

He got up and followed his friend into the kitchen, plopping down into the chair. Tucker remained in the examination room with the injured man, and Bixby had retired to his room.

"Just so you know, part of this mess with Charity running off lies at my door. I should have returned her letters promptly. She'd written several in my last months at school and then here, and I didn't get back to her. She may not show it all the time, Brandon, but she's sensitive. She was worried about me."

Brandon waved him off, obviously not ready to let his anger go. "That's a croc—"

He stopped abruptly. "Said I wasn't going to talk about her." Several moments passed. "How you like Rio Wells?"

John stirred up the coals in the woodstove and put the coffeepot filled with water on to boil. He then scooped a half cup of grounds from a can and carefully put them in the coffee basket, placing that into the pot. "It's not Y Knot, if that's what you want to know," he said with a chuckle, then looked over his shoulder at his friend. "But, it's not that bad, either. I'm getting to know the people and that helps. Sure is hot, though. That's hard to like."

Brandon leaned back in his chair, relaxing. "Understandable. What the heck is that smell?"

John came and sat while they waited for the coffee to perk. "Sulfur spring just over on the next block. It's not always so bad, but sometimes it stinks to high heaven." He leaned forward toward Brandon and lowered his voice. "There is something I need to discuss with you. Actually, your showing up today was like an answer to a prayer."

Chapter Thirty-Three

He now had Brandon's attention. "Bixby told me about the fiancée." Brandon's brows knitted together in thought. "What's her name?"

"Emmeline Jordan."

"I'm flabbergasted. Nobody from the ranch said anything about her."

"That's because I haven't broken the news yet. Only Charity and my relatives here know. I was going to tell them in my next letter."

Brandon grunted. "The ones you never write?"

John shrugged noncommittally. "Yeah, but, that's not what I'm talking about now. A bounty hunter showed up in town a few days ago looking for a stolen jewel and the person who took it. Just so happens that I have that said item locked up in my safe."

His friend's eyes narrowed. "Does he know?"

"No. I'm not sure he's not after it himself, to steal. Or else, perhaps he's trying to fix a botched job."

"How did you come by it in the first place?" Brandon asked, life coming back into his eyes with the subject at hand. He was a lawman through and through.

"Lily Anthony found it in her aunt's possessions after coming into town on the same stage I did. It was soon after the Comanchero attack. She's certain it doesn't belong to her aunt because they were down to their last penny, and her aunt would have said something about it if she'd had something of that value. If I say anything about having it, one of us will be suspect, or maybe all of us will. I don't know. Maybe you can do some digging without it looking suspicious."

Tucker came out of the room.

"He still out?"

"Yeah." Wearily, the boy headed for the stairs.

"Thanks, Tuck, you're a real help."

"First thing in the morning," the boy mumbled, "I'll let the undertaker know he has a body to pick up." He slowly ascended to the upper floor, leaving John and Brandon alone.

"Go on," Brandon said.

"The man's name is Lector Boone. Boone said it was a robbery in Boston and he was working for the owner on getting it back. I have no way of checking out his story, or any of the information, because the telegraph lines have been down since I've arrived. I've been wondering about *that* too."

"Well, you wouldn't want to send a message from here anyway. I'll go back to San Antonio tomorrow, and send some wires and do some checking around. See what I can dig up."

"Tomorrow?"

"Yeah. The way I see it, the sooner the better."

John didn't like butting into his friend's business any better than he liked anyone butting into his. But if Brandon up and took off before Charity had a chance to speak with him and set things straight, she was going to be an emotional mess. John had enough experience with his sisters-in-law, and Charity herself, to understand a bit about how the female psyche worked. "I agree—"

"But?"

Brandon was looking straight at him with a "keep out of it" look in his eyes. His jaw was set in a determined expression John knew all too well.

"Just take a moment and speak with my sister before you do. She really wants to explain some things to you. Have a heart."

"Like she did?"

John held up his hands. "I understand."

"No. Don't think you do." Brandon opened the hand he had fisted on the table and worked his fingers. "What went through my head when I couldn't find a trace of Charity in Denver? Because a certain ticket operator was out with the pox, it took me days to learn she'd purchased a ticket to Rio Wells. Once I figured out she was on her way down here, my fear turned into something completely different. Can't stop my feelings, John Jake. They're just there."

"I guess she didn't think anyone would be checking up on her so soon."

"Well, she guessed wrong, didn't she?"

John figured this was a stone wall he wasn't going to get over tonight. The pot was now perking rapidly and the smell of coffee permeated the air. John got up and sliced some day-old bread, then retrieved the crock of butter and the small jar of peach preserves. He set it all on the table and grabbed two cups. After filling both cups, he set the coffeepot back on the stove.

Horses stopped in front of the office. Moments later, Dustin strode in the door. "John," Dustin said, looking Brandon up and down. Chaim followed.

"Dustin. Chaim." John stood and shook their hands in welcome. "Guess you heard about the excitement in town tonight. The woman's dead and the man will most likely make it. These are my cousins, the Texas McCutcheons, Dustin and Chaim," he said to Brandon. "Brandon is our sheriff back home."

The men pulled out chairs after shaking hands and John went for two more coffee cups.

"We came into town as soon as Pete Miller left our house," Dustin said. "He's riding out to all the ranches. It's been some years since there was such a brutal killing in town. I'm not speaking of the atrocities committed by the Comancheros in the badlands. This is different."

Chaim took a sip of coffee, then set his cup on the wooden tabletop. "Ma sent us into town. She's worried about Charity staying at the hotel alone. Said she'd never forgive herself if anything happened." He removed his hat and pushed his fingers through his shaggy brown hair, placing the Stetson on his knees. "She wants her to stay at the ranch with us, where it's safe. At least for a while, till all this passes."

"I had that same thought, actually," John said. "Originally, she wanted to stay in town to be closer to me, but under the circumstances, I think that's a reasonable idea."

"Good. We can collect her up and take her out later today. After school," Dustin added quickly.

"So, you've heard," John said.

He nodded and shrugged. "You'll come to find Rio Wells is pretty small. News travels fast. She can use the buggy to go in and out of town and we'll send a ranch hand along to escort her. She'll be safe."

"You have a man to spare?"

He nodded.

"Thanks." John smiled and was surprised when Dustin returned it. "I'm wondering something else."

Dustin sat back, relaxed. "Go ahead. I'm all ears."

"Is there room at the ranch for someone else?"

Surprised, Dustin looked at Brandon.

"Not me," Brandon said grumpily.

"Emmeline is here. She arrived today."

Both his cousins' brows shot up in surprise, followed by a smile.

"Your fiancée?" Chaim asked, surprised.

"That's right. I don't want her staying at the hotel alone, either. She and Charity could share a room."

"That won't be necessary," Chaim said. "The house is big enough to fit all of us and then some. Of course she can come. Why, she's practically family."

Dustin's eyes were expectant and his smile broadened. "I do have to say that things have sure gotten more interesting since you've come to town, cousin."

Brandon almost spit out the coffee he was sipping. "I think that goes along with the McCutcheon name. A never-ending rollercoaster of fun, fun, fun." He wiped his arm across his mouth.

A horse nickered outside and soon there were more footsteps on the boardwalk. Several men's voices rumbled in conversation, and Chaim got up and looked out the window. "Sheriff's back."

Dustin stood. "Tell Charity and Emmeline to get packed. We'll bring the buckboard into town later on today and pick them up. Ma's going to be delighted."

"Thanks," John said. "I appreciate this. I'm glad you two dropped in, even if it is before dawn." He followed the men out and watched them mount up. There was a lantern burning next door in Lily's shop, but he'd not bother her now. Feeling confident she was safe and sound, he headed back to check on his patient.

Chapter Thirty-Four

It wasn't even seven in the morning when Charity came into his office, looking around.

Dawn was just breaking outside, and John was surprised—and more than a little annoyed—that she'd walked the short distance from the hotel alone.

"Good morning." Her gaze went around the room and out the door, toward the stairway. Surely she hadn't dressed so carefully today for her three students. She was looking for Brandon.

"You're up early," John replied, before taking a sip of his coffee. "Were you able to get any sleep last night?" Before she could answer Emmeline appeared and came over and gave him a small kiss on the cheek. Her eyes were red and a little puffy.

"Good morning," she offered.

He was taken aback by her melancholy. He'd understand if she'd acted frightened from the killing, but other than that he didn't know why she'd be upset.

Before he could say anything Charity asked, "How are the man and the woman from last night? Did either of them make it?"

Guilty for feeling relieved to get back to footing he knew, he answered, "The woman died soon after they brought her in. There was..." He stopped, a bit overwhelmed by frustration. So far, he wasn't doing a good job of paying back his debt. Nothing he and Bixby had done to try to save the woman's life had made the slightest difference. She'd slipped away right before their eyes, just as Bob Mackey had.

He shook off the morbid thoughts. "...nothing we could do to save her. But, Mr. Reece looks like he's going to make it. That is, barring any new complications setting in."

Charity shook her head. "It was frightening last night. We didn't know what was happening. The scream woke me up and I ran over into Emmeline's room since it's just across the hall."

Worried about Emmeline, he took her hand and was just going to go into the other room for a little privacy so they could talk when Chaim came through the front. He was clean-shaven and bathed and smelled better than he had a few hours before.

"Mornin', all."

John nodded.

"Came early into town on an errand. Wanted to see if the ladies want me to pick up their things now."

"John?" Emmeline looked at him in confusion.

"For the time being, Emmeline, you and Charity are going to go out to the Rim Rock Ranch and stay with my relatives. Until the killer is caught and things settle down in town."

Charity stepped forward. "I'm not going out to the ranch."

John knew she'd put up a fight. He could see her mind going a mile a minute. Of course, she'd want to stay in town to be closer to Brandon. Well, she was headed for a shock when she learned Brandon had already left, ridden off to San Antonio around five that morning.

"Charity, I hope you're not going to make a big fuss about this. Aunt Winnie really wants you and Emmeline to come out and stay with them. It will be one less thing for us to worry about with all these new faces in town, and now the stabbing. Can you please just say you will, and we'll talk about the details later? Chaim here is good enough to take your things now, if you want."

He turned to Emmeline, who was standing by his side. "Is that okay with you, Emmeline?"

She nodded, but he could see there was still something troubling her. "I'll go pack my things and be ready in just a few minutes." Before John could stop her she let go his hand, breezed past his cousin and went out the door.

"I'll pick you up in a few minutes," Chaim called after her. His cousin hitched his head. "That must have been Emmeline."

John wanted to follow after and see what was troubling her so much, but he needed to stay with Mr. Reese today and monitor his progress. With all the blood he'd lost, it wouldn't take much of a setback to hamper his recovery and put his life into jeopardy.

Charity's face was red, but she looked as if she was going to comply as she watched Emmeline go. "I'll go pack my things too, before I have to head over to the school, and leave them in Emmeline's room."

"That'll be perfect," Chaim replied. "I'll get them when I pick her up."

"I'd like some time here after class before heading out to the Rim Rock. Will that also be okay?"

Chaim nodded. "Just give me a time and I'll have a man here to fetch you back to the ranch."

Charity gazed out the school house window deep in thought. She hardly noticed Theodore, across the street at the livery, pushing a wheelbarrow in and out as he cleaned out the stalls.

How could Brandon have ridden off this morning without giving her a chance to explain her reasons for running off? Just thinking the words made her cringe inside, now seeing well the thoughtlessness of her actions. But couldn't he have given her a chance to clarify?

He'd be back, she reminded herself for the thousandth time. John had assured her of that. And when he was, he'd be less mad now that he knew that she was safe, and he'd had some time to cool off. Oh, how she missed him.

Jane's hand went into the air and Charity got up and went to her side. "Do you have a question?"

"No matter what I do I can't get this to cipher right. Every time I try it comes out different."

"Let me see." Charity pulled up a vacant chair next to the little girl and looked at the numbers on her slate. "You're not carrying over the two in the third column. Watch how I do it."

With her finger, Charity smudged out the four-digit answer that Jane had and started figuring the problem slowly, explaining what she was doing as she went. When she looked up, the four other children were watching her.

Two new children had shown up today. Candy Brown, the little girl John had performed an appendectomy on, and Mark Miller, the deputy's son. Both children were ten years old.

When she was done, Jane's face brightened. "I see now."

"Good. Do it again for me three more times."

Charity stood and noticed Mark looking over Harland's shoulder at something the banker's son was drawing on his slate. Both boys were whispering behind their hands. Charity moved quickly and Harland didn't have a chance to cover it before she looked over his shoulder too. She snatched up the slate angrily.

"How can you be so mean, Harland? You too, Mark. Have you no empathy for others at all?"

On the slate was a picture of a boy with only one hand and it looked like he was falling out of a tree onto his head. There was no mistaking who the banker's son was making fun of.

Harland sat back and crossed his arms defiantly. "Ain't no harm done."

"Yes, there is. You're making fun of someone behind their back. When they're not even here to defend themselves." She looked at the new boy who at least had the decency to look ashamed. "And you, Mark. What would your father think?"

Harland stood as if to leave. "Tucker is a dumb, one-handed gimp no-account. Why are you getting all riled up? The doc just feels sorry for him and took him in. I don't see why he don't have to come to school too."

Charity's back went straight, bringing her eye to eye with this bully. *Probably because of shortsighted, ignorant people like you.* "That is none of our business. Now, sit down in your seat or suffer the consequences."

Harland's face contorted into a sneer. "And just what consequences do you have in mind?"

"Don't cause more problems, Harland," Mark said. He was smaller and two years younger than Harland, but was stockily built. His voice wobbled.

Jane looked like she was about to cry.

Being this close to Harland, Charity was all too aware of the boy's size. The last thing she wanted to do was get into a fight. "You can be sure I'll be speaking with your father today! The moment class is over."

"Come on, Harland, sit down. You run off the last teacher and my pa said it was shameful," Mark said, standing as he took Charity's side. He only came to Harland's shoulder, but anger had won out over fear and bravery shone from his eyes. "Quit being so mean."

"Either sit down this instant and be quiet, or leave," Charity added pointing to the door. "The choice is yours."

"No. I don't have to sit down or leave or to do a thing you say."

There was a satisfied smile on his face now that he was sure she didn't have any means to back up her words and discipline him in earnest. With his foot he shoved over Jedediah's chair and the boy fell hard on to the wooden floor. He gave the young boy a kick in the side and shoved Mark before anyone saw it coming. The deputy's son fell, tripped by his desk, and hit the back of his head.

Chapter Thirty-Five

Fear welled inside Charity. She fought the urge to step back. To give him room.

Harland laughed, and pointed at Mark, who sat curled on the floor, holding the back of his head in stunned silence. With Harland's next step toward Mark, Charity whirled and ran up to the chalkboard, snatching up the yardstick that leaned against the wall. In an instant she was back and with a mighty swing, slapped Harland on the side of his face so fast nobody knew what she was about to do. Tears gushed from Jane's frightened eyes as a big red welt formed on Harland's left cheek.

"Get out," Charity shouted. "You've hurt Jedediah and Mark and made Jane cry. I won't stand for your ugliness, you bully. Get out now before I smack the other side of your face. I don't care where you go as long as it's out of my schoolroom."

For a moment Harland stood transfixed, his fists clenched by his side. His cheek puffed up right before Charity's eyes, and she realized this would most likely be her last day as teacher. Still, she wouldn't take her action back even if she could. It was plainly apparent the banker's son had been getting away with murder for some time, even running the former teacher off. Everyone was afraid of him. It was time someone took him to task, even if she had done so in a shockingly juvenile way. Her mother would probably be stunned with her way of handling the situation, but her brothers wouldn't. They would be proud of her.

She pointed to the door.

Harland walked out of the school room and disappeared. Charity looked around the room, then went over to Mark, righted his chair and helped him up. Then she picked up the frightened Jedediah and hugged him to her. Jane, overcome with emotion, wrapped her tiny arms around them both.

John went out on the boardwalk and leaned his palms against the railing, looking up and down the mid-morning street. Two weeks had passed since the murder, and Lector Boone had left town, to where John didn't know.

From the west, a cloud of dust preceded a herd of cattle being driven past on its way to the stockyard. The Texas Longhorns nonchalantly trotted by, their docile temperaments in opposition to their huge horns. Every now and then one would snag a post, causing a traffic jam of sorts.

Dustin came around the corner and stopped for a moment to watch the cattle, too. His cousin nodded to John when he saw him outside the office, but said nothing before venturing inside Lily's shop.

They were falling in love. It was plain to anyone who had eyes. And the question was—why wouldn't they? Furthermore, he thought irritably, why should he even care? Wasn't he engaged to be married to someone else?

John went back into the office and picked up his black bag. It was time for him to go check on Harriett. When he entered the shop, Lily was exactly where he thought she'd be, hard at work stitching Madeline's gown, the exact spot she'd been in for the past two weeks. Her chair near the window, allowed plenty of light as she stitched the huge piece of fabric rumpled by her feet and draped across two padded sawhorses. Dustin leaned against the cutting table, talking with her.

"Mornin'," John said, pretending the sight of the two of them together didn't mean anything at all. "I've come to check on your aunt."

Lily's face brightened. "You will be happy to hear that Tante is up this morning and taking some tea in her chair. Some color has come back into her cheeks and she almost seems like her old self."

John stalled, taking in the sight of her. Her hair was swept up on her head and she looked lovely, if a bit tired. "You didn't work on that dress all night, did you?" He came closer as she turned away from his scrutiny. "You did. Lily, you're going to make yourself sick if you keep up this pace."

"He's right," Dustin added. "You'll be finished in time for the Fourth of July celebration. You needn't work so hard."

He gave John a look that said he'd not be left out.

"John, is that you I hear down there?" Harriett's voice came from the upper level. "Come up here, young man. I have something I'd like to discuss."

Dustin smiled.

Lily laughed and shrugged. "See what I mean? She's almost back to normal."

"John?"

"I'm on my way, Harriett. I'll be right there."

Dustin waved his hand at his cousin. "Go on, already."

There was nothing left to do but go upstairs. As John put his foot on the first step, he heard Dustin's deep voice, "Have you thought about the Fourth of July celebration coming up, Lily? There're a host of…"

What did he expect? He was engaged to Emmeline. He had no rights or expectations over Lily. Dustin had a lot to offer a wife, and Lily had grown fond of his parents and sisters as they made frequent visits to her shop. There was nothing, *absolutely nothing*, standing in the way of Dustin and her getting married.

At the top of the stairs, he saw Harriett watching for him expectantly from a chair in the small, upstairs parlor.

"Good day, John," she said, her shrewd eyes searching his face.

With gnarled fingers she set the teacup she was holding on the table and closed the book in her lap. She looked over the top of her spectacles at him and smiled. "I've been waiting for you to come by and see me." Her tone was teasing and he knew she meant well, but today he didn't feel much like talking. He set his bag on the footstool and gazed at her. "Is something bothering you, John?"

He gave himself a mental shake. "I'm sorry. Just thinking about my day. How're you feeling? I'm glad to see you up and about."

Laugher from downstairs twisted his gut such that he had to look away from her face.

Harriett leaned forward. "What do you expect her to do?" she asked quietly.

Surprised, he just stared at her.

"She's young and in the prime of her life. One adapts when one knows one has no choice."

Anger surged to the surface of his feelings. He couldn't hurt Emmeline like that. Only the most callous of cads would even think of it. She'd done nothing to bring this on and yet...

He had as many answers this morning about the whole relationship as he'd had yesterday—none. He took his stethoscope out and listened to Harriett's breathing, then examined her eyes and reflexes.

"You're much stronger today. I'm glad. How are your thoughts? Your concentration?"

"If you mean do I still think about the drug, yes, I do. Not an hour goes by that I don't desire it. But, with prayer and perseverance, I think the craving isn't as strong as it once was."

"That's good. I'd say your next step would be to come down into the shop where you can help Lily with small things and socialize a little. Would you like me to help you down now? It would give you a chance to get to know *Dustin* a little better."

The edge in his voice was impossible to hide.

"Jealously doesn't become you, Doctor. Actually, you have nothing to be jealous of, if you'd only open your eyes."

John packed up his things and stood. "I don't know what you're talking about. Are you going downstairs with me or not? I'm sure Lily would also enjoy your company."

With surprising ease she stood and waited for him to offer her his arm. "Well, if you insist. I don't want to disappoint you."

He led her to the stairway and preceded her down, making sure she had a firm hold on his arm. At the bottom she looked around. "Oh, my. The shop is beautiful, Lily."

Lily hurried over and met her aunt with a hug. "This is a happy day for me."

Lily took Harriett by the arm and helped her into the main room, but not before letting John know of her pleasure by the look in her eyes. Lily slowly led her around the room, stopping to explain each carefully planned spot.

They ended by the window and the yards of fabric for Madeline's gown.

Harriett bent forward and fingered the material. "And this is Madeline's dress for the celebration on the fourth? Lily, it's beautiful so far." She lifted it up and turned it over in her hands, inspecting the work carefully. "You've done a marvelous job on the bodice. Exquisite." She looked into Lily's face. "You've learned well. Your stitching is incredible, exceedingly straight," she said, now examining an arm seam closely as if she loathed putting the garment down. "I'm so proud of you."

Lily's face clouded up with emotion, so John quickly said, "I'm off now to the ranch to see Emmeline and the family." With black bag in hand, he walked slowly to the door.

"Isn't today Madeline's fitting?" Harriett asked in all innocence. "Perhaps you could give Lily a ride out. She's been cooped up for days working her heart out and I think the fresh air would bring the roses back into her cheeks."

Dustin straightened quickly. "I heard Madeline and Becky talking about coming into town today a little after noon for that exact purpose. You don't need to make the trip out, Lily."

He'd inched closer to Lily and her aunt, and the look he shot to John said *don't you dare*.

It was only fair. John nodded and left, feeling unease spreading through his body and out into each limb. He'd put it away for now and enjoy his first time out of town in days. He'd let Bo run to his heart's content, and perhaps it would ease his heart a little, too.

Chapter Thirty-Six

John gave Bo his head and the gelding surged up the incline, sucking in big gulps of air. He laid the reins against the gelding's neck and the horse swerved off the trail and bounded up a steeply slanted slope, through brambles and shale, coming out almost on the hilltop. Even though the weather was still cool, warmth from the animal's hide sent the scent of saddle leather and blanket wool up to John's senses, bringing with it a deep longing for home.

The detour he'd taken on the way out to the ranch veered off the main road. His destination was the top of the mountain, where he'd get a feel for the lay of the land. The weight of his Colt 45 rested comfortably on his thigh, and his Winchester was in its scabbard. In the next few feet the land leveled out and John reined to a halt, stopping in front of a great drop to the valley floor. Off in the distance was Rio Wells. Beyond that was another mountain range, much larger than the one he was on.

A handful of clouds gathered in the west over the far range. Perhaps later today they'd get some much needed rain. John rested his arms on the saddle horn and felt his horse cock his hip, relaxing too.

Emmeline. His intended. He loved her, he told himself.

He held onto that thought for a moment, as if suspended in time, and then slumped in the saddle. No, he corrected himself. He didn't. He needed to face that fact, as awful as it was, and as much as it was going to hurt.

John removed his hat and ran his arm across his moist forehead, then placed his hands on the saddle horn, his Stetson still dangling in his fingertips.

Time seemed to stop. He welcomed the cool breeze that moved across his face, ruffling his hair. Emmeline was a good woman, one deserving a husband who adored her. Someone to love and cherish her. One to give her children and take the best of care of her...and a multitude of other things as well.

He just wasn't that man.

John sucked in a deep breath, taking consolation in the feel of the wind as it picked up, tousling Bo's mane and rolling the thunderheads closer. Angry with himself, he put his hat back on, knowing he wasn't the one who needed soothing.

It would be Emmeline. Today. After they talked honestly and openly.

Without warning, his thoughts wandered to Lily, and what she was doing right now. *She and Dustin.*

But his feelings, or the lack of them, had nothing to do with Lily. Even if he'd never met her on that stagecoach to Rio Wells, he fully believed his feelings for Emmeline weren't deep enough for them to marry. Even without Lily, he would have realized that they'd made a mistake.

Emmeline deserved more than that. There was no getting around what he needed to do.

Charity rushed from the ranch house as John tied his horse to the hitching post. Without giving him a chance to say anything, she embraced him in a fierce hug. "I was going to come into town to see you today."

He laughed, enjoying her enthusiasm. "You were? Well, I beat you to it."

"Did you come to see Emmeline?"

"Yes. And you too, of course."

"Of course." Her tone said she didn't believe it for a second.

"I did," he said more forcefully. "Hey, I'm sorry about the teaching position. The parents thought you were doing a fine job."

Charity shrugged. "I wasn't surprised when they let me go. With Norman Shellston and Fred Billingsworth on the school board, it was no wonder. What's Harland up to these days?"

"Don't know. I haven't seen him since the incident."

"Any news from Brandon? It's been two weeks since he left."

They were halfway to the house already so he stopped, knowing this meant as much to her as his problems meant to him. She'd been putting on a good show, but he knew she was hurting, wondering what Brandon was thinking. John needed to remind himself that she'd come all the way out here to Rio Wells for him alone, to check on him when she felt he needed her. That was a real act of love and he intended to remember it. His little sister may act tough, but her heart was as soft as butter on a warm day.

"I haven't heard anything yet."

A little of the light went out of her eyes.

They again started for the house. "But, two weeks isn't that long when you're investigating…"

John nearly cursed when she snatched his arm and stopped him.

Her eyes narrowed. "What do you mean investigating?"

"What? Nothing."

"*John Jake McCutcheon*, you spit it out right now."

He feigned innocence. "Nothing. All I meant was that he said he'll be back. He didn't give me an exact date but if he said he'd be back, he will."

"You know where he went though, don't you? I can see it on your face. If you don't tell me right now, I'll think you don't have a conscience at all."

John took her by her shoulders to settle her down. Brandon had made him swear he wouldn't tell her anything more than that he'd ridden out. John was just trying to stay out of it, but knew now that he had to say something.

"Brandon asked me not to say anything, Char. I'm in the middle of you two and I don't like that one bit. But there are some other circumstances, too, that kept me from telling you the whole story, and they still won't let me."

She searched his face, as if trying to figure out what he wasn't telling her.

"He'll be back, Charity. That I can say with confidence. Shouldn't be much longer, either. But, honestly, that's all I can tell you."

He could have added that concerning the two of them, Brandon hadn't told him what he was thinking.

Her eyes turned dark. The gusto she'd displayed when he first rode up was gone. "Come on," he said, lifting her chin with his finger. "It's going to be all right. And when it is, you're going to wonder why you were so upset."

"If Brandon is doing something for you then it must have something to do with the law. What else could it be," she went on stubbornly, not ready to give up.

The door opened and Emmeline looked out.

"Char, I need you to keep this to yourself, okay?"

"Okay. But you better tell me if you're in any danger. I knew I had a strange feeling about you."

Both hurried to the house where Emmeline waited. Her dark eyes assessed him questioningly. He took her hands in his and she went up on tiptoe so he could kiss her.

"I didn't know you were coming out today," she said, a bit breathless.

"Sorry it's taken me a few days."

"That's okay. I've been very busy. There's hardly time to think."

"That's true," Charity agreed. "Yesterday Chaim and Uncle Winston took us for a tour of the ranch that lasted all day."

John stepped through the door and removed his hat, hanging it on a peg. "You rode?" he asked with surprise, looking at his fiancée.

"No," Emmeline laughed, moving farther into the room. "Chaim drove me in the buggy and Charity and your uncle rode beside."

"Well, good. I did notice the pretty pink in your cheeks."

Emmeline clapped her hands together, resembling a little girl. "It's lovelier than I'd have ever thought West Texas could be. I really love it here. We took along a big basket of food and had a picnic."

John had been hoping that maybe the topography, with its heat and cacti, not to mention rattlesnakes and scorpions, would not be to her liking, and might make this transition a little easier if she wanted to go back to Boston herself.

"John!" Chaim said as he came into the room. He wore a blue and white cotton shirt with the sleeves rolled up over his powerful forearms; his pants were tucked into his tall, hand-tooled boots. He stood next to Charity and shook John's hand. His boyish smile split his face as he squeezed John's hand in a grip like a bear's. "You just get here?"

"I did. Emmeline and Charity are just telling me about the outing you all had yesterday. Sounds like I missed a heck of a day."

Oddly, color came up in Chaim's face.

"We did have a good time," he answered. "It would have been better, though, if you had come along, too. You've yet to see it all."

"That's true. I hope to remedy that soon. Where is everyone? Seems deserted around here."

John followed Chaim and Emmeline into the parlor and seated himself on the sofa. Charity stood in the doorway, looking a little downcast.

"Not really," Emmeline said, taking the seat next to him. Her gaze followed Chaim across the room until he sat in a leather chair by the window. "Becky and Madeline are upstairs doing something and I think your uncle is out working with Dustin."

"Nope," John said, relaxing next to Emmeline. "Saw Dustin in town this morning in Lily's shop."

Becky came in the room all smiles and took a seat on the green velvet settee. "Yes, that's right. I think he intends to ask Lily to the Fourth of July celebration. He was asking me all sorts of silly questions about women. Can you imagine? Dustin?"

Everyone laughed except John.

When he looked over, Charity was watching him closely.

"I'm not surprised," Chaim said. "I saw that coming."

So he wasn't imagining it. Dustin had feelings for Lily. Could he blame him? He was astounded that there weren't more men beating a path to her door.

"I've been hearing all sorts of wonderful stories about the celebration coming up," Emmeline said softly. "There's a bronco riding contest, pie eating contest, and shooting contest. I'd like to know what the women are supposed to do. Just watch?"

"I'm not watching. I'll compete in the shooting," Charity said boldly, her chin tipping up. "I might try the horses, too."

"I can understand the shooting," John said. "As a matter of fact, if they're taking wagers I'll put my money on you. Just stay off the horses. I don't want to be patching up any broken bones—or your head, either."

"We get to make a box dinner, Emmeline, and the men have to bid on them and then eat it with you," Becky added, her face lighting up. "It's so much fun. I'm going to fry chicken and bake a cherry pie."

Chaim shook his head in disbelief. "Aren't you a little young yet?"

Becky's eyes flashed a challenge. "I participated last year, don't you remember?"

"Oh, yeah, now I do." Chaim chuckled. "You had to share with Poke and Bill, our ranch hands."

"That's because Pa wouldn't let any other boys bid. This year will be different. A secret glimmered in Becky's eyes.

Chaim laughed. "Lord, protect him—whoever he is."

"You'll just have to wait and see." She straightened her skirt.

John said, "I had no idea it was such a big deal."

"Well, it's coming up fast," Becky said. "I have my dress already and everything else I need."

Emmeline looked to John expectantly, as if waiting for him to say that they were going.

Hell.

He wished there wasn't such a big social event coming up. She would be crushed if they didn't go, but he knew he couldn't drag this on a day longer. It was one of those impossible situations.

Her eyebrow arched, and he knew what was coming. "Should I be thinking about my dress, John?"

John felt his face go hot. What the devil should he say? "Certainly, Emmeline. I'm sure the whole town is going."

She was searching his face again with her big brown eyes.

"Chaim, I'd like to borrow your buggy and take Emmeline out today. We've hardly had a moment to ourselves."

Chaim stood and strode over to the door. "Of course. I'll tell Poke to get it ready now."

Chapter Thirty-Seven

Lily folded up the collar of Madeline's dress and set it on the worktable next to her chair. The work was intricate and took her full attention. Her eyes ached and the tips of her fingers were numb. She needed a break, just for a few minutes, and then she'd resume in earnest.

Dustin still relaxed against her cutting table where he'd been for the past hour, reading the day-old paper, and Tante sat in the kitchen area, her chair in the spot of sun coming through the window.

"All done with the lace?" he asked when she stood. He folded the paper in two and set it aside.

"Not yet. But I will be later today. Then I will fit the pieces together with the rest of the dress and stitch them on. I hope to be completely done by the end of the week."

Dustin had been waiting around, as he did often these days, as she worked. He was nice enough. Handsome, too. She liked his reserved sense of humor when he came up with outrageously funny comments, so unlike his serious, contemplative nature. And the timbre of his voice when he laughed reminded her exactly of Roland and made her a bit homesick for all her siblings so often of late. It had taken a few weeks, but she finally felt as if she knew him quite well and understood why he was here. He had designs on her and would soon bring up the subject of courting.

Courting. What would she say? What *should* she say? The man she loved was an impossibility? She'd resigned herself to that fact the day Emmeline had shown up in town. Until then, the dream of John falling in love with her had been a constant in her heart.

Now, it was on with life. Life *without* John. But, did she want to go on alone when there was a wonderful, handsome man interested in her? Her practical self told her to consider Dustin. Her heart would hear none of it.

Dustin followed her over to the cutting table where the frame stretched with green velvet hung on the wall, still completely blank. She reached up to take it down but Dustin beat her to it and laid it on the counter.

She smiled into his face. "I need to work on this so it will be finished by the time the celebration is here. I have been meaning to sew something onto it each evening yet I cannot seem to keep my eyes open long enough."

She laughed, reaching for her button box under the counter, and the drawstring bag holding the stray crystal and sequins her aunt had collected over the years. She spread them on the counter with the palm of her hand and began picking out the most colorful and appealing pieces.

"Have you always been such a hard worker?" Dustin asked as he watched her put several brightly colored buttons off to the side. "This is supposed to be a break and now you're working on this..."

"...piece of art," she finished for him.

Selecting a pretty mother-of-pearl button, she set it in the center of the velvet and moved it around until she was satisfied with its position, then quickly stitched it on.

"Lily, there's something I'd like to talk to you about."

At that instant, the bell above the door sounded and Martha Brown and her daughter, Candy, came into the store. Martha's eyes lit up a fraction when she noticed Dustin but quickly shifted to Lily's face. Lily had met the petite woman once before and liked her very much. Candy's too-short brown calico dress was ragged from use, but she was clean and her hair glistened prettily.

"Good morning," Lily greeted. "Is there something I can help you with?" she asked, thankful for the distraction.

"We're just looking, thank you."

Lily nodded. "Just let me know if there is something I can show you."

Martha took her daughter's hand into her own as the girl reached for a roll of lace. "Don't touch," she whispered softly.

Lily smiled and went back to her sorting and began laying some of the buttons and glimmer onto the velvet. She glanced up at Dustin to see if he was going to finish what he had been about to say.

He just smiled a crooked grin and shrugged.

"Mama, can I have some lace for my doll's bonnet?" Candy asked. "It would make it much prettier. Can I, Ma, pleeease?"

Lily quickly set her project aside and went over to the lace rolls where the child and her mother were looking.

"Let me show you," she said, taking a thick roll and handing it to Martha.

Candy, whose eyes were opened wide in awe, gazed at the beautiful lace in rapture.

"How much is it?" Martha asked.

"Twenty-five cents a foot."

Martha's expression fell but her daughter had no idea of knowing that luxuries such as hand-tooled lace were expensive.

"Can I, Ma?"

"No. Not today, Candy. You promised you just wanted to look." Martha quickly placed the bolt back where it had come from. "We'll come back some other time."

The disappointment in the child's face was more than Lily could bear. If she didn't have such a hefty self-imposed debt to pay off to Dr. Bixby, she'd give the child the lace. As it was, it was going to be hard to make that money up before she died, even if she sold a hundred dresses. Maybe the tiny scraps she'd snipped from the collar she was working on for Madeline would be something the child could use.

Just then Dustin stepped forward. "Consider this a Christmas present in June. Lily, could you please measure out a foot of lace for the young lady. Will that be enough?"

"Mr. McCutcheon," Martha gasped, as her daughter's angelic face looked back and forth at the adults. "That's a lot of money. We couldn't accept such a gift."

Lily moved into action when Dustin nudged her. "How would I sleep remembering the yearning in Candy's eyes? It's my pleasure, Martha."

Lily quickly measured off the lace, cut it and folded it carefully. She wrapped it up in a piece of soft brown paper and tied it up securely with a string. After handing it to Candy, she gave Dustin a smile that mirrored how her heart was warmed. What an incredibly nice thing for him to do. He pulled the coins from his pocket and placed them in Lily's hand.

"Thank you," Candy said, excitement beaming from her eyes as she clutched the small package to her chest.

Martha nodded once more, then smiled nicely at Dustin as she hurried to the door, propelling her daughter with her hand between Candy's shoulder blades.

When the door closed, Dustin turned to Lily. "Before I'm interrupted again I have something I want to ask you," he said, glancing at the kitchen where her aunt sat.

Lily smiled, knowing she couldn't put him off forever. The glow of the moment from his good deed was still fresh in her mind. "Yes, Dustin?"

"I'd like you to go to the Fourth of July celebration with me, Lily. Be my guest. I'll buy your box dinner and we can eat together. What do you think?"

She looked away. Now that going was a possibility, she wasn't sure she wanted to. Not without John. "I have nothing to wear. And no time to sew."

"I don't care what you wear." His mouth dropped open, astonished. "Wear this." His hand swept to her side gesturing to the work dress she wore. "You're beautiful in anything you put on."

She didn't care what she wore, either. Silly as it seemed, because she was a dressmaker, that was the last thing she thought about. She had said it just to buy a little time. She could go and have a fun time she was sure, but would that just be leading him on? If she could not have John, she felt certain she wanted to stay a spinster, like her aunt.

"Well, at least don't say no this instant. Think about it. You don't have to give me your answer today. I'm leaving tomorrow for Sweetwater to take some stock over to a rancher. I'll be gone for about a week. Think on it and give me your answer when I return."

What else could she do? John had Emmeline. Loved her. Was going to marry her. She needed to forget about the charming doctor with the beautiful eyes. She needed to force him from her heart.

She looked up at Dustin and nodded.

Chapter Thirty-Eight

John clucked to the buggy horse and flipped the reins over the animal's back. Emmeline sat next to him, parasol up and lap robe folded nicely over her legs, even though the weather was balmy. She waved happily to Charity and Becky as the buggy pulled away and then to Chaim, who watched from the darkened doorway of the barn.

John was sick inside. He must tell her what was going on in his head. She deserved the truth. Not some silly, sweet talk that would only lead them deeper into trouble. This was the right thing to do even if it was difficult.

He glanced up at the clouds, the same ones that had been over the far mountain range this morning, and noticed that they blocked out a majority of the sun.

Emmeline was lost in thought.

"Hungry?" His voice seemed to surprise her.

"Yes. I am. I can hardly wait to see what surprises Maria has packed for us in the hamper. There's been nothing but good smells coming from her kitchen all morning."

He nodded. "Did you have any breakfast?"

"I did."

He nodded, again glancing forward. Small talk seemed all he could wrangle out. She looked beautiful, as usual, but he could sense something was different today and wondered if she could feel his uncertainties.

They traveled at a leisurely pace as the coffee in John's stomach thickened. Seeing a good-sized plateau with several large cottonwoods, he pulled up. "I didn't eat, though. Mind if we stop and lay out the blanket and food?"

"Not at all. This spot is lovely."

John set the brake and tied off the long reins. Hopping down, he hurried to the opposite side of the buggy and helped Emmeline to the ground.

They headed for a pretty spot and shook out the blanket together, encased in a bubble of silence. John went back for the wicker basket.

A bit nervously, he sat down next to her and removed his hat, setting it to the side.

"Emmeline."

"John."

They spoke at the same time, then laughed, breaking the tension between them.

"You first," said John, taking a napkin wrapped chicken leg she offered, but made no move to eat it. "Please."

"All right." She scooted around, getting comfortable. "Well…" She dabbed at her forehead with her napkin, taking away the weather's sheen. "I've been thinking. Thinking about us."

Her, too? Does she want to set the date? Firm up our wedding plans? But, if that's the case, why is her brow furrowed in worry?

It was like a gargantuan horseshoe fell down from heaven and conked him on the head as realization dawned.

"John, are you okay?"

There it was again. An undercurrent of remorse coloring her words.

"John!"

He shook his head, wondering if what he was thinking could possibly be true. "I'm sorry. What were you about to say?"

She looked at her hands for a long moment. "I said I've been doing a lot of thinking about us," she repeated in a soft voice.

Honor demanded that he speak up now. Say something. Anything.

"About us getting married."

"About us getting married?" Again they spoke at the same time, his a question, hers a statement.

This time neither laughed.

The misery behind her eyes told him clearly what her next sentence would be. He couldn't let her take the whole responsibility of breaking up on her shoulders. Her conscience. That wouldn't be right.

Her hands began to quiver and she wiped at her eyes with the napkin, and then crumpled it in her palm.

John hastily discarded the chicken leg and took her hands between his own, quieting them. "I'm breaking our engagement, Emmeline," he said gently. "I hope someday you will be able to forgive me."

Her eyes widened for a moment, and then she let out a little sigh. "You are?"

He nodded.

She dabbed at her eye again, then gave him a tremulous smile.

"To be honest, John, that is what *I* was going to say. That I wanted to call off our wedding. Can you ever forgive *me*?"

Ashamed for the tremendous relief he felt, he struggled to think.

"Emmeline..." He pulled her a little closer. "There isn't anything to forgive. If what you said is what is in your heart, then that is truth. And the truth will set you free."

He didn't want to ramble on. He wanted the right words. For them. For what they had once felt. For what they would feel going forward.

She looked down where his thumbs were moving back and forth across the backs of her hands. "You do forgive me then?"

"I'd not have forgiven you if you'd gone forward knowing your feelings had changed. *That* would be unforgivable. Not this."

He threaded his fingers through hers and brought her hand to his lips, kissing her fingertips. "I think you're an incredibly brave and wonderful woman. It takes courage to do what you set out to do."

Her face flushed. "I've been worried sick about what I would say, and how you would take it," she offered. "I think you're wonderful, too." She looked up into his face, all traces of her smile gone. "Everything felt different when I arrived in Rio Wells."

He nodded. "I'm sorry. I should have brought it up sooner."

She looked as if she was rallying. "No, don't you be sorry. I feel better now than I have for a couple of weeks." She leaned forward, wrapping him in her arms. "Friends?"

John closed his eyes and held her, thankful for the way everything had worked out. "Always."

A moment passed, then they both sat back, the same and yet after a simple, five-minute conversation, completely different.

Her gaze slowly roamed his face and settled on the spot Lily had stitched. "I'm sorry about your face. Was it horribly painful?"

He shrugged. "Some. But it's almost healed now."

Emmeline's lips trembled. "The scar will shrink, you'll see. Please don't worry over it."

She seemed to be searching for the right words. He waited.

"John, knowing that you're not brokenhearted over this— *me*—is a whole lot easier to live with."

"What will you do now?" he asked.

"I haven't decided yet. Guess I'll cross that bridge when I find it."

His heart squeezed, but for what he didn't know. She looked so young. And sweet. He could see why he'd fallen for her in the first place. "Guess you will."

Chapter Thirty-Nine

With John and Emmeline out for the afternoon, Charity decided she couldn't sit around another moment. Madeline and her Aunt Winnie were tending the garden, but that held no appeal for her. Becky was holed away in her room making some sort of secret plans for the Fourth. Chaim had mentioned he was going into town in a few minutes and if she wanted to go along, to meet him in the barn. That was right where she was headed, dressed in her riding skirt and duffle bag in hand.

"Knew you'd decide to come," Chaim said, handing her reins to the horse she'd ridden the day before. It was groomed and saddled, and nudged her when she came close.

She threw the stirrup up over the saddle and checked the girth, giving it a small tug. With little effort she mounted and waited for Chaim.

"You okay?" he asked.

"Sure. Just getting homesick, I guess."

That was part of it but, even more than missing her family, she was missing Brandon. She tried to remember back if they'd ever been apart this long before, not running into each other in Y Knot or on the ranch. The wait was getting taxing.

Chaim put his boot in the stirrup and swung aboard his mount. He gestured to her bag. "What's that?"

"I'm staying in town tonight. That way I'll get to eat supper with John and also see Lily. I'm sure she needs some help on Madeline's dress since her aunt is still sickly and the Fourth will be here before we know it."

Charity sat easily in her saddle, enjoying the wide open space. Her mount, a grey mare, moved with a comfortable stride. Yesterday, Chaim stayed busy keeping the buggy on level ground and away from any potholes. He and Emmeline had chatted for hours. Surprising for a man of such few words. Now was her opportunity to learn more about the family.

Charity glanced over before asking, "Does Uncle Winston ever talk about his youngest brother, Gideon? He's younger than my pa, and from what I know he disappeared when he was fifteen. Pa says they don't know any more than that. Not even if he's dead or alive."

Chaim wagged his head back and forth. His hat was tipped up casually, giving her a good view of his face. A cross between John and Luke, he was quite the charmer in a shy and wholesome way, and a darn good-looking fellow indeed. And, in her opinion, much more approachable than Dustin, who was guarded and a little hard to get to know.

"Nah. Dustin and I used to wonder about that, but after getting stonewalled time and again, we gave up. I'd like to know the full story, too. I'm sure there's an interesting tale there. Or a scandal, or somethin' they're hidin'. How old would he be now?"

"Late forties, I think. I know what you mean. We all used to speculate, too. He just up and vanished and was never found. Strange. Sad, too."

"And there is, or I should say was, Uncle Rudolph McCutcheon. The oldest of the four boys. Our grandfather, Augustus McCutcheon was only sixteen when he came along."

Charity laughed. "I know. Thank goodness Grandma Sarah was sixteen too, and not younger. I'm eighteen. By their standards, *and* my mother's, I should already have a passel of kids. Our grandparents moved to Texas in 'thirty-six, right after Texas was annexed into the States, but before even my pa or Uncle Gideon was born."

"You know a lot."

"My father has it all written down in a ledger he made when he was a young man," Charity said. "Has dates and names and all sorts of interesting stuff. Says it's important to know who you are and where you came from. Also, to remember the mistakes your forefathers made, so you don't repeat them yourself. Now he's recording all the grandbabies and such and what and where."

Chaim grunted as if thinking over what she'd just said.

"Come on, I want to show you something." Chaim reined his horse off the narrow, well-worn road and guided it up a good-sized incline. Charity had to lean forward and give her mare ample rein as the horse scrambled up the shale and rock. He pulled up in front of a cliff that overlooked the whole valley and had a nice view of Rio Wells.

"Beautiful," she said softly, taking it all in.

"Glad you like it. Kind of puts everything into perspective, doesn't it?"

"Sure does."

She sat there drinking in the pinks and corals of the rugged land. The olive hues of the cacti and ironwood bushes blended nicely with the dry, earthen brown of the floor of the valley. A cricket of some kind buzzed behind her as if upset at the intruders in his area. A bald eagle glided across the horizon.

"Your brother Luke?"

Charity snapped around, looking at Chaim and not sure what to make of his question. "What about him?"

"He was always off-limits in our household, too. I know he's a half-breed, but not much more than that."

She stared at Chaim for a few more moments, then faced the valley in front of her. "Maybe that's because it's none of your business."

"Okay. Didn't mean to offend."

Several minutes passed. She could feel that soon they would venture on and she didn't want to leave the tenseness between them. Besides, Chaim was family and in a way had a right to know. It was out of ignorance that most anger and suspicion was born.

"Chaim, I'm sorry. I've just had my fill of stupid questions about Luke from people who didn't have any reason for asking. You're family. You have a right to ask."

She hunkered down into her saddle and crossed her arms over her chest.

"My mother, when Matt and Mark were just little fellows, was taken off the ranch in an Indian raid. Back then, Y Knot was nothing more than a one-cow town. Since there wasn't any sheriff," a pain jabbed Charity in the heart, thinking about Brandon, "it was hard for my father to find anyone to help search for her. Plus he had his little sons to care for. At first, he didn't have any choice and left them with a neighbor for a few weeks so he could go after my mother. Returning without her, he found Matt and Mark grimy and thinner than before. When they saw my father they clung to him like a tick on a dog's ear, and he was resolved to do better for them."

"That's when he brought them out here to Rio Wells?"

"Yes."

"That was before any of us were born," Chaim said quietly.

Again, she nodded.

"Does your mother ever talk about what happened?"

"Never."

They sat in silence as the eagle made another pass across the horizon.

"What's Luke like?"

Charity had to remind herself that Chaim, or the rest of the family, had never met Luke. And since it was a subject no one ever talked about, they probably had all sorts of strange ideas about him. Perhaps they thought he had hair down to his waist and rode around shirtless, looking for scalps. Or that he pitched a tepee next to the ranch house. She pushed down a surge of anger.

"He's just like the rest of us. No different."

"What's he *look* like?"

Charity had to count to three. "Chaim," she said, turning to face him. "Now you *are* starting to make me mad. What the heck do you think he looks like?"

Chaim sat up, making his dozing horse jump in surprise.

"He looks like Matt. He looks like Mark. Heck, he even looks a little like *you*."

Even as she said the words, she knew she wasn't being completely honest with him. Luke did have a wildness about him that made him stand out. No matter if the three boys dressed identically, with the same haircut—Luke always got the second look.

"Okay, I can see I've said too much. Let's get moving." Chaim turned his roan gelding and started for the trail.

Charity waited a good minute before she followed. It all just stuck in her craw. She'd never be ashamed of Luke—ever! She loved him and wanted to protect him from hurtful words. Just like she did with John, when people went to whispering about what happened when he was just a boy. How they looked away, causing darkness to pass over his expression.

But even worse than that, and boy did it gall her, was how so called friends would ask questions, or let slip a little comment, oh so innocently of course, as if they didn't know what they were doing. Did they really believe they were fooling anyone? Shameful. But, she didn't fault Chaim for trying to familiarize himself with family. That was different.

Charity clucked and the mare, already antsy to follow Chaim's horse, plunged eagerly down the hill, sliding on her haunches and breaking her speed with her powerful front feet. Charity leaned back in her saddle, dropping all her weight into her stirrups.

When she was close to the bottom, a gunshot rang out. Almost instantly, another blast ripped the air, and a bullet whizzed past her ear, embedding into a tall saguaro cactus with a thud. She ducked to the side of her horse and spurred hard, wanting off the face of the hill where she was vulnerable to take a bullet herself.

Chapter Forty

Charity reined up behind some rocks. With a thumping heart, she pulled her Colt 45 from her bag and spun the chamber, checking to see that it was loaded. All still quiet, she looked carefully around, holding the gun close to her chest. Where was Chaim?

Descending the hill, she'd been deep in thought and hadn't seen what had happened.

She waited a moment longer. Still nothing.

"Chaim!" she shouted.

Carefully, she nudged her horse forward, warily scanning the edge of the brush as she went. Twenty feet in front of her she spotted the roan with Chaim slumped over his neck.

"Oh, my God!" A shiver of dread spiked through her. Forgetting her own safety, Charity galloped up to her wounded cousin. His chest was soaked in blood.

"Chaim, can you hear me?" She gave his shoulder a shake. "Chaim! Please, say something!"

Some garbled words came out of his mouth before he sank forward again, and like a one hundred-eighty pound sack of grain, almost tumbled to the ground. She grasped his shirt and fought to keep him in the saddle of his spooked horse. Galloping hoof beats over the crest of the hill made her want to give chase. Give the devil, whoever he was, a taste of what he'd given Chaim.

But she couldn't. Chaim was in a bad way. If she didn't do something fast, he would die. Reaching for her bag, she tossed her gun in and pulled out her nightshirt and rolled it into a ball. She stuffed it under his shirt next to his chest and then pushed firmly to stop the flow of blood that now glistened on her hands like liquid rubies. With her home-made bandage in place, she took his horse's reins and started forward, but Chaim slipped to the side again.

This wasn't going to work. She'd have to ride behind him and try to keep him aboard. Without dismounting, Charity slipped over behind his saddle and settled onto the roan, praying the gelding was broke to ride double. She reached around Chaim with one arm, holding him as securely as she could, and took the reins with the other, all the while still holding the reins to her mount.

Dear God, she felt the need to hurry, but knew if she did, it would risk Chaim falling. She was thankful they were already off the side of the hill, because now it should be smooth riding all the way into Rio Wells. If she could just keep him in the saddle. The roan moved forward steadily. And her horse came along, too.

A small sigh came from Chaim as he tried to sit up.

"Just stay down. You've been shot." A plop of rain landed on Charity's rein hand. When she glanced up, another splashed her face and one landed on her thigh. Time was of the essence.

All was eerily quiet, then without warning, a bright flash lit the area and Charity prepared for the crack of thunder that would follow. When it hit, both horses tried to bolt but Charity fought to keep herself and Chaim aboard, as his horse danced around. Hers jerked free and ran off in a frenzied panic.

"Lily," Harriett called from the kitchen, "I've made you a nice cup of hot tea. Come drink it before it gets cold."

Happy that her aunt was feeling so much better, Lily set her work aside. "It's starting to rain," Lily remarked, opening the back door to look out. The musty smell of wet earth wafted in on a warm breeze as the tin roof started to sing. "Let's leave this open for a while and let the fresh air in. I love the smell of rain."

She scooted a chair over by her aunt and went to pick up her cup.

"Yes, let's." Harriett peered out into the alley. "I'm actually anticipating a trip to the mercantile—soon."

Lily looked at her in surprise. "You are? Would you like to go today? I could close for a few minutes and we could go over now."

"Oh, no." Her aunt's face clouded over and Lily realized that going to the mercantile was just hopeful thinking on her aunt's part. That was okay. One day at a time. At least she was here now, downstairs, having tea in the kitchen.

The rain started coming down in earnest and soon was a deluge, splashing on the wooden step and onto Lily's shoes.

"I need to close this," Lily laughed as she went to the door. Just then the little white cat bolted inside as if the devil was on its tail, almost tripping her. "Come in, come in, before you drown." She was looking down at the cat when she heard her aunt gasp.

"Close the door. Quickly."

Her aunt was out of her chair and pushing it closed. With shaky hands she bolted the lock and quickly drew the window curtains closed.

"What is it?" Lily asked in alarm, following her aunt as she shuffled toward the stairs.

The sound of the rain was now deafening. "Just a summer storm," she replied, looking over her shoulder. "I feel tired, Lily. I'm going upstairs."

The fear in her eyes was evidence enough for Lily that her aunt was not telling her the truth. At another sound of thunder, the frightened cat, her back arched and her eyes wide, dashed up the stairs in front of them.

Lily placed her hand on her aunt's shoulder, stopping her. "Tell me what's wrong."

"Nothing, dear, just the storm."

The back door rattled as someone knocked with force.

"Don't answer it."

"Why?"

"Please, Lily, just do as I ask. And go and lock the front door and close the curtains. No one else will be shopping in such weather. Go quick."

Tante Harriett's expression held such concern; Lily had no choice but to do as she asked. She ran over to the front door and yanked the metal rod into its slot with force. Then she drew Mrs. McCutcheon's heavy drapes across the front window just before she saw a figure in a black coat hunched in the rain, hat pulled low, come out of the alley next to the store and approach her front door.

Harriett motioned to her from halfway up the stairs. "Come upstairs with me, Lily," she whispered, as a loud knock rattled the front door.

Lily looked back and forth, not knowing what she should do.

Perhaps her *Tante* was hallucinating from the drugs. Maybe they weren't out of her system yet. But that didn't seem possible, for it had been quite some time and John felt sure she was better. Could she have gotten into his safe?

"Lily!"

This was only the second time Lily had ever heard anything but love in her aunt's tone. Now there was fear, laced with authority, demanding that she obey.

In the darkened store, Tante Harriett's face was an unreadable mask.

"I insist you leave that person and come upstairs with me."

Lily turned away from the door, praying it wasn't a matter of life and death. Was John hurt? It could be anything in the world.

Chapter Forty-One

John and Emmeline were almost back to the ranch. They were huddled on the buggy seat beneath the blanket they'd used for their picnic trying to ward off the rain. Suddenly, a horse came out of nowhere, galloping up from behind, and passed them with ease. It was saddled and the reins flipped around wildly. John pulled up on the startled buggy horse as it tossed his head and pulled on the bit, calming him with his voice. "That looked like Charity's bag on the back of the saddle."

Emmeline grasped his arm. "That's the grey horse she was riding yesterday. Something must have happened to her."

Without another word, John hauled on the left rein, turning the buggy around. "Heeaaw," he shouted.

Leaning forward, he slapped the reins on the wet back of the distressed horse, sending it galloping back toward town.

"You watch your side and I'll watch mine," he shouted. "And hold on."

The buggy fairly flew down the road, not meant to be driven so fast. It bounced over ridges and groaned loudly as the wheels were punished in potholes. John prayed it would hold together long enough for them to find Charity.

As the panic inside him grew, John scanned the area. He had to pull up and walk at the part of the road that was washed out, a place they hadn't gotten to on their drive today. It wouldn't be far before they'd reached Dry Street, which would mean they'd missed Charity somewhere between the ranch and town. If that happened, he'd continue into town and gather some men to go out on a search. They'd seen everything they could from the road.

Emmeline touched his arm as he pulled into town.

He slowed the horse from a gallop to a trot.

"What now?" she shouted.

She'd long since let go of the blanket she was holding so she wouldn't get bounced out. Her hair was one blob of black and she pushed it out of her eyes with shaky fingers.

"I'll stop at the livery and gather some men. Maybe you could run down to the sheriff's office for me."

"Of course."

John pulled up in front of the livery, bounded out of the buggy and ran to the other side to help Emmeline. The horse was lathered, and his eyes were glazed in fear after their breakneck journey.

Just as Emmeline held out her arms to John, she pulled up. "Look." She straightened and pointed down the street. "That's Chaim's horse at your office. Maybe they were together."

John hopped back into the buggy, scrambled overtop Emmeline, and picked up the reins. He flipped them up once and brought them down across the tired horse with a loud slap. The buggy lurched forward.

Charity must have seen them drive up because she met them outside.

"Thank God, you're here," John shouted, as he wrangled the horse to a stop. "I thought something had happened when we saw your horse galloping back to the ranch alone. What's going on?"

Standing in the buggy, he paused for the first time since he'd seen the racing horse, and took a deep, calming breath.

She held the door open and frantically waved him in. "It's not me. It's Chaim. He's been shot."

At Charity's words many emotions flashed through John, fear being the strongest. It could've been an accident, or... *who would want to kill Chaim?*

Not waiting for Emmeline, John leapt from the buggy and ran inside.

Chaim was laid out on the examination table, shirtless, with a bullet hole in the left side of his chest, nerve-wrenchingly close to his heart.

Tucker dipped a cloth in the water basin and wrung it out as he cleaned the excessive blood from Chaim's torso, and Dr. Bixby shuffled around the room, getting ready to go after the bullet.

"I'm glad you're here," the old doctor said without looking up. Charity must have told him who had arrived before he entered the room.

Emmeline followed him into the office but stopped at the door, tears streaming down her face. Slowly, she walked forward and pressed her palm to Chaim's cheek as she looked longingly into his face. A sob escaped her. Charity took her by the shoulders and led her out of the room.

John pressed his finger to Chaim's neck, feeling for his pulse. "He's awfully weak."

"Yeah, lost a lot of blood."

For the first time ever, Dr. Bixby's voice sounded shaken and old. Or, the likelier probability was he was showing the love he had for Winston and Winnie's second eldest. Most likely Dr. Bixby had delivered Chaim and seen to his needs for all these years. He no doubt felt closer to Chaim than John did.

"Looks like it went deep." John leaned forward to get better look.

"By all that is holy, I think you're right," Bixby responded tenderly in what John thought was a prayer. "It doesn't look good for our Chaim."

Both doctors washed up and Tucker went into the kitchen to get the tools out of the boiling water. When Bixby took the opposite position his hands were shaking vigorously. As Bixby attempted to take the tray of instruments from Tucker, he almost spilled the lot.

John looked up at the old doctor.

The old timer shook his head. "It's no use. I can't seem to make 'em stop. Never happened like this before."

The shaking got worse and his whole body trembled right before John's eyes.

"Why don't you go out and talk with Emmeline? She and Charity looked like they could use a friend right about now. Someone who knows what's going on and can ease their fears."

Bixby's face was ashen, but he complied and soon it was just John and Tucker left in the room. John stared at Chaim's face for a long, thoughtful moment. He sure didn't want to go this alone. Some moral support and assistance would help immensely. He remembered Lily's steady hand as she stitched up his face, never squeamish about what she had to do. Just resolute on the job that needed doing.

He glanced up at Tucker. "Go ask Charity to fetch Lily for me. Tell her to hurry."

The boy nodded and ran out the door.

It had taken Lily a good half hour to calm her aunt. The woman had refused to tell her who she thought she'd seen, or why she was fearful of him. She'd stubbornly stuck to her excuse that she was tired and wanted to get some rest without anyone coming into the shop to awaken her. But she'd never complained about noise before and had slept undisturbed for many hours during her recuperation. Lily knew it was just a cover for what she didn't want to say.

Thank goodness she'd finally fallen asleep.

Now Lily rested in the upstairs sitting area, holding the cat. The trusting little animal purred contentedly, now dry and warm and snuggled on Lily's lap. "What to do, kitty? I wish my aunt would tell me what she fears. Then maybe we could fix whatever it is."

The cat looked up at her with adoring eyes and Lily couldn't help but smile.

A rapping on the front door made her jump. The pouring rain had stopped and Lily could hear female voices whispering softly. Setting the cat on the cushion, she hurried down the stairs.

"Lily," Charity called through the door. "Open up! Chaim's been shot and John needs your help."

Lily opened the door.

Strain and tears marked Charity's face and her clothes were completely soaked. A large red stain covered the front of her shirt. Fear rocked Lily when she realized that it was blood. Charity held Emmeline by the arm and the poor woman looked beyond her wits. "They're in his office."

"Of course. But, my aunt was—scared by the storm. I cannot leave her alone."

"We'll stay here."

Lily hurried out the door.

Entering the doctor's office, she was shocked to see Dr. Bixby sitting at the kitchen table, his head resting in his hands. He didn't even look up when she ran past and into the examination room.

"Thank you for coming, Lily," John said softly, trying to hold back his relief at seeing her.

She looked at Chaim briefly, then up into his face. "Of course. Anything. What should I do?"

If she was squeamish over assisting, she didn't show it.

"Get washed up as quickly as possible."

The surgery he was about to perform, so close to Chaim's heart, was a damn risky one. He doubted any arteries or veins had been hit, though, or there'd be more blood. Now, looking down into the face of this cousin, John knew he was shaken to his core. Chaim was too young to die. It would be such a waste.

Tucker stood at Chaim's head with the can of chloroform and a cloth just in case Chaim actually woke up during the operation. He also kept his finger lightly pressed on the artery in Chaim's neck, monitoring his pulse.

John looked at Lily, then at Tucker. "Here we go."

With tweezers in hand, John probed around the exterior of the wound slowly, knowing full well he had to go down into the hole and look for the bullet. The possibility of nudging it in a wrong direction, even the tiniest bit, could claim Chaim's life.

"You can do this," Lily said in a soft voice.

Her spoken encouragement was a balm to his nerves. Her nearness gave him strength. Without glancing up, he nodded his thanks, acknowledging to himself how her presence here fortified him. Helped him.

He *could* do this, and with God's help, he would save Chaim's life.

Lily dabbed at the blood that flowed steadily from the wound. As John went deeper, pulling some muscle and tissue out of the way with the needle nose tweezers, a bright red stream spurted up and welled, about to spill over.

"Let me get that," Lily said, soaking it up.

With his finger, John pulled the hole wider to get a better look, not minding the feel of his cousin's warm blood.

Chaim moaned, and his eyes fluttered.

"Sorry, cousin," John said quietly. "You're young and strong. It'll take more than a little bullet to bring a McCutcheon down. You're going to live to tell about it."

So far John hadn't seen the bullet. Typically, extraction of a projectile didn't take long. The loss of blood was usually the cause of death in a shooting. You had to get in and get out fast, then plug the hole. Charity's makeshift bandage had done a darn fine job at stemming the flow until she'd gotten him here.

Tucker looked up sharply, the sudden movement drawing John and Lily's attention. "He stopped breathing."

Chapter Forty-Two

John immediately grasped Chaim's neck and pressed his forefinger into the flesh, smearing it with blood while barely able to feel even the slightest sign of life. He watched Chaim's chest, willing it to rise. Moments ticked by.

Although he'd only seen it done once, he'd read about artificial breathing in his studies. There were many cases cited and right now, it was his only option. But, before he tried, he'd quickly extract the bullet.

Lily looked at him with scared eyes and Tucker seemed to be in a trance. "He's not breathing so we have little time. First, I'm going to find that bullet, and then…"

Lily nodded although he could see she was shaken.

"Swab away the blood," John said.

Gritting his teeth, he went in like a bat after a mosquito, unwilling to retreat without the hideous ball of lead. "I feel it." Slowly, he opened the tweezers wider until he felt them around the bullet and brought it out, tossing it aside.

"Only light pressure, Lily."

John stepped to Chaim's head and tilted it back, making his mouth drop open.

Before his eyes, and in a flash of inspiration, John saw the face of Bob Mackey lying dead on the ranch house floor, all those years ago as the man's life blood leaked from his body, slowly sapping his energy away. Once again John felt the weight of his Colt 45 in his hands and the burden of guilt on his soul. Was *this* the reason that the accident had happened?

So he'd be here as an educated doctor with the newest procedures, and prepared, to save Chaim's life?

Could that possibly be?

Something good will come of this, you will see, his mother had insisted many times through the years. *As horrible as that sounds, that's how God works. It's hard to understand and to accept, but it's true. And when it does, you'll know it.*

John gave himself a mental shake. Artificial breathing was virtually unknown to self-taught doctors. It was just now becoming a talked about subject in the medical schools. Would Chaim die here and now, even with its possibilities to bring him back to life?

Not if he had anything to say about it!

With renewed purpose, John gripped Chaim's chin and nose and placed his mouth over Chaim's, blowing a large breath into his cousin's mouth. From the corner of his eye he saw Chaim's bloody chest rise under Lily's hands, bringing a startled gasp from her.

Tucker stepped back several feet and watched.

John said nothing but waited a few moments and repeated the process. After five more breaths, John paused to feel for a pulse in Chaim's neck, hoping, praying, to feel something substantial.

A flutter...

Determined, he kept at it, three breaths, and a quick check of his pulse. Three breaths, and a check of his pulse.

"You are doing well," Lily said solemnly. "So much air going into his lungs is truly amazing."

She touched John's shoulder for a quick moment, in support, he was sure. Just having her close kept him grounded.

"His color looks better, John. It is working. I am sure."

A handful of agonizing minutes ticked by. Ten turned into fifteen. Tucker came forward and wiped the sweat from John's brow. Resigned that Chaim wasn't going to start breathing on his own, knowing he should probably give up and face the fact that they'd lost him, he heard Dr. Bixby's voice from somewhere in the room. "Keep going, boy, don't stop."

John took a moment and glanced around. At some point, Charity and Emmeline had entered the room unannounced. They huddled in a corner with their arms around each other and eyes as big as saucers, staring back at him.

Lily stood firm, her hand pressed upon the folded towel over Chaim's chest.

Twenty more minutes passed—but felt like twenty hours.

John finally stepped back. He straightened his aching back, feeling lightheaded and downhearted. He swiped his arm across his sweaty face and heaved a deep sigh.

They all stared at Chaim.

Without any help this time, his chest lifted, then slowly went back down. It rose again.

Everyone gasped.

"He's breathing!" Tucker said enthusiastically, pointing at Chaim as if anyone needed direction.

John placed his finger on Chaim's neck one more time and smiled. "His heartbeat is strong. I think he's going to make it."

The group clustered around the kitchen table in a hushed silence. Charity and Emmeline, with teeth chattering, did their best to drink the hot peppermint tea Dr. Bixby had prepared for everyone. They'd been draped with a blanket and looked like a pair of ragamuffin bookends as they sat in stunned silence.

As soon as the emergency had passed, they'd told Lily that Louise Brown had been walking past her shop after closing up the Post Office early and they'd begged her to stay in the store with Harriett. After hearing why, she insisted it was the least she could do to help, being her and Chaim had practically grown up together. She'd sent her prayers and promised to come and get them the moment she heard Harriett wake up.

Exhausted, John gazed out the window at the evening street deep in thought. Overhead clouds made the town darker than normal. Tucker was taking the first shift sitting with Chaim to keep a close watch on him. He, too, had a cup of tea to soothe his frayed nerves. None of them, with the exception of John, had ever witnessed a person being brought back to life.

"Will there be problems later?" Dr. Bixby asked, looking much older than his years. His hands still shook as he had the cup sandwiched between his palms, almost as if he'd forgotten he held it.

John dragged his attention away from the window to look at his friend.

"Impossible yet to tell. Cases vary. It's the opinion of many doctors that it depends on the length of time his brain was deprived of oxygen."

Emmeline's cup rattled badly and she quickly set it down. Her silent tears had not stopped flowing since they'd come into the kitchen and it was clear to everyone in the room that things had changed considerably since she'd gone out to the ranch to stay.

"But, we'll not think of that now," John added. "Besides his wound, Chaim's strong as an ox. If infection doesn't set in, he even may be up in time for the dance. I'm not saying he'll be able to participate, but at least he'd be able to go. We'll shoot for that."

Charity glared at his choice of words.

She had reported to the sheriff what had taken place, and he'd ridden out to the Rim Rock to let the rest of the McCutcheons know what had happened. If the runaway horse hadn't made it completely back, perhaps stopping in some pasture to graze, they'd have no way of knowing anything was amiss. John was sure it wouldn't be long before the family would be arriving in a panic.

Bixby set his cup down heavily. "I've heard of artificial breathing from time to time, but haven't yet read about it. And I surely wouldn't know how to do it. I'm flabbergasted."

Lily rose and went over to the stove to get the kettle of hot tea, then went around the table refilling everyone's cups. The sweetness of peppermint filled the air.

"That was the most amazing thing I have ever seen," she said. "Breathing for another human being. Imagine that. If not for you putting air in Chaim's lungs—" She shook her head in disbelief and it was a second before she continued. "He would be gone. You saved him as surely as I stand before you now."

She gazed at John, pride shining in her eyes, and it was impossible for him not to smile. There was something else there, too.

A promise of things to come?

More like my imagination.

John swiped a tired hand across his face. "I've never done it myself before. I could only hope I was doing it right."

"I think there was something bigger watching over you today, brother," Charity whispered. "It was miraculous."

"She's right, John," Emmeline said. It was the first words she'd spoken since coming from the store. "I'm thankful you didn't stop. It felt like a dream."

John didn't know how to respond. Although artificial breathing was a fact of medical science now, he too felt as if there had been, at that moment, something else, something supernatural, guiding him.

Thundering hooves clamored from down the street; everyone stood.

It didn't take but a second and Dustin burst into the room, followed by Winston, Winnie, Madeline and Becky, all dressed for hard riding.

"He's alive, but tenuous," John said gravely. "We have to keep a close watch on him for a couple of days."

It was Aunt Winnie who spoke first. "Can we go in?"

John nodded.

They went in single file, as quiet as a parade of mice. They gathered around the examination table and Tucker backed away.

Uncle Winston tenderly touched the bandage over his son's chest, and for a moment squeezed his eyes closed.

"You got the bullet, then?" he asked in a strangled voice.

"Yes. But he's weak."

"Look!" It was Becky as she stroked her brother's forehead. "He's opening his eyes."

John pushed forward and again took Chaim's pulse, thankful that it appeared as strong as it was before. He leaned closer. "Chaim, can you hear me?" A moment passed. "Chaim?"

Chaim's eyes fluttered and then opened slowly. He looked around at the faces of his family standing around him and tried to smile.

"No. Don't smile," Becky admonished, sounding like a little girl. "Save every ounce of energy you have for getting better. I love you." Her face clouded up and she had to quickly back away. Once out of sight, she ran out of the room.

Uncle Winston took Chaim's hand and leaned in close to his face. "Can you hear me, son?"

Chaim's nod was almost imperceptible, but it was there. The family wasn't aware that Chaim's waking up this soon was a good sign. And the fact that he'd responded to his father's question, even in such a small way, spoke volumes.

Winston looked up sharply. "He just squeezed my hand."

Winnie pressed forward impatiently. "Let me talk to him."

She leaned forward and gently kissed his cheek. "I love you, Chaim. I love you." That's all she said as Chaim gazed up at her. She looked as if she was going to say something else, then stopped. "Just rest, son. Get stronger." She kissed him again and let Madeline take her spot.

Madeline gazed down at Chaim with tears pooling in her eyes. "I'm happy to see you, brother," she said affectionately. Then, teasingly: "You're always one for stealing the attention, aren't you? But this time you've gone too far." Her expression wobbled and John placed his hand on the small of her back. He feared this many visitors was wearing Chaim out.

Dustin came up and just stared at his younger brother lying so helpless on the table.

"Chaim."

The name came out like a croak. He cleared his throat, and then sniffed loudly. John almost swore Chaim was tearing up at the sight his big brother was making. "Chaim," Dustin tried again, without any better result.

"I think we should let Chaim get some rest," John said, starting for the door. He looked at Tucker with a silent request to stay watchful.

Emmeline inched into the room, then tiptoed to Chaim's side. She gazed at his ashen face, eyes closed, for several long moments. Kissing the tip of her finger, she placed it on his forehead.

Turning, she looked at John. "Will you forgive me?" she whispered so only he could hear.

"I'm happy for you, Emmeline. For Chaim, too."

Several shouts came from the alley, then a string of curse words.

Dr. Bixby went to the back door, opening it wide.

Everyone watched as the sheriff and his deputy pulled Harland Shellston from his horse and shoved him toward the back door of the sheriff's office.

Sheriff Dexter looked over to the group watching. "Got your man."

Chapter Forty-Three

"**H**arland Shellston?" Bixby was the first to say.

"We found him hiding out in the brush between Rio Wells and the ranch," Pete Miller, the deputy, responded. "Don't take age to pull a trigger."

John could attest to that fact. "Did he have a gun on him?"

"Yes."

The boy sat sprawled on the ground, glaring at anyone who dared to look his way. His hands were bound and his face showed signs of a fight, with blood dripping from his nose and his clothes were covered in dirt. As much as he hated to do it, John would go over there after things had calmed down and see to his scrapes and bruises. Make sure he hadn't suffered any broken bones.

"Go get my father," Harland shouted defiantly, as the deputy attempted to lift him to his feet. He slumped down like a sack of potatoes, refusing to go into the sheriff's office and be locked in a jail cell. He kicked out at the deputy viciously, connecting his boot heel to the man's shin, making the deputy curse in pain.

Dustin pushed between his family members crowded in the doorway watching and made a direct line for Harland.

"Hold up, McCutcheon," Dane bellowed. "I'll have no vigilantly justice in my town." He pulled his gun and cocked the hammer, pointing it in Dustin's direction. Everyone in the doorway pulled back.

"The hell you won't. Just try and stop me from teaching this piece of scum a lesson he'll never forget. He bushwhacked my brother! I aim to see him in no better condition than Chaim, who is fighting for his life as we speak," Dustin shouted.

When Harland saw the rage in Dustin's eyes he turned over and scrambled, trying to get to his feet. Instead, he fell and accidentally rolled under a horse, spooking it. He was tromped on several times before the deputy and sheriff could pull him free.

Dustin took a step forward and the sheriff fired off a shot that landed in front of his boots.

"I meant what I said, Dustin. Go back inside until you cool down."

Winston came forward and grasped Dustin's arm at the same time Lily came up behind John. He felt her presence before she even spoke. "Do you think Harland Shellston could do it?" Her voice held a certain amount of surprise and sadness rolled up together. "He is not much more than a boy."

John turned. Fatigue lined her face, but still she managed a smile for him. Everyone else's attention was on the commotion outside, so John took the opportunity to take Lily by the hand and lead her back toward the table. He'd done his part for Chaim. Now Sheriff Dane could do his part controlling Dustin. John didn't have the strength, or volition, to try to do it himself.

"Don't know about Harland. I guess anyone is capable of anything they allow themselves to justify in their mind. From what Charity says, he's pretty used to getting his own way."

She nodded but didn't move away from him.

"You were amazing, Lily."

Her face blushed in pleasure and she glanced away.

"I mean it. I was shaken to the core when I saw Chaim so close to death. I don't know if I'd been able to do what I did without your support."

Their moment was gone as everyone filed back around the table, taking seats. Dustin leaned against the drain board, his expression one of great distress as his gaze sought out Lily's.

Charity watched John excuse himself from Lily's side and go into the other room to be with Chaim, closing the door behind him. Trouble was brewing. She'd seen it coming for weeks. Even without John saying anything, she could tell he had feelings for Lily. The way he watched out for her well-being, the many visits he made to her shop, and mostly, the way his gaze always sought out Lily's first. Charity was actually a little shocked that he hadn't figured it out sooner.

To confuse the matter even more, Emmeline and Chaim seemed to be warming up to each other. Then there was Dustin and Lily…

With all this craziness going on, Charity sort of wished she were back at The Heart of the Mountains. At least there, she was certain of who loved whom.

With a deep sigh, she realized the only rollercoaster relationship back in Montana was Brandon and herself. The thought of Brandon made her heartsick and she glanced out the window longingly.

When is he coming back? Perhaps he'd changed his mind and had gone back to Y Knot already, happy to be rid of her. After the stunt she'd pulled, she wouldn't blame him in the least.

"You really need to get out of those wet clothes before you get sick." Deep in thought, Charity hadn't heard Lily's approach. "Emmeline, too. Come over to my place and you can borrow something."

"I'd appreciate that." They both looked over to where Emmeline sat next to Aunt Winnie and Becky. Her eyes were red from crying and she was in a daze. "I'll go with you and then bring something back over here for Emmeline. She doesn't look like she's going to go anywhere."

They turned to go but Dustin met them at the door. "Going to your shop?"

"Yes. I have to check on my aunt and also get Charity and Emmeline some dry clothes."

He nodded. "With everything that's happened, I'm not going to be taking the livestock to Sweetwater after all. I'll come by later. After Chaim—"

His voice broke and he had to look away.

Lily reached out and touched his arm. "Chaim is going to be fine."

Upstairs in her shop, Lily peeked in at her aunt, who was still asleep. Tonight, after she'd made Tante Harriett a light supper, she was going to get to the bottom of this mystery. Have the whole thing out. Maybe it was her aunt's fears, warranted or not, that were keeping her from getting better, even more so than her dependence on drugs. Lily had been trying to be careful of her feelings, trying to protect her, not upset her. Tonight she'd set everything aside except getting some answers. This had drawn on long enough.

Getting back to the task at hand, she chose a yellow dress for Charity, and a blue skirt and blouse for Emmeline. She found Charity in the kitchen, huddled next to her stove.

John's sister took the garment from her hands. "You're not going back over?"

"No. If my *Tante* was feeling better I would, but all the thunder and lightning really rattled her nerves."

And, Lily thought, I'll have some answers tonight, whether the questions upset her or not.

Chapter Forty-Four

John sat at the desk in the examination room with an open book in front of him. He'd started reading about infection, and the newest treatments, but he couldn't seem to keep his thoughts focused. The whole family, with the exception of Dustin, had gone to the hotel and secured rooms for the night to allow them to be closer if there was any change in Chaim's condition. Worn out, all but Dustin had left an hour ago and checked in. John promised he'd let them know the moment there was any change. Dustin now sat close to Chaim, feet and arms crossed, in a deep sleep.

The door squeaked open. "You want any supper?" Bixby asked.

John stood and stretched. "No. I'm not hungry. I'll fix something later."

He glanced at Dustin and Chaim and followed the old doctor into the kitchen, closing the door behind him. Tucker sat at the table eating a bowl of soup.

John went over to the stove, took the lid off the pot, and sniffed. "What is it?"

"Beef barley. Sure you don't want any?"

He shook his head. That sounded about as appealing to him as week-old catfish. Too many things on his mind. Like, where was Brandon? Or, more to the point, where he wasn't. He'd been gone much longer than John had expected, and now with Chaim getting shot...no, he wouldn't go there. That wasn't a possibility.

Then there was the jewel, or whatever it was. It still sat in his safe and he knew nothing more about it than when he'd put it there. Was it Harriett's? That was a possibility.

Now today, Harland Shellston had tried to kill Chaim. Would he do such a thing because Charity had shamed him in front of the other students?

And then there was Lily.

Lily and Dustin.

He couldn't forget about them even if he tried.

If he were honest, that was what was torturing him the most. It had been a hard day with Emmeline, but from what he could see, things had worked out and it looked as if there was a future for her with Chaim. Now that he thought about it, they did make an extremely compatible couple. Chaim being lighthearted and fun and Emmeline being immature, in her incredibly sweet way. Seriously, he couldn't have found a better match for either of them. But where did that leave him and Lily?

If it would have been unforgivable for him to go forward with Emmeline, knowing his feelings for her were not what they'd once been, was it unforgivable to never tell Lily how he was feeling about her now? Especially knowing how Dustin felt?

"You want to talk about it?"

Bixby stood before him. "Nothing to talk about."

"Suit yourself. I'm going to bed. Come get me if there's any significant change."

"Will do."

Several minutes passed before John heard loud voices in the alley. Going to the back door and looking out the window, he saw Norman Shellston in a heated argument with the sheriff.

Deputy Pete Miller looked on.

John opened the door.

"My son said he didn't shoot McCutcheon. That should be proof enough for you to release him."

"Can't do that and you know it. He'd take off, never to be seen again. If McCutcheon dies, he'll be tried for murder."

"I told you I've signed this paper promising to keep him in Rio Wells, in our home." He waved a paper in front of the sheriff's face.

Shellston looked over at John, refusing to go on in front of him. "This isn't any of your business, Doctor."

Sheriff Dane took Shellston by the arm and was able to propel him a few feet away before Shellston violently shook him off. They stood staring at each other for several long moments.

"Come back tomorrow," Sheriff Dane finally said. "After you've had some time to think. Maybe then you'll be making a little more sense."

"Pa. Pa, don't leave me here." Harland's voice came from within the building, hoarse from shouting and crying.

"Go on now, Norman. He'll be okay. If he's going to act like a man, he better be ready to accept the consequences."

John closed the door and headed back to the examination room. Something about what Shellston had just said was rolling around in his head in a way that made him think it had some significance. He had signed a paper for Harland? He'd signed. No, maybe it was something about his signature...

Dustin was now awake, standing over Chaim.

John put his hand on Chaim's forehead, pleased to find that his cousin's temperature still felt normal. "Good. He needs to rest. It's the best way for him to recover."

They looked at each other for a long moment across Chaim's body.

Dustin's voice was gravelly and low when he said, "Emmeline told me what you did to save his life."

"I was glad to be able to do it."

"I suppose Chaim was lucky that you'd come to town."

Dustin raked his fingers through his hair, then massaged the muscles in the back of his neck. He rotated his shoulders and rolled them several times. "What are his chances?"

"That's impossible to say. We just have to hope infection doesn't set in, and that the bullet didn't damage his heart. As much as I hate to say it, it could go either way."

Dustin just stared. "Thanks for being honest."

Lily paced the floor, waiting impatiently for her aunt to wake up. The white cat followed her back and forth across the upstairs rug, mewing hopefully as if wishing her adopted mistress would sit down so she could jump into her warm lap. It wasn't but a moment when Lily heard a small sound on the front porch, and then a whisper.

Gathering her courage, she blew out her lantern and carefully sneaked down the stairs to the front door. Even with her ear pressed up tight, it took a moment before her heart stilled enough to be able to make out what was being said.

"You're sure?" the sheriff said quietly.

"Without a doubt."

Lily would recognize Lector Boone's voice anywhere. It was as black and foreboding as what he wore. "I've done my due diligence. It's in the safe."

"And if he resists?"

"I'll have the jewel, Sheriff. One way or the other."

"There will be no killing, Boone."

Lily almost gasped. Did he mean he'd shoot John, without even trying to find the truth, just to get the reward?

A tremor begotten of trepidation began in her hands and traveled all the way down to her feet. She must get the jewel out of John's safe. John was everything. She loved him with the depths of her being. It didn't matter if he didn't feel the same about her. She'd do anything for him. Anything to keep him safe. She had brought this trouble down on his head, and she would fix it.

The men walked away, their heavy footsteps fading into the night. She had to think of some way to help. Could she tell the sheriff about Tante Harriett? What if they wanted to lock her up in the penitentiary? As Lily hurried to the stairs, she could hear her aunt talking to the cat.

Tante Harriett had finally woken up.

Chapter Forty-Five

Lily knocked on the doorjamb. "May I come in?"

Tante Harriett looked up. "Of course, dear." She patted the quilt.

"How are you feeling?" Lily asked, sitting on the bed.

"So much better." Harriett paused to listen. "I'm glad that horrible storm is over. I don't think I've ever seen it rain so hard."

The last thing Lily wanted to do was bring up the jewel, and what it was all about, but there was no other way around it. Time was running out. Come what may, she needed answers tonight.

"Tante?"

"I can see the dark clouds in your eyes. Something is troubling you, my dear. Tell me what it is."

Lily nodded.

Her aunt gazed back.

Perhaps the old woman was stronger than she thought. "It's about something I found in your belongings. Something incredible."

The color drained from Harriett's face.

"A jewel. I didn't mean to go through your things, but it was when I found you passed out and went for John. Remember?"

"Of course."

Lily waited for her to continue.

"As you must have guessed," the old woman said in a shaky voice, "the gem does not belong to me." She reached out and took Lily's hand. "I never wanted you to find out. I'd hoped coming to Rio Wells had settled that problem. But after seeing that man tonight, I know there's nothing left for me to do but tell you the whole truth. Actually, I think I'm relieved the time has finally come."

Harriett sat up in the bed and gazed out into the darkness of the night for a few moments, thinking.

"When I sent for you in Germany," she said in a small voice, "I didn't have enough funds. I thought I had, when I first wrote to your mother and father, but it turned out to be double what the shipping company had first quoted me. Since the plans had already been made, and you were getting ready to set sail, I decided to take out a loan rather than disappoint you or the family."

She squeezed Lily's hand softly. "At first, there was no problem. I made payments over the months and was close to having the loan paid off. Then, when that new shop on the east side opened, our business fell off considerably."

"Was that when we began to take in laundry, too?"

Harriett nodded.

"And you worked night and day, and wouldn't tell me why. Your health started to deteriorate."

Harriett smiled sadly.

"Why was the bank so uncompromising? Wouldn't they help you at all?"

"That was the problem, Lily. I didn't go to the bank for the loan. I went to a local pawnshop. I knew the owner. We were friends. But when money is involved, people change."

Harriett reached over and rubbed the sleeping cat that had snuck onto Lily's lap during the conversation. It was a moment before she continued.

"When I made the last payment I was told the interest rate had changed, that I owed almost as much as I had in the beginning. He warned me that if I said anything to anyone, something horrible would happen to you. I went along with it for a while, but could see what was happening as my money dwindled away. He was never going to stop blackmailing me. So, I began plotting an escape. Before all the money was gone, I found the shop for lease in Rio Wells, and I sent the year's rent money to Mr. Bartlett."

Harriett took a deep breath, closing her eyes.

"What happened?"

"Before it was time for our escape, the pawnshop owner demanded my debt be paid in full. He assured me he'd sell you into white slavery, after maiming you for life, making any escape for you impossible. I was frightened. Didn't know what to do. Almost all the money I had, I'd already sent to Rio Wells.

Harriett paused, taking a deep breath.

"Then, that day, when I was delivering the red velvet ball gown to Mrs. Lowerby, I saw the expensive looking jewel on her dressing table. All sense flew from my mind—except for the temptation of having a way of paying the loan off. Before thinking twice, I slipped it in my pocket. At first I was relieved, thinking I could just hand the jewel over for payment and no one would find out where I'd gotten it. Then, when a few hours had passed and I'd come to my senses, I knew I'd made a horrible mistake. I was sick with worry. Ashamed and horrified with what I had done. But, I couldn't think of a way to reverse my actions. The Lowerbys had gone away for a few days and I couldn't get back into their house. Then, the man I saw tonight came to the shop asking how I knew Mr. and Mrs. Lowerby. I knew then we had to flee."

"I am so sorry you went through this. And all because of me."

Harriett scowled.

"Hush now! You're the daughter I never had. I love you and take full responsibility for my actions."

Tante wouldn't live very long if she was locked away in a prison. Someone so caring and loving should not spend their last days like that. "But, the Lowerbys love you. I remember time and again their saying it. They will forgive you when they hear why you did it. I know they will."

"Perhaps they would. But the law has been involved. Lawyers and judges don't make exceptions for silly old ladies."

Tante Harriett was right. Just as Boone did not care if he got to the truth as long as he got the jewel and his reward. This was an awful mess.

Lily knew what she had to do. She patted her aunt's wrinkled hand.

"Thank you for finally telling me. You rest for now. We will figure this out."

"But, the man in black?"

"All will be well."

Tante Harriett sank back down into her bedding, exhausted, almost as if she were a little child trusting in Lily to take care of things.

Lily kissed her forehead. "Don't breathe a word of this to anyone."

John shut the door behind Dustin, thankful his cousin decided to join his family at the hotel and get some rest. It was almost midnight and John trudged up the stairs to his room, exhausted. He needed to wash up and change out of his soiled clothes. After that, he'd take his rest in the examination room with Chaim.

John poured water into his basin and splashed his face. The cool liquid refreshed his flagging spirits, so he repeated the process, this time rubbing it all the way over his head and through his hair. He grasped his towel and dried vigorously, trying to chase away his fatigue.

Glancing up, he spied the porcelain figurine on the shelf. It looked so much like Lily he had to smile. He remembered what she had told him about all her sisters in Germany. A dull ache in his chest almost made him wince.

John pushed aside any thoughts of her for now, then stripped off his shirt and pants, going to his closet for fresh clothes. As he finished buttoning up his shirt, he thought he heard a noise downstairs. He quickly pulled on his pants and hurried back into the examination room.

All was quiet and Chaim was sleeping peacefully.

Still, a prickle of unease taunted him. Going to the window he glanced out, but saw nothing but the dark street. Slipping from the room, he was surprised to find Lily by the front door—as if his earlier thoughts had conjured her out of thin air.

"Lily, is everything all right?"

He glanced at the clock. It was only fifteen minutes since Dustin had left. He took her hand and led her into the dimly lit kitchen.

"Yes, I...I just wanted to see how Chaim was. I guess I should have waited until morning."

John pulled out a chair, careful to pick it up rather than sliding it across the wood floor. "Here, sit for a moment," he whispered, "and I'll give you an update on his condition."

She hesitated, looking either frightened or nervous. "Lily?"

"I really should not, John. Tante was shaken badly by the storm. I cannot remember her ever being so upset. If she calls me and I am not there, she will be even more frightened."

"Is she doing okay? I can come check on her."

"No, that is not necessary. You look tired." Her soft laugh seemed strained. "I think we all are. It is just the thunder and lightning that has her rattled. You need to get some sleep, too."

He nodded, then realized he still had hold of her hand. "Okay. Well, Chaim seems to be doing well. I'm happy with his condition. His temperature is good and he's sleeping soundly. All we can do now is wait and hope that infection doesn't set in."

With that news she finally smiled. "Good. I am relieved to hear it." She softly took her hand from his and turned. "You get some rest too, yes?"

John didn't want her to leave. He wanted to tell her about him and Emmeline, and what had happened between them. And, about Emmeline and Chaim, too. What a difference a day made. But it seemed she was determined. "I will."

He went with her the few feet over to her shop and opened the door. "You get some sleep, yourself. Doctor's orders." He leaned over and pressed his cheek to hers. "If you need anything, Lily, just ask," he said softly into her ear. "I mean it."

Charity lay in the hotel bed, staring up at the crack in the ceiling, listening to the sounds of Becky sleeping by her side. So many things were rolling around in her head. Chaim, with blood covering his chest, as she tried to keep him in the saddle. Harland Shellston trying to kill her. She slammed her eyes closed when Brandon came into her thoughts. He'd given up on her. Ridden out of her life for good.

Everything will look better in the morning, she tried to convince herself. It was a tactic her mother always used to cheer her up, but unfortunately it never really worked. Problems were problems, period.

Unable to lay still another second, she lifted the blanket, careful not to awaken Becky, and cautiously got out of the bed. It squeaked loudly, causing Becky's breathing to stop for a moment; then the girl rolled over, lost again to her dream world.

In the cool room, Charity slipped on her coat, carried a straight-backed chair over to the window, and sat down. Careful not to make a sound, she pushed the pane open a few inches, welcoming the chilly night air.

Darkness pervaded the sleeping town. The sign at the Black Silk Garter creaked softly, and was the only sound until the footfalls of a horse coming up the street caught her attention. The rider was still too far away for her to see who it was through the shadows, but something about the rider's outline kept her attention.

In another few moments he would be directly in front of the hotel.

She stifled a gasp. No need for him to come closer. Even from this distance she'd know that silhouette anywhere. She'd been studying it for all of the ten years she'd known him. And that of the big, solid horse he rode, too.

Chapter Forty-Six

Brandon was back!

A wallop of adrenaline made Charity's limbs shake. She ran to the door and pulled on her boots with unsteady hands, not caring that under her coat were only her pantaloons and chemise. Flattening her ear to the door, she checked for anyone in the hall. Time was of the essence.

Before Brandon vanished again, she'd throw herself into his arms and beg his forgiveness. She'd tell him everything in her heart, holding nothing back.

She hurried down the green and pink carpet runner in the hall, past the room in which Uncle Winston and Aunt Winnie slept, then past the room they'd gotten for Dustin. Reaching the stairway, she glanced down, thankful there was no one in sight.

At least five minutes had elapsed. By now Brandon could be anywhere. Charity ran down the boardwalk past the saloon, wondering where he'd been heading. At the corner she looked over at John's office, but Brandon's horse was nowhere in sight.

She looked up the street in the direction toward the bank and the church. She'd go that way first, then if she didn't find him, she'd come back to this block. She ran across the street avoiding the puddles, then hugged the side of the buildings as she went, passing the barbershop and the tannery.

A chicken darted out from an alcove and, in a multitude of feathers and frightened clucking, tripped her up. With a cry, she landed hard on her side, knocking the air from her lungs. Charity lay in the alley, dazed.

"What was that?"

Norman Shellston's voice was easy to recognize. A door opened. Through the haze of her pain, Charity slowly rolled as close to the side of the bank wall as she could.

"Nada, Señor. Sounds of the night."

Whoever was with the banker had a chilling voice. It flowed over Charity like something evil, threatening harm. The door that had opened now closed, leaving her to catch her breath. She crawled to her knees and then a crouching position.

What was going on in the bank in the wee hours of the morning? Whatever it was, she felt sure, was meant to remain hidden.

She wished she had her Colt 45. She felt naked without it. She glanced down at her legs, feeling the breeze.

"Si!" A voice boomed. Whoever it was, he was exceedingly angry.

"Keep your voice down."

Did they have Brandon against his will? Surely not. He wasn't one to get waylaid unawares. But, what if they did? There was no way she could leave now without knowing for sure.

With her back pressed against the white bat-and-board siding, Charity inched along carefully, feeling her way with the palms of her hands. She stopped next to the window. It was chin height and, if she were careful, she might be able to see inside. The rumble of an argument taunted her, a little easier to hear, but she still couldn't make out what was actually being said.

Curiosity burned, and more—fear for Brandon drove her on.

She gripped the sill, peeking through the window, trying to stay low and out of sight. The room was dark, with only one small candle burning.

Mr. Shellston was arguing, his hands waving in front of a man with a Mexican blanket slung over his shoulder. He looked like an outlaw. When he turned, two bandoleers and a large knife were partially visible underneath the mantle.

Charity quickly pulled back. She hadn't noticed the dog coming up the alley until it let out a bark. In her surprise, she banged her head against the wall, then turned to him pleadingly.

"Shhhh, boy. It's okay," she squeaked in a panicked whisper. She held her hand out to him in invitation.

The dog growled. He lowered his head, taking a step closer.

Charity let out a yelp as rough hands gripped her from behind. She was swung around and slammed up against the wall of the bank. Stars danced before her eyes. Blinking to clear her sight, she was face to face with the Mexican.

He took her arm and pulled her inside.

Norman Shellston closed the door.

"What's going on?" she demanded, summoning the sternest voice she could from her fear-fogged brain. "I'll have you know Uncle Winston is not going to like this one little bit!"

"Sit down, Miss McCutcheon. And be quiet."

Charity gasped, pretending outrage. She snugged the coat around her and drew herself up until she was eye to chin with the rough-looking character. She shoved her panic aside, sneering right back into his face. She *knew* the predicament she was in was far more precarious then she'd first thought.

"I will do *no such thing*, Mr. Shellston. I *demand* you release me this instant."

The Mexican laughed. He pushed her into a chair, causing her hip-length coat to hike up, giving the men ample view of her legs. He ran the toe of his boot up her pantaloons, and the sharp, spike-like spur glimmered dangerously in the candlelight.

She sprang to her feet and bolted for the door.

As quick as a snake, the bandito gripped her wrist and wrenched her arm behind her back, almost bending Charity to the ground. She hated sounding weak, but stopping the cry that tore from her throat was impossible.

"Now, you will listen to me, Señor Shellston," the Mexican hissed, turning back to Shellston. "*You owe me.* Time is *past.* We stopped that stage. My men died. You pay, or she will be next. Then, your son. And you."

He jerked Charity's arm viciously. "And, I assure you this, it will be slow and painful. Si?"

"B-b-but," Shellston stammered. "You didn't get me the letter. Without it, the deal is void." His voice was weak, pleading. "I could lose everything." His face was red with anger or fright, Charity couldn't tell which.

"*Screw* the letter! You have one day. Then—" he made a slashing motion across Charity's neck.

Shellston was shaken. "All right. I'll get you the money. Look for it in the planned spot. Just make sure she never makes it back to town."

Charity gasped.

The Mexican shoved her roughly toward the door. "*Vamos.*"

Tucker rounded the corner of Main Street at a dead run. He stumbled, caught himself with his good hand, and sprinted on. He crashed into the doctor's office, banging the door against the wall so hard it rattled the picture, almost sending it crashing to the floor.

John and Dr. Bixby jumped up from their seats at the table, alarmed.

"What the hell is wrong with you, boy," Dr. Bixby whispered loudly as he stared at him in disbelief. "We have a patient in there."

"Char—"

Tucker gripped his side as he struggled to talk and breathe at the same time. "Charity..."

John pulled out a chair. "Sit down until you catch your breath."

Tucker shook his head. "No! We have to help her..."

John put his hands on the young man's shoulders, giving him a little shake. "What are you talking about? What's happened to Charity?"

Tucker's face was still bright red, his breathing labored.

"She was taken by a man I've never seen. A *Comanchero*." He spat the last word out as if it was something dirty.

"When? Which way did they go?" John was already halfway up the stairs to get his gun and hat.

"Few minutes ago. East on Church Street. Riding double."

John took the stairs three at a time. In moments, he loaded his Colt 45 and strapped his holster to his leg, all the while remembering the killing lust he'd seen from the top of the stage. He grabbed extra ammunition, shoved it into his saddlebag and crammed his Stetson on his head.

Hurrying down, he was surprised to see Sheriff Dane waiting for him at the bottom of the staircase. Just as he was about to tell him about Charity, something struck painfully against John's skull and sent him crashing to the wooden slats. He broke his fall with his hands and his gun slid across the floor.

Chapter Forty-Seven

"Going somewhere, McCutcheon?" Boone asked as he stepped over John's body from behind the staircase. He bent and picked up John's gun, stuffing it in his belt.

John fought the blackness that threatened to take him down. When Tucker ran to his side to help, Boone lashed out with his boot and sent Tucker to the ground, smashing up against the door.

Bixby, stunned into silence until this point, stepped forward. "Sheriff, do something!"

Boone hefted John up by the arm and pressed the barrel of his gun against the side of John's chest. "The heat getting a little too much for you, Doc? Leaving town?"

John struggled to stand on his own. "What's this about?" he asked groggily.

The sheriff looked about helplessly.

"Mr. Boone, uh, has some questions for you, John." The sheriff's voice wobbled and he took a step back. "I suggest you answer 'em."

Boone shoved John into the other room. "Open your safe."

John felt queasy as the image of Boone wavered before his eyes. Once he opened the safe and the others saw the jewel, the sheriff would take him into custody and lock him up. He needed to get to Charity. Before something horrible happened to her. He turned to the safe, trying to focus on what to do next.

Wiping the moisture from his fingers, he spun the dial to the right several fast turns, clearing it out. Squeezing his eyes, he tried to focus on the small numbers. Carefully, he stopped on the number ten. He turned the dial to the left, stopping on ten again. Then to the right a second time, passing thirteen once, then completing the action on the number thirteen. Jerking the handle down, the door swung open. He turned.

As best he could, John blocked anyone from seeing inside.

Boone stepped forward and pressed the muzzle of his gun firmly to John's forehead.

"Hold on, Boone," the sheriff said, trying to calm him. "There ain't no reason—"

"*Shut up,*" Boone shouted. He swung around and smashed the sheriff's head with his gun. The sheriff crumpled to the ground.

White-faced and shaking, Dr. Bixby bent down and checked for a pulse. "He's dead."

"Move aside, McCutcheon."

John did. With gritted teeth and a blinding anger, he watched Boone scatter his things, as his gut kept screaming his need to go after Charity. The packages of morphine, two clean vials, and several slides fell to the floor in a clatter.

Boone turned around. "Where is it?"

"Where's what?" John shot back, regaining a little of his strength.

Boone had *missed* it? Somehow, the bounty hunter hadn't found the jewel? John's mind was racing. "You never told me what you're after."

"You're full of it, McCutcheon. You know exactly what I want. The blue sapphire. Two full carats."

In a fit of rage, Boone's face flamed red and John saw his hand tighten on the gun. "Get it."

John went to the safe and shuffled the few remaining things around, looking. Finally, he turned around in astonishment. The jewel was nowhere to be found. "I don't have it. You've seen for yourself. Now, I'm walking out of here so stand aside."

"I don't think I'm going to let you do that."

The man backed away a few feet as if he didn't like the thought of getting splattered with blood. "Harland Shellston saw it." Again, the gun was pointing at John, but this time it was shaking from Boone's uncontrollable rage, then he smiled. "Let's go ask your girl. The one who stole it in the first place."

He took his eyes off John only long enough to look at Tucker and Bixby. "You're coming, too."

At gunpoint, Boone marched the three of them over to Lily's shop. "Knock on the door, McCutcheon."

John didn't want to let this dangerous animal anywhere near Lily. He stood his ground. "She doesn't have the jewel. I'll get it for—"

Boone pulled Tucker to his side, placing the barrel of his gun on the boy's temple. "One, two…"

John knocked.

Footsteps sounded from within.

He searched his mind, trying to think of a way to overpower the man before Lily was put at risk.

The door opened. "John?" Lily's eyes went wide as she took in the scene.

Boone shoved them all into her shop. "Where's the jewel?"

Stunned, Lily looked from Boone to John. He could see she was deciding what to do.

"Once he has it, we're all dead," John said, guessing that she'd come in at some time and taken the jewel from his safe. "He won't want any witnesses."

"Shut up," Boone screamed, spittle flying from his lips.

"He killed the sheriff," Tucker said under his breath.

Boone went to the cutting table and began pulling things from under the shelf. He dumped out the button box on top and spread the contents out with the palm of his hand, all the while keeping his gun trained on the group.

"I know it's here." He swung around, pulled the dressing room drapes from their rod, tossing them to the side.

John could hear Lily's breathing, ragged and strong behind him, as she huddled with Tucker.

Boone struck a match. "You'll talk."

He held the tiny flame to the curtain in the kitchen window. "Or the old granny upstairs will cook like a turkey at Thanksgiving."

The muslin ignited slowly, the flame licking up the fabric.

John gathered himself and launched, taking Boone by surprise and shoving him to the floor. The two men rolled in the kitchen and John smashed Boone's face several times with his fist, driven by a violent rush of anger. Fury fed by fear for his loved ones surged up, powering his strength.

Bumping next to the iron stove, Boone smacked John's head with his own, momentarily knocking John off the fight.

Ducking when Boone tried again, John felt the bulge of his Colt 45 wedged between their bodies, stuck in Boone's belt. Instantly and instinctively he reached for it, squeezing the trigger even before pulling it clear.

Boone hollered in pain, then yanked his pistol from its holster as the two men rolled over again.

John grabbed his arm and hammered it on the floor, trying to knock the six-shooter from his hand.

"Drop it!" Brandon demanded from the doorway.

He stepped in and pointed the muzzle of his gun at Boone's head. "*Now!*"

Tucker bolted out the door and returned with a bucket of water he'd scooped from the horse trough and heaved the contents up on the window, dousing the small flames. As he did, John struggled to his feet and Lily rushed to his side.

"Are you hurt?" The words gushed from her as she took his arm, steadying him. "Oh, your poor, poor face." Her hands softly examined the punishment his face had taken, and her face blanched when she touched his scar. "I am so thankful he did not shoot you, John. I could not have stood that."

Gently, John took her hands in his, holding them close to his chest. "Good to see you, Brandon," he said, never taking his eyes from Lily's. "You've the knack of showing up at just the right time."

Finally, he turned. He motioned to Boone lying on the floor, grasping his bloody side. "Let's get him locked up. Charity's in trouble."

The sun was just coming up when they finally stopped. The Mexican slid from his horse and jerked Charity's arm so that she fell into the dirt. Bloody and bruised from her attempted escape, she blinked several times, trying to focus.

Earlier, she'd leapt off the galloping horse, figuring the fall would be better than what her captor had planned. But he'd caught her easily and slapped her around. Thank God, he'd been in too much of a hurry for anything else. Her main regret was that she'd lost her coat, and the little protection it gave.

Through squinted eyes, she watched her captor hand his reins to a woman, then drink from the jug he was offered. Several other women gathered, waiting to see what was going to happen.

Another man approached. When he saw Charity in the dirt, he stopped short, anger darkening his eyes. He was older, with sinewy arms and long black hair. He glanced at her again, then cursed furiously at the younger man, spitting into the dirt.

Scrambling to her feet, she met her captor face to face. He spun her around, then pushed her forward. They climbed a rocky hill where more of the outlaw's encampment was visible. A few small fires still burned and horses were tethered about.

They stopped at a structure half carved into the rocky hillside. The man opened the door and shoved her in, closing the door and snapping the lock. She tried to block her fall, but she hit hard, taking gravel on her face and in her mouth. She lay there, giving into the luxury of a groan as she looked about the room. It was small, a ten-by-ten box at most. The ceiling would barely clear her head if she stood.

She shivered. The images of her loved ones back in Montana flitted through her mind in jagged pieces. Her mother and father. John. Luke. The rest of her family.

Brandon.

Oh, how she loved them all. Would she live to see them again? Would she ever have another chance to tell them just how much they meant to her?

Chapter Forty-Eight

Dustin bolted into the jail just as John and Brandon swung the cell door closed. Winston wasn't far behind his son. "What's going on? We heard a shot. Saw the lights from the alley."

"Boone's killed the sheriff," John answered, motioning to the back of the sheriff's office where the body of Sheriff Dane was laid out on the cold stone floor.

Pete Miller, the deputy, looked dazed, and Harland sat in his cell, watching.

Winston sucked in a big draught of air, his expression shifting from sleepy to alarmed. "Why the hell…"

John held up his hand for silence. "It's a long story, Uncle Winston, and one we don't have time to go into right now. Charity's been taken by a Comanchero and we need to rescue her. How many men can you round up quickly?"

Brandon started for the door.

"Hold up, Brandon," John barked.

"I'm going after her. The longer we sit here talking, the likelier—"

"You're right." John jogged to his friend's side and Dustin followed.

"Go on," Winston agreed with a wave of his hand. "I'll gather together a posse and follow as quick as I can. My best guess would be to head northwest. To the boarded up ghost town. It's been rumored on and off for years that the Comancheros sometimes use it for a hangout. Could be a goose chase but without any other direction, at least it's a start." He looked uncertain. "Don't know..."

When the three men exited the sheriff's office they found Tucker and Theodore waiting with John and Dustin's mounts, saddled and ready to ride. The boys had also retrieved Brandon's horse from around back. Theodore was mounted on his own horse and Tucker swung aboard another, clearly intending to come along.

Brandon mounted up, as did John and Dustin.

"Tucker. Theodore," John said, quickly taking stock of the rifles and ammunition the two had gathered together. "I know you want to come, but too many riders will be conspicuous. You're needed here to watch over the women. Until we know *why* Charity was taken, the rest of the town could still be in danger, too."

When Theodore opened his mouth to protest, Brandon intervened. His face was stern. "John Jake is right. We may not make it back. If that's the case, you'll be the next line of defense."

With that, he turned his horse and took off at the gallop, John and Dustin fast on his heels.

From her bedroom window Lily watched the men ride away into the night, then said a silent prayer for their safe return. She squelched a shiver at the thought of Charity in the hands of those horrible men.

"Godspeed," she whispered, her hand against the cold pane of glass. She wasn't sure if her desire for John was creating something out of nothing, but it seemed as if things had changed between the two of them. She'd seen it in his eyes. Felt it in the way he'd held her hands next to his chest. She'd wanted to stay like that forever and just let the world pass them by. But time had been of the essence, and they needed to find Charity.

The tumult Boone had caused in the shop had awakened Harriett. She'd been so scared that Lily had helped her up even though it was the dead of night, settling her in her chair next to the window, wrapped in a warm quilt. She was there now, still agitated, with a pair of knitting needles forgotten in her hands.

Tante Harriett had been terrified after John and Brandon had taken Boone away. It was as if her worst nightmare had come true right before her eyes. She'd heard the screaming and the fight. And then the gunshot that rattled the walls and sent the acrid smell of gunpowder throughout the place. Confused, she'd called to Lily by Lily's mother's name, alarming Lily tremendously. And there had been no convincing her otherwise. Finally, Lily had had to agree with her, affirming she was someone other than who she was, just to calm her down.

The teakettle was warming and as soon as the water was hot, Lily would make a cup of tea for both of them as there'd be no sleeping again this night. She expected Emmeline, Becky, Winnie and Madeline to be coming over to the shop at any time.

She peeked into her aunt's room and asked, "Tante, are you doing okay?"

Harriett's head jerked up with a start, as if she'd been deep in thought. "Oh, it's you, Gretchen. Yes, I'm fine."

A niggle of unease crept up Lily's spine. "It's me, Tante. Lily."

"I've been thinking about all the things I have to do this day. So many, I fear I will never be done. Just look," she said, holding up the knitting needles, the ball of string forgotten on the rug. "I may never get this sweater done in time for Mother's birthday. It's taking me forever. And the carpets need beating, and I promised to take some fresh milk to the market."

Lily nodded and backed away, her heart breaking. When she saw the kitten, she picked it up and took it to Harriett, laying it on the older woman's lap. "She will keep you company until I return with our tea."

"Thank you. I've always said you're the most thoughtful sister anyone could ever have."

With shaking hands, she stroked the kitten now curled in her lap.

A noise by the alley door drew Lily's attention. "The others are here. I'll go down and let them in, and bring you back a nice cup of tea."

Relieved to have company on this strange night, Lily hurried to let the others in. When she turned the knob the door flew open, and hit the wall with a bang.

Boone burst in, holding his side.

"Hold up," John shouted to Brandon, still riding hard in the lead. "It's not going to do Charity any good if we run our horses to death. We have to stop. Let them breathe."

A few seconds went by before Brandon's large bay gelding began to slow down. John reined in Bo, and Dustin followed suit. Soon the three sat their mounts side by side in the early morning light; an amber yellow glow limned the horizon.

The horses' chests heaved and frothy white lather dripped from their sides.

John was the first to dismount and loosen his cinch. He walked his horse slowly in a circle.

They'd been following Dustin's directions and would be at the ghost town within a quarter hour. "How're you feeling about this town Uncle Winston has sent us to?"

"Hopeful," Dustin answered. "Without this lead, we'd be buggered up. I just have a feeling he's right about this."

"If he's not?" Brandon was distracted. He gazed out over the quiet landscape as if he could see Charity through the miles and darkness.

"We have to go with it, for now," John said. "I have a feeling that it's right, too."

Brandon felt his horse's hide. "Or, could turn out the same as it did for your ma, John Jake. Held captive for a year, was it? It's a miracle Flood got her back at all. History may be repeating itself."

John placed his hand reassuringly on Brandon's back. "That's not going to happen. We'll get her back, Brandon. I'm betting my life on it. I'm not returning to Rio Wells without her. She's always been there for me, and now I aim to repay her."

All three tightened their cinches and remounted. "We need to take it more slowly from here," Dustin said. He pointed to the rise above the abandoned road that they were traveling on. "We'll go up and stay behind the rise until we get closer. Then, we should split up and make a quick sweep of the town, then regroup."

"Sounds good." Brandon's horse tossed his head in agitation, then pulled on his bit. "Let's go."

Chapter Forty-Nine

Lily gasped as Boone grabbed her and clamped his hand over her mouth, backing her into the kitchen. A gun hung threateningly from his other hand. Closing the door behind him, he never took his eyes from her face.

"Now," he whispered. "I'll have the jewel. I haven't come all this way and worked all these weeks to leave empty-handed." He winced in pain.

John's words of warning ripped through her mind. *Once he has the jewel we're all dead.* Was he right? If she gave it to Boone, would he leave without hurting her or her aunt?

She wasn't sure.

"We can do this the easy way—" he reached around and grasped the back of her hair and yanked down, bringing her upturned face within inches of his, "—or not. Your choice."

He quickly let her go, his gaze darting around. He opened the drawers and dumped them out, scanning the contents. He fingered through her cupboards.

She glanced to the closed door to the alley and wondered if she dare try an escape.

"Forget it," he chuckled. "You know you're going to give it to me. May as well make it easy on yourself."

"How did you escape?"

"The old man thought I was hurt worse than I was. Came in to doctor me."

Her blood pulsed. "Is he...dead?"

"*Shut up.* I'm asking the questions."

He'd already moved rapidly about, searching all he could downstairs, pulling the bolts of fabric and lace from the walls and dropping them into a pile on the floor.

"I want that jewel," he shouted. After rifling through her book of sketches, he threw it across the room in a fit of rage, raining pages down like leaves in the fall.

He clenched his side and groaned.

After a moment, he grasped her arm and propelled her up the stairs, bumping the walls in the confined space as they moved. At the top, he shoved her down, then began searching. He ran his hands through the seams of the upholstered chairs, turned things over, and left nothing unexplored.

Lily wanted to run to her aunt, make sure she was okay, but Boone kept her close to his side. In Lily's room, he dumped out her highboy drawers, picking through her things. When he found her box of personal keepsakes he all but shook with excitement, but again was disappointed. All that was left to check now was her aunt's bedroom.

Harriett gasped when Boon pushed open the door, one Lily felt sure she had left open when she'd gone downstairs. Her aunt, still sitting where Lily had left her, blanched when she saw the gunman.

Angrily, he opened her armoire, pulling out her aunt's belongings, then tossing them to the side. Tension crackled in the air and Lily felt sure he was ready to explode.

When he spotted Harriett's satchel next to her chair, he stopped. "Here," he said, in a frenzy. "It has to be here."

When that didn't produce the gem, he turned on Lily, murder glistening in his eyes. Pushing her roughly to the bed, he towered over her as she strove to remain steadfast.

She would not cower.

"I don't think you want to give your old mother here a show that will shock the life out of her." He reached for his belt buckle. "You better start talking."

Pop. Pop. Pop.

The sound didn't register to Lily until she saw Boone's eyes go wide.

He tried to turn to see what had happened, but instead pitched to the right, hitting the wall and sliding down until he was on the ground, motionless.

Tante sat in her chair, the tiny derringer still smoking in her outstretched hand. "You won't hurt my Lily," she said calmly as she started to shake uncontrollably. Her eyes, set deep in her wrinkled face, were riveted on Boone's body, her contorted expression one Lily had never seen.

Voices boomed from below, followed by the sound of someone running up the stairs. Tucker, Theodore and Emmeline burst into the room before Lily could even move to get herself together.

"What happ—" Tucker began, gaping first at Boone's body, then at Harriett.

"I killed the man in black," Tante Harriett whispered. "He was going to hurt my Lily."

She'd be ready for that black-hearted snake—Charity stopped the direction of her thoughts. Luke always said anger hampered one's thinking. Be smart. Think. *I'm a McCutcheon. And McCutcheons don't die easily.* She'd not be distracted when the door finally opened. She'd be ready for *anything.*

Charity felt around the floor. She almost smiled when Lady Luck placed her hand over a rock that fit perfectly in her palm. Tenaciously, she began scraping under the door in the hard-packed earth. Over and over, she pummeled with vengeance, then brushed the dirt away.

Shellston's words rankled. He wanted her dead. She'd heard too much in the candlelit bank. For some reason, Shellston had had the stagecoach attacked. Innocent people had died. John, Lily and Harriett could have been killed, too. After what seemed like an eternity, she had to stop to catch her breath. Perhaps they were planning to leave her here forever, to die of thirst where no one would even know. In the heat of the day that wouldn't take long.

Again she attacked the ground. Sweat poured down her face and stung her eyes. Her arms throbbed. The dull ache radiated from her wrists up to her shoulders. She pounded and scraped the earth, but it seemed part rock, too. Frustrated, she flung the rock to the side and, like an animal, scratched with her fingernails until the pain was too much. She stopped, then felt the insignificant dent she'd made under the door.

Panting, Charity collapsed against the wall. She closed her eyes, and fingered her sore jaw, then let her hand drop down to the dusty earth floor.

What she wouldn't give for a cup of cool water. She licked her dry lips. Tried to swallow.

For several long minutes she just sat. Her heart slowed. Time passed. A prayer of deliverance took flight. With so much going on in her head, she never heard the soft shifting of pebbles and sand beneath the door beside her.

Dustin was already back from his search of the west end of the ghost town when John came running in to their meeting place. They'd left the horses and had ventured out on foot.

"Nothin'," John said, feeling desperate. He reached for the canteen on his saddle. After a long drink, he swiped his arm over his mouth and stood looking at the town in the early morning light. "I found nothin'. You?"

John's anxiety-turned-fury was getting the better of him. He didn't know this area. He felt impotent, useless. Charity had been gone too long. She could be dead. Or, on the back of some horse headed for Mexico, never to be seen again. He *wouldn't* let that come to pass. She was his baby sister. It was his job to keep her safe.

"I got nothin' either," Dustin said crossly. He paced back and forth like a caged wolf, rings of sweat on his shirt, anger blazing in his eyes. "I've been thinking, though."

"And?"

"If I were those Comancheros, I wouldn't hang out here. Too easy for raiders to swoop in and kill everyone. But living out on the desert all the time would get old. Maybe they're close. Somewhere they could get to the town easily when they wanted to, but not live there all the time."

John gave him a look.

"Up on that hill." Dustin walked through the group of horses and pointed up behind the town.

"You may be right. Let's go check it out."

"What about Brandon?"

"It's been over twenty minutes since we split up. I don't feel comfortable waiting any longer. I think he'll figure out where we went and follow."

It took ten minutes for the two cousins to climb the hillside overlooking the deserted town. With Winchesters in hand and their guns strapped to their thighs, they crouched behind some rocks and took in the Comanchero's camp, just waking from the night.

"There's a lot of 'em," John whispered, scrambling up farther onto a big rock, careful to stay hidden. He removed his hat and wiped the excess moisture from the inside hatband. "Any sign?"

She had to be here. If not, they wouldn't have any idea of where to start looking.

"No." Dustin scanned the camp in the opposite direction. "That doesn't mean she isn't here."

John slid back down the rock. "I agree. Looks to me like they're breaking camp." He looked over to his cousin. "Does it to you?"

Dustin nodded. "More women and children than men."

"I've counted five men, although some are pretty old. Still, doesn't mean they can't shoot." Or do other things, John thought. Like cut off the hands of a small child. "Let's get closer and see if we can see Charity."

Charity came awake slowly. She blinked, and for a moment she didn't remember where she was. When realization dawned, she clenched her jaw and pain exploded through her head. Her fingertips felt bloody. She couldn't have slept more than a few minutes. A trickle of sweat eased down her temple and she brushed it away. She leaned over to the crack between the door and jamb, intent on getting some air, when a rattling sound erupted in the far corner.

Rattlesnake!

As slowly and as carefully as she could, Charity turned back around, trying to move as little as possible. Squinting through the dimness, she could make out the outline of the reptile coiled up in the corner. Above its raised head was a tail that held a good three inches' worth of rattles. As the deep timbre indicated, this snake was a granddaddy, and huge, much like the one that had been in the outhouse.

After a few moments, it stopped rattling as it stared back at her.

Her pulse quickened until she feared she would pass out.

Dear Lord in heaven. What now?

Charity fought to keep a rein on her fear, which was vivid, rank and rapidly welling up inside her. What would she do if it started her way? Where could she possibly go? There wasn't anywhere to climb to get out of its reach. She dared to take her gaze away from the hideous reptile for just one moment, long enough to quickly scan the low hanging ceiling. To her utter dismay, it was completely smooth.

The door. Her only avenue of escape.

Charity peered again at the door handle she'd checked countless times since being imprisoned. Was it substantial enough for her to wedge her foot onto? Perhaps she could scramble up and somehow balance on the handle while garnering some sort of hold at the top of the doorjamb. Still, if the diamondback wanted to, she was sure he was large enough to reach up and strike her.

The creature was still quiet. It lowered its head and tail. It must have come in looking for a shady spot to sleep away the day. There was movement outside and a few voices. The snake raised its head.

In a panic, Charity dared a look out the crack by the door, praying it was her captor finally coming to get her. At least with him, she'd have a fighting chance when he went to kill her. In here, she was totally defenseless.

Guttural voices wafted in, then somebody walked by, leading a horse. The snake's tail started to slowly move. It wasn't like the first explosive rattle when she'd surprised it. This was soft, almost like the dance of raindrops on a tin roof—but still, a warning no less. It saw her. And, didn't like her. In two seconds it could cross the room and sink its long fangs into any part of her it wished.

Charity swallowed, wondering if anyone would hear her if she screamed. Maybe they knew the snake was inside with her. An accidental death would be convenient; the law wouldn't be able to pin it on anyone.

A scuffling sound outside made Charity look again.

A child. A child stood next to the door. He was looking in.

"Please," she whispered frantically. She stuck her fingers through the crack a small way, wiggling them at the little boy. "Here, honey, open the door. Open the door. *Please*."

He was about three feet tall. His eyes went wide and he quickly ran off.

Tears sprang to the surface and Charity had no defense against them. "Come back. *Please*, come back." Her throat, tight from trying to hold in her emotions while still getting her desperate whispers out, felt as if it would snap.

"Charity." The voice was low and urgent.

Stifling a gasp, Charity turned so fast the snake began his low warning once again. "Brandon," she said under her breath. "You're here. You've found me."

Emotion flooded her as tears sprang from her eyes and streamed down her face. Fearing to move any more than necessary, she didn't try to brush them away. "There's a huge rattler in here. Quickly—open the door."

Charity could see he held a large tumbleweed over him as a cover. He was in peril every moment he stayed outside her door. "Shhh, honey, don't cry. I can't open it. Yet. It's bolted and locked. If I shoot it off, it'll bring the whole camp down on our heads."

"What are you going to do?"

He drew his Colt 45 and tried to push it under the door. The gap was too small. "Not sure yet. John and Dustin are here, too. Somewhere."

He paused, then looked around.

"What? What are you thinking?"

"If I can find a large enough rock, I may be able to bust this off."

His face was so close to the crack she could see the gold-colored flecks in his eyes that she knew so well. He felt the lock, testing it. "No. It won't work. Shooting is the only way."

"Then shoot it off! But get me out quickly. We'll make a run for it."

She looked over her shoulder. The snake wasn't coiled any longer, but stretched out on the back side of the wall, its head turned in her direction.

"Brandon. Shoot it off!"

When he looked at her through the gap she didn't like his expression. "What?"

"I'm going to have to leave for a little while until I find your brother and get some backup. If I try to bust you out now, we'll both be killed."

He paused, still looking at her. "I'll be back."

She stuck her fingers out and he caressed them. "I'm so sorry I didn't tell you what I was doing," she murmured. "Please forgive me. I…"

"Shhh, Charity. There'll be time later."

He stopped and quickly flattened himself to the ground. Two men talking loudly passed by and were gone.

"Brandon," she whispered as seriously as she could. "No. Don't go. *Don't leave me here.* The snake has moved. It'll come at me. I just know it."

"They sleep in the day, Charity," he whispered back. "Stay still. I'll be back as fast as I can, darlin'. Trust me."

"Brandon?"

"*Brandon!*"

It was no use. He was gone.

Chapter Fifty

With John gone and Dr. Bixby injured, Lily kept a close watch on Chaim as the morning sun climbed higher in the sky. Mostly he slept, but once he'd awakened and Emmeline had fussed over him like a mother dog over her pup. She spoon-fed him soup and held his head when he asked for water. There was a slight sheen to his skin, but, all in all, seemed to be on the road to recovery.

And poor Dr. Bixby. Stretched out on a cot in the doctor's office, he eyed her each time she walked by. He had a lump on his head and an awful headache and felt humiliated from being tricked by the killer.

Winnie, Madeline and Becky all helped, as did Emmeline. Somehow, Lily found herself in charge, so to speak, and she attributed it to having been John's assistant with Chaim. Winston McCutcheon had rounded up a sizeable posse and had ridden out over an hour ago, with Deputy Miller and Cradle Hupton.

Harriett, still shaken, sat in silence by the kitchen stove, sipping a cup of tea. Seeing her aunt made Lily think of the jewel she had hidden away. As soon as she had one spare second, she would wrap it up and send it back to Mr. and Mrs. Lowerby, saying that Harriett had taken it and that she wanted to give it back.

They were good people, and surely after they had it back they would forgive her. If they had gotten the law involved, she would tell them about the pawnshop owner and what he had tried to do to her aunt. No need to involve John ever again now that she had a plan. She'd put his life in danger once; she would not do it twice.

"We're taking Harland his lunch," Tucker called from the back door. "He must be spitting mad by now since we forgot about him this morning."

"Be careful. We don't want any more patients to tend to," Madeline said, her brows arched knowingly.

"I'm going, too," Theodore announced. "We'll be especially careful. No one else will be escaping from the jail today."

They went out the door with Theodore carrying the tray of food and Tucker following behind with a Colt 45 in his hand.

It wasn't but five minutes and the boys were back. Becky took the now empty tray from Theodore, glancing adoringly into his face.

Lily looked up, surprised at the perplexed expression on Tucker's face. "Is everything all right at the jail?"

"For one thing, Harland confessed, so to speak," he answered as he came into the room and put his gun on the sideboard. "Mr. Shellston was over there. It was just him and Harland. He was rooting around in Sheriff Dane's desk. I think he was looking for the key to open the cell. He was furious with Harland and before they knew anyone else had come in, Harland kept saying he was sorry for shooting Chaim. Soon as they saw us he shut up."

"Taking him out would be breaking the law," Becky said slowly.

Winnie shook her head in disbelief. "He wouldn't do that, would he? The boy's only been there one day. For all the trouble he's caused over the years, it's hardly a punishment at all. Especially in light he almost killed Chaim."

Madeline harrumphed. "I'm not surprised. I've never trusted that man."

Lily waited for the women to finish. "What happened when you went in and found him?"

Theodore threw a glance at Tucker. "Tuck asked Mr. Shellston what he was doing. Boy, that really got his dander up. I guess he didn't like being questioned by a kid. He demanded to know where the key to Harland's cell was."

Lily and the other women had gathered around. Hearing a noise, Lily turned to see Dr. Bixby standing in the doorway, interested in what Tucker was about to say. She ran to his side and helped seat him at the table.

"Go on, Tucker," the doctor said, looking old and feeble. "What did he do then?"

"After I informed him the sheriff usually keeps the key on him and I was sure the deputy must have it now, he went into a hollering fit. Even Harland looked scared. For a minute, I thought he was actually going to come after us. Finally, he stormed out the door muttering all kinds of crazy things. I think he's gone mad."

Dr. Bixby cleared his throat, still looking wan. "I'd feel better if everyone stayed close to this here office until the posse and the rest get back. So many strange things going on. I don't like it one bit."

Emmeline rushed into the kitchen. "Chaim is awake again. Come see."

"Look," John said to Dustin and pointed. "Brandon. Three o'clock."

Both men lay on their bellies under some thick underbrush at the north edge of the Comancheros' camp. They watched Brandon as he came around a deserted tent, staying low and moving in the direction where they'd first left the horses. John gave the bird call they'd used for years. Brandon stopped and lunged behind a large granite boulder. A few moments went by, then the call was returned. John repeated once. Slowly then, Brandon came from behind the rock and picked his way toward John and Dustin, being careful to stay hidden.

"I'm glad you saw me," Brandon said, rolling in next to Dustin. He was covered in dirt and sweat. "I found her. She's locked up with a rattlesnake."

"You couldn't get her out?" Dustin said.

"No. The door is bolted closed and the lock will need to be shot off. I didn't want to get her killed in the process of rescuing her."

"Where?" John was having a hard time keeping himself from running straight into camp. He remembered how frightened Charity had been when the snake was in the outhouse.

"Close. Just past the horses, where the hill starts."

"We need a plan," John interjected. "Dustin, you go back and get the horses. Bring them straight up from the town and leave them out of sight on the north edge. Brandon, do you know where I'm talking about?"

"Pretty much. I'll find it."

"Good. Now, Dustin leaves the horses there and circles back halfway, by the rock where we first came in. I'll be there. We'll create a diversion, draw the men off. Hopefully, that will leave it clear for Brandon to run in, shoot the lock, and get Charity before anyone realizes what's happening. We'll all meet back at the horses and make a run for town."

"Okay," Dustin said.

John nodded. "When Dustin is back, I'll give the call, long and loud. It won't matter if they hear since we're going to make our presence known moments after that. Just be ready."

"You know I will be," Brandon said.

"Yeah, I do. Let's move."

The snake had come halfway around the wall since Brandon had left. As it moved, Charity did too, barely inching along to keep as much distance between them. As it edged forward, she backed away, and she was now a good three feet from the door—her only source of fresh air.

It was stinkin' hot. Dehydrated and dizzy, Charity tipped her head back against the wall and closed her eyes. Nausea swirled inside. Not daring to keep her eyes off the slithering devil for more than two heartbeats, she opened them and glanced across the room.

Where is Brandon? And John and Dustin? How long had it been since he'd left? Nothing made sense. She couldn't quite remember how she'd come to be in this stifling tomb in the first place. She wiped her hand across her face, longing for her space by the door. She inched in its direction before remembering about the hideous creature waiting to sink its fangs into her leg. She pulled up clumsily, but not before the reptile had lifted its tail and rattled.

"Oh, be quiet," she scolded. "You're not so damn tough. So what if you're a snake." She began to laugh uncontrollably but stopped abruptly when she heard a shout from somewhere. Then a shot. "Brandon?" she whispered, shocked back to her senses.

Several more shots. Women screaming. What was going on? The same muffled sound she'd been hearing all day whenever the snake made a move caught her attention. He'd coiled again and was rattling loudly. Soon the room was filled with the terrifying sound.

A blast threw her to the ground. The door flew open. Brandon stood in the opening. He lunged in her direction at the same exact moment the snake lashed out with lightning speed.

Charity flung herself back. The sight of the six-foot-long reptile stretched out like a lance was terrifying. It knocked Brandon down at the same time he swung his arm around. He pulled the trigger a second time, the report almost breaking her eardrums.

The diamondback's heavy body was blasted back against the wall. The next instant Brandon was pulling her into his arms.

She couldn't stop her sobs as she clung to him, running her hands over his chest, wadding his shirtfront into her fists. She needed to make sure he was actually here with her, holding her, not just a figment of longing she'd dredged up from her fevered imagination.

"The snake bit you," she gasped.

"No. It hit my spur."

He silenced her by pulling her scantily clothed body close. They melded, and heat surged inside her. All the days of torture of the unknown, when Brandon had angrily left Rio Wells, bubbled up. She pushed closer, needing the feel of him. She ached to show him just how much he meant to her, how much she loved him. His fingers scorched her skin as they traveled down her arms, around her back, straying lower still. He gazed into her eyes, reaching into her soul.

Then, his lips found hers and he kissed her hungrily, fervently as if she was his sustenance after a ten-year fast. She whimpered when he started to pull away, not wanting to lose this sensation, this yearning burning deep inside.

He buried his face into her hair, breathing deeply. "We don't have much time," he said low.

He turned and, taking Charity by the hand, approached the door with his gun outstretched. When she wavered, he scooped her up and dashed outside. She buried her face into his neck and closed her eyes. If she died now, she didn't care. At least it would be in the arms of the man she loved. He ran swiftly, dodging among horses, rocks and cactus. There was shooting somewhere else, and shouting. Confusion all around. He stopped and put her on her feet.

Hand in hand, they started down an incline, her sliding and lurching and trying to keep up. Right before they hit bottom, Charity fell onto her buttocks, but kept sliding until they stopped.

A rifle fired close by with a deafening sound. All at once, she found herself enfolded in John's arms; and she felt as she had as a young girl—love and cherished by her older brother.

Not wasting a second, Brandon mounted up and John lifted his sister onto the back of Brandon's horse. Charity clamped her arms around Brandon's waist and locked her fingers, burying her face into the solid presence of his back. Without another word, the three horses turned and bolted off through the dense West Texas brush, as if the devil himself was on their tail.

The horses thundered back into town, sliding to a halt at the doctor's office. John dismounted and carefully took Charity from the back of Brandon's horse and carried her inside, shielding her from curious gazes of bystanders that had gathered.

Aunt Winnie and the rest of the women watched as he crossed the room without saying a word. He went straight up to his room and shut the door, not yet knowing what his sister might have endured in the hours she'd been captive. He laid her on his bed and covered her with his blanket.

"Are you okay?" he asked, taking in her scraped and bloodstained face. His heart feared the worst.

"I am now." She sat up, keeping the cover pulled tight to her chest. "Thank you for rescuing me."

Unable to stop it, John heard a sound like a hurt bear escape his throat. He sat on the mattress next to her and enfolded her in an embrace, marveling at how small and delicate his usually tough little sister felt.

"*Of course* I'd come for you. If hell froze over I'd come for you. If Texas broke open creating a vast cavern a thousand feet deep, I'd come for you. Find you. Nothing could stop me.

I hope you realize that." He had to know more. "Did they hurt you—" he paused for a heartbeat, then sat back and looked into her face, "—more than what I see?"

There was a light knock, then the door opened slowly. Brandon stood there for a moment, then came in and shut the door.

John stood and Charity looked from one man to the other. "I'm okay. I mean, they didn't have their way with me."

The relief on Brandon's face mirrored what he was feeling.

"Thank God," John said. "I think I've aged about twenty years since Tucker came running into the office to tell us you'd been kidnapped."

"Is that how you found out?"

John nodded. "Did the Comanchero take you from your room at the hotel?"

Charity looked away, breaking eye contact.

John could tell she was hiding something. "What? Where were you, Charity?"

She wouldn't look at him. He knew her stalling tactics all too well. Finally she said, "I was outside. On Main Street."

"In the middle of the night?" Brandon's expression darkened. "In your unmentionables?"

She nodded, watching him closely. Despite her tough demeanor, her cheeks pinked.

John didn't want the wall between the two of them to go back up. "Why?" he asked hurriedly, wanting to get to the bottom of it before Brandon did. "Why would you go out by yourself in a town like Rio Wells?"

"Because..." A look of consternation crossed her face. She glanced up at Brandon, then stood, boldly letting her covers fall away. Stepping close, she had to tip her chin up to look Brandon in the eyes. "Because I saw you riding down the street, Brandon," she whispered, inches from his face. She reached out and laid her open palm on his chest. "I wanted to talk to you, tell you everything, before you got away again."

"That was foolish," Brandon replied softly, with no trace of his usual sternness.

"I agree," she said. She inched forward.

John cleared his throat. "That explains it, then." He took Brandon by the shoulder, a smile tugging at his mouth. "Let's go. Little sister, I'll have someone bring you up some warm water and clothes."

"Wait! I almost forgot. Shellston," she said, looking from one man to the other, the spell broken. "He had the stagecoach attacked."

"Are you sure?" John asked. "What else did you learn?"

"It's something about a letter somewhere. The Comancheros were supposed to stop the stage and get a letter, then take it to Shellston."

In her excitement she was talking with her hands, waving this way and that. Her eyes, opened wide, sparkled with the passion of youth, and every time she looked in Brandon's direction, her lips curled just a tiny bit, pleased to be able to help in Brandon's occupation as a law man.

"But, they failed," she went on. "The banker hasn't paid what he promised, and that's why the Comanchero kidnapped me. He thought Shellston would pay to get me back." She laughed. "He didn't know Shellston couldn't care less if I was dead or alive. That's when the Comanchero said he'd kill Harland next, then Mr. Shellston himself. He's paying the Comanchero today."

John exchanged a heated look with Brandon.

"I'll take the deputy and go arrest him," Brandon said.

Charity grabbed his arm. "Just so you know, Shellston told the Comanchero to make sure I never made it back to town."

John tamped back his temper, feeling the urge to reload his Colt 45 and take down the murdering banker himself. "I know what letter they're after."

Both Brandon and Charity's heads snapped around to look at him.

"At least I think I do. Jeremiah Post had a letter for the sheriff in his breast pocket the day he and his brother were killed. I put it with his belongings, which I hope are still at the Wells Fargo office waiting to be shipped to his next of kin. I'll go get it while you go arrest Shellston."

"Can I go with you, Brandon?" Charity asked with solemn urgency.

"*No*," both men said in unison.

Chapter Fifty-One

Jeremiah Post's letter was still at the Wells Fargo office in the duffle with the rest of the murdered brothers' belongings. With a little persuasion—specifically, informing the clerk the sheriff was dead—they let John take the letter in question. He assured them that as soon as it had been shown to the circuit judge, it would go back to its rightful place. For now, it was needed for important business, John said, and he'd lock it in his safe until that time.

Brandon apprehended Shellston with no problems and the banker was now locked in the cell next to his son. He'd been on his way out of town with a travel bag filled with hundred dollar bills, confirming Charity's story. Brandon had also told John that he'd not found out too much about the gem, but did learn that Boone was known in the East for his murderous ways. He was an outlaw and wanted for more than one crime. John had yet to speak with Lily about it, but intended to as soon as everything settled down.

When John returned to the doctor's office, Lily was there with the rest of the women around Chaim. Dustin was by her side.

"He all locked up?" Dustin asked.

John came in and looked Chaim over, then put a thermometer into his mouth. "Yeah. He won't have long to wait for the judge. Pete Miller said he's due next week. I wouldn't want to be in Shellston's shoes." John was addressing

Dustin but his gaze kept drifting to Lily. "This will interest you, Lily. The letter was from Mr. Bartlett."

"Owner of the shop on Spring Street?"

He nodded. "One and the same. The shop that you and your aunt were on your way to Rio Wells to lease."

She smiled at his reply. "What did it say? How ironic that everything comes full circle to the person who brought us here in the first place. John, that seems like so long ago, does it not? In reality, it has only been two months. So much has happened since then."

Dustin stepped closer to Lily's side, as if feeling the sudden connection between the two.

"From what we can gather," John said, "Mr. Bartlett had taken a loan from Shellston. Then the banker raised the rate, making it hard for Bartlett to fulfill the contract. Mr. Bartlett spelled out how Shellston had been acquiring property unlawfully by using his position at the bank. It sounded like he wasn't going to go along nicely, like others here in Rio Wells had, and so Shellston had him beaten to death and put in the river. Thing was, he didn't die.

Jeremiah and Cyrus Post were his attorneys, on their way here with proof of a document signed between the two of them, and testimony from others he had done the same thing to. Without the letter, Mr. Bartlett wouldn't have a case."

"What will happen to Mr. Shellston and Harland?" Becky asked.

John shrugged. "Only time will tell. But as the facts come out, and in light of the fact he ordered Charity's demise, I think he'll feel the full extent of his crimes. The boy, I don't know. Seems he was after Charity for her standing up to him in school. I'll bet he's never been told no."

Bixby hadn't said more than a handful of words since John had returned. The old man sat in a chair by the window, gazing out. John went over and looked at the lump on the back of his head, then palpated the area gently.

"How you feeling, ol' timer?" His tone was soft although he was trying to elicit a response. "Come on," John said. "I thought you were tougher than being put down by one conk on the noggin."

Bixby shrugged. "Just feel like a damn fool. That man Boone could have killed Lily and Harriett. What really makes me mad is that he was smarter than I was." Bixby sucked in a deep breath of air and let it out slowly, rocking his body. "No fool like an old fool."

"You were just doing your job," John said, although he'd been utterly terrified when he'd heard about what happened with the gunfighter. Lily hadn't been hurt, and now she was here, in the room, beautiful as ever. "You couldn't know he was playing possum. I'd have done the same thing," John finished.

Bixby shrugged again and John patted him on the shoulder. "Okay, everyone, I think Chaim is due some rest from all this attention." John said, gesturing to his aunt, female cousins, Dustin, Emmeline, and Lily. "Unless you all think I'm wrong." Chaim rolled his head and gave him a thankful look. "Come on, out with you."

"You're right," Aunt Winnie agreed. "It's time we all went home and got some rest. I'm about ready to fall over." She looked at John. "That is, if you think it's a good idea."

"I do. Chaim's made a remarkable recovery so far. His fever is about gone and his coloring is almost back to normal. It's amazing considering how much blood he lost yesterday."

"It's a miracle," Emmeline said, nodding at John. "As was your saving his life like you did." She was the only one still close to Chaim's side. She bent down and kissed him on his cheek, then blushed profusely when she realized everyone had seen her.

Chaim held her hand in his.

"I guess you're wondering about us," Chaim said softly. "Well, Emmy and me, well…we're a couple."

Everyone smiled as if this was news to anyone.

"And, we intend to get married as soon as I'm able. John knows and has given us his blessing."

"Chaim's right," John said. "Some things are just meant to be." He looked up and found Lily looking at him. Boldly, he winked at her, then continued. "Congratulations, Chaim. You're getting a good woman."

Now it was Lily's turn to blush. Didn't John know everyone had seen that wink? Her cheeks burning, she turned, heading for the door. She'd left her aunt alone for as long as she felt comfortable and needed to get back to her store.

"Not so fast," John whispered, close to her side. "I'll walk you back."

"I need to—"

"I know. Check on Harriett. I'll go with you."

Chapter Fifty-Two

"Thought I'd find you here."

Brandon looked up at the sound of Charity's voice. She saw the mask descend over his expression, his eyes go dark. She walked into the livery with poise, hoping she looked more confident than she felt. Welcoming scents of hay and leather bolstered her spirit. But mostly the sight of the man who'd been her every thought since their kiss. They'd shared chaste little pecks before, and a touch here and there, and longing gazes. But mostly they'd been the best of friends. Steadfast. During the kiss, she felt consumed, desired and loved. And, she wanted more.

"Charity." He tossed the brush he was holding into a box of grooming tools and met her at his horse's stall door.

"Can we talk for a minute?"

"I'm busy right now," he said, turning and closing the gate. He latched it slowly, methodically, rattled it, and checked its strength, as if he was fearful his steed would escape, taking so much time Charity almost laughed.

"I'm on my way over to the jail," he said. "I don't put too much stock in Deputy Miller."

Her heart sank. He hadn't forgiven her. He was still brooding over her running off. She wished she could make things right, do it over, but unfortunately that wasn't possible. She took one step closer, until they were almost face to face.

"I thought you'd forgiven me. Today, upstairs in John's room, it felt like you had. I guess I was wrong."

Brandon shrugged his large shoulders and looked out the livery doors, avoiding her gaze. "It's just—"

His mouth was a straight line.

"What? Tell me."

"No, you weren't wrong—I have forgiven you. I'm thankful we got you back alive."

She had to do something before he talked his way right back into his anger. He looked so unhappy. Miserable. Just like she felt. Warmth pooled inside at her close proximity to him. She reached out and ran her hand down his chest, amazed at the strength she felt beneath his shirt. His expressive eyes had a hint of vulnerability, his lips enticing. "What are you, then?"

"Resigned. I've known you for way too long to think you'll ever change. For me."

His last two words gave her courage. "What do you mean?"

"I've been waiting a long time for you, Charity. A damn…long…time. I've given you every opportunity to let me know how you felt, but you haven't. Not really. You've strung me along. I'm done. Tired of it. I'm a new man."

She sucked in a breath. "But, what about the kiss?"

"Didn't mean anything. Just a reaction to a tense situation."

Charity squared her shoulders and planted her hands on her hips. "I don't believe you."

He tipped her chin up with his finger and came so close she would swear his lips were on hers. "Believe it. I'm just a plaything to you. Not good enough for a McCutcheon. It's true I don't come from some blueblood lineage, but I'm honest and I've loved you more than anyone ever could."

Charity was overcome with emotion at his proclamation. She leaned forward, needing desperately to feel his lips on hers, but he pulled away, just out of reach.

Hurt, she shook her head. "That's not true. I just thought you wanted to be part of our family. Any part. I imagined you'd do whatever it took to make that happen. Even so far as to marry me. I never believed you wanted me just for me."

Brandon's eyes narrowed for a brief second, then he laughed long and loud. Finally finished, he wiped the moisture from his eyes. "Is that so?"

"Y-yes," she stammered, not quite knowing what to make of him. His expression, a mixture of bedeviled annoyance and little-boy mischievousness was one she'd never seen before.

Before she had time to say anything else, he scooped her up and flung her over his shoulder, heading for the ladder leading up to the hayloft. Charity screeched, then beat her fists against his back. She kicked her feet wildly, but there was no way out of his strong grip. He climbed swiftly, reaching the top in the blink of an eye.

Before she could let out a gasp, he laid her back in the hay, took her face between his palms, and crushed her lips with his own. She squirmed and pushed at his chest, twisting her head.

"Stop it," she tried to say, but she was pinned tight beneath his chest.

This kiss was nothing like the tender kiss earlier; that kiss had been filled with passion and wonder, promise and meaning. This kiss was angry, filled with questions. Her heart lurched at what it might mean.

All at once, he stopped. He pressed his forehead to hers but didn't open his eyes. He rolled onto his back and slung his arm over his face. Long moments passed. She had no idea what he was thinking. She looked over at his profile in the darkened rafters of the barn. Strong jaw and chiseled face, so handsome, so alone. She thought about what it must be like not to have any family to call your own. Her heart shuddered painfully inside her chest.

She was his family.

She had been all those years ago, and she still was now.

"Brandon," she whispered, snuggling deeper into his side and walking her fingers across his chest. She leaned forward and kissed his earlobe lightly, unsure, taking liberties she'd never dared before. Picking up his arm, she placed it over her side, and tugged softly.

He turned a little and gazed into her eyes. Then he rolled, taking her into his arms. He kissed her again, this time so gently it stole her breath, her heart, everything that she was.

Oh, how she *loved* him. Every confusing part of him. He rolled farther until he was above her once again, breaking the kiss and moving his lips to her ear, then proceeded down her neck, branding her skin with the fire of desire.

Charity's breathing was heavy, her thoughts disjointed. *This* was Brandon. *This* was her love. Never in her wildest dreams had she known it would feel like *this* to be his woman.

"Charity." Her name came out gruff and endearing.

"Shhh." She struggled to open her eyes, feeling as if she'd been drugged. He was intoxicating. His touch, magic. His face, everything that heaven must be made of. "Let's not talk. I want to keep kissing."

"No. We need to talk. All these years you thought I just wanted to be part of your family? So much so that the feelings we have—"

He stopped. His expression now brought her excruciating pain as he struggled to say the words. "That I *thought* we had. That *I* had... Really?"

She wished she could just tell him a little lie to make it sound better, save his feelings, but she couldn't. *Never* again to Brandon. "Sometimes I did. But not all the time. I'm sorry. I'd get so confused I'd get angry with you, or put distance between us, or some such silly thing. Everyone in my family is so significant. All my brothers are smart and successful and..."

There was a long pause before Brandon nudged her. "Go on."

"They're loved by *everyone*. I can see why you'd like being a part of that, Brandon. But, when I get married, I want to be loved for just being me. Charity."

She searched his face to see if he understood what she was trying to say. "Without the McCutcheon name, the ranch, or all the fanfare that comes with it. I know that sounds really horrible because I love my family—and everyone in it. I do. But, I can't help it. It's how I feel."

He gathered her closer and Charity thought she'd die from the joy of finally being in his arms. "I do love you for just being you. If you don't know that by now then I don't know how else to prove it to you. Even as aggravating, headstrong, outspoken and downright—"

She stiffened. "Okay, I get it."

"—infuriating as you are sometimes," he whispered next to her ear, then chuckled. "I do love you. God help me, I do. You think I'd tangle with a monster-sized rattlesnake for just anyone?"

His eyes darkened and he pressed closer, taking her lips again with his, kissing her slowly, showing her just how much he wanted her. She was drowning in desire when he whispered, "I'd go anywhere with you, darlin'. Just name the place. We don't have to go back to Montana. If that is what it'll take to prove my love, then so be it."

Charity sought his lips, blissfully happy by his avowal of love. Before the kiss could heat up, she couldn't stop a little laugh from slipping out.

Brandon pulled away. "Something funny?" His hair was mussed and a strand of hay fell over his eye. She thought he'd never looked more handsome.

"Just something Luke told me once."

He went up on his elbow and gazed down into her face. "And what was that?"

Again she laughed, unable to contain her happiness. "To be careful who I rolled in the hay with."

Brandon's eyebrow cocked up humorlessly. "You make a habit of this?"

Right then the barn doors banged open and Charity all but gasped.

Brandon's eyes widened, then sparkled with mischief.

"Come on, Chester," Cradle said. A creaking sound attested to the fact Cradle was taking Chester out of his stall. He clucked to the old gelding, then there was a jingling sound as the livery owner went about harnessing him. "Hey, Theodore, you mind mucking out Chester's stall while he's out?"

"Nope. I'll do it now."

Brandon pulled Charity closer. "So, you want to marry me?" he asked quietly.

Charity was terrified of getting caught in the loft, and by Brandon's expression, he knew exactly what she was thinking. She tried to shush him but he came in closer and resumed where he'd left off, kissing the corner of her mouth and nibbling on her lips.

His spell once again wrapped around her and she almost forgot the threat of discovery from below. She leaned in, then drew back quickly when Theodore laughed at something.

Brandon whispered, "It's just kissing."

She clamped her hand over his mouth.

"Did you say something?" Cradle called from the other side of the barn.

"Nope," Theodore answered. The squeaky wheel from the wheelbarrow screeched out, followed by the shuffling of straw.

"Hey, boys. I need to get our horses rigged and a buggy hitched. We're going home. Winnie is plain wore out and I'd rather drive her than have her ride. How long will it take?"

Charity's mouth went dry. *Uncle Winston!*

"That's what I'm doing now. Saw Tucker out on the street and he said you'd be wanting a buggy. I'll have Chester ready in a couple of minutes, then I'll tack up your horses. Won't take me long."

"Thanks, Cradle, appreciate it. How is Theo…"

Charity felt something crawling up her leg and kicked out in reflex. The hay rustled loudly and the talking in the livery stopped.

"Oh, damn," Brandon whispered into her ear. "That may've done it."

Charity lifted her head, frantically looking for somewhere to hide. Muffled voices floated up from downstairs past her panicked senses, then she heard the barely audible scrape of boots on ladder rungs.

Brandon sat up and pulled her up with him. He quickly brushed long strands of hay from her hair, then waved at Cradle when his head poked over the wooden landing.

The livery keeper's eyes went wide in surprise, then crinkled in understanding. He looked from one side to the next, then shrugged. "Nope. Nothing up here, Mr. McCutcheon," he called down. "Must have been a mouse." He chuckled, then stared back down the ladder. "Or, maybe two."

Chapter Fifty-Three

John was aware of Dustin watching as he escorted Lily out the door and over the few steps to her shop. He felt bad, but not all that much. Life was hard. Hurt was an everyday occurrence. Something had to give between him and Dustin, and as he opened the door for Lily to go in, he knew it wasn't going to be him.

The place was quiet, the smell of smoke strong. He still couldn't believe Boone had broken out of jail and come back for the jewel. So much could have gone wrong. He was thankful that it hadn't.

"She must be sleeping," Lily said softly. "She usually calls down if she hears the bell."

"She's been sleeping a lot lately, hasn't she?"

Lily nodded. "And there is more."

"What do you mean?"

"Tonight she was very confused. She thought I was her sister, not her niece. She insisted on calling me Gretchen. I did not know what to do and I did not want to upset her, so I just went along."

"Maybe she's just shaken from the events tonight. I'm sure it was very traumatic for her. Or—"

"What?"

"She may be slipping into senility. We need to remember Harriett is old. Plus, coming off her dependence to morphine may have added to her confusion. It's hard to know for sure. I just want you to be prepared if she should get worse."

Lily nodded. "I am prepared, John. I hope she is not becoming senile. How sad for her. And us."

When she started for the stairs, John reached for her hands. "There's something I want to tell you."

Lily looked at him with a thousand questions in her eyes. He'd never felt compelled to share this with anyone, not even Emmeline when they'd gotten engaged. Now he was almost eager to get it off his chest.

"When I was a boy I killed a man. A good man." He took a deep breath. "A friend of our family."

Lily didn't turn away in horror or disgust, but waited for him to continue.

"He was a merchant delivering some panes of glass for a broken window. I was nine years old, home alone. When I heard a crash down in the livingroom, I thought someone was breaking in. I grabbed my gun and ran downstairs. I didn't mean to shoot him, but I did. Killed him in cold blood."

"Why are you telling me this, John? I do not understand. I am sure God knows you were just a boy. Let it go. Forgive yourself. God has long ago."

Overwhelmed, he closed his eyes. He felt an unfamiliar stirring. Something flittering in his gut until he recognized it for what it was…the forgiveness he'd been holding back. After all these years, he was able to forgive himself and that forgiveness flowed within, and brought with it an indescribable joy he'd never experienced before. Overcome with something surreal and bright, something bordering on extreme ecstasy, he said, "You heard Emmeline tonight? And Chaim?"

"I did."

"Well?"

"What are you asking me?"

Her face flushed. He wasn't so sure he wanted to know the answer to his question. Had more happened between her and Dustin than he'd realized? It easily could have.

She straightened as he waited for an answer. The words jumbled in his head and he cursed himself for not planning out the best way of going about this. He'd jumped in like a...

"Just wondering—well—if—I want to tell you—that—"

Damn, this was harder than he thought. With Emmeline, she'd always helped. Naturally flirtatious, she'd been able to read him like a book, and liked the fun of the chase. Lily was the opposite. Her naiveté was as real as the thudding of his unexpectedly shy heart.

"I was curious," John began again, "if you realized that if Chaim and Emmeline were sweet on each other that meant, well, I was now free."

Annoyed at how assuming that sounded, he snorted. *Here I am, Lily. Come'n get me.*

Appalled, he raked his hand through his hair. "I didn't mean it to sound like that." He shrugged and tried again: "What I'm trying to say is that I'm no longer engaged. And, since I'm no longer engaged, I was wondering if you'd consider—" What? Being my wife? Marrying me tonight? He almost laughed at the absurdity of how that statement sounded—even more outrageous than his last one, even if it was true.

Since meeting Lily, he'd changed. He'd never felt more sure about anything in his life. "—going to the Fourth of July celebration with me?" he finished, chickening out.

"Is that what this is all about? You silly goose. That is two weeks away."

"I know." He gave her hands a gentle tug and pulled her into his embrace. She fit perfectly and felt so right.

"Lily, I can't lie," he said into her hair that smelled like sweet honeysuckle. "I've been drawn to you since we first met. I tried to deny it to myself. Tried to stay away, stay honorable to Emmeline, but I must admit, it's been difficult. Then when I went out yesterday to talk to Emmeline, determined to break it off, well, I don't want to betray a confidence, but let me just say, she was in total agreement about ending our engagement."

Lily took a step back, needing a little space, a moment to absorb everything John had just said. In one split second, it was as if all her prayers had been answered. Did he have any idea that she had felt the same attraction to him since boarding the Wells Fargo stagecoach? Could he possibly know about the butterflies that practically lived in her stomach whenever he was close?

"You're killing me," John stated, seriously. He hadn't taken his eyes from her face since his unexpected statement. "You have noticed Emmeline doting on Chaim at every moment, haven't you?"

In that instant, the realization of the situation sunk in. She began to shiver in excitement and shock. "I have. I didn't know what to think."

John closed the distance between them, desire easily recognizable in his eyes. "But, you still haven't said anything about us."

He pulled her close, and she felt sure he was going to kiss her, but she wanted to say something first. She stopped him with a hand on his chest and almost giggled when his brows fell in disappointment.

"Lily?"

"I have many, many feelings for you, John. So much more that I thought possible to feel for a man. It has been difficult not to let them show, or come to the surface. I did not want to do anything that might hurt you if your destiny was with Emmeline."

John wrapped her in the safe haven of his arms. His lips found hers, warm and inviting. The kiss was gentle, questioning. She leaned into him, needing more—something to prove she wasn't asleep and this was a dream and she'd soon awaken to utter disappointment.

A thousand times she had dreamt of this moment, been tempted to allow her thoughts to wander and make believe—

but she knew thoughts like those only led to heartbreak. So she had stayed her desires, wishing only the best for him. But now, because dreams sometimes really do come true, she did not have to imagine what it would feel like to be in John's arms anymore, imagine what it felt like to have his lips on hers and to kiss him passionately.

Now that she was here, she never wanted to leave this spot, this moment.

John cupped her face. "There's more I want to say to you. Much more." His hands strayed down her back. "Lily, I love you. I want you to be my wife. Before you say anything, just listen to what I have to say. I know you think this is sudden, but it's not really, not for me. I've never been surer of anything in my life. We were meant for each other. Of that, I'm confident."

"Marry you?"

She wanted to pinch herself.

"I can't live without you." He kissed her again.

Lily realized this was her destiny calling. Tomorrow she might be dead. Look at poor Sheriff Dane. He surely did not realize today was going to be his last.

She nuzzled closer, knowing John was the only man she'd ever want. "Yes. I will marry you. I...I love you, too." Joy burst inside her at finally being able to tell him. "But, what about Chaim and Emmeline?"

"What do you mean?" he asked. His face was radiant.

"Will we be stealing their thunder, so to speak? Especially if we marry so quickly?"

"They won't care. They're just so happy that they found each other they probably won't even notice. It's amazing, isn't it? All the things that have happened. When are you thinking? The sooner the better."

Lily glanced away. Her *Mütti's* loving face came into her thoughts, reminding her of her mother's request. Others might get married by a justice of the peace, but that prospect made Lily's heart heavy. She just had to bring it up, and suddenly realized she didn't know everything about John after all.

"What?" he asked softly.

"It would mean everything to me…"

"Yes, Lily? Tell me."

"My parents asked only one thing of me before I left Germany. That when I got married, to do it in the church. By a priest. It is the faith I was raised in. And means so much to me. I know there is a church here but…"

"Of course! Anywhere you want. By anyone you want. You just say where and I'll do my best to make your dreams come true."

"Is there a mission nearby?"

"Not too far. San Antonio. It's a little over a day's ride by wagon. We'll make a holiday of it, and then go back every year on our anniversary. I think it's a wonderful idea. Everyone will be happy for us, Lily. You'll see—extremely happy." He stopped. "Well, maybe Dustin won't. What about him?"

Dustin hadn't even crossed her mind. "I feel for him, but I tried not to lead him on."

"What about your family? You once told me you'd return to Germany someday."

She kissed his cheek, then brushed her lips to his, enjoying his reaction to her caresses. "You are my family now, John. I only want to be where you are. I could never have understood that before I fell in love with you, of course." She smiled. "I will just have to bring some of my sisters to West Texas, where they can find their own cowboy husbands to love."

He smiled. "And, the jewel? I assume you've talked to Harriett and found its origin?"

"All is well. I know everything and you need not give it another thought."

"You're sure?"

"Yes. Now that that horrible man is dead, all is fine."

She hoped that was the complete truth. For now, she thought it was.

John looked at her for a long moment as if deliberating on her words, then kissed her thoroughly, passionately, until her senses thrummed with anticipation.

Everything else in her life paled in comparison.

Chapter Fifty-Four

Lily hurried to the wagon where John was loading her travel bag, and Brandon and Charity sat their horses, ready to go.

"Up you go," he said, taking her hand and helping her in. "The morning couldn't be more beautiful. Look at all the stars."

She studied the dark canopy above. "So much has happened in three days. It seems like a dream. I am excited to see San Antonio. And the mission too, of course."

She snuggled close to his side.

"Is that all you're excited for? I was hoping there might be something else occupying your thoughts."

He tweaked her nose, then laughed as he gathered the reins. Uncle Winston's eight well-armed men mounted up. His uncle wanted to make sure they made it to Mission San José y San Miguel de Aguayo and home again in one piece. The cowboys, all in extremely good humor, were somewhat flummoxed at their extraordinarily fine fortune. Three days of hanging around San Antonio—a town filled with restaurants, saloons and beautiful women—hardly felt like work at all.

Being early, Dr. Bixby was the only additional person on the boardwalk to see the group off. The others had said their farewells the night before in a small pre-wedding celebration.

John waved to Bixby. "See you in a few days, old-timer. Take good care of everyone."

"You can count on it, young rooster," was his gravelly reply. "Just don't get to crowing too loud." He watched the wagon and horses pull out of sight.

"I'm relieved Chaim is doing so well," Charity said, riding next to the wagon.

"He's rallied like a true McCutcheon," Brandon added, astride his horse on Charity's other side. "And why wouldn't he, with Emmeline and the rest of the family doting on his every whim. I think he's actually enjoying his convalescence."

John nodded and smiled. Unfortunately, he'd had to dash Harriett's idea of coming along. The trip would be too strenuous. She'd finally seen the truth in his words, relenting.

"I will be there with you in spirit," she'd said, overjoyed at their decision to marry. Madeline had generously volunteered to take care of her, promising them she'd watch over her as if she were her own. And, not to be left out, Theodore and Tucker had vowed that by the time they returned, Lily's shop would be as good as new.

"You sure you haven't forgotten anything?" John asked. He liked the way her face deepened in color thinking about the intimate things he was sure she'd packed away in the suitcase. Ever since the announcement, the women folk had been abuzz with excitement, all but keeping Lily hidden from him, filling her head with who knew what. "We're going to be in San Antonio for three whole days."

"Your aunt made sure I have everything I could possibly need. And then some. She is a real help to me, along with your cousins—and sister, of course."

"Of course," he teased. "And it doesn't matter if you did forget anything, because I'd buy you whatever it was, or anything else your heart desired."

Lily hugged him tighter. "Then you will not have to part with any of your money because my heart only desires you."

--------⟨∿⟩--------

John tucked Lily's hand into the crook of his arm and started for the mission in the town square. From the corner of her eye, Lily saw several people stop to smile at them in the late afternoon shade. She carried a small bouquet of daffodils and early spring roses held together with a pink sash, giving a splash of color to the ivory dress that John's aunt had borrowed from one of her friends. It fit her perfectly and had a lovely cape that draped over her shoulders, then hung midway down her back, making her feel beautiful.

A woman called out to them, seemingly overcome with emotion. She blew them a kiss, followed by some kind of greeting in Spanish as she watched their promenade to the church.

John nodded, and pulled Lily's hand up to his chest, drawing her closer. "Excited?"

"Yes," she replied. "This is the day every little girl dreams of."

Looking up into his eyes, she felt incredibly shy. His eyes sparkled with warmth, and a promise of things to come. Gently, his thumb grazed across her trembling fingers, and he gave them a little squeeze.

He was breathtakingly handsome in a suit she'd never seen before. His hair, ruffled by the balmy breeze, shone in the sun and smelled wonderful. Even his scar, something they shared between them and would always remind her of their first true encounter, was attractive to her. She stayed her hand from reaching up and caressing it.

John stopped before the mission's gigantic stone steps. The aroma of something sweet being fried nearby wafted on the air. He turned Lily toward him and looked down into her face.

"What's troubling you? I hear it in your voice," he asked amid the flowers, the buzzing of bees, and brightly colored canaries hopping around in the tree branches.

Lily glanced away from his gaze, not wanting to put a damper on their special day. Her heart thumped inside her chest. She *was* happy. *Excited. Thrilled* beyond her wildest dreams. In less than an hour, she would be Mrs. John McCutcheon. John's bride, to have and to hold, till death did they part. At least, that was what Charity said the minister would say. In Germany it was a little different, yet much the same, too.

"Lily?" he coaxed, tipping her face up to him with his finger. Worry creased his forehead as he searched her face. "Are you having doubts? It's not too late to change your mind."

"I would never have doubts about you. Or about us getting married. It is just that I wish my family were here for this day. My *Mütti* and *Vatie*. All five of my sisters. My two brothers."

"I was afraid you'd regret not having a big wedding. If you want to wait—we can do that. We can even travel to Germany and get married there. Anything you want."

As usual, his words were a balm to her. "No, I do not want to wait. That is why I did not want to say anything. I knew it would hurt you, or make you feel sad. I love you. Today is the happiest day of my life. Just thinking how happy my family would be for me made me long to see them."

"If you're sure?" He started up the steps, bringing her along, too. "I'm ready and willing. Let's go—the others must be wondering what happened to us."

On the landing, John opened one of the huge wooden doors and held it as Lily passed through into the cool vestibule.

All was quiet. On one side of the entry, a metal stand held a multitude of flickering candles, which gave off a warm, spicy scent. Like a welcoming sign from God, the sunlight beamed through a small stained glass window, making a splash of crimson and gold at the beginning of the wide aisle where they would begin their life together.

Brandon waited on one side of the aisle in the sanctuary, Charity on the other. The priest came out of a side door and positioned himself in the middle. He nodded once, then the strains of Ave Maria floated out from one of the side alters where a young man drew a bow slowly, reverently across the strings of his violin.

If he wasn't the luckiest man in the world, then he didn't know who was. Lily's hand trembled when he tucked it protectively into the bend in his arm, and she looked up into his face for support.

"I love you," he whispered as they walked. "Never doubt that for as long as there are stars in the heavens."

They walked down the aisle slowly and stopped in front of the altar.

The music faded away.

Charity beamed. "Here," she whispered, gesturing to Lily to come and stand by her. She took the bouquet from Lily's quivering hands.

The priest smiled. "Let us begin. In the name of the Father..."

Lily had a hard time concentrating on anything the priest said. Glancing down, she marveled at the beautiful gold band John had placed on her finger moments before. It had been a surprise, something she hadn't expected until he was slipping it on. When the priest raised his hand to give them a blessing, somewhere high in the rafters, a bird trilled out joyfully, another sign that the heavens were jubilant over their union.

"I now pronounce you man and wife."

Like magic, the church bells began pealing, the magnificent sound announcing their love across the whole city of San Antonio.

"You may—"

John pulled her into his embrace, and kissed her passionately until the priest made a small sound in his throat.

Charity giggled.

When they came apart, Brandon grasped John and embraced him for a good ten seconds while Charity hugged her. As if he couldn't stand to be away from her for even a moment longer, John pulled her back close to his side as congratulations were given all around.

Chapter Fifty-Five

"**W**hat do you think of it," John asked as they followed the maitre d' to their table. Yesterday, he and Brandon had scouted the most renowned restaurant in San Antonio and reserved the best table in the house. It overlooked a stone courtyard alive with a barrage of blooming flowers. Butterflies flitted here and there, much to the women's delight. A three-tiered fountain bubbled in the center of the patio, making the afternoon feel cooler by a few degrees just by the sound of running water.

"It's stunning," Lily said as she oohed and aahed over everything. "I do not think I have ever seen any place like it."

"Me either," Charity agreed. "Mother would love this."

Three musicians strummed their guitars under the shade of a wisteria-covered lattice, smiling whenever Lily or Charity looked their way. John pulled out Lily's chair and helped her get seated as Brandon did the same for Charity.

A handsome young man with dashing eyes and olive colored skin approached. He wore snug-fitting pants and an immaculate white shirt adorned with ruffles. A black silk vest added a finishing touch.

It was apparent to John the rake played his roll well as he made his way across the semi-crowded room, smiling fetchingly at every lady who caught his eye. A white linen cloth was draped over his arm and he held out a bottle of champagne for John to inspect. "Our finest, sir, as you requested."

John nodded and the waiter promptly opened it and poured a small taste into John's glass. After the approval, the waiter filled the glasses and set the bottle in an earthen jug that he placed in the center of the table.

"May I offer you my congratulations, Señora," he said, his eyes dancing as he boldly admired Lily's beauty.

When he walked away, Brandon raised his glass. "I'd like to make a toast to the bride and groom. May they share many happy years together. May they produce a passel of new McCutcheons to populate West Texas—and—and—to a lot less drama in all our lives for at least a few days."

The four laughed, as did a few of the people seated close enough to hear the salutation.

Charity made a salute of her own, and again they all drank heartily. The waiter was back with a platter of mushrooms stuffed with some sort of meat, herbs and melted butter.

After serving Lily, he leaned down and smiled into Charity's face. "*Señorita* ..."

By the time they were finished with their dinners and the waiter brought a small cake to the table, Lily knew she was tipsy. She sucked in her breath at the creation, then, for no reason at all, giggled like a schoolgirl.

The waiter handed the knife to her and John to make the first slice, then he finished the cutting and served it.

"How did you have time to arrange all this?" Lily asked, leaning onto her husband's shoulder and looking up into his face. "I am amazed. You can do anything."

"Which question would you like me answer first?" His gaze held hers. "The one you just asked or the one lurking behind your enchanting blue eyes?"

She laughed nervously at his question, then felt her face go hot when he brought the tips of her fingers to his warm, pliant lips and kissed them.

Charity gaped at the romantic gesture. "I can't believe my eyes."

"It's a good thing this celebration is almost over," Brandon added, chuckling as he forked in the last bit of his cake.

The other patrons had dwindled down to just a few as the four of them lingered over each course of their dinner, taking time not to rush. Aunt Winnie had given Lily and John specific orders to enjoy every moment, as a wedding day was once in a lifetime.

"I have one more surprise for Lily," John said, extracting a small, wrapped box from under the table.

He set it in front of her.

"For me?" He looked so handsome she had to drag her gaze from his face.

"Go on, open it."

She unwrapped the paper, being mindful not to rip it too much. "I have no idea what's inside," she murmured. With shaky hands, she opened the little wooden box to find a delicate porcelain figurine that looked remarkably like her. "John, I don't know what to say. It is beautiful, it truly is."

"See," he said, pointing. "The flower is the exact color of your eyes."

A moment passed, during which she gazed at the lovely thing and gathered her thoughts. "Thank—"

A burst of voices came from the cantina, then a shout.

Lily straightened and they all looked toward the other room.

"John McCutcheon!"

John jumped up and pushed Lily back gently when she tried to rise.

Brandon followed close behind.

"McCutcheon!" the voice hollered again, followed by the murmur of other voices inside the bar. "I have a bone to pick—"

Before John could cross the floor, Dustin burst into the dining room dragging a handful of ranch hands who were struggling their best to hold him back.

His face was flushed from anger or drink.

John held up a hand to Brandon. "I have to take care of this myself or it'll never be finished."

Brandon nodded.

"You!" Dustin shouted, pointing at John. "You're about as low down as a man can get! A snake in the grass. The wors' kind of—" he slurred, yanking his arm free.

He lunged at John, who was just a few feet in front of him. The handful of diners in the room fled in a panic.

Lily gasped in horror as the two big men, locked in a bear hug, careened across the tile floor and crashed into the wall, causing a shudder that rained shawls and hats down everywhere. Tangled in a ball, they smacked into the maitre d' as he scrambled to get out of the way, sending the man spiraling into a tray stand filled with water pitchers and wine bottles.

The crash was deafening, drowning out the man's angry Spanish curses.

John and Dustin rolled. When they stopped, Dustin straddled John and slammed a powerful fist into his face.

Charity grasped Lily as she started for the two. "You've got to let them have it out, Lily. It's just their way."

John dodged the next punch and Dustin hit the tile floor, bringing an enraged shout of pain. John punched Dustin in the eye, then jumped to his feet, pulling his cousin up by his shirt.

Not ready to give it up yet, the older McCutcheon yanked himself free and picked up a chair and swung.

John ducked and lunged, and the chair sailed over his head, across the room, shattering the mirror on the opposite wall. John locked his arms around Dustin's waist and the two men propelled backwards, colliding into the very table he'd dined at, almost knocking it off its legs. Glassware rattled and the leftover cake rocked back and forth.

Dustin grabbed a handful of the sweet and ground it in his cousin's face, letting out a howl of satisfaction.

Not to be outdone, John managed to get his fair share of frosting and smeared it over Dustin's smug look.

Having seen enough, Lily broke free of Charity's grasp, ran to the table with a pitcher of water, and drenched the two.

They sputtered and blinked, looking up at her in surprise.

"Lily!" they both cried in protest.

"Enough! That is enough!" she shouted. "You are acting like little boys! Shame on you!"

The handsome waiter was back, towing the reluctant sheriff by the arm. "Arrest them," he shouted, pointing at the men.

Brandon quickly withdrew a wad of cash from his pocket. "Sheriff, I'm sure we can settle this another way."

"You want to go with them?" the sheriff answered, finding his voice. "There's plenty of room in the jail for you, too."

"Wait a minute, sheriff," John said, struggling to his feet. Dustin followed. "It's my wedding day—"

"Might've thought of that before bustin' up the place. You need some time to cool off."

The sheriff clamped both McCutcheons into handcuffs.

Brandon's brows arched up over his amused eyes. "You boys sure know how to throw a party," he drawled slowly. "But, don't worry about a thing tonight. I'll make sure Lily and Charity are safely tucked in."

The sheriff shoved John and Dustin toward the door.

"Nighty night," Brandon quipped as they trudged away.

The next morning, John spotted Lily and Charity through the hotel window, having breakfast. He stopped, and for a moment, just took in the sight of her. Last night was the maddest he'd ever seen his bride. He wondered if she'd forgiven him yet.

"Go in, I'm hungry," Brandon said, giving him a nudge.

Brandon had bailed him and Dustin out, then helped settle up the charges with the sheriff. Dustin had ridden off without a word, and John had headed for the bathhouse where he'd divested himself of the sticky, sweet icing.

"I wonder if she's still mad," John said, pulling the door open.

"I guess you'll find out soon enough."

They approached the table. The moment Lily glanced up, John could see that all was forgiven and forgotten. She jumped up and hurried to his side, checking to see how bad his injuries were. Before she could say a word, he swept her into his arms and kissed her, taking his time to make sure she knew just how much he'd missed her last night.

She sighed, leaning into him. Diners whispered behind their hands.

"I did not sleep a wink," she whispered close to his lips. "I was overcome with worry. I wanted to go to the jail, to check on you, but Brandon said you wouldn't want me to. Are you hurt badly?"

He held up his hand. "Just a few sore knuckles, sweetheart." He wanted to make a mad dash for their room, but knew propriety would frown on that. "And, a sore jaw."

She reached up and stroked his face.

Brandon seated himself next to Charity, turning over his coffee cup. "You two going to sit down and join us, or not?" The look on his face said he knew exactly what John was thinking.

"I don't know. My head still hurts some and was going to see if Lily would mind having breakfast sent to our room, where I could lie down for a spell."

"Of course," she responded quickly. "I am sure you did not get much sleep in that horrible jail cell." She fingered the ripped pocket of his new suit jacket. "I think it is a fine idea."

After leaving Charity and Brandon in the restaurant, John and a conspicuously quiet Lily climbed the three flights of stairs to the bridal suite. John withdrew the key he'd fingered all night in his pocket and opened the door, letting it swing wide, revealing candles and flowers—all things he'd had sent up yesterday.

He swept her into his arms. Her face flushed, more gorgeous than anything he could remember. She tried to hold his gaze, but failed miserably. Chuckling when the corners of her mouth pulled up shyly, he couldn't resist kissing her again in the hallway, taking all the time in the world.

Finally, he pulled back just far enough to see into her eyes. "Hello, Mrs. McCutcheon," he whispered. Stepping over the threshold, he softly closed the door.

Chapter Fifty-Six

The days after returning from San Antonio were a blur of happiness for Lily. She worked in her shop, counting the seconds until John would be back for lunch, and again for dinner, then the long, blissfully happy evenings and nights were spent getting to know him fully. Someone had moved his things over from the doctor's office when they'd been away, and for now, they were scrunched together in her little room across the hall from her aunt.

Now, only a day before the big Fourth of July celebration, she rushed around helping Charity with her dress and cooking up a storm for the box dinner auction. Thank goodness she was married and didn't have to participate. She knew who she'd be eating her dinner with—and the thought brought a new round of butterflies as several recent memories sent naughty tingles racing up her back.

"Lily, do you think it's done?" Charity asked, pushing the chicken parts around the big frying pan with a metal fork. "I don't want it to be dry. Brandon always says my mother makes the best chicken ever, and I want mine to be just as good."

Lily looked into the bubbling hot oil. "I think it is. I would take it out and pat it dry." She wrapped a potholder around the hot handle, and was in the process of dragging the heavy skillet off the heat when John came in the back door.

"Careful now," he said as he hung his hat on a peg by the door and wrapped his arms around Lily's waist, kissing the back of her neck.

"John, let her be. Can't you see she's busy?"

"I like it when she can't defend herself."

"Go sit with Harriett at the table; your lunch is already there," Charity ordered. "We have work to do."

Lily wasn't complaining. She would've liked nothing better than to run up the stairs with John and take a little nap. She leaned back into his embrace, drinking in the feel of him, sorry when he finally let her go and went to the table.

"Harriett," he said, as he sat. "Glad to see you're up."

Harriett slowly set her cup into its saucer with great difficulty. "I had to come down and visit with—" she paused for several seconds, thinking, "—Lily. You keep her all to yourself when you're here."

"You complaining?"

She laughed and patted his hand with her wrinkled one. "No, no. I'm happy the two of you are getting on so well. Won't be long before there's a baby to welcome."

He dug into his plate of cold meats and bread, taking note of her feebleness. She was growing weaker by the day, and he thought the end wasn't far off. He glanced at Lily. "Wouldn't surprise me any," he said around a mouthful of food. When Lily turned to look at him, he winked. "Would it you?"

"Not really. And, I hope it happens soon," she replied, removing her apron and folding it. "But, talk of babies can wait for now. We are all done here. Finally." She went to the drain board and lifted the cloth napkin off the bowl of potato salad so John could see, repeating the process with the chocolate cake and loaf of fresh baked bread.

He whistled. "That's a lot of food."

She wiped her arm across her moist brow and wilted into the chair next to him. "I just hope you men can hold up your end of the bargain tomorrow."

"Don't you be worrying your lovely little head," he replied, tapping the tip of her nose lightly with his finger. "It'll be a grand celebration. You should see the dance floor we've built. It's huge. And everything is decorated with lamps and streamers. I think a good time will be had by all. By noontime tomorrow, Rio Wells will be filled with citizens, all looking to have a fine time when the competitions begin. Chaim is even strong enough to come, as long as he stays sitting down."

"That's wonderful," Charity gushed. "I hadn't heard."

"Yep, I was out there this morning and gave him the go-ahead. As long as he doesn't overdo things, he should be fine."

Charity looked between John and Lily. "What about Dustin?"

John glanced at his plate for several moments before finding Lily's gaze. "No. He's gone to Sweetwater to deliver some livestock. He'll be gone for about a week."

Charity came over and rubbed John's shoulders and said, "Mayor Billingsworth came by a little while ago. He's added fifty dollars to the jackpot in the shooting competition, bringing it up to two hundred dollars. Said he's trying to take the attention off of Mr. Shellston, and the scandal of the bank."

John gave another whistle, longer this time. "That's a fair amount. You shooting?" He looked over his shoulder, into her face. "I know before you said you were, just wondering since Brandon was back if you'd changed your mind."

"Are you kidding? He was just here a little while ago, too. I'm shooting against him."

With Lily on his arm, John surveyed the throngs of people milling about the streets of Rio Wells, laughing and talking in the highest of spirits. The weather had cooperated and it was actually one of the cooler days that they'd had since they'd come to town. If a person stayed in the shade it wasn't bad at all. Still, the water stand was doing a great business, as was the saloon.

The bronco riding contest had just concluded, and John was returning to his office to drop off his black bag. Thank goodness Chaim was unable and Dustin was out of town. He was tired of his loved ones being in danger, or getting busted up. Chaim, Charity *and* Lily.

He'd all but threatened Charity within an inch of her life to drag a promise out of her that she'd stay out of the bronco contest. He didn't want to be setting any broken bones today. He intended to have a nice quiet time at the celebration, eat a fine dinner with his beautiful new bride, then go home and get a full night's sleep, that is—after showing Lily just how much he loved her.

Was that too much to ask?

"John," Uncle Winston called, waving him over to a group of people. "I want you to meet our good friends, Martin and Malitta, from over in Sweetwater. They make the trip each year."

John stepped forward and gripped the man's hand in a firm shake.

"This is Lily McCutcheon, John's new wife," Winston added, introducing Lily.

They chatted for a few minutes when John noticed Bixby watching their group from a few feet away. More to the point, the old man watched Aunt Winnie with great interest. The years seemed to melt away from his expression, and adoration was the only word John could think of to describe what he saw.

Abruptly he knew why Chaim's brush with death had been so hard on the doctor. If his assumption was correct, Bixby had been in love with his aunt, and maybe still was a little bit. Anything precious to her would naturally be precious to him, too.

He sucked in a breath.

"What is it?" Lily asked as they excused themselves and walked on.

"Just a little surprise, nothing important." Not to us, he thought, wondering how Bixby had coped with it for all of these years.

Tucker came dashing up. His face was flushed from running, and his hair flopped into his eyes. "Shooting competition is about to start." He pointed with his arm down the street and past the school. "Everyone's down in the wash and the targets are set. If you don't hurry, you'll miss it."

"Come on," John said to Lily. "I may as well hold onto this," he added, holding up the medical bag. "As much as I hate to think it, something could go wrong." He chuckled as they hurried through the crowd. "I guess a doctor's work is never done. It's either feast or famine."

By the time they arrived, over fifty spectators were gathered behind the five shooters, and five targets were set out one hundred and fifty feet away. They waved to Chaim and Emmeline, who were sitting in chairs placed in the back of a buckboard.

Charity and Brandon stood at the front of the crowd, as well as his aunt and uncle, his two female cousins, and Theodore and Tucker. Although Charity was the only woman in the competition—and a young woman at that—she held her rifle by her side proudly and smiled at them all.

"You all know the rules," Mayor Billingsworth called out loudly. He was sweating profusely and wiped his face with his handkerchief. "When I give the signal, you'll all shoot together, one shot only, at the target in front of you. The person farthest from the center of the target will be eliminated. Good luck to all of you. Get set, shooters."

Charity looked around until she met John's gaze. He gave her a wink, and then a wave to Brandon.

"Who do you want to win?" Lily asked, so no one else standing close by could hear. "Your best friend or your sister?"

"Seems I'm in a predicament, doesn't it?" He pulled her close. "How about I just concentrate on you," he said next to her ear, giving it a kiss as he finished. "I don't think I've told you yet how beautiful you look." He let his hand slip down her side just a smidge, feeling her shiver and draw a deep breath.

"Oh, you," she laughed, her eyes sparkling in the sunshine. "Always the tease. I am going to tell…"

"On the ready," Billingsworth shouted. "Fire."

Five shots split the air. Everyone laughed and clapped as the mayor and another fellow made their way down the hard-packed dirt until they were at the first target. Walking briskly, the two marched down the line, stopping to inspect each contestant's work. Soon the man came running back and the mayor walked a good distance away to a safe waiting spot.

The man asked one of the shooters to leave.

"On the ready."

Chapter Fifty-Seven

Charity lifted the rifle to her shoulder and took aim.

"Fire."

When the smoke cleared, she watched as the mayor and the man walked down the line again. She glanced over at Brandon, who had his hat pushed up and an easy grin on his face. He'd been waiting for her to look his way. She gave him a saucy smile, then looked back at John and Lily, standing in the front row with the rest of her relatives. Brandon was feeling pretty big for his britches. She'd been considering letting her aim stray just a hair, but not now. She knew *that look* when she saw it.

The helper was back and dismissed the man to Brandon's left. There were three shooters left. She glanced over at the older man between her and Brandon and wondered at his ability. His clothes were tattered and her eyes widened when she saw that he was barefooted.

"On the ready. Fire."

Charity's rifle kicked back on her arm. She lowered her gun, and drew her bottom lip in between her teeth and chewed. Her concentration had wavered. It was possible she'd pulled up. No, the runner was back and dismissed the elderly man, who shook his head in great disappointment.

"Sure could've used that money," he said as he walked away and took a spot to watch the outcome.

"Good luck, darlin'," Brandon called to her.

She turned.

His grin was mischievous. "May the best *man* win."

Before she could respond, the mayor called out, "On the ready."

She hefted her rifle, knowing this was it. She was good, but so was Brandon. She honestly didn't know who would win.

"Fire."

Mayor Billingsworth and his helper studied the targets as they went back and forth between them. The man said something, pointing to the center of one, and Billingsworth shook his head, then walked to the other. It seemed it was a tie. The man came running up.

"We can't tell. We're going to back 'em up a bit and shoot again."

The crowd cheered loudly and Charity took a deep breath, settling her nervous heart, squelching a burning temptation to look at Brandon again.

"On the ready."

She sighted down the long gun just like her pa had taught her and held her breath. She pulled the trigger.

Again the men stood at the targets. They shook their heads. They picked them up and kept on walking. She hadn't any idea how far they'd gone, but it was going to be a true test of her ability.

"I really mean it, Char," Brandon said, close to her ear and making her jump. She'd been concentrating on the mayor and the targets, and hadn't heard him approach. "Good luck." He looked deep into her eyes. "And, don't you dare let me win. Honestly—I'm happy whatever the outcome."

The admiration in his voice made her soften. She smiled. Without warning, he stepped closer and kissed her square on her lips right in front of everyone, making the onlookers cheer loudly.

"That's not fair," Uncle Winston called. "He's distracting her."

"I think she's distracting *him*." A scantily clad saloon girl waved vigorously in their direction. "Helloooo, Brandon."

Amid the laughter, Brandon held up his hand as if swearing to tell the truth. "I'm innocent, honey, believe me."

"On the ready."

Charity took aim, wishing this crazy competition was over and done with. It was as if she could feel the onlookers staring down her back, and the sun was taking its toll. What the heck was taking the mayor so dang long? Her hand tensed.

"Fire."

There. This would surely decide it. Most likely Brandon had won, and she didn't care. She turned around and shrugged at John and Lily.

Both men came hurrying back as fast as they could.

"I've never seen anything like it before in my life," Mayor Billingsworth stated. "They're exactly the same. We've decided that since the pot is so big, we're going to split it between the two of 'em. That way everybody wins." He pulled out the wad of bills and counted out half to Charity and half to Brandon. "Congratulations, you two."

"But—" someone called out.

"It's done. Final ruling from the judge."

"She'd beat me eventually," Brandon said. "This way saves my pride. Thank you, Mayor."

The crowd had dwindled by the time friends and family were finally finished talking about the competition. Charity smiled and listened, once in a while offering a comment. Brandon had a healthy sheen on his skin. He took off his hat and fanned his face. "Sure is warming up. How about we take a stroll to the water stand and get a drink, then go put these rifles away? I want to have some fun."

She couldn't hold a grudge against his earlier teasing. "Sure. That sounds good. They might even have some lemonade."

They started to walk.

"Hold up. I'll be back in a second." Brandon zigzagged through some people until he'd found the old man who'd come in third.

Charity hurried over when she realized what he was doing. "I'd like to give you mine, too," she said, slipping the money into his pocket. The look on his face was one she'd never forget.

"Thank you, kindly," he said, overwhelmed. "I don't know what else to say except that."

"Well, we're just visitors, after all," Brandon replied gently. "It makes all the sense in the world that you'd have won if we hadn't decided to come to town. We just wanted to have a little fun."

Brandon snatched up Charity's hand and they hurried away.

"There, that looks pretty." Charity stood back, admiring the yellow bow she'd tied around the box dinner she'd prepared for her and Brandon. She and Lily had spent the last hour resting and prettying up after the busy afternoon they'd had. That left them a whole ten minutes to hurry over to the town hall for the auction that would be followed by the dance. "You think he'll like it?"

Lily laughed at the silliness of her sister-in-law. "Brandon would like it if you had filled it with cold liver and stale bread."

"You think so?"

"Oh my heavens, Charity, yes. That man sets the sun on you. John and I are having so much fun watching the two of you together. *Finally* together, I should say. He has told me of your long and complicated courtship." She ran her hands down her blue silk dress and took a quick look in the mirror at the hair fashioned half on her head and half falling to her waist. "Give me one second to run up and check on my *Tante*, and I will be ready to go."

"Okay. Hurry."

In the bedroom, Lily sat on the side of the bed and her aunt smiled up into her face. She had her knitting needles out again, but she never seemed to complete a stitch. That was all right, just as long as she was contented.

"You're set to go, Lily?"

"We are. I just wanted to tell you goodbye. I will be back off and on to check on you."

"You needn't worry so. If I feel more energetic later on, I may don my ball gown and come down and join you. It's been many years since I've danced a waltz."

Lily's heart trembled. She pushed away the melancholy and pointed to the window. "You should be able to hear the music when it starts."

"You can be sure I will be listening."

Lily bent down and kissed her aunt's wrinkled cheek. "Do you need anything before I go?"

"Just a promise that you will always keep a joyful heart. Foster an innocence of mind and body, and love John each and every day that you are alive."

Lily laughed nervously at the beatific-sounding request. "I promise."

"Happiness is the greatest good, Lily. *Be happy.*"

"Finally," John whispered into Lily's ear. "I was just on my way to see what was taking the two of you so long. Everyone is waiting." He took their box dinner from her hands.

Lily glanced around as they proceeded to the front room. She noticed Cradle with Theodore and Tucker, all three washed up, shaved nicely and hair conspicuously slicked back. John's aunt and uncle were sitting at a corner table with Chaim and Emmeline, the latter's shining beauty and glow of happiness Lily recognized immediately as love. She waved and Emmeline waved back. After all, when she and Chaim married, they would be in-laws. Brandon was at the back of the room, talking with Dr. Bixby and probably tormenting Charity by acting as if he'd not seen her enter.

A row of six pretty girls stood in a line along the wall, waiting to have their box dinners auctioned off. Becky fluttered a napkin in their direction, getting Charity's attention while Madeline watched quietly.

"There, Charity," Lily said, pointing discreetly. "Becky is signaling for you to join her."

Charity stopped dead in her tracks. "I can't believe I wanted to do this. I must've been possessed by demons." Her face had lost its pretty glow and was now pasty white.

"Why? Are you scared?" Lily couldn't believe her sister-in-law was afraid of anything. But a tiny nod affirmed her suspicions.

John turned around. "What are you doing, Charity? Everyone is waiting on you. Get up there."

"She is scared."

"*What?*"

"It's true. I can't go up there." The box in Charity's hands was quivering noticeably. "You know Brandon—and how he likes to tease me. He won't bid on my dinner. I'll be left standing there like a fool."

"That's the most ridiculous thing I've ever heard," John replied.

"Well, then do not do it," Lily offered. "Tell them you changed your mind."

John looked at Lily as if she'd lost her wits. "She can't do that."

"Of course she can."

John leaned close to Charity's face. "Can't be as bad as when Luke stole your clothes from the swimming hole and you had to run home naked right past the bunkhouse porch filled with ranch hands. Right?" John gave her a gentle little push. "Go on. It'll be fine."

Chapter Fifty-Eight

Moving like a turtle, Charity made her way over to the girls and was the last to draw a number from the hat Mayor Billingsworth held out.

"I would not like to do this either," Lily whispered as she and John found a good place in the crowd to watch. "I think I would faint straight away. Look at Charity. I have never seen her so wan."

John chuckled. "You're right. She looks like a snowwoman."

Lily turned on him. "Are you making fun of your sister? How mean of you."

"Now, Lily, I was just having a little—"

"Welcome, ladies and gentlemen. Today is the twenty-second anniversary of our grand Fourth of July celebration," Mayor Billingsworth proclaimed proudly. "Tonight we kick off the Cattlemen's Ball with the ladies' dinner auction and picnic. You all know the rules. All proceeds will go to our fund to make the hot springs into a tourist attraction, and thereby help generate income for our good town. A ladies' dinner can sell for as high as it can go. Have fun." He waggled his finger at the first girl and she marched to the middle of the room.

"Who would like to start the bidding on Sarah's dinner? Do I hear five cents?"

Within a minute, Sarah's dinner sold for three dollars and seventy-five cents, won by the teller from the bank.

"Why, it is the young man from the bank," Lily said, getting her first look at the buyer as he paid the mayor and escorted Sarah to the back of the room. "He could have offered a little more than that." She stilled her desire not to like the man who had worked for the horrible Mr. Shellston.

"Now, Lily, where is your charity?"

"Nowhere to be found when I think of Mr. Shellston or anything else to do with the bank."

The youngest looking girl took the center stage. She couldn't be more than fourteen, if Lily had to guess. Her dress was worn, but she was pretty and her eyes shone as she looked around the room in anticipation.

A heavyset woman leaned over to Lily. "She's an orphan. Lives on the edge of town and does washing."

"I did not know."

"Let's start the bidding on Maisy's dinner. Do I hear five cents?"

The room was conspicuously quiet and the girl looked down at her feet.

"A dollar," a voice shouted from the back and Lily saw Charity's head snap up.

"Uh, oh." John looked to the back of the room. "That was Brandon. Maybe Charity knew what she was talking about."

"Dollar twenty."

Lily strained to see. "Tucker is bidding, too."

"One fifty."

"Two dollars!" Tucker's youthful voice was easy to recognize.

A moment passed. Then another. "Sold to the young man who works at the doctor's office."

Tucker hurried forward and whispered something to Maisy, and she smiled. He took the box in his good hand then ushered her away with his other arm on her back.

"Well, I'll be." John looked at Lily in surprise. "I didn't know. This is actually fun."

Madeline came forward in her reserved, beautiful way. Lily smiled at her when she looked their way and offered a small wave of encouragement. She couldn't help but feel proud at the way the gown had turned out. It fit Madeline perfectly, and she was a vision of loveliness. Lily just wondered if there was anyone here brave enough to offer for the eldest daughter of the richest rancher in the county.

"Who would like to start the bidding? Do I hear five—"

"Ten dollars."

There was an audible gasp, then silence. Everyone looked around to see who'd made such a bold offering. Ten dollars was a lot of money. Uncle Winston's table was all abuzz.

Mayor Billingsworth looked around. "Any more bids? No? *Sold* to the unknown gentleman in the back."

Lily leaned close to John as the man came forward. "Who is he? I cannot see."

"Don't know. And by the looks of it, neither does anyone else."

He was tall and well dressed. His black hat was new, and had never hit the dirt, Lily was sure. When he stopped in front of Madeline, he tipped it, as if meeting her for the first time. Madeline, always the model of propriety, let him take the box from her hands, and they moved away.

"This is getting better by the minute," John said, chuckling. "What else can happen tonight?"

Two more box dinners sold in quick succession made by young women Lily had never met, to men she'd never even seen. She reminded herself there were still many wonderful discoveries to be made in her new town. She chanced a look over at John who was smiling from ear to ear, clearly enjoying the evening. It was amazing that she turned out to be the lucky young woman to marry him. She would never forget that for the rest of her life.

"Charity's up," John said, nudging her. "And she doesn't look too happy about it." He looked around. "Now where did that Brandon go?"

"Quiet, please." The mayor held up his hand. "Who will offer five cents for our sharpshooter?"

"Ouch." John withdrew his hand from Lily's tight grip, and gave it a shake.

"He did not have to say *that*," Lily gasped.

"What?" John questioned. "Sharpshooter? Well, she is."

In the longest second of Lily's life, she watched Charity's face go from stark white to a painful bright crimson. "Where is Brandon?" She craned her neck, scanning the room. "John—do something. Make a bid."

"Two dollars," a youthful voice offered. Theodore proudly waved his arm.

John made a deep sound in his throat. "Uh oh. This is bad. Very, very bad. Charity will kill Brandon if he lets Theodore buy her box dinner." John was just getting ready to put up his hand when another voice called out.

"Four dollars."

It was a cowhand from the Rim Rock. The one who'd escorted Charity to and from town the short time she'd been the teacher.

Theo's face clouded. "Four fifty."

"Five."

"Five and a quarter." Theodore's face looked uncertain; clearly, he was getting close to his limit.

"Seven."

Again the crowd gasped, then laughed at the entertainment. Charity stared face forward, not daring to make eye contact with anyone.

Theo shook his head and backed down into the men, and Charity's eyes went wide.

"Do I hear any other bids? No?—"

"Twenty," a deep voice boomed out.

Brandon stood in the back of the room, in the doorway, having just come inside.

"Twenty-one," the cowpoke said with a look of surprise that someone had joined in the bidding so late.

Brandon took long, slow strides into the room and proceeded to the front. "Twenty-five."

The room was deadly silent now and the faces bounced back and forth between the two men.

"Thirty." The cowboy's buddies were handing him bills, encouraging him not to lose out to Brandon.

"Forty."

"Mm, mm, mm," John whispered, shaking his head. "They're both going to be fit to be tied when this is over."

"Forty-five." The cowhands surrounding the bidder let out a round of laughter.

Brandon was within ten feet of Charity and still she wouldn't look at him. His nostrils flared in anger. "Fifty dollars," he said barely over a whisper. The onlookers whispered behind their hands, wondering if they'd heard him correctly. Brandon drilled the mayor with a look that said if he didn't close this down *right now* he'd never close anything down again.

"Sold," Mayor Billingsworth shouted. "To the *other* sharpshooter."

Thunderous applause broke out as Brandon stepped forward and withdrew his money clip. Slowly he counted out the bills and handed them to the mayor. Without a word between them, he and Charity walked away.

Becky's was the only box dinner left and she looked defeated after what had just taken place. Lily remembered how excited she'd been over tonight and how she hung on every word Theodore uttered. She whispered into John's ear, and he hurried to the back of the room.

"Only one more to go, fellas. This is your last chance for a delicious home-cooked meal tonight. Who will offer five cents for Becky's box dinner?"

"Two dollars," an older cowhand Lily had seen at the ranch called out.

Becky's smile faded.

"I bid three," said another, standing close by his side.

John hurried back to Lily.

"Well?"

He shrugged.

"Who are those men bidding?"

"Cowhands that work for Uncle Winston. They bought Becky's dinner last year."

There was a lull. "Any other bids? Going once—"

"Five dollars." Theodore had stepped forward and wore an unsure expression on his face. When a smile lit up Becky's face like a ray of sunshine, he ducked his head in pleasure.

"Any more bids?" The mayor looked around. "Going, going…"

Lily stomped her foot. "What is he *waiting* for?"

"Sold. Thank you, ladies and gentlemen. That concludes the auction for another year. I must say this was better than all our other years combined. *Thank you* to the generous bidders. Go have a nice dinner. The band will commence in half an hour."

Chapter Fifty-Nine

Under a starry canopy, the band tuned up as folks materialized out of nowhere, finished with their dinners and ready for some much-anticipated entertainment. Men's eyes searched the crowds for a possible partner, and girls ducked their heads shyly when gentlemen looked their way. The evening had cooled, bringing with it a soft breeze and the earthy aroma of springtime in Texas.

John glanced around, noticing that Brandon and Charity were nowhere to be seen. Were they off somewhere arguing again, or had they made up? He pulled Lily close. "May I have this dance, Mrs. McCutcheon?" he crooned, as the trio, comprised of a guitar and two fiddles, began a waltz. "I'm tired of worrying over everyone but you. Tonight belongs to us."

"You may." Smiling, Lily slipped gracefully into his arms and they began to move around the large dance floor the men had built. The floor, constructed especially for this occasion, gave gently with each step, and was illuminated by sparkling lanterns draped gracefully between poles.

Soon there were other couples gliding with the music, and John couldn't see from one side to the other. When Theodore and Becky twirled by, her face brighter than any of the lanterns, John grinned at Lily and winked.

Prompted by the feel of his wife in his arms, the beauty of the night, and how grateful he was for the turn his life had taken, he nuzzled Lily's ear. "I love you," he whispered, hoping she realized just how much he meant it. She held him closer, and he memorized the feel of the moment. "You're *everything* to me."

Still moving with the music, she leaned back and gazed up at him innocently. "I love you, too." Her eyes roved lovingly around his face, as if in question and her tentative smile warmed his heart. "What has brought all this on, John? You sound sad."

"No, not sad. Not sad at all. I just feel so blessed that we have finally found our way to each other. I'm an incredibly happy man." He enfolded her in his arms again, her head and soft hair smelling of flowers fit perfectly in the hollow of his neck. He rubbed it with his cheek. "Shall I go find a plate so you can demonstrate how you can dance with it on your head?" he whispered next to her ear. He felt her giggle.

The music faded out and stopped. Some dancers walked back to the edge of the dance floor, while others stayed, holding hands as they waited for the music to continue. John placed his arm around Lily's shoulder, when someone behind them quite obviously cleared their throat. They turned to find Dustin, hat in hand.

"Dustin. Hello," John said. He tried to hide his surprise. Dustin had the shadow of a shiner on his eye.

"John. Lily. Just wanted to offer my congratulations on your marriage since I didn't get the chance the last time we spoke."

"Well, thank you, Dustin. It means a lot to hear you say that."

In that moment, an understanding passed between them. John saw the hurt in Dustin's eyes, yet there was resignation and acceptance there, too. When Dustin offered his hand John grasped it quickly, in a firm hold, and a bond was sealed.

"When did you get back?"

"About an hour ago," Dustin replied. "Decided I didn't really want to miss the celebration. But, from what I hear, I already did." His gaze strayed over to Lily, and he smiled warmly.

John chuckled. "You're not exaggerating. It's been quite the day. One people will talk about for years to come, I'm sure."

"Fifty dollars for a box dinner?" Dustin shook his head.

John snorted. "Yeah. I'm sure it's gonna be a while before Brandon will be able to swallow that with a smile."

"That is almost as much as the two of you had to pay in San Antonio, to the owner of that fine restaurant, if I am remembering correctly," Lily said, a mischievous glint in her eyes.

Dustin laughed. "Yeah, you're right about that, Lily. That night hurt too, in more ways than one."

John rocked back on his heels. "Let's not forget I had to spend my weddin' night *in jail*," he shot back, feeling his temper starting to warm. He inched forward. "That still rankles when I think about it, *cousin*." He looked Dustin in the eye.

Dustin laughed a bit too forcefully. "That pales in comparison to what *you did, cousin*, right under my very nose."

Lily stomped her foot and scooted in between the two tall men, pushing them apart like a mouse between two hedgehogs. "There will be no fighting tonight! Do you hear? You two just made up. Let bygones be bygones."

She looked so small, John had to smile at the picture she made, one hand on each of their chests. No, he didn't want to fight, either. "I'm thirsty. Let's go get some lemonade."

At a group around the drink stand, Cradle was talking with Martha and her sister Louise, and Tucker and Daisy were standing hand in hand. John made his way through, handing a cup to Lily, then Dustin, and taking one for himself.

"Who's the newcomer who bought Madeline's dinner?" John asked, taking a sip. The tart juice made his cheeks pucker.

"Don't know. They're still over at the picnic tables, eating. Ma and Pa are camped out a few tables away with Chaim and

Emmeline, keeping an eye on them. I have to say, it's been a while since I've seen them so excited over something."

John felt Lily's attention wander as she looked down the street to her shop.

"Did you want to check on your aunt?"

He was rewarded for his astuteness with a grateful smile. "Yes. I was just thinking that. I can go and you stay and talk with Dustin."

"You two go," Dustin quickly said. "We'll catch up later."

John grasped his hand again and they shook for a long moment. "Absolutely."

Walking away, John hugged Lily's arm tightly to his chest. "Well, that was—"

"Nice," she finished for him. "I am so happy the two of you have come to an understanding."

"The three of us, you mean."

They were almost to the shop when Brandon walked up from between the buildings and met them. "Don't you dare say a thing," he said, warding off any teasing about his auction extravagance.

"Okay, I won't," John laughed. "Where's Charity?"

"Putting some prizes in your office that I won for her at the fishing booth."

Lily glanced up. "You stay," she said to John. "I will check on Tante and be right back. You can watch me the whole way down the street." When he tried to protest, she waved him off.

Lily slipped the key in the front door lock and opened the door, tinkling the little bell above. She looked up at the four-leaf clover Dustin had given her on her opening day, acknowledging that it had indeed brought her luck. She now had utter happiness she would never take for granted, plus John, the most wonderful husband in the world.

Turning, she stopped short at the silhouette of a man leaning against the wall in her dark kitchen. He lit a match, putting the small flame to the wick in her lantern until it glowed, and she was able to see his face, hard-lined and hawk-like. She didn't recognize him.

"How did you get in?" she asked breathlessly.

"I have my ways."

"My aunt?"

"She's unhurt. Asleep."

Lily started to back up toward the door she'd just entered. If she dashed quickly, maybe she could get out before he pulled the gun strapped to his thigh.

"I wouldn't try that," he said, stopping Lily in her tracks.

John was so close, yet so far. She wondered if he'd hear her if she screamed. And what if he came barging in? Would this man shoot him in cold blood? "What do you want?"

"I think you know, Miss Anthony. You didn't just think everyone would forget about the jewel, did you?"

From three buildings down, John watched Charity close the door to his office, pause for a few moments as if listening to something, then stride over to him and Brandon. He smiled at her nonchalance, but saw she was waiting for the teasing words they both knew were coming. "How was your dinner?" he quipped.

"Better than yours, I bet." She threaded her arm through Brandon's and he smiled down into her face with adoring eyes, the earlier incident all but forgotten.

"Oh, brother," John said, chuckling inwardly at the sight of the lovebirds. "I don't think I'd be able to eat a bite after dropping that kind of money. My hat's off to you, Charity."

Brandon picked up her hand and kissed the back of it. "It was worth every penny, John Jake. You just need to learn priorities."

Charity looked around. "What are we waiting for?"

"Lily. She's in the shop checking on Harriett."

"Who's with her?"

"No one. Why?"

"I heard her talking to someone. A man."

John's heart stopped. "You sure it wasn't Harriett?"

They all turned, and started for the shop. "No. Definitely not her aunt."

John had debated about wearing his gun today, but was relieved now that he had. He flipped back his coattail and lifted it once. Wearing his firearm was a habit he'd never been able to break, and he'd felt it especially well-advised tonight, considering all the newcomers to town. Lily hadn't been happy about it, but he was glad for it now.

He stopped and held up a hand. "We'll go through the front since it's probably still unlocked. I'll go and you cover. I'm not waiting. Charity, you stay—"

"Don't even think about it."

Sneaking up to the door, John could hear Lily's voice but not what was being said. Adrenaline thrummed through his veins. He turned the knob, relieved when it clicked open, then dove into the room, rolling and drawing his gun at the same time.

The other man also drew, jumping behind the protection of the wall partition.

"United States Marshal, throw down your weapon," called out the man in a firm voice.

Brandon was now in the shop, too. "What's your name?" he shot back.

"Talence Smith, Boston."

A heartbeat passed in silence, then John asked, "Lily, you okay?"

"Yes," she replied from where she was pressed up against the wall.

"I'm a sheriff from Y Knot, Montana," Brandon said, still not holstering his gun.

"Then you're Brandon Crawford," the Marshal said. "Clarence Hockmeier sent me your way. I've been looking for you."

"Let's all just come out into the open, nice and easy," Brandon said.

When the two lawmen stood eye to eye, Lily came over and slipped into John's arms.

Charity, who'd been waiting outside the door, came in too, and went about lighting several lamps until the room had more than enough light to reveal everyone's faces.

"What's all this about?" John asked roughly, unable to quell his anger. "Why did you break into our home?"

"I'm here for the jewel stolen from the Lowerbys. It's worth a lot of money. A fortune, you might say. And, to arrest the perpetrator."

Chapter Sixty

Lily felt the accusing stare of Marshal Smith, and the uncertain looks on Brandon's and Charity's faces. She couldn't bring herself to look at John. It might break her heart forever to see what he was thinking.

"What's he *talking* about?" Charity gasped. "Lily hasn't done anything wrong."

Smith's face hardened. "Someone's going to stand trial."

John sucked in a breath. "First off, Smith, it's Mrs. McCutcheon now. Secondly, my wife would never steal anything, let alone a priceless jewel."

"Are you telling me you know nothing of the gem's whereabouts?"

Lily glanced up at John then, unsure of what he would say. Their eyes met, and locked. Perhaps he thought she'd been lying to him all along. That she was the thief, running to a new town, trying to escape justice.

His eyes softened, then he went over to the table and pulled out a chair. The time had come to tell them everything. Lily took a seat and John sat beside her.

The others followed suit.

John reached out and took her hand into his own. "Go on, Lily. Don't worry. Everything is going to be okay. Let's get this whole thing out in the open."

He looked so handsome, so sincere. She didn't know if she should try to say that she did it, to protect her aunt. God only knew how long Tante would actually live after being incarcerated. Not long at all, she was sure.

His eyes were encouraging, his smile bittersweet. "Just tell how it happened, sweetheart."

Lily took a deep breath as she sent a silent plea to God for help. For wisdom. To direct her words. To tell her what to do. She didn't want to lose John, or this happiness that she'd so recently found. She didn't want anything awful to happen to her aunt either, in these last few years of her life.

She kept her eyes on John's thumb as it grazed back and forth across the back of her hand. "The night of the big storm, I finally asked my aunt where the jewel had come from. She was sad and ashamed over what she had done."

Lily went on, retelling the story just as her aunt had told her, never stopping until the whole thing was out. When she was finished, she went to her cutting table, withdrew a box from underneath, and hurried back to the table.

Everyone was so quiet; she couldn't imagine what they were thinking. From the box she withdrew a folded piece of paper.

"Here is the letter I wrote to the Lowerbys saying how sorry we were and explaining why Tante Harriett would do such a thing. I was going to send it, along with the jewel, as soon as I could get their address in Boston."

Lily then went over to her art piece hanging on the wall. Taking a pair of small scissors from her cutting table, she reached up, and, from between the many pretty beads and buttons, snipped off the jewel. She walked back and placed it in the marshal's hand.

Smith stood up, his gaze still hard. "I'll need to talk to your aunt, this Harriett Schmidt, and see what she has to say."

Lily looked at John, and he nodded. "It can't be helped, Lily. It'll be okay."

They went up the stairs in silence, John leading the way with the lantern and the others following single file. John stopped just outside the bedroom door.

Lily turned to look at the marshal. "Let me go in first and wake her up so she is not frightened," she whispered. "When she sees you, she will think you are here to arrest her."

"She would be right."

"Easy, Smith," Brandon said crossly. "You don't know that yet."

John nodded. "I'll go with you."

Lily drew a deep breath, knowing her aunt was going to be frightened to death no matter what. At the side of the bed, she reached down and nudged her shoulder, whispering, "Tante Harriett. Tante Harriett, wake up."

John stood behind her, the room dim in the one lamp's light. When nothing happened, John stepped forward and set the lamp on the bedside table.

The old woman looked incredibly serene.

A small smile lifted her cheeks, and she somehow looked years younger. The peacefulness on her face was that of an angel. As John and Lily gazed at her, the realization of what had happened hit them both at the same time. Turning into John's embrace, Lily wrapped her arms around his body, letting out an anguished cry.

Strains of a waltz wafted into the room through the open window, the hauntingly sweet song of a lone violin.

John pulled Lily closer, running his hands down her back in comfort, nodding to the others in the hall to leave them alone.

"Shhh, Lily, sweetheart. It was her time. Look how happy she looks."

"I know," she choked back, leaning into him. "It is just that I will miss her so much. She has done so many wonderful things for me. She brought me to you."

John heard the downstairs door click closed. He sat in the corner chair, pulling Lily onto his lap. He stroked her hair as she buried her face into his neck, her tears warm on his skin.

"Go ahead and cry, darlin'. It's okay," he whispered, gazing over Lily's head at Harriett's body in the bed. After several minutes Lily's cries lessened, and she stilled in his arms.

"Did you hear that?" she asked. She stood, stepping to the window.

"What?"

John followed his wife to where she gazed into the black sky. "Tante Harriett. She said to be happy. I heard her, John, as plain as if she were still here in the room. Didn't you hear it?"

John wrapped his arms around her as they looked out.

Lily gasped. "Look."

He glanced up. A shooting star streaked across the sky from one side to the other, sparkling as it went.

Lily turned and buried her face into his chest. "It *was* her! Tante Harriett said goodbye."

The following Monday, after the funeral, a small group gathered outside the Wells Fargo office, waiting by the stage. The marshal, who was riding along until Denver, was already mounted, and Charity and Brandon held the reins of their horses as they said their goodbyes to the whole McCutcheon clan and all the friends who'd gathered. They would travel with the stage, all the way to Y Knot.

Tears streamed down Charity's face as she hugged Lily, then turned into her brother's embrace. John held her close. She was special, this sister of his. She'd come all this way through hardship and danger just to see him, to check on him after she'd feared he was in trouble. A tightness formed in his chest.

"I'll miss you," she said, still enfolded in his arms.

He cleared his throat painfully. "And, I you. Thank you for making the trip all the way to Rio Wells."

She pulled back. "You better come to Y Knot soon. Mother and Father will want to meet Lily. And so will everyone else."

"We will."

"Promise?"

He tweaked her red nose and noticed her watery eyes as he struggled not to tear up himself. "You know I will. I have a hankering to see the ranch and smell the high mountain air."

She nodded. "I know what you mean."

"What about you and Brandon?" he asked, glancing at his friend watching them with interest from a few feet away. "Will the two of you be tying the knot soon?"

Her face flushed.

"Charity?" He pulled her chin around with his finger so he could see into her eyes. "What *aren't* you telling me?"

She shrugged in the mischievous way she had, but wasn't able to keep a smile from her face.

"Five minutes," the little man called out in a scratchy voice. Several people climbed aboard the stagecoach, waving to their loved ones.

"Charity, it's time to go," Brandon said, walking up and extending his hand to John. They shook, then embraced for several long seconds.

"Take good care of her," John said with a teary voice. "And yourself."

"I plan on it, John Jake," Brandon answered. "Let us know what happens with Shellston and his son when the judge arrives."

Charity looked around. "Where's Theodore? If he doesn't hurry, he'll miss the stage."

"Didn't you hear?" John said, chuckling. "He's decided to stay in Rio Wells." At Charity's surprised look he added, "I guess you're not the only fish in the sea."

Everyone laughed and Lily slipped under his arm.

In a bubble of happiness, John picked her up and swung her in a wide circle to excited cheers and shouts from everyone. He made sure her feet were securely on the ground again before he kissed her passionately for anyone under God's blue sky to see.

The moment was sweet. His eyes filled as he set her away. Never was there a woman so beautiful. Her eyes danced and the sweet curl to her lips told him he was the luckiest man in the world.

"Come on, darlin'," he said, tenderly tucking her hand in the crook of his elbow. "We have a life to live. I'm itching to get started."

ACKNOWLEDGMENTS

Heartfelt gratitude to my sister, Jenny Meyer, for her expert editing and good advice—over all the years, over all the projects. We make a good team. Thank you!

Fond appreciation also to my critique partners for the help, encouragement and insight given so generously on this story. Each of you is talented in your own way, and this book would not have been completed without you: Theresa Ragan, Leslie Lynch and Sandy Loyd. Thank you!

A huge hug of thanks to my five beta readers for their gifts of time, talent and super-sharp eye. I value your sincerity for the project along with your kind words: Jennie Armento, Mariellen Lillard, Kandice Hutton, Patricia Fyffe and Michael Fyffe. Your suggestions have made this book so much better! Thank you!

To my wonderful author friends on the web and in my RWA chapters, whose support and willingness to lend a helping hand, encouraging word or velvety soft piece of warm chocolate in times of desperate need—thank you!

To all the readers who've written to me with enthusiasm and love—thank you, too! You're the reason I write.

About the Author

Caroline Fyffe was born in Waco, Texas, the first of many towns she would call home during her father's career with the US Air Force. A horse aficionado from an early age, she earned a Bachelor of Arts in communications from California State University-Chico before launching what would become a twenty-year career as an equine photographer. She began writing fiction to pass the time during long days in the show arena, channeling her love of horses and the Old West into a series of Western historicals. Her debut novel, *Where the Wind Blows*, won the Romance Writers of America's prestigious Golden Heart Award as well as the Wisconsin RWA's Write Touch Readers' Award. She and her husband have two grown sons and live in the Pacific Northwest.

Sign up for Caroline's newsletter: www.carolinefyffe.com
See her Equine Photography: www.carolinefyffephoto.com
LIKE her FaceBook Author Page:
Facebook.com/CarolineFyffe
Twitter: @carolinefyffe
Write to her at: caroline@carolinefyffe.com

Made in the USA
Middletown, DE
10 January 2017